Milk Te

Amrita Mahale was born in Mumbai. She was trained as an aerospace engineer at IIT Bombay and Stanford University. This is her first novel.

debut with all its back and forth with the ease of a spin-doctor. The prose is meticulously lyrical, almost set to a metronome.'

—*Hindustan Times*

'Mahale brings to life a city in transition, its residents straddling convention and aspiration, hoping to be free someday in a city that promises the fulfilment of everyone's dreams... Her vivid and convincing depiction of Mumbai is a treat.'

—*The Wire*

'Mahale draws three plausible human beings, along with their motivations and indecisions, their neighbours' gossip, their mothers' banalities, and their bosses' delusions. Above all, she is spot on with the lies and truths we tell ourselves when we are in love.'

—*India Today*

'*Milk Teeth* lives up to its title in a number of ways—it alludes to that innocent first romance which often evolves into something a lot more complicated, the feelings around a first home that everyone must come to terms with and the process of reconciling with who you are and what you want.'

—*The Indian Express*

'Mahale's first novel is a very good one, brought alive by a Mumbai swirling with life, idiosyncrasies and Indians eyeing modern ways of being.'

—*Outlook*

'Even if you've never set foot in the city, this novel will transport you to Mumbai with its sidewalk chaiwallahs and breezy beach fronts.'

—*Huffington Post India*

Milk Teeth

AMRITA MAHALE

antxi

cntxt

First published in hardback in 2018 by Context, an imprint of
Westland Publications Private Limited
First published in paperback in 2019 by Context, an imprint of
Westland Publications Private Limited
1st Floor, A Block, East Wing, Plot No. 40, SP Infocity, Dr MGR Salai,
Perungudi, Kandanchavadi, Chennai 600096

Westland, the Westland logo, Context and the Context logo are the trademarks
of Westland Publications Private Limited, or its affiliates.

Copyright © Amrita Mahale, 2018

ISBN: 9789387894228

10 9 8 7 6 5 4 3

This is a work of fiction. Names, characters, organisations, places, events and
incidents are either products of the author's imagination or used fictitiously.

Typeset in Arno Pro by SÜRYA, New Delhi
Printed at Manipal Technologies Limited, Manipal

For Avanti Desai

Raj and Nargis sit on the beach
The beach is all they've got

Nargis feels a little dreamy
Seeing a bottle drift ashore:
They break the bottle like a coconut

Out pops a genie:
Feeling happy they ask for a Home

A home in Bombay! Says the genie

And now you've broken the only one I've got

– Hoshang Merchant,
'An Old Bombay Film Story (1950s)',
Collected Works, Volume 3: Place/Name, A Sextet

PROLOGUE

SOMETIME LATE IN THE AFTERNOON, a man rang the bell at the Desais' ground-floor flat in Asha Nivas and asked if Mr Desai was at home. Any Mr Desai, father or son. When Mrs Desai said no, her husband was out, and both their sons lived abroad, the man handed her an envelope. A message for her husband. She asked him who he was and he repeated, Aunty, just give the envelope to Uncle. Somewhat alarmed, she reached for the door, but he stretched out an arm to keep it open. No strain or effort, just a hand on the door.

Don't worry, he will know who it's from. A smile spread slowly across his face like a spill. Okay, Aunty, see you. As he spoke, the man balled his right hand into a fist, then straightened two fingers before her frozen face. He tapped this finger-gun on his temple, twice, and grinned, feasting on her terror before he dashed out of the building.

The envelope, which she didn't dare open till her husband was back from the market, contained a folded sheet of checked paper; it appeared to have been torn hurriedly from a child's maths notebook. Scrawled in an unintelligent hand were two words: GET OUT.

Part One

IRA & KARTIK

1

MATUNGA, THE YEAR IS 1997, a muggy evening in late April.

The milky clouds of the past weeks had curdled into thick cheese, blotting out the evening sun, raising hopes for a spell of unseasonal rain. The air felt slightly stale. Being outside was like taking an evening local train cramped up against a mouth breather. Yet, on the terrace of Asha Nivas, thirteen residents had congregated—ten men, two women and a child—representatives from the ten flats in the building. Among them, Ira Kamat and Kartik Kini. Each resident had brought along a chair to sit in; you couldn't simply plonk yourself down, the terrace was not what it used to be. The floor was missing several dozen tiles, and the ones that remained were cracked or chipped. The whole building had an air of disrepair, but it was the terrace that bore the brunt of the landlord's neglect. Many of the men had come to the meeting wearing lungis, some also donned undershirts with sweat towels on the shoulder—the neighbours had known each other for twenty, thirty, forty years, there was no need for niceties—and they all wore grave expressions. They had been summoned by Mr Desai to discuss and dissect that event, the ultimatum. Bipin Desai, a retired electrical engineer, had been leading the residents' efforts to negotiate a redevelopment deal with their landlord. That it was his flat that was targeted made sense; that it had happened at all did not.

'This goondagardi is unacceptable,' said Mr Desai. 'We are all decent family people. How dare he send a goon to the building?'

'Absolutely ridiculous,' Mr Naik barked. The Naik family of seven (father, mother, son, daughter-in-law, grandchild, grandchild, daughter) lived in the flat across the terrace. It was a one-bedroom flat, and how the family had grown to seven with such a shortage of privacy was unclear. 'If he wants to scare us into taking his rubbish deal, does he think a man miming a gun with his hand is all it will take!'

'I hope he thinks it's *enough*,' Kusum Kini pointed out. 'Who knows what he will send next time—I certainly don't want to find out.'

Mrs Kini was the only woman at the council, apart from Ira. She was a couple of years shy of sixty—older than the afternoon's victim, who was too shaken to attend—but it was hard to guess her age. Her hair was impeccably dyed. She did not have those tell-tale burnt orange roots, nor was her crown the too-dark coal that bled into the forehead like a child's colouring. She was said to use only a natural black shade of dye from an expensive French brand. In some ways, age had improved her appearance. Her long face had finally started to look regal, its expanse cut by fine lines that announced a life of more laughter than worry. Kusum Kini had once been notorious in the building. She was called pickle-tongued and too proud, was envied for her wardrobe full of chiffon sarees with matching bindis and purses. The peerless chiffons had given way to cottons, but her pride was intact, for she was also the mother of the building's most successful export, Kartik Kini. But that her neighbours were comfortable with.

'Now the question is,' Kartik's mother continued, 'how do we make sure this does not happen again? Should we go to the police?'

'The police is always mixed up in this, Kaki,' said her neighbour Ajit Shanbhag. 'Why don't we approach the Shiv Sena office? Last year, my wife's mangalsutra was snatched by two men on a motorcycle and they got it back in two days— with no leads. Just two days.' He held up two fingers. Of all its current inhabitants, the Shanbhags had lived in Asha Nivas the longest. Ajit was the first resident to be born in the building, and now he had two teenagers of his own.

'Why fight violence with violence—what does that achieve? You know, a dharna outside his house might shame the landlord into apologising.' This was Professor Rajwade, the Desais' ground-floor neighbour. A principled, ponderous man, he was the building's newest tenant, and had lived in Asha Nivas for nine years.

Kusum Kini cut him off with a snort. 'Really, Professor, you and your non-violence!'

'Me and my non-violence? *We* and *our* non-violence.'

'Yes, yes, I know,' she said impatiently. 'Ira, don't you work closely with the municipal corporation? Surely you know the right people who can bring this landlord to his senses.'

That was the reason Ira was attending the meeting—she was a reporter on the municipal beat for a city newspaper—but she had not spoken at all so far. She had tried to keep up with the drama unfolding before her, but her attention was tied up with one man among those present, the friend who had returned after years. Each time she looked at him, her mind leaped across memories: a gun pointed at her own face a long time ago, the weapon and its wielder stripped of power only moments later, a power they had swapped back and forth for years.

It was not clear to Ira how Kartik, gang-leader, first friend, fabulist, had become this shy, self-conscious man of thirty. She would have asked him herself but in the week since he had returned to Mumbai, they had spoken only once. Not spoken really, just exchanged flat pleasantries. She had run into him on the stairs a couple of times after that but he had rushed ahead each time, making a great show of appearing absorbed in his thoughts. Only once did she know that he was not pretending: when she saw him walk up slowly, dragging his fingers along the banisters, even drumming them absently every three or four steps, just like he used to as a child.

Knowing this would discomfit him, Ira looked in his direction every now and then and threw him wide, impish smiles, while his gaze remained tentative, hovering a few inches beyond her even when he smiled back from four chairs away.

'I do, Kusum maushi, my BMC contacts can certainly help,' Ira said. 'But I should first talk to the landlord, no? See what he has to say?'

'I already said I called him. He denied he had anything to do with it,' said Mr Desai. 'I suspect this was a builder's doing.' *Builder? What builder?* This new angle provoked a round of murmurs. 'He has been trying to get us out for five years. Do you think he has not had talks with any builders? We all know how these builders are. I think we should take another look at his proposal.'

'Builder or landlord, nobody can threaten us like this. We have rights as tenants. Not to mention that this kind of intimidation is completely illegal. If he doesn't back down, I promise I will make it a page one article.'

Her bluster amused her. It had been two months since she'd had a story on the first page. Still, she wanted to make a good impression on Kartik, show him that she had made something of herself in the years he had been away.

Kusum Kini smiled at Ira before turning to Mr Desai. 'There is no question of looking at his proposal. I don't think we should settle for anything less than a new flat. Right, Ira?'

Ira smiled but made it a point not to nod. Her father would throw a fit if he heard that she had publicly agreed with Kusum maushi on this matter. He wanted nothing to do with these negotiations, he wanted to ally with neither camp. Shankar Kamat claimed he only wanted to enjoy retirement in peace, at least for a few years.

'A larger flat,' added Mrs Kini.

Ajit Shanbhag and Mr Naik made noises of agreement while Mr Desai frowned. Professor Rajwade shook his head sadly. Alliances were already forming, dissolving.

Ira knew that in the weeks to follow, every conversation in Asha Nivas would course back to the gun incident. Occasionally directly, she imagined, like while talking about the monsoon and how much worse the building would get after another season of neglect by the landlord, that desperate and shameless man who had sent a gunman to scare families he had known for decades. More often that course would be winding: for instance, chitchat about tax returns would become a discussion on standard deductions and life insurance premiums, then someone might bring up a relative who had become an LIC agent, how the job entailed being pushy, showing up at people's houses to sell insurance policies, sometimes uninvited. And at the mention of any uninvited visitor, the interloper who had visited Mrs Desai would come up again. This incident was going to become a fold in the dull pages of their days; no matter how one flipped through the volume, one would land on this dog-eared episode.

Monsoon would arrive in a little over a month. Patches of moss had already started to sprout on the low wall around Asha Nivas. Over three months of rains, the green-grey would spread, devouring all spaces in the ceramic lattice that covered this wall: tiles with bright images of gods, goddesses and gurus, even a mosque or two. The pantheon had been installed the year before to dissuade passers-by from urinating around the building. No one wondered what it meant for the residents of Asha Nivas to live their lives with the backs of two dozen gods turned on them.

The gods had smiled upon Sundar Sadan next door, the first building in the lane to be torn down and rebuilt. After its redevelopment, it had a new name too. Belle View. Every flat in the six-storey Belle View had window grills: metal bars flowing this way and that, no two windows identical. Each window wore its ornamentation as a badge of distinction, a mark of the riches it contained. The most visible riches were the shirts, nightgowns and brassieres hung to dry in the windows.

Unlike its neighbour, Asha Nivas was rent-controlled. Most tenants paid a few hundred rupees in rent, less than a hundredth of the going market rate for a flat in Matunga, or any other part of central Mumbai. The landlord had been negotiating with the tenants for years, tempting them with a lump sum settlement which swelled every year, but so had real estate prices and the expectations of the tenants. When his incentives failed, he slowed down the regular repair work and maintenance, eventually stopping altogether. He hoped that the crumbling shared areas would finally drive his sticky tenants out, so he could replace the portly three-storey with a modern mid-rise like Belle View next door. Now it appeared that he was willing to adopt more desperate measures.

Just before the meeting wrapped up, evening prayers started at one of the nearby temples, the sounds of cymbals and singing mingled with that of bells. Some of the meeting attendees folded their hands and bowed their heads. The less pious felt obliged to follow. Ira promised again to talk to her contacts at the municipal corporation who were well-versed in these matters. The neighbours got up and started to leave, dragging their chairs behind them.

Professor Rajwade had cornered Kartik and was holding forth to his class of one. 'We think our privilege shields us from the violence of the city, and it does, of course, but there are limits to it. Think about the horrors the poor have had to face for years. Not only *real* guns but worse—bulldozers, arson, riots. The claim for space in this city has always been in the realm of self-reliance, you know, and self-reliance means struggle, and the struggle has reached our doorstep. What do you think the '92 riots were—an armed struggle for space! How long could we middle-class people have shut the violence of the city out?'

Switching to Marathi, he added that the link between land and violence was the theme of a paper he had been working on for a few months, for a sociology conference at Kartik's alma mater in Powai. It was an *international* conference, he beamed.

Ira, who had been eavesdropping, was greatly amused. Shut the violence of the city out, what was the professor talking about! It was his teenage daughter who had invented mosquito cricket—where every mosquito swatted was a run, and three no-kill claps in a row got you out—and the bloody game had spread through the building faster than malaria. Next door to the professor, Mrs Desai, otherwise a paragon of wifely stoicism, was known to stamp on cockroaches repeatedly till they had disintegrated into atoms. Upstairs, the Shanbhag children fought among themselves to drop live crabs into boiling water each time their mother cooked kurle ambat. Meanwhile, the Ganesans had a leather chaabuk hanging in their hall. Mr Ganesan liked to joke that the sight of this horse-whip alone had got his daughters through college, first-class with distinction, and then straight to their husbands' homes without detours, and he had never had to even take it off its hook. And what about the wife-beaters, the dog-kickers, the tyre-slashers and rabble-rousers, how common those afflictions were. Rage and bloodlust thrived here, casually disguised as order, as eccentricity, as sport and hobby.

Kartik was listening to the professor and nodding earnestly. He held a chair in each arm. There was more muscle on his sloping shoulders than she remembered. Gone was the neat side parting of his childhood, his thick hair appeared uncombed but not untidy. She was going to wait for the professor to finish speaking, but when she caught Kartik's eye, she saw his face twitch and read in his expression a plea to be rescued. This was her chance. He lit up with relief when he saw her walk towards them.

'Hello, Uncle, what are you two talking about? Kartik, you picked an exciting week to come back, didn't you?'

'Good evening, Ira. I was telling Kartik about a paper I am presenting at his college next month. Such irony about this gun situation in the building, it's the very subject of my paper: space and violence.'

'Space and violence? It's about Star Wars?'

From the corner of her eye, she saw Kartik cringe.

'What? No—oh! Ira, you are too funny. I meant space in the city. Land, homes, plots.'

'In that case, we must have a longer discussion—you know about my reporting on slum demolitions, right? But let's not bore Kartik. How about I come over on Sunday? Tell Aunty to make sabudana vadas for me.'

Kartik saw an opening. 'Best of luck for the conference, Uncle. Ira, do you need help carrying your chair? Here, let me help. I can stack these two, no problem.'

He grinned, suddenly friendly. Only because he saw her as the lesser of two evils, she thought, feeling a nip of irritation.

'You are welcome,' she said after the professor left.

'It looks like you are going to save the building too—look at you, big-shot reporter and all.'

'We know who the real big shot is, *scholar*.'

He winced, and shook his head lightly. Kartik had once topped every subject, every exam in school, scoring perfect marks in the most insuperable of classes. While parents chanted the word fawningly, *scholar, scholar*, making it a cudgel to hold over their children's heads, the harangued kids had flipped it into a term of scorn with a little turn of tone. *Such a scholar.* Ira knew how much the word vexed him. He once told her it sounded like a disease. Cholera. Sclerosis. Scholar.

'Finally,' she said.

'Finally what?'

'I finally get to talk to you. Or do you have an errand that you forgot about?'

'No, no such thing, of course not.' But the way he said no-no-no made her think that that had indeed been his plan. 'How have you been, Ira?'

Finally, but after so many years, where does one even begin?

2

IN THE SIXTIES, THERE HAD been an exodus of retirees from Asha Nivas and from Matunga. Their departure to newer suburbs in the north, to bigger homes, created a vacuum that young couples filled, and their broods followed soon. Vasant Naik, whose family lived in the flat across the terrace, was the oldest of this new generation, born in early 1967. Kartik was a few months younger. Ira and a slew of other playmates arrived over the next couple of years.

The children of Asha Nivas were each other's first friends and second family. They went to the same school and many were classmates, some even desk-mates. In the hours after school, the building belonged to the children. Doors remained open and the kids flitted from one house to another. They slid down the cherry bannisters to borrow salt and sugar, to sample the food at different houses and decide whose mother was the best cook. In the evenings, after their naps, they got together in the foyer. Either they went to one of the many parks in the area, or they played on the terrace, or in the street. After the sun set, when their mothers started calling for them, they had to return home, where they were made to wash their hands and feet before prayers and dinner.

Sometimes, playtime did not end there. Like in the game called Emergency that Kartik made up. He decided upon a list of words they were forbidden from saying. The game had no boundaries, it went on all day and evening, at school, at home, on the terrace. If you were caught saying any of the words on the list, you were out. The children tried to trip each other up with cunning questions, waiting for the silver thrill of a friend or a sibling uttering a taboo word. The older children knew that the prime minister had imposed something called the Emergency. Their parents sometimes talked about her and her new rules, like the one which made it compulsory for buses and trains to run on time, or another which did not permit any loose talk. And yet another that let her put all the rascals of the country in jail. It had taken a woman to rule like a man, one of the mothers was said to have remarked, to rule like the patriarch the country needed. The children were only glad they had a new game to play, that Kartik had more straw to spin into gold.

Kartik, the wizard.

Each year on his birthday, Kartik invited his building friends to the Udupi restaurant his family owned. His birthday was in April, when even the early evenings were plump with sunshine. At around five, the children left for the restaurant in neat files, a ten-minute walk under the watch of Kartik's mother, and it would still be bright when they returned an hour later. The name of the restaurant, Saraswat Bhawan, was painted in bold letters in both English and Marathi, flanked by a painting of the goddess Saraswati on one side and the Indian flag on the other. Unlike the Udupi restaurants at King's Circle, it was usually quiet at the Kinis' restaurant. Saraswat Bhawan stood next to a cinema hall that showed Hindi and Tamil movies. Its patrons ebbed and flowed, peaking every three hours between movie shows. Kartik's father and grandfather sat at the cash counter, one perched on a stool, the other sinking into a more comfortable chair. The cash counter had a spike through which several pieces of papers—bills and receipts—were pierced. Each year when the children arrived, Kartik's father, whom Ira called Ashok kaka, brought down his hand on either side of the spike, rapidly and rhythmically, then asked if there were any volunteers for a repeat act. Each year they laughed nervously, hoping he would not pick a volunteer himself.

On the wall behind the counter were framed black-and-white photographs of Kartik's great-grandparents. The frames were garlanded, to mark that they were both dead. A painting of Mahatma Gandhi hung a foot above these portraits, also garlanded because he was dead too. A few years later, the frame of Gandhi would be moved below the great-grandparents' portraits. Once Ashok kaka had taken over the restaurant, the picture would be removed altogether.

Two steel tables in a corner near the kitchen were joined so the children could be seated together. For the next hour, waiters brought them whatever they wanted to eat, any number of times. If one of the younger waiters was on duty, there was some chance of secretly getting coffee. The older staff usually refused and repeated what their parents said, that coffee made children darker. It was the only opportunity most of them had to eat at a restaurant, and some of the mothers fed their children before so they would not appear greedy. So their eyes would only be as big as their stomachs. The kids still stuffed themselves, but also kept an eye on how much their friends ate.

There was a long history of war between manners and greed, between need and want. If one did not line up at the milk booth sharp at six in the morning, the family had to go without milk until the next day. So if the queue looked long, you would jostle somebody to get to the booth first if you had to. There was a six-year wait for a car, a ten-year wait for a scooter, even longer for a telephone. If you could pull favours to cut the wait, you would do it. The fair price shop in Matunga stocked unpolished rice. For polished rice one had to travel all the way to Mankhurd, two hours away, and for only five kilos of rice a head. Fathers dragged their children to the black market in Mankhurd on Sunday mornings for those five extra kilos, so the children certainly knew it was not a time of plenty, not for most.

So, at their neighbour Rama Ganesan's wedding, they collected fistfuls of coloured rice from the plates of akshat being passed around. Instead of showering it upon the newlyweds to bless them, they carried it home stuffed in their pockets, wrapped in handkerchiefs borrowed from parents. They played house with it for weeks. This had also been Kartik's idea. The rice was stored in a biscuit can and stashed under the water tank, where it slowly turned to dust. When it was gone, it took away some of their imagination with it—how could they pretend any more that air was food? So Kartik found stubs of old crayons at home and they used a pencil sharpener to reduce these stubs to flakes, their rainbow groceries for weeks. No other child that Ira knew had imported crayons and nobody she knew would part with such gifts so easily.

Kartik, the generous.

The children in the building were close in age, but respect was not apportioned in accordance with one's years. Vassalage was declared to only one. Kartik Kini was the star of the building. They were happy being planets in his orbit, perhaps in the belief that his brilliance would reflect off them.

It was thus a matter of pride for Ira that, of all the children of Asha Nivas, Kartik was closest to her. Their friendship had begun long before their births. Its seed was sown when a bored housewife rang her neighbour's doorbell, a timid new bride who had arrived in Bombay the week before. An unlikely friendship had sprung up between the two Konkani women, and a few years later, it was passed on to the fruits of their wombs. Kartik was nearly two when Ira was born, and he spent his afternoons watching over the baby while the mothers listened to Binaca *Geetmala* on Radio Ceylon. For the women, these afternoons were an escape from the drudgery of housewifery. It was in this air of lightness, of confidences, that Kartik and Ira had become friends.

Kusum maushi had once told her that the other children gave her a headache with their shrill voices and loud games. Only Ira was allowed to play with Kartik in his house, a place of many wonders. The Kinis were the first family in Asha Nivas to own a television set. Above the TV, which outside of programming hours was covered with a lace doily, were glass shelves full of porcelain figurines. Women wearing bonnets, children with puppies. A cow, a windmill. Instead of the usual

pictures of gods and goddesses, the wall calendar had paintings
of storks and snowy mountains. It was a Japanese calendar,
Kartik told her, a gift from his uncle who lived abroad. The
centre table was covered with magazines: the newest *Reader's
Digest* and older issues of foreign glossies. Her favourite was
the Christmas catalogue of an American department store: over
a hundred pages full of things she could not conceive existed.

The larger of two bedrooms was for Kartik and his parents.
This bedroom, to Ira, was a monument to excess. The double
bed, crowned with a carved wooden headboard, was always
covered in a beautiful sheet that stretched from the head of
the bed to the foot like a shroud. It was a bedspread, Kartik
told her. His mother removed it at night when they slept and
put it back in the morning. There was a dressing table where
Kusum maushi kept a large number of bottles and jars arranged
in neat rows: talcum powders and lotions at the back, then
perfumes and creams, and a box of lipsticks right in the front.
But the most remarkable thing about the room was the slatted
box in the window which purred when turned on, a beast with
icy breath.

'An AC in the bedroom?' Ira had heard her father say.
'Kusum's dowry is a gift that never stops giving.'

Till Ira turned six or seven, they were allowed to play in
his parents' bedroom unsupervised. She had enjoyed those
visits more, when she could pore over the contents of the
dressing table, or go through Kusum maushi's sewing box, a
cornucopia of small treasures: threads and buttons, rolls of
lace, cloth patches in the shapes of animals. Kartik's books and
playthings, however, were off limits. He liked his things to be in
fixed places and could not risk the intrusion of other children
into his ordered world. Instead, he offered her his stories. The
tales he composed were almost always about a pair of friends,

a boy and a girl, who went on all sorts of adventures: they helped orphans, found buried treasures, fought off smugglers and mythical beasts, and made friends with talking animals. Their names changed across stories, always names like Johnny, Tom, Mary or Anna. Kartik said Indian names didn't sound *proper*. The only Indian characters to appear were heroes or demons from the epics. Interesting things only happened in other places, in other times.

Another favourite game had been planning picnics to different parts of the world.

'I have hard-boiled eggs, scones and clotted cream,' he declared once, on a picnic to London. 'What did you bring?'

Whether those were really foods or not and how he knew about them, she did not know. Nor did she know the names of any exotic foods herself.

'I brought pulao,' she stammered, her voice softer than usual. Pulao was what her mother cooked on special occasions, on birthdays, on Sundays when her father was in a good mood.

He burst out laughing. 'Nobody eats pulao outside India, you ghati!'

It stung when he called her a bumpkin. Still, this playtime was precious. Outside his flat, the games the Asha Nivas children played began to acquire an edge of hardness. Gangsters, policemen, jails appeared in their play-acting, adventure was now tales of loot, treachery, even murder. A game called hoppingo-battingo had become popular among the boys at school, in which you could punch somebody if they did not say hoppingo or battingo each time they sat down or stood up. It was not a game open to girls. Already the older boys, Vasant and Arjun, had started looking at the girls as unwelcome, dead weight on the group. If Ira or Arjun's sister, Anjali, suggested they play one of their old favourites, like lock-and-key or London-Statue, they looked at each other and pulled faces and after a moment or two, even Kartik shrugged the idea aside. When it was just the two of them, he became her old friend again.

Ira had always known that there was something about Kartik that was just beyond her grasp and beyond his years. He had been a bit of a crackpot all along. It was a side he kept hidden from his other friends, especially the older boys.

She remembered that as a six-year-old he had asked her, 'Who are you?'

'My name is Irawati Shankar Kamat.' Like she had been taught many times by her mother.

'That's your name, but who are *you*?'

'I told you—I am Irawati,' she offered again.

He then pointed at her hand and asked what it was.

'This is my hand.'

'Yes, *your* hand, but who is this *you* whose hand it is?'

'Irawati,' she mumbled, growing more confused.

'Forget it, you are just a child.'

He had walked away, leaving her in tears, and in all likelihood, she followed him and asked him if he would still play with her. It had been a common occurrence at that stage of their childhoods, he made her cry and she ran after him teary-eyed, her world painted in impressionist strokes, Kartik the only part sharply in focus.

And after some years, the tables had turned, and then again, the seesaw of their friendship had seed-and-sawed plenty, never getting a shot at the equilibrium that adulthood sometimes brings to childhood friendships.

Boy–girl friendships were tricky, and rare, even at their age. A divergence of interests and concerns was inevitable, it was believed, and when that happened, what else but romance could hold them together? Such friendships were only for the bold, the reckless, those who scoffed in the face of disapproval. But for Ira and Kartik, there was no such thrill. They called each other's mothers maushi and each other's fathers kaka, as if their mothers were sisters, and their fathers, brothers. She tied him a rakhi for a few years and in return he vowed to protect her like brothers do.

Not that she needed any protecting.

There was that incident in Five Gardens. She still felt the scald of shame when she thought about it. The children often went to the garden with the playground in the evenings; it was only a twenty-minute walk from Asha Nivas. The gang waited to hear what they would play that day. It was Kartik who came up with games: play which absorbed available props, which allowed competition but also collaboration so there was a winner but no losers. For weeks, Ira had been demanding a game which involved climbing the jungle gym, but his younger constituents were afraid of its height. Escape from cannibals, Kartik announced, and laid out the course to be followed. The running track, the swing, a few park benches, the seesaw, and the last hurdle, the jungle gym. For the young children alone, he offered an alternative: three times on the slide instead.

Before long, a ragtag group of children appeared on the playground. Their skin the colour of burnt biscuits, hair a sun-bleached brown, bellies pressed against unwashed cloth. For a few minutes, this group merely watched the children of Asha Nivas at play. Then one of the new arrivals whispered to another and they both sniggered. This joke spread, there was more laughter. Somebody pointed a finger at the jungle gym and the whispers became louder, turned into teasing. One of them began to imitate the overweight Vasant running out of breath as he scrambled from one obstacle to another. Two others shouted words of mock encouragement to Arjun, who was stuck at the peak of the jungle gym. Don't look down, whatever you do, don't look down, they howled, or you will fall and break your neck. They left his confidence in tatters.

To Kartik they said: look at your eyes, big like an owl's and probably only as good in the day.

To Ira, who was wearing a frock: go on, climb up, give us a good show.

Imaginary cannibals were one thing, but a real confrontation left the Asha Nivas children stumped. When they did not rise to the provocation, one of the urchins threw a pebble in their direction. It landed a few feet from where Kartik and Ira stood. The one who threw the stone raised an eyebrow at them. *Now your turn.*

Ira looked to Kartik to defend his friends, to shout back a volley of insults, to pick up a bigger stone and aim it better. Instead, he said, 'Ignore them.' So, for some time, they did. When that did not work, Kartik looked at the street children sternly and asked in Marathi, what do you want? That provoked louder laughter, *kaa paije, kaa paije,* they parroted with glee.

'Go away,' Kartik said. 'Leave us alone.'

'Is this your father's playground? We will play wherever we want to.'

'Fine, play here then, but don't bother us.'

'Oh, we are bothering you? Poor you!' said one of the boys.

'What is this fancy game you are playing?' asked the oldest boy in the gang. 'Can we join—or are you afraid we will beat you, you pansies?'

This gave rise to another torrent of laughter. The back-and-forth went on a little longer and, finally, the little boy who had spoken to Kartik dug from his nose a large ball of snot, clouded like a pearl, and after briefly holding it up for all to see, flicked it in Kartik's direction.

That was enough, thought Ira. The Asha Nivas children, or at least Kartik, might have had no counter to quicksilver street barbs, but Ira was aware of what they did have. She stepped forward before the oldest boy, who was a year or two younger than she. Looking him in the eye, she said in her best English: 'Don't you understand—we don't want to play with you.' She paused to produce a sweet smile. 'It is getting late, you should go home and eat dinner, or do you not have food at home? Do you even have a house to go to, or do you sleep on the road?' She mimed the sharpest words. House, sleep, road, eat. 'Why don't you answer, don't you understand what I am saying? No? You don't speak English? No English? You *poor, poor* boys!'

The boys went quiet, they looked at each other and at their leader, the boy Ira had addressed, before slowly walking away, leaving the playground to the other kids. Her friends remained silent for some time, relieved and also confused. They knew they had witnessed something shameful, but it was not their shame that hung in the air. It was Vasant who spoke first. He smiled and patted her on the back. Well done, he said.

She glanced in Kartik's direction and saw him looking at her with bewilderment and disapproval. He moved closer before he spoke.

'Why did you do that?'

'They insulted us.'

'That was not a nice thing you did.'

She could not help but smile. 'Why not? I didn't use any bad words.'

He shook his head and she saw his mouth tighten. She thought he was going to shout at her, but instead he began to tell everybody to get back to their positions so they could start again. Every couple of minutes, he looked around, perhaps anxious that the urchins might return. Kartik did not speak to her for the rest of the evening. On the way home, she apologised doggedly till he succumbed.

Ira had known even then, at the age of eight, that it did not matter that she had not sworn at the street children. The content of what she said had been unimportant; English had been the weapon that caused annihilation. In thinking of the incident later, Ira recalled first—above the initial provocations, above her choice of words and the reactions of her friends, which would all fade with time—the young boy she had spoken to. His face, his bright eyes, the flame she had snuffed out with such little effort. She never forgot Kartik's disapproval either. For years, buried within the folds of her guilt was a different thought: she continued to wonder whether Kartik had disapproved of her cruelty—her childlike but crushing cruelty—or of her success where he had failed.

3

I N SOME WAYS, THE LANE that housed Asha Nivas had remained unchanged over the years. Its three temples continued to mark the passage of hours with prayers and bells, faithful timekeepers that served the devout and the unbelieving alike. A flower market had run along one flank for decades, and it turned the strip into a scented blur of coral, ivory and fuchsia. To look up was to see many shifting hues of green; giant gulmohar and peepul trees butted heads across the road. The lone palm cutting into the footpath was still wont to shedding a dry frond or two every couple of months. Only now, unlike twenty or thirty years ago, there was a high chance there would be a car parked under it.

The changes had crept in slowly. A shiny new bank, an ATM, a shop that sold only Western outfits, a travel agency specialising in tours to Europe. The influx of Gujaratis meant shop signs in a new language, a new script. Sundar Sadan had become Belle View and a new building was planned in the single empty plot. One could see posters advertising drivers, full-time nannies, French tutors. People had begun to fight over parking. Every few weeks, a tyre got slashed.

Some changes were more welcome than others. One of the two tapris around the corner from Asha Nivas had got a facelift: in the place of a ramshackle booth selling chai, biscuits and cigarettes now stood a proper fast food stall. Those too impatient for the brusque sit-down service of the restaurants at King's Circle gathered here for a twist on the same south Indian fare: idli, vada, dosa (plain, masala, Mysore, Schezwan, et cetera). From time to time, Ira found herself among them. There were no tables for the diners here, only half a dozen plastic stools blocking off part of the footpath. All the stools were occupied that day by a clutch of schoolchildren sharing two dosas between them. Between bites they discussed the solutions to a problem set: *Apply this theorem, that's it—But the problem doesn't meet the conditions—It does, if you reduce it to the right form.* Ira could make out familiar phrases from another era. Sine, cosine, their squares. She had presumed that the students were younger but now she noticed the tell-tale signs of teenage: the fuzz on the lip, a sprinkling of pimples, the outlines of a bra, the girls who had already begun to go quiet and defer to the louder boys. But they were all so tiny; did each new generation of teenagers look younger?

'Paneer dosa!' yelled the man at the counter.

She walked to the stall to collect her order and was hit by a thump of heat from the dosa pan, on which four dosas were cooking at once. Bowls of lurid fillings were cramped next to the stove. The cook's hands moved in rapid circles to spread the batter, and as soon as it began to set, he scooped on the fillings without missing a beat. It was like watching a video in fast forward. Her plate in hand, she was about to step away when she recognised the customer at the next kiosk.

'Kartik!' she called out.

He turned around. She saw a shadow of alarm cross his face before his smile revealed itself. He waved at her, and after paying the tapriwala, he walked over.

'What are you eating?' He held up a pack of cigarettes. 'Care for a smoke?'

Her mouth fell open.

At the age of fifteen Kartik had smuggled a cigarette up to the terrace, one that a careless uncle had left behind. He had tried to smoke it in his bathroom when he was alone, but he had no idea how to light it, or even which end to light for that matter, so he had gone to Ira for help.

'How can you not know how to smoke a cigarette?' she had exclaimed. 'Do you not watch movies? Here, let me try.' Ira had put the cigarette in her mouth and lit a match, before drawing on it hard and deep. The fire raced up through the cigarette and ran down the length of her body making her tremble. When she handed it to Kartik, he looked down, and she was left holding her hand out, the cigarette slowly turning to ash.

'What's wrong?'

'I can't do this, Ira, I am not that kind of boy.'

'What do you mean *that* kind of boy? What kind of girl am I then?'

His voice dropped. 'I can't do this to my parents.'

'But your parents won't even know.'

'It doesn't work that way. I am sorry.'

'You are such a scholar na, useless!'

She had stubbed out the cigarette even though he insisted she didn't have to. For weeks she had cursed him and teased him in turns.

Now here he was, some fifteen years later, offering her a cigarette.

'Yes, Ira, I smoke. Don't look so surprised—and please don't tell my parents.'

So not much had changed. 'Thanks, but maybe later. What happened, mister scholar? Remember that little lecture you gave me about smoking?'

'College happened. Life happened.' Kartik shrugged. 'And how does Shobha maushi feel about you eating dosas right next to home?'

It was something that irked her mother—why waste money when home and dinner were only minutes away? Home-cooked meals, Ira had tried to explain, could not match the contact thrill of street food, that gratifying melange of spice and sweat and sizzle. Her mother had retorted that perhaps they ought to make her contribute to running the household. Having less money to spend might automatically make the meals at home taste better.

'I brought her here last week and it took her two bites to conclude she could make this at home. Not the Schezwan one though, which she declared was too unhealthy anyway.'

He laughed. 'My mother embraces gaps in her cooking skills. She says even mothers need a break.'

'So how do you hide this habit from your parents?' She pointed at his cigarette with her chin.

'I'm still figuring it out. Buying cigarettes is the hardest part.'

'Why?'

'You mean your mother doesn't go through your cupboard and shelves to make sure everything is tidy?'

Of course not, she wanted to say, because I am an adult, but she did not wish to embarrass him. Besides, it was not like her parents really let her be, just that their intrusions were different.

'I have to answer half a dozen questions each time I step out,' he continued. 'I can't even make up errands—Ayee says she doesn't want me to lift a finger, I have to sit back and enjoy my *vacation*.' He rolled his eyes. 'What vacation? More like the Spanish Inquisition.'

'You are living at home after, what, ten years?'

'Thirteen.'

Thirteen years since he left for college, since they stopped being friends.

'May I?' Kartik asked, pointing at her plate.

He scooped a piece of her paneer dosa into his mouth. There was only a little left, but he had neatly torn off a small morsel, leaving her the last bite. Under the sweet, smoky scent of tobacco she caught a whiff of his aftershave.

'Will you wait while I smoke another one? Give me company?' he asked her.

'Gladly. Let's go for a walk.'

Anything to lengthen the evening, delay going home.

They asked for a glass of water, rinsed their fingers over the plate. He lit another cigarette and offered her one. This time, she accepted. She saw a frown on the face of the boy who collected her plate. It was not all that common in Matunga, a woman lighting up in public.

The sky was still a rich blue, deepening little by little. They crossed Asha Nivas and rambled towards the flower market, where the flower sellers were packing up for the day, locking away plastic buckets filled with softly drooping blossoms. A plump stray dog sauntered next to them till the end of the lane; at the crossroads, the border of its kingdom, it sat down with resignation.

'Left or right?' she asked. Then, thinking that she might have been presumptuous, she added, 'Or back?'

'How about we keep going straight? We can walk to the station and back.'

Squat greying buildings rimmed the road in front of the Matunga railway station. A splash of colour came from the ground-floor shops with their printed flex signs. Hawkers occupied half a lane on each side, which meant that Ira and Kartik had to squeeze themselves between a honking jumble of evening traffic and wooden carts overflowing with plastic knick-knacks: combs, mirrors, hangers, mugs and pegs. Behind the hawkers were saree and dress boutiques, beauty parlours and haircutting saloons, variety stores, photo studios, textbook depots. *The sum total of middle-class aspirations*, Kaiz had once said of this assortment.

Along the way, they talked about inconsequential things: the brutal humidity, the thirty-one flavours of ice-cream at the new Baskin Robbins, who among the newer crop of actors they thought had staying power, the rapidly-cycling coalition governments at the centre, the four prime ministers that India had had in the past year. She was reminded that Kartik at his most social was a well-adjusted introvert, deftly weaving questions and small talk into conversation that gave away little about him. A master of deflecting attention from himself. Ira had always enjoyed his inscrutable inwardness, even if she was also confounded by it. The two times she had run into him on the stairs came to mind; it was hard to believe that it was the same man walking next to her. Either she had earned his confidence in just one meeting or he'd had a very good day.

'Ira, can I ask you something?'

'What?'

'Why does your father not want to move out of Asha Nivas?'

She hadn't expected that question at all. She blinked and stared at him for a few seconds.

'I don't know,' she replied, somewhat truthfully. 'He says he will move out of the building when he wants to. Not for money, not out of fear.'

'Hmm,' said Kartik.

'He wants to savour retirement without the hassle of a big move.'

'For a few months presumably? Surely not indefinitely?'

'It's not only him. Professor Rajwade does not want to move either. His daughter has board exams next year.'

Board exams were the Indian epidemic that afflicted entire families at once. Cable connections were disconnected, social lives were paralysed, and all big decisions were suspended till the end of the exam season.

Sukhada and her younger brother were only a year apart. One of the Rajwade children would be writing board exams for the next four years.

'I understand wanting to wait for a better deal, or for a better time, but to choose to not move at all? I find that—' he paused '—interesting.'

It was clear that he thought her father was crazy but was too polite to say it. That word had been used to describe her father with alarming frequency in the past months.

'You seem to be fully caught up on the issue.'

He looked a little embarrassed. 'You know my parents. I have told them I don't want to get pulled into this. I won't have any time once the job starts.'

It was his father who had started the demand for a new

flat. Mr Desai had been angling for twenty to thirty lakhs as settlement, enough to cover the deposit for another rented flat in the neighbourhood, and most of the residents had once believed that even that was an ambitious demand. Now the Reges and the Shanbhags agreed with Ashok Kini that they should not settle for anything less than a new flat, and Kusum Kini was working on the Naiks too. Only her father refused to be drawn into either camp.

Ira and Kartik turned towards King's Circle. On the way, they saw a fenced-off plot with a giant hoarding: Santorini Towers, world-class luxury apartments in the heart of Matunga, 3 and 4 BHK. Underground parking, air-conditioned gymnasium. Separate service elevators. Your own *private* island, ready in 1999.

'Santorini, really?' Ira sighed. 'There's Belle View next to us, and a building called Eiffel Enclave on the way to Wadala.'

You could put all the French or Italian you wanted in their names, but you couldn't take Mumbai out of the buildings: the clothes drying outside the windows would remain, and so would the mud streaks from flowerpots on windowsills.

'Separate service elevators,' she continued, 'so you can't even see the *lowly servants* who run your houses and bring up your children.' She scanned the hoarding for the developer's name. 'Sonawala Builders. Well, with *that* name...' she said and let her words trail off.

'Actually, they might be one of my clients,' he said sheepishly. 'The consultancy has a large real-estate vertical.'

'You have to help them come up with better hoardings.'

'That's not what I have been hired for, but I promise I'll try.'

'Remind me again what you do?'

She didn't fully understand his line of work: the world of profit and loss, strategy, optimisation, turnarounds. There had been such few options before them when they were growing up; brilliant children became either doctors, engineers, lawyers or professors of some sort. Then the economy had grown suddenly, like a magical tree from a fairy tale, sprouting countless new branches. Branches laden with money it seemed, waiting to heap riches on anyone standing in the right spot. Anyone, but why him? She had once believed that Kartik was made for greater things, that he would enter the world of Einstein, Newton, Nobel Prizes. How loosely they had used that word, greatness, how little they had known about the world, about the changes to come. That the certainty of wealth, of upward mobility, would trump the possibility of greatness, whatever it meant.

Perhaps he realised this, for he did not meet her eye when he described his new job at a management consultancy. He would be like a doctor for struggling businesses, diagnose their troubles and help them recover. And a sort of coach and guide too. A variety of foreign companies were interested in entering the Indian market and they needed local experts. Some of his firm's multinational clients were already in the country. What did she think of this new fast-food chain, he enquired, and what about that soft drink, and did she remember life before such-and-such product became available in India?

She nodded vacantly and gave him short answers. She had little interest in talking about the shifting sands of the new economy, or even about the attendant shifts in their own lives. She wanted to go back to the small and safe space of childhood, give in to the tug of nostalgia that his presence inspired.

'Remember that game we used to play where we went on picnics to different countries?'

He put his hands up. 'Fine, I admit it. I lifted all the foods from books.'

'That I don't care about. You once told me that pulao is not eaten anywhere outside India. I now know that's not true.'

'Umm, congratulations?'

She punched him lightly in the side.

They prodded the long-ago memory together till forgotten details came tumbling out. Buttery scones, jam tarts and liquorice candy. Meatballs, pickled herrings, split-pea soup. A short-lived variation that involved different Indian states, which proved too commonplace to hold their attention. At the turn-off towards Asha Nivas, they marched straight ahead, wordlessly buying ten more minutes together.

Ira and Kartik made their way back home just as the street lights were flickering to life. After taking leave of him on the first floor, she climbed another flight of stairs to her own flat. The brass nameplate on the varnished door announced her father's name. Shankar V. Kamat. WELCOME, said the coir mat at her doorstep. When she could no longer put it off, Ira braced herself and rang the bell.

Her mother opened the door. The television was on, her father was watching a police show with rapt attention.

Ira looked around till she spotted it.

A beige-and-gold envelope on the sofa.

On the cover, *Amit weds Sushma.*

About a year ago the groom's father, a former colleague of Ira's father, had sent over his son's picture and horoscope. Ira had laughed the match off. The boy looks like the ape from *Dunston Checks In*, she had said, couldn't they at least have taped his ears back for his matrimonial photo? Her father had to hem and haw, and politely turn down his co-worker. A year later, the son was getting married but there had been no more proposals for Ira.

The groom's father had called that morning to ask if the Kamats had received the wedding invitation. So Ira knew that the card was on its way. What she did not know was how her parents were going to react. What ruse would it be today, she wondered, how would her mother bring up the issue of marriage this time?

Ira was asked to set the table for dinner. They ate without much conversation, listening to the news playing on the television in the living room. Almost an hour had passed since she returned and there had been no talk of matrimony, but she remained suspicious. Her mother had worn a feeble smile all evening. It was a warning.

Shobha Kamat was a petite woman who appeared apologetic about even the little space she occupied. She was a head shorter than her daughter and her narrow shoulders were usually a little hunched, her gaze pooled around her feet. Ira's mother was no lamb though. The sweet smile and small frame belied the strong will and craftiness she had accreted over the years.

'Pramila called me over for tea this evening,' her mother said as she began to clear the table. 'It took her a whole minute to let me in after I rang the bell. They have three locks and two chains on their door now. Poor thing.'

Pramila Desai had already repeated the story of the gun to all the women of the building many times, summoning new details with each retelling. The boy barely out of his teens in one version became a pukka north Indian goonda-type in another. To some, she said his swarthy complexion raised her suspicion first, to others, she recalled her panic at the rising menace in his face when he was handing her the envelope, even before he threatened her. Elsewhere, she grabbed her two mangalsutras and thanked the gods her husband was not at home that afternoon. What if the goon had decided to deliver a stronger message had a man been present?

'Pramila thinks Kusum has waved a magic wand over the Naiks,' her mother continued. 'Naik told Desai they are willing to wait till the landlord agrees to give everybody a new flat. And you know what? Pramila said the landlord is planning to get the building certified dilapidated,' said her mother. 'If that happens, we will all have to vacate. No compensation. Everybody loses.'

'He can't just do that. It's not that straightforward.'

'Then you have not seen the Naiks' flat. You believe it'll survive this monsoon in one piece? What more does he need?'

'And you must think my work with the BMC amounts to nothing. I know enough engineers who can certify the building safe if he tries any tricks—and he knows that.'

Ira had called the landlord the day after the residents' meeting. On the phone he had repeated his apologies about the incident, while also claiming ignorance of who was behind it. But she had made sure that he took note of her connections at the municipal corporation.

That was when her mother revealed her true agenda: 'Whatever else needs to be done, do it quickly, who knows when you will marry and move away.'

Ira looked at her mother in disbelief. 'Even if I do, you think I will cut off all ties with this building, with you and Pappa?'

'That I won't let you do even if you want to. We didn't raise you for twenty-eight years so you could abandon us. Still, your priorities will change—why will you care about our building disputes?'

Because it was the only home, the only life she had known. The song of the temple bells, the smell of sun-warmed flowers, these peculiar neighbours, to live with the din and bustle, to know all the hawkers in the street.

'Don't worry, I am in no hurry to get married. And think

about it, if I move out, you will be left alone with Pappa. Do you want that?'

Her mother made an expression of mock anger. Her father was out of earshot, back in front of the television.

'Is this because of that wedding card? I had rather remain single than marry a monkey.'

'That monkey is a chartered accountant. That monkey just bought a two-bedroom flat in Vile Parle.'

'And he is off the market.' A sly smile. 'So what do you want me to do?'

Her mother hesitated. 'If you have a friend, you can tell us.'

'I have many friends. Orso, Vasudha, Anjali, Aman. You know them.'

'You know what I mean. And if you don't have one—uh, a friend—why don't you look among the people you work with? If he's a journalist, he will understand your odd working hours, the outstation trips. It will be hard for a normal boy to adjust to your job.'

'You want me to find someone abnormal?'

Her mother looked exasperated. She did not enjoy this jousting.

'Okay, let me find someone I work with.' Ira paused, as if to think. 'Will a BMC contractor do? Most are in their forties or fifties, but they make a lot of money. All black money, but so what? Or how about a chapraasi? I count many BMC peons among my sources. That way, I'll also get every scoop in the municipality—reserved exclusively for Ira Kamat, daughter-in-law of the BMC. Wow, what a great idea!'

Her mother tried to purse her lips in disapproval, but her mouth cracked into a smile. 'My life has become a comedy show. We might as well disconnect the cable and save some money, no?' She looked towards the living room, where Ira's father was switching channels, jumping from one cloying advertisement to another at a too-loud volume.

'And live like Pappa's only ally, Professor Rajwade?'

'Can you imagine that—going back to only watching Doordarshan on TV? No way! But promise you'll tell us,' her mother pleaded, 'if you have a friend.'

Ira's mother was not aware of the *friend* she had recently parted ways with, or the ones before. Her mother had been right about her odd working hours; the outstation trips, however, had been spent not at work but in the company of these friends. Her parents would have liked Vinay, the boyfriend she had broken up with three months ago. He was the perfect match. On paper, that is. A year older than Ira, he worked at a foreign bank and his family owned a flat in Mahim. Most importantly, he was, like her, fair-skinned, Konkani-speaking and of the same caste.

Goud Saraswat brahmins, GSB to themselves, were brahmins who had originally settled on the banks of the river Saraswati in north India. Upon its mythical disappearance, they had moved eastwards to Bengal and then south to Goa before slowly fanning out along the western coast of India, the Konkan coast. Behind them was a long history of migration and escape, from persecutions of nature and man: famine, drought, forced conversion. Once high priests, they now ran Udupi restaurants, managed banks, set up schools and colleges, became worker bees in the service economy. They bowed, among countless other deities, to the god of commerce.

They were the insular sort when it came to marriage, as many communities tended to be, but with time, like loosening a belt through a big meal inch by inch, the emphasis on Goud Saraswat brahmin matches had been relaxed, first shedding the goud, then dropping the saraswat, and for those who called themselves broad-minded, even the brahmin became optional, *any* upper-caste Hindu match was suitable. These *radical* changes aside—and perhaps because of them—a conventional GSB match was a prize catch.

She and Vinay had dated for a year, but she had mentioned him to her parents only once, and had to watch the tight coil of tribalism spring to life.

'Vinay Prabhu? That's a GSB surname. Did he say what his native place was?'

'I think he said Kumta.'

At the mention of her hometown, her mother's eyes began to shine.

'There was a Prabhu in Kumta who owned a chemist shop. Is your friend related to Srinivas Prabhu? No, wait—all his sons are settled abroad.'

'My neighbour's wife in Hubli used to be a Prabhu from Kumta, married to a Shenoy,' her father chipped in. 'Her family had a hardware shop opposite the church.'

'That must have been Shashgir Prabhu's oldest. But he only had daughters, so no, cannot be him.' Her mother tapped her forehead, a ritual of recollection. 'There was also a Suresh Prabhu who lived behind the post office. I'm sure one of his sons moved to Mumbai after college. When did he say his family came to Mumbai?'

'He didn't say—because no one from our generation talks about all this nonsense!'

A half-lie. There were other forms of tribalism, other signs of allegiance they searched for. For example, the brand of your jeans, the fabric of your clothes, the party you voted for, how you pronounced tomato, whether you said Bombay or Mumbai.

'You can ask him next time.'

'He is Vasudha's colleague, I just met him once. How will I see him again?'

Ira was more indignant than she needed to be. She was going to have coffee with him the next day. Ira had met Vinay at her friend's birthday party, and asked him a harmless question about how he liked working at a foreign bank. He had launched into a confession: he had been trying to immigrate to America till the previous year, but had finally given up and taken a job at an American bank. The work culture was better than that at the Indian ones but he did not believe it was as good as the real thing. Just like the censored American television shows on Star TV, watered down. That is why he went to Lamington Road every month to pick up CDs of the originals, even the ones not on Indian channels yet. He had watched every TV serial of note, he said with pride. His friends even called him Christopher Columbus, he told her, for bringing America to the shores of their lives.

'My mother thinks I was born in the wrong country,' he said. 'I tell her it was the right country, just a few years early. At least the economy is now open. Think of our poor parents—they wasted their youth in a rotten system with none of the comforts we are already beginning to take for granted.'

It was then that she noticed he was dressed in brands from top to bottom, a lemon-yellow polo t-shirt with a tell-tale crocodile, tucked into blue Lee jeans, black-swooshed sneakers, and peeping from his pocket, black-and-gold Ray-Bans. His hair was combed neatly to one side, he was clean-shaven and had bright, white teeth. Vinay wore an earnest, good-boy look which, to her surprise, she found herself drawn to. They chatted for an hour and made plans to meet again. Ira found an undemanding comfort in the conversation. That palliative was exactly what she needed at the end of a stressful period at work: for three months, she had worked with a corporator from the opposition party to expose a multi-crore scam in the buildings and factories department of the BMC, an exhausting investigation for which she had received a bit of acclaim in the journalistic community.

The coffee was followed by more coffee dates, then dinners, and more. His company continued to be undemanding and comfortable. There were times when she found him trite, or felt that he was contradicting himself but, for the most part, she was happy. It was in their time together that she began to realise that she was ready to marry. Perhaps what had drawn her to him was a particular idea of a husband. With him, she could slip into speaking Konkani at a moment's notice. He was caring and patient, an attentive listener. Vinay had no political views beyond believing that Power Corrupts and that every politician was a scoundrel guzzling the taxpayer's money, so hearing about her work, her investigations into corruption pleased him greatly. They confirmed his world view and he lapped them up, little nuggets to be repeated: *trust me, this is how bad it truly is.* Each time his eyes brimmed with excitement when she told him about her work, she could see the appeal of spending a lifetime with him. Her friends liked him when they met him in large groups. Ira suspected that they too had adjusted their expectations of her romantic prospects.

A shadow on the relationship was that Vinay was an eager but lousy lover. When they kissed, he sipped at her like a kitten. He insisted on going down on her—she imagined he prided himself on participating in what he saw as a bold, Western act—but in this department, much like Columbus, he had trouble telling apart India from America. She did not think this was a deal-breaker.

Ira met his parents for the first time at a restaurant near his house. His mother said that inviting her home was out of the question because his grandparents lived with them.

'Vinu's grandparents don't understand this love-marriage business, they are quite old-fashioned,' she explained, 'but you can come home after we meet your parents to make things official.'

Ira learnt that Vinay's father did not speak much, and that his mother's preferred conversation topics did not go far beyond her family, but she tried to talk to Ira about her job as a senior reporter.

'It is important for a woman to keep her brain sharp,' his mother said with an air of benevolence. 'I devoted myself to the family all my life and it's only now that I am dabbling in the stock market. I know I don't have to worry about my children anymore, Vinu's sister is married, and he has found someone to look after him.' Vinay and his father laughed. 'Let's order? We could get butter chicken and one vegetarian dish. I love their baingan bharta—we *must* get that.'

'Aunty, do you mind if I order the bhindi fry? I don't like brinjal.'

'You'll like this dish, trust me.'

'I have never liked brinjal, sorry.' Ira made a helpless face.

'Oh, I see.' She appeared concerned. 'Three dishes might be too much for four people, no? Do you not like brinjal at all, Ira?'

'Brinjal, eggplant, aubergine. One vegetable, so many names,' said Vinay's father. It was the first sentence he had spoken. Might it be a coded plea to his wife, Ira wondered.

'Never mind, Aunty. I'll have the chicken. There's no need to order bhindi.'

'No, no, if you like bhindi, we'll get the bhindi fry. I just hope it's not oily. Vinay has a slight acidity problem—has he not told you?'

'Really, the butter chicken is enough.'

When the food arrived, his mother insisted that Ira try

the baingan bharta, but Ira did not like brinjal at all, so she politely refused.

The next day, Vinay told her that his mother had been peeved at Ira's refusal to even taste the dish. She had read into it a too-strong will, an aversion to any compromise.

'Why did you have to be so stubborn, Ira?' He sounded exasperated.

A few days later, he appeared even more worried. His parents were not convinced she was a good fit for their family, so they were planning a trip to their family temple in Goa, where they would pose this question to the deity. They would place flowers on both arms of the idol, he explained, and the one which fell first would indicate the god's preference; it was like a divine coin toss.

'Don't worry, I will meet them again,' she said to comfort him. 'I am sure they will change their mind.'

'Why didn't you just eat the fucking brinjal when you had a chance?' he cried, losing his temper at her for the first time.

The night after Vinay's parents left for Goa, Ira could not sleep. She pictured the temple, its carved wooden pillars, the idol dressed in silk and gold, a single flower on each arm, a priest chanting, his parents with their hands folded and heads bowed, their hearts exploding with a single question: should their son marry the girl too pig-headed to eat brinjal even when asked repeatedly?

In that moment, she hoped and wished and prayed for the right flower to fall off, the one that said no, the one that screamed no. Abso-fucking-lutely NO.

The next morning, she broke up with Vinay, telling him she did not want to be a source of strife in his family. He put up no resistance. She suspected the deity had already delivered its verdict.

'How could I have loved somebody so spineless!' she exclaimed to her friends.

But she had not loved him, not really. She would not have loved handsome Vinay even if he had stood up to his parents, even if he had been a better lover.

That title, love of her life, she had given away to someone who had neglected to return it when he left. How was it possible that she still believed she loved him? That after more than three years, if even a single thought of him crossed her mind, it bored deeper and deeper, not stopping till it reached her heart, gnawing at her insides like Pacman?

Kaiz, oh Kaiz, where was he?

4

IRA HAD TO WEAVE THROUGH a long sheet of suburban traffic to cross the road. Even outside peak hours, four lanes of vehicles were pinched into three as they entered a narrow subway under an overhead rail line. The rattling of train tracks drowned all sounds and the smell of sewage deepened the assault on the senses. A storm-water drain ran along one side of the road, filled with a green-grey sludge with a dull vitreous sheen. For a long moment, she could see reflected in this glassy film a flock of egrets flying above.

Glass is a liquid that flows very slowly.

It was only the illusion of flow: nothing would actually move through this channel. She covered her nose and mouth with a handkerchief to lean forward for a final look before she stepped away. An auto-rickshaw driving dangerously close to the edge of the road honked at her. The shrill, adolescent horns of rickshaws made the suburbs sound different from the island city.

Ira had spent the morning walking along storm-water drains around Bandra and Santa Cruz, appraising them with a former municipal civil engineer who had volunteered to help with the assessment. The rains were only a week or two away. There had even been a few flashes of thunder the previous day. So far, her source Sanjiv Shinde was right: most nullahs in the western suburbs had not been cleaned for the monsoon. In many places, the dredging hadn't started. Where the drain had been desilted, the silt had been left in piles by the side of the road.

Shinde was clad in a light grey safari suit. A dank, darker grey marked the outlines of a vest. He travelled in an air-conditioned Sumo, but even five or ten minutes spent outside were enough for the humidity to leave its mark.

'Last year, Miss Ira,' he said, 'I started work on the fifteenth of April and we had wrapped up by this time. And look at this—nothing has been done. A contractor was selected a full two months ago but he stopped after a few weeks of work and no one followed up. How can the BMC not know that this is the most flood-prone area in Santa Cruz? As a concerned citizen, I feel that all Mumbaikars should know what their elected representatives are doing to their city.'

'Only as a concerned citizen, Mr Shinde?'

'What, Madam—are you taking my phirki?'

He smiled, flashing small pearly teeth. Shinde was among the youngest BMC contractors and was the relative of a three-time municipal corporator from Santa Cruz. He had built a modest fortune carrying out civil works projects in Santa Cruz and Vile Parle, but in the most recent elections, his uncle had lost his seat. Since his uncle's defeat, Shinde had many leads for Ira.

'At the Saiwadi nullah in Andheri East, the tender was for seventy labourers and the contractor is using only ten. Yes, seventy to ten, write it down please.' He shook his head solemnly. 'Everything is in a shambles this year. All we can do now is sing that nursery rhyme: rain, rain, go to Spain, don't come and give us pain.'

Then he appeared to have a change of heart. In penance, he slapped his hand over his mouth a few times.

'What am I saying? We need rain, lots of it. If only the BMC would do its job. My friend knows of jhol in the Linking Road concretisation project too. Multi-crore scam, Miss Ira, at least two crores this year itself. Can I put you in touch?'

She didn't have to ask who his friend was: also a contractor who was smarting from losing a plum project, and a share of this multi-crore pie. It was this lightness of pocket that gave her more leads than any lightness of conscience.

'Yes, Sir, please. I'll call you if I have any questions.'

'I am going VT-side for a meeting now; can I drop you somewhere?'

'Thank you, Mr Shinde, but I have meetings nearby, I need to stay longer.' As tempting as the air-conditioned ride was, she did not want to take favours from someone who could be—no, would be—on the other side of a report another time.

After Shinde left, she spoke to a few residents. They all had the same things to say, that the BMC was corrupt and incompetent, that the city was bad enough for the rest of the year but was truly unliveable during the monsoon when the city whirled in a slurry of rainwater and sewage, gifts from heaven and hell. Newspapers tore into the BMC. Fingers were pointed, enquiries ordered. But the year after, reporters found themselves asking the same questions of the same people, receiving the same answers. At least this year promised some new excuses: the late civic elections could explain the delay in forming the municipal standing committee that was supposed to sanction the pre-monsoon work.

At times it felt like there was nothing new left to say about Mumbai. More often than not, work had become one routine story braided into another, this meeting and that scheme, delays and excuses. The special reports were few, and even those were the usual tales of corruption, incompetence, politics. The big stories appeared to be in hiding. The elusive aha moment skulked around her, invisible and biding. In its place there were only false starts and dead ends. All thunder and no rain.

Or all fart and no shit, as Kartik had said the past weekend to describe a new movie that was heavily hyped, only to release to terrible reviews and empty theatres. What an odd sense of humour the guy had, she thought, and found herself smiling.

She reminded herself that the public loved these stories of corruption, like Vinay had, even if they had heard them a hundred times before. They liked stories that confirmed what they believed: that their venal leaders were the ones standing between them and greatness. Between them and a modern city, between them and a first-world nation. These scams enraged them, and from the crucible of their fury, they themselves emerged pure. They wanted corruption removed from the root, so that honest people could prosper for a change, as if they had no role to play in the shape of their lives, in the fate of their cities and their country, as if these stories of graft unfolded in black vacuum.

At Santa Cruz station, Ira boarded the Churchgate local and found a place to sit. There was a young woman reading *The Fountainhead* by the door of the train. She was wearing yellow plastic earrings, the kind you could buy for Rs 5 a pair in the train itself, to match her taxi-yellow shirt. This was a common sight in the local train: junior college student flirting with Ayn Rand. If she finished the book, she would find an idol and role model in Howard Roark. For a week or two, she would believe that all her dreams were within reach, she only had to apply herself to them fully. She would even briefly look down upon friends who didn't read, who were content with bunking classes and hanging out at the canteen. Eventually, one hoped, with time or after reading *Atlas Shrugged*, her youthful foolishness would become visible to her. The teenager in yellow was only about fifty pages in.

A woman breastfeeding her baby had sat down cross-legged next to the door, narrowing the exit like plaque in an artery. Two stops away was Dadar, where there would be a surge of passengers. Women had started making their way towards the door, and passengers bound for farther destinations were retreating from the exit. These were unwritten codes that the mother was breaking. Stations like Dadar kindled fights, the crowds rubbing together like stones. An argument broke out between the nursing mother and two middle-aged women who asked her to move away from the door. Fights were a daily occurrence in the ladies' compartment, but these women fought in Gujarati, which Ira had never witnessed before.

'Why should I move? Nobody is complaining other than you two.'

'No one cares about you, it is the baby we are looking out for.'

'I can look after my child, ladies. Leave me alone.'

'Maybe you deserve to get a shoe or two in your face.'

'Fuck off.'

'Oh really? You are lucky we are just *asking* you to move. The likes of you should cross a Marathi passenger—they will cut you down to size in two minutes. One tight slap, that's what you need.'

Ira went back to reading her book. Train fights followed a template: a provocation, usually stemming from the endless struggle for space, the tension rising to a simmer that both parties were comfortable with, and the end of the fight when one of the parties got off the train, sometimes even before. But this fight was different, the shouting continued even after the train pulled into Dadar, women started alighting, and others climbed in to take their place. When the train started moving again, and her middle-aged antagonists were halfway up the stairs to the overbridge, the young mother stood up, her baby in one arm, and started shouting into the crowd.

'Go die, you horse's whore, dog's cunt, you dried-up asshole of a pig.'

Some passengers gasped, a few giggled.

There was plenty of anger on offer in Mumbai and it was easy to look away. But every once in a while, someone with imagination crafted their fury like origami into something delightful. These were the times when even train veterans like Ira were forced to drop everything and look. Her mood brightened again, briefly.

When she came home from work, she found her parents in the middle of a fight. She had entered the house at a moment of repose, the lull before a storm, but she could smell, taste and feel the acrid afterburn of conflict. She had barely sat down when her mother started to tidy the small shoe rack near the door, making more noise than a person not trying to make a point would make: slapping slippers on the ground as if dusting them, piling shoes one on top of another, muttering and shaking her head.

'Give me a minute, I'll put my sandals away,' Ira said.

'You will, but what about the other people who live in this house?'

She suppressed a smile. 'Which other people?'

Her mother glared at Ira. 'Someone bought new shoes today. Ask him why he needs another pair when he already has two. Why does a man need more than one pair of shoes, huh? What is he, some Lord Falkland?'

These were the second pair of shoes her father had bought since he retired four months ago. Old age was supposed to be a second childhood, but in her father's case it was his second youth. It was not uncommon now to find him trimming his eyebrows in front of the mirror in the morning, whistling a tune to himself, after which he combed, back-combed, side-combed his hair, searching for an angle that would hide the thinning patch on his crown. A tube of Fair & Lovely had appeared in the bathroom cabinet. This he applied to his face morning and night in tender outward circles. Freed from the toil of ten-to-six, Shankar Kamat had turned his energies to himself. A few nights ago, he had even complained to his wife about eating rice for dinner every day, to which she had replied that their people had eaten rice for every meal for generations. If it was good enough for their daughter, who had not yet found a husband and hence had a reason to worry about her *figure*, it should be good enough for him. Embarrassed, he made some noises about diabetes, cholesterol, heart disease. Who said anything about the figure, he sputtered.

'Tell your father that the next pair of shoes he buys I will have to keep on my head, there is no more space in this house,' Ira's mother announced. 'This house that he does not want to leave.'

Instead of answering her directly, or conveying a retort through Ira, her father got up and walked around the living room with his eyes on the ceiling, then he paced around the kitchen before stopping next to the fridge. He looked at the wall, then towards his wife, then the wall, and back, chin bobbing, lips curled at the corners. Ira followed his gaze to a small cluster of cobwebs on the walls.

Her mother did too. 'What does that look mean?'

'It means you mind your business and I will mind mine.'

'How you spend your money—our money—*is* my business.'

'Yes, given how hard you have worked to earn it.'

In no time the fight started becoming familiar: they had only three lakhs saved up; it was comfortable enough for retirement; how long would that last, his pension barely covered expenses; she had not earned the money and had no right to question him over it; the pay-out for the house would be at least twenty lakhs. A new flat, were the landlord to agree to it, would be worth much more than that—no, he would not move under any condition, that was final. Her parents had had the same fights dozens of times. Even she knew their arguments like the map of a familiar neighbourhood, which streets to avoid, which alleys not to turn into. And yet, her parents retraced their steps day after day. Her mother would finally look at her, exasperated, and say, 'Tell him, Ira, tell him to be less stubborn and think about us too.' It was unbearable to witness, so she decided to get out of the flat. The sound of her parents' squabbling was gone as soon as she shut the door, and so she went up to the terrace.

Most of the terrace was covered in sawdust, thanks to the Naik family. Every monsoon the rainwater seeped into their ceiling and cracked the plaster into hundreds of pieces. Afraid that their ceiling would not stand even one more shower, the Naiks were getting wooden beams hoisted to support the ceiling, both inside their flat and outside in the landing. Each beam was a skinny brown Atlas holding up the sky.

The Naiks had the most to lose if the negotiations with the landlord stalled for any reason. Which proved that the Kinis were remarkable people. They had managed to make Mr Naik waver in his long-standing support of Mr Desai's demands. Kini, Rege, Shanbhag, Naik. The four Saraswat brahmin families other than her own had flocked together. In the battle for Asha Nivas, it was the Konkanis versus the Gujaratis and the South Indians. If her father could be persuaded to join the Kinis, they would outnumber the Desai camp. Kusum maushi had already brought it up with her mother a couple of times. These money matters are men's matters, her mother had told her friend, they have no place in our friendship. But Ira knew that Kusum maushi was not one to give up, and that her mother could only put on the act of being her husband's ally for so long. Privately, Shobha Kamat was already cracking.

Ira felt her stomach stir when the smell of fried onions wafted in from the Naik home. Suddenly it looked to Ira like buddhi-ka-baal was growing from the walls. The sawdust from the carpentry job had covered all the cobwebs on the terrace and turned them orange, almost like candy floss. Her stomach made rumbling sounds, like rain clouds rolling in. She hadn't eaten since lunch, and now she was seeing food everywhere.

Going home immediately was out of the question; then again, it wasn't like the mood at home would improve if she stayed away longer. Kaiz used to describe the way his parents fought as white-hot, all blaze and blitz like the Delhi summer. Her parents never shouted or swore, but their petty bickering seemed to go on day and night. Each needled the other plenty, and in turn, rose to the smallest provocation. It made the air in the house feel mildly toxic. It was a soft, simmering, suffocating heat, no different from a summer in Mumbai.

Had it always been like this, she wondered. She knew the answer was both no and yes.

That first fight she still remembered. Whether her father

had slapped her mother, twisted her arm, or simply shoved her, Ira was not sure, not even twenty-two years later. Her parents had been in the bedroom and she outside, only six years old at the time, but she'd known that something had happened because their bickering suddenly stopped, and her mother yelped and started crying. It was the first quarrel between them she had heard. It might even have been one of the first quarrels they'd had, for her mother only started talking back to her father much later, when Ira was in her teens. Putting together the chronology later, Ira surmised that the incident had been around the time her father resolved to say no to promotions because bank officers could be transferred around the nation. He said he was done with other people deciding where or how he lived. Her mother might have protested his decision, or pointed out that as a clerk-cum-cashier he wasn't exactly the Lord of Matunga either. Either would have been enough to invite his wrath.

Ira's father was a quiet but short-tempered man. It had added greatly to his aura when she was a child. His aura came from his position as the head of the household, from his absence from morning to evening, like a weekday vampire. Unlike her mother, he had never struck her or twisted her ear. He didn't have to, an angry stare from him was chastising enough. It was he who decided whether her mother and she went to her grandparents' house for the summer, and her mother only cooked fish when he asked for it. She had always sensed this power her father held. She would name him first in her evening prayers and hold in any news from her school day till he was home. If someone said that her smile was like her father's, or that she got her light eyes from his side of the family, she would swell with delight. And if he did hit her mother, she forgave him, feeling only a mix of shame and anger towards her mother.

For provoking her father, for losing, for getting punished like a mere child. For the first ten years of her life, she thought her father could do no wrong.

Even his job had once seemed of grave importance. When someone put their money into the bank or took it out, he explained to her, they had to go through him. He made sure that one person's money did not get mixed up with another's—it was the key to keeping everybody's money safe. Before long, she had figured out that her father's account of his role at the bank was greatly exaggerated. Nor was he a powerful or feared man outside the house. This appearance of power was something he put on before he came home, like a pair of house slippers.

Her father's stand on the Asha Nivas issue was another appearance of power, she believed, a type of tantrum. She wanted to move no more than he did, but at least she had her reasons, as silly as they were. Ira suspected he was enjoying holding the other residents hostage, watching them plead and cajole. It made no sense otherwise; he had never displayed any particular love for the building they lived in. It was no more than the sum of its walls to him, no more than a roof over the head. And yet, she could not bring herself to confront him about it, or ask him what was really on his mind. The blind adulation for her father was long gone but its seed remained. She argued and fought with him but there were gloves involved. There were rules. She could not point out to him that there was nothing iconoclastic about his decision to remain a clerk all his life, or about his recent refusal to engage with the redevelopment. She would not correct his pronunciation of an English word, or make fun of his new-found vanity. It was easy to believe that a mother's love was unconditional, which made it alright to challenge her, correct her, laugh at her. Fathers were more complicated. Their love, once earned, had to be sustained. It had to be sheltered from the glare of truth.

Her thoughts were interrupted when she felt a hand on her shoulder. It was her mother.

'Come, eat.'

Ira looked at the door expectantly as she walked towards the staircase. Still no sign of Kartik. She had run into him on the terrace around this time a couple of times in the past weeks. He had warned her that his new job was demanding, that he would have to plunge into work right away. It looked like his long days had already begun. She would not see him today.

The throb of disappointment that followed took Ira by surprise.

5

IRA WAS NOT SURE WHETHER it was the playground episode with the urchins that had marked a shift in their friendship and her idea of Kartik, or if it happened a few months later when the camera incident occurred.

Their school had asked students to submit science projects. The best entries would represent the school at a citywide science fair. She had been too young to participate, and the children of Asha Nivas had pegged their hopes on Kartik anyway. A rival of his had bragged about how he was certain of victory. This boy was said to be building something magnificent. His silly boast passed from student to student and reached the Asha Nivas gang at lunch. They were sitting at their favourite stoop close to the school, the spot where they had their tiffin every day. It was an open challenge to Kartik and, by extension, to all of them; rivalries were among their greatest entertainments and were actively fanned.

Ira was the first to react. 'How can he say that? As if he can come up with anything better than you.'

'Three projects will qualify, not just one,' Kartik answered.

Ira frowned. 'But you have to come first!'

Somebody else asked, 'What are you building, Kartik?'

He hesitated. 'I don't know yet.' Reading concern on the faces of his friends, he added, 'But I have lots of ideas.'

'You have to submit your project next Friday!'

'You think he doesn't know that? He can build something much better than that boy in half a day.'

On the day of the submission, Ira happened to leave for school early. At the gate of their building, she met Kartik, who was carrying a cloth bag in his hand. He was leaving earlier than usual as well.

'Is that your project? What did you make?'

'A pinhole camera.'

Her face lit up. 'Can it take photos?'

'It's not that kind of camera.'

'Can I see it?'

'It's delicate, I don't want you to break it.'

'I'll be careful. I promise.'

He looked annoyed but opened the cloth bag to produce a long rectangular box with thermocol walls held together by lots of tape. One of the ends had foil on it and the other was sealed with white paper.

'This?' Her tone did not mask how let down she was.

'You look through this end and see an upside-down version of whatever you point the other end at.'

'Let me see.'

He said it needed to be darker for the camera to work properly but she had already taken it from him. It rattled lightly in her hands. She looked at the screen. Nothing. She swung around, pointing the camera in different directions. Nothing. She looked through the other side, through the pinhole. Nothing again.

'I think this doesn't work.'

'You don't know how to use it.'

He tried to explain to her what a pinhole camera was, something about the principle of cameras and lenses. Midway through his explanation, he thrust his arm out to take the device back from Ira, but she was quicker, she pulled it away before he could grab it.

'Let me try one more time.'

'Give it back before you break it. Now!'

He snatched the thermocol box from her hands with great force, a brief bright gleam in his eye, and inspected it—his invention was intact.

'What'll you do? It doesn't work.'

He said nothing. He put it back into the cloth bag and ran ahead to school.

The projects were due at the end of the day. At recess, Kartik did not join the gang for lunch. They traded descriptions of the contraptions they had seen: a clap-activated light bulb, volcanoes, kaleidoscopes and periscopes. Did anybody know what Kartik had built, someone asked. The children shook their heads one by one. Ira did too.

Two periods after the recess, she asked her teacher for permission to go to the bathroom. A few students sniggered and a backbencher made hissing sounds. How many times does she need to pee, somebody whispered. She had a healthy bladder, but also restless limbs and a straying mind. Sitting in a classroom for hours at an end was difficult, boredom would begin to press in on all her bones. These five-minute breaks were the only remedy. She ambled along the corridor to delay her return to fractions and decimals, stepping only on every third tile, till the sound of footsteps made her turn around. A figure caught her eye: Kartik coming out of his classroom. She knew the room was empty—she had walked past it on her way to the toilet—his entire class was on the playground for the physical training period. Kartik glanced at both ends of the corridor. Before he could see her, she hid behind a column. He ran to the staircase and disappeared from her view. She did not know what made her hide, or why she did not ask him what he was doing, but in her heart of hearts she understood that she had witnessed something she was not supposed to see, that she had accidentally swallowed a slice of a secret.

In the evening, when she went out to play, her comrades wore solemn expressions. Somebody had broken Kartik's project, Vasant reported, his entry had been destroyed while he was in the school playground and he was too upset to meet anybody. The teachers were shocked too; they had threatened to punish the whole class if the offender did not step forward. The children pursed their lips and shook their heads in sympathy but came to life when they began to discuss various theories: they listed his rivals and looked for clues to indict or acquit each one. While the teachers were focusing on his classmates, what if the culprit was not from his class at all? Or what if it was someone from another school? Don Bosco was an old nemesis and Kartik's reputation had spread far and wide. Ira remained quiet. The image of Kartik slinking out of his empty classroom had bothered her all day, like a mango fibre stuck between the teeth. A slice of a secret. She felt an illness coming on, her skin was now hot, now cold. These flashes slid along her body to settle in her stomach where they continued their dance. She told her friends she had a stomach ache and returned home.

Kartik joined his friends on the terrace the next evening.

His friends were relieved to see him in good spirits again. He asked everybody what they wanted to do, and they decided to play gangster-gangster, a game inspired by their most famous neighbour, the Tamil gangster Varadharaja. Kartik sorted the kids into pairs, and each pair was given a challenge at which they competed with each other. The winners won favours with the crime lord while the losers were punished. Kartik played Varadha, the don of Matunga. He had a plastic gun in hand, a water pistol which he said spewed acid at those who displeased the don. From time to time he shot in the direction of the younger children, which made them squeal and scatter like chickens.

Kartik asked Ira and Manoj to arm wrestle. They locked palms and began to push with all their muscle and might, teeth gritted. The veins in Manoj's reed-like arm were visible, his brow was knitted, hungry for victory. Even the younger siblings won more challenges than the scrawny Manoj. Why it mattered who won or lost, nobody could answer. There was nothing at stake other than Kartik's approval. Kartik, their leader, their friend. Ira scanned his face for residues of what had happened at school but found none. In the moment that she was looking away, Manoj squeezed out a cache of strength and pushed Ira's arm down.

'I want a rematch, I was distracted,' she protested.

Vasant had been denied a rematch a few minutes ago. Everybody looked at Kartik to see if he would make an exception for his closest friend.

'You can't ask for a rematch if you don't win. It's not fair.'

She paused, dropped her voice. 'But it's fair to lie when you know you won't win?'

'What are you talking about?'

'Who broke your camera—your project?' This time her question was loud and clear.

'How do I know? Must be someone who was jealous.'

She looked into his face in challenge, in mute reproach, unable to say what she had left unsaid. He stared back, looking straight into her eyes. Her eyes, like marbles, hard and green.

'Don't waste everybody's time, Ira.'

Kartik took Manoj's hand and raised it into the air before announcing Ira's punishment: she had to rub her nose against a wall ten times. This was considered a grave insult.

'I won't do it. Give me another punishment.'

'You don't choose the punishment, I do.'

'This is a stupid game. I don't want to play.'

Loath to be challenged again before the gang, Kartik stepped back into character. 'If you don't do it,' he said, pointing the gun at her face, 'I will shoot.'

'Then shoot. It's just water.'

Kartik frowned. 'It's acid.'

'Varadha uses guns and knives, you think he uses acid? He is a gangster, not a toilet cleaner.'

The challenge to his fiction was the final straw. His face hardened. 'Get lost. You are no fun to play with.'

Only Ira heard the tremor in his voice, it was small and wounded. Then he did something he had never done before—he stepped forward and shoved her. She stumbled to the floor. The other children looked on saucer-eyed. Ira got up and brushed the dust off her palms. A scrape at the heel of her left hand burned and she felt a dull ache all over. She walked away slowly, nobody stopped her.

It was a few weeks before it become clear that Ira and Kartik had really stopped talking to each other, that neither was willing to blink first. Ira stayed away from the group for a few days after the confrontation and when she returned, it was Kartik's turn to not show up. When they were both present, they carried out only minimum communication, and even that through others, complicating their evening games. This feud was thrilling at first. From it bloomed hours of debate and discussion: it was insolent of Ira to speak to an older kid like that but Kartik should not have asked her to rub her nose against a wall, it was too much. Unrelated grievances also came up for air. Ira thought too highly of herself, didn't she? As for Kartik, why was he still their leader? They were not little children to indulge in the play-acting he favoured. And what about that unanswered question: who had destroyed his science project? Was it possible that he himself—no, no, he would not, would he?

Eventually a volunteer was dispatched to inform their mothers. The women sat their children down and forced them to shake hands. When that did not work, her mother broke down the calculus of forgiving and forgetting for her: don't be too proud to say sorry, this much pride doesn't suit a girl. The words bounced off her skin like a rubber ball, leaving only a faint sting, but it made her more determined not to be the one to buckle.

Kartik caved first, five weeks later. He never lent anybody his books but brought her one he thought she might enjoy. At first, she remained frosty, she did not reach for the offering. When she saw his face crumple, Ira could not keep up her act anymore.

'I did not do it, I promise,' he pleaded. 'I won't lie to you. You are my best friend, aren't you?'

Neither of them talked about the pinhole camera again.

Even if he did destroy it, she reasoned, it was only a lapse of judgement. He was still the same boy as before, at worst a shade more fallible. A more twisted child might have even resorted to sabotage. So she did not ask him why he had been sneaking out of his classroom.

Only one problem remained. The question she had posed before their friends, how long had it lingered in the air and rung in their ears—long enough to lodge in their heads? *Who broke your camera?* In the months that followed, as she saw old friendships transform and wither, she carried an abiding sense of guilt.

Perhaps it was not her fault at all. The star of model students tends to fade after adolescence. So, really, Kartik's hold over the gang might have weakened anyway. The gang itself was dissolving, breaking into smaller factions. The older boys, the older girls, the younger children who in time would split further. There was no group he could easily ally with, no games he could smoothly insert himself into. So Kartik began to retreat into the world of textbooks, exercise sheets, novels. Cricket and football matches continued without him, as did badminton, walks, gossip sessions. A new nickname emerged. Scholar. An incantation, a jibe. Under its unsparing glare, a friend began to fade away.

Except from her life.

This was to become a new chapter in their friendship, one that was not encumbered by the dynamics of the building gang, one in which they were also rapidly becoming the people they were going to be.

6

IT APPEARED THAT THE MONSOON was only crawling towards Mumbai. There were false alarms but rain eluded the city. Gusts of wind that made you run to take wet clothes off the clothesline. Low clouds that teased you and quickly retreated, like kabaddi players. The air smelled of moisture but there was only dust, no water. The city simmered, the hopeful and the weary alike waited for the first rain. It was the biggest event looming on the horizon: the break of monsoon was easy to shape into a sign from the skies, a promise of change. For Ira, the lull at work continued but there was an unexpected, albeit small, victory. After her report on storm-water drains, the BMC had started fining contractors for the delay in desilting. The fine of ten thousand rupees for each week of delay had earned the municipal corporation four lakhs already.

A few days later, another surprise awaited her, this time at home: Kartik had left a message asking her to call him.

'What did he want?' she asked her mother.

'Pick up the phone and ask him yourself.'

'You didn't ask him?'

'So you can call me the CBI again? I said nothing to him. What is it to me?'

Her mother's new indifference struck Ira as phoney. The previous week, she had invited her friend Vasudha for dinner, and then spent a considerable portion of those two hours subjecting the guest to a blunderbuss of questions. Among them: how much did MBAs earn, how well did MNCs pay, was it common for them to have their offices in five-star hotels, did Vasudha have any idea about this new type of job called management consulting? Ira was appalled to learn that, through these circumlocutions, her mother had been trying to work out how much Kartik earned. It was not just her, she confessed to Ira, Mrs Desai and Mrs Rege were curious too. Kartik's mother had told them that, on his first day of work, his office took him to lunch at the Taj Mahal hotel, where the bill had come to Rs 15,000. And his boss had moved back from America for this job. The willing return of an emigre was unheard of; the job must pay a fortune. Vasudha was not sure how much management consultancies paid their project managers. Nonetheless she lobbed a guess at them: three times what her father had made before he retired. Four times Ira's salary.

So what, Ira repeated to herself before she called him, money was not everything.

Kartik wanted to meet for a smoke. 'And I haven't seen you in a week,' he said, which pleased her. They agreed to meet on the terrace, but only after Ira assured him that nobody would catch him smoking there. It was amusing, a thirty-year-old man afraid of his parents finding out that he smoked. But many of her close friends over the years had been the goody-goody types: god-fearing, mother-revering, hair-oiling, hormone-defying beacons of decency who brushed their teeth twice a day, who forgave and forgot, who said thank you but found more opportunities to say you are welcome, and when they read the paper they started from the front. But they were also often the biggest rascals, which explained why they were her friends. The adult Kartik she was only beginning to unpack.

Kartik stood away from the edge of the terrace, still nervous about being seen. In the street below, a knot of temple-goers was haggling over flowers and coconuts, pouring in and out of temples, sifting through the mass of shoes outside. There was a faint but continuous echo of bells. Ira could not tell if this was unceasing devotion on display or whether she had developed tinnitus from living near three temples her entire life. She waited to bring up the matter on top of her mind.

'I heard that your office is in the presidential suite at the Oberoi.'

Kartik blushed. 'Our team in India is still small and a hotel suite is cheaper than renting a full office. Real estate in Bombay is ludicrous.'

'Don't you dare complain! So what is it like going to a five-star every day?'

'It's not that big a deal. You get used to it.'

'*You get used to it,*' she repeated in a child's high voice. 'No, tell me, how does it feel?'

'You haven't changed one bit,' he said. 'But really, it is startling how quickly it begins to feel normal.'

His first day at the consultancy had been surreal, he explained. He had worn his best clothes, a suit with a silk tie, but had still hesitated when he entered the hotel to report to work. The name of his firm and the suite number he carried on the tip of his tongue and the offer letter was within reach in a folder in his briefcase. But the doorman had merely given him a salute and opened the door for him, no questions asked.

'Do you remember how we used to stand in the corridor of the Taj Mahal hotel and look into the air-conditioned shops when we were children?' he asked.

'And we would wait for somebody, *anybody*, to open a door, for the cool air from inside to hit our faces.' She closed her eyes and smiled, soothed by the memory of this draft.

Once a month or so, a few hours after their Sunday lunch, Ira and Kartik along with their mothers would take the train from Matunga to Churchgate to spend half a day around Colaba. Starting from Churchgate station, they would take in the grandeur of Eros Cinema and the apartment buildings around it. It wasn't the bold palettes of art deco or the architectural leap towards modernity that they admired, or even grasped, it was the glow of old money that they marvelled at. They walked through Oval Maidan, where gothic towers and palm trees cast tall shadows on boys playing cricket, and through the basalt arcades of office buildings on the way to Kala Ghoda Circle and Regal Cinema. Then to Colaba Causeway, in and out of the warren of pavement stalls peddling antiques and bric-a-brac, occasionally stopping at Kamat restaurant for a dosa or a lemon soda, or at Tibbs for a chicken frankie whose orange gravy dribbled down your chin like a henna beard, and onwards to the Gateway of India, near which the Taj Mahal Hotel was located.

'To think we could have just walked in,' said Kartik.

'Not a chance.'

'You might be right, it wasn't possible then. Some of the people who walk in today, they come wearing shorts, ripped jeans and t-shirts. I am talking about Indians, not foreigners. When did we become so confident? Where has this sudden self-assurance come from?'

'Maybe they too have got *used to it*. Let's see what you wear to work a year from now.'

He chuckled. 'True. The suit is already off. The tie too might be gone soon. What next?'

Her pulse quickened at the image of Kartik undressing piece by piece.

'I do think it is deliberate,' he said.

'Sorry, what is?'

'The choice of clothes, the indifference.'

He opened and closed his mouth a few times without saying anything, as though he were struggling to articulate something he felt deeply.

'Think about how we grew up—we were comfortably middle-class, yes, but we never had much,' he said, finally. 'And it didn't matter, there wasn't that much to have anyway. There were a few symbols of wealth scattered around us even then—the five-star hotels, the sea-facing apartments—but nobody told us they were within reach. They were like distant stars that exerted no great force on our lives.'

It dawned upon her then, from how he said we and us, that Kartik had not grasped the difference between their circumstances. He remembered their families' joint excursions to South Bombay but seemed to have forgotten that it had been Ira's mother who decided where they stopped for a snack, that it was she who dictated whether they would take the ferry at Gateway of India or if the children got to ride horses at Bandstand. Kusum maushi had always generously let the Kamats go first so they could set a budget they were comfortable with. The much better-off Kinis would then follow. Nor had he registered that he alone made nearly twice as much as her father and she put together. She had spent a whole day the previous week appraising sewers, she knew little of the luxuries he had got used to.

Still, it felt like he was confiding in her. This air of intimacy pleased her.

'Go on,' she said.

'You might say that they are used to these places—the shabby young men and women I was talking about—that they see no need to impress. But when I look at them, I think about when we were children. Their indifference is not in the least the same as ours. Going to a five-star hotel is no marker of wealth anymore. Too many people can do that, so you want to announce that you have made a habit of opulence, make a show of this disregard. Because this disregard of wealth feeds back into it—you could even say that the performance of indifference actually inflates wealth, adds depth to it. You know what I mean?'

'New money shouts, old money whispers?' she offered, by way of summation.

He smiled a small, sheepish smile. 'Sorry, I did not mean to deliver a lecture where one line would have sufficed.'

Kartik put his hands on the low wall around the terrace before pulling away almost immediately. Sawdust and whitewash. He swore and wiped his palms on his jeans. She wondered if she had bruised his feelings.

She spoke after a long pause. 'Someone once said to me that try as hard as you may, the first coat of paint shows.'

The muscles in her face contracted at the bitter memory. The urge to add a disclaimer arose: not about me, about somebody else. But she wasn't sure of that, was she?

'*Someone*, I see. Was it an ex?'

How sheer some memories made you, how powerless you were before them.

'No,' she said, 'but close.'

'Someone close to an ex, hmm. Boyfriend you are thinking of breaking up with?'

Ira smiled. 'No, Sherlock, literally someone close to an ex. His best friend.'

'So, no boyfriend?'

'Is my mother paying you to spy on me?' she said with mock outrage. Then, the glimmer of another possibility. 'No boyfriend. Go tell her.'

'I will,' he said. 'But only if you tell me why you don't want to leave Asha Nivas.'

That came out of nowhere, she thought.

'Who told you I don't want to move? You are thinking of my father.'

'And you agree with him.'

'Go ask my father when I last agreed with him. Neither of us remembers.'

'You have never told me what you think of this redevelopment business. It can only be because you have a contrarian view.'

He was right. She did not want to move, did not want Asha Nivas to be torn down.

'Fine. I love this building,' said Ira. 'I like how we live. I like how we fit into this lane, how Matunga fits into Mumbai.'

'Surely you don't want things to go on like this? Look at how the Naiks are living. The state of the terrace is appalling. The parapet outside my own bedroom window is close to falling off.'

In short, there was life beyond nostalgia. But surely there was life beyond greed too, beyond sucking your city dry.

'Of course not. I understand that Asha Nivas has to be repaired or rebuilt. But I don't look forward to what will come next. Modern buildings that most of us will not be able to afford at all.'

'Unless?'

'Unless your parents succeed. Right. But the fact remains that there's something special about this part of Mumbai that's being stripped away piece by piece. The wide green roads, the open spaces, an understanding that every building is part of the city's fabric.'

'What do you mean?'

'We can't cut ourselves off from the street here, unlike, say, in Santorini Towers with its separate service elevators. The street is the very soul of this city.'

Oh shit, she thought, she was parroting Kaiz's words. What had he called the new office buildings around Fort? Generic, soulless. She had laughed at him then. Was it possible, she wondered with a shudder, that what she thought was a vision for the city was only a phantom memory, a borrowed dream? The idea was appalling.

'It won't be that bad, Ira. Everything will be more or less the same—just a slightly taller building, some new neighbours.'

'Kartik, I know how this story unfolds. It's a book I read

every day; this is what I do for a living. Just because you know something's going to happen doesn't mean you look forward to it.'

'Alright, let's talk about something else. What *do* you look forward to?'

'Hmm, let's see. To monsoon, to litchis, to three Shah Rukh Khan films releasing in the next four months. And what do you look forward to?'

'These days, only to weekends.' He sighed loudly.

'But, Scholar, you started your five-star job just three weeks ago.'

'You have to stop calling me that. How did you even come up with such a dumb nickname?'

'You know why. And it wasn't just me. Everybody in the building called you Scholar.'

'Not to my face.'

'Of course they did.'

He shook his head.

'I can't believe you don't remember that!'

She learnt over the weeks to come that the differences in their accounts of their childhood ran deep. He claimed the episode with the street children had happened in the King's Circle park itself, not all the way in Five Gardens where he said they were not allowed to go by themselves. When she reminded him of that savage game that had gripped the boys one summer—hoppingo battingo—he was astonished that he had forgotten it, for he still felt a thump on his spine upon hearing those words. They both remembered the game where they climbed the water tank to spot shapes in the clouds, and she made him confess that he had cheated often.

They marvelled at how their childhood playmates were now parents, and she filled him in on whose kids were the worst behaved and which ones were carbon copies of their parents. Soon they were gossiping about the adults in the building too: Anjali Krishnan had walked out on an abusive husband after four months of marriage and had been dispatched to her grandmother's house in Chennai, word had only got out after the Krishnans' maid told the Shanbhags' cook. Manoj Doshi was still waiting for his parent's blessings to marry his girlfriend of seven years, but they were aghast that she was not vegetarian. Ganesan uncle, the disciplinarian whose big ruddy eyes they had once feared, had adopted a puppy in his late sixties and was seen walking it around the neighbourhood morning and evening.

Neither brought up the camera incident, the first break in their friendship. Nor did they speak of the reason they had not spoken for thirteen years.

In getting to know Kartik again, Ira began to look at that very mistake as the event that had allowed them the chance— now, as grown-ups—to be friends. The clean break had let her preserve the friendship as something precious and exalted that could be put together again if suitable amends were made. How would they have reversed a more commonplace separation, a slow drifting apart?

7

EVERY OTHER SUMMER KARTIK'S GRANDPARENTS left for America to stay with his uncle's family in New Jersey for three months. When they were away, Ira's mother spent most afternoons in the Kinis' flat. Kusum maushi switched on the air-conditioner for twenty minutes, enough for the bedroom to cool down a bit, after which the women took naps. On particularly hot afternoons, Ira dropped in too, to read a book or finish her homework in the cool lung of the Kinis' bedroom.

Her mother seemed to sleep lightly there. At the slightest noise, she would wake with a start and look for Ira. Most times she went back to sleep but, if Ira had stepped out of the bedroom, her mother would follow her out. She might get a glass of water from the kitchen or pretend she had forgotten something in the drawing room, but her intentions were transparent: to keep an eye on Ira.

When Kartik was not around, her mother slept like a baby.

Her mother had no reason to worry, Ira wanted to assure her. She was thirteen that summer. She was aware of the soft swells of her own body, still new but already drawing the curious, the twisted. Other girls had begun to hunch, trying to bury their breasts back in their chests. A futile attempt to deny, to delay their burgeoning womanhood. They still got you, didn't they, so what was the point? The accidental bumps and grazes, the gaze held for too long on some parts, words ripe with double meanings. Older cousins, classmates, even some old playmates were guilty of these trespasses, but never Kartik.

The two had begun to make for an odd duo. Their friendship seemed inexplicable even to their old building gang. Childhood friendships could be like that, people reasoned, a deep love and loyalty unaccustomed to such accounting. Kartik had grown into a cautious adolescent and then an even more cautious teenager. Many layers of deliberation seemed to separate the desires in his mind from their corresponding resolutions in the outside world. Ira saw rules as gauzy, and as she grew so did their translucence. It was easy for her to look through the things that stood in her way. She liked to imagine that her presence was the momentum driving Kartik forward, spurring him into action. She had pushed him into climbing the water tank on the terrace when they were younger, even though he had been terrified of being caught. When he was thinking about smoking his first cigarette, he had come to her for help. She knew he loved making up stories, so she urged him to write them down. When he finally wrote a short story, after years of pestering, he refused to show it to her: he said he was too embarrassed to share it.

It did not take much to embarrass him. Sometimes she told him dirty jokes only to watch him squirm. There was one doing the rounds in her class: a girl who spent a summer in America picked up the habit of ending every sentence with man. *How are you, man? I am doing well, man. I forgot to do my homework, man.* When her parents gave her a watch for her birthday she wore it all day, not even taking it off when she went to bed. The next morning at school, her friend asked her about the marks on her wrist.

'What was her reply?' Ira asked him, a glint of mischief in her eye, her lips compressed to stifle a giggle.

'I don't want to say it.'

'Then you don't know the answer. Admit it.'

'I slept with my watchman?' He was blushing a beet red.

'What a dirty mind you have! She slept with her watch *on.*'

Whether she held more power than he did, whether their childhood roles had been reversed, she was not sure. After all, it was still she who hankered after his attention. She learnt that she got it only when she demanded it, when she became loud and sharp, when she interrupted him and gave him no choice.

'Stop bullying him,' her mother might say if she caught Ira teasing Kartik but Kusum maushi laughed it off.

'Ira is doing him a favour,' she said. 'My poor bookworm

will have a hard time in the real world unless he toughens up.'

One evening years before, the four of them had been in the Kinis' flat. Ira was reading a book about birds and a particular species had come up that mated for life. What does that mean, Ira had asked Kartik.

Kusum maushi looked at her friend and smiled. 'Mate for life? Ask your mother, she's the zoologist.' Her mother winced. Ira was struck by how easily her mother could be unsettled, even bullied. How had she learnt so little from Kusum maushi after so many years of knowing each other, so many afternoons spent working side by side?

Their mothers worked in harmony in Kartik's house as in hers. One wiped the washed vessels, the other put them away in the correct drawers. One squeezed the water out of the laundry and the other hung it to dry, smaller clothes on the outer clothesline, bigger ones inside. Even when they cooked together, they settled into roles and recipes with ease; they seemed to agree on the level of spice, on who would stir the kadhai and who would set the plates. An unspoken harmony, choreographed over years, allowed them to work together in the smallest of spaces, to divide up the smallest of mandates. Ira was never sure whether they wholly agreed on these domestic routines or whether her mother was only following, mimicking, half a beat behind.

But she knew there was a hum of competition under the hood of this friendship. No matter how many hours they spent in Kartik's house, her mother used the bathroom only when she returned home. Sometimes straight after unlocking the door.

'Kusum is an expert in every aspect of housekeeping,' her mother said, 'but their toilet is never very clean. I suppose not everybody cares about a clean bathroom as much as I do. Look at ours, always spick-and-span.'

So this is how friendships went. Why then, she wondered, did she never begrudge Kartik his success, his genius?

Kartik had not been her only friend. The room for a more attentive presence in her life had been filled—of course, it was a girl—by her classmate, Rukmini Nair, who lived a lane away from Asha Nivas. Girls of their age were divided into two camps that year: between two star sons who had made their movie debuts, between a chocolate-faced hero and a bad boy with a drug problem. Ira and Rukmini were the only two girls in their class who favoured the latter. It was reason enough to be friends and confidantes, though Ira suspected that her friend only said she preferred the bad boy for the waft of notoriety it carried. Rukmini's image was snow-white otherwise. She was one of the class toppers and her mother was the school's strictest teacher.

Ira had never seen a home with more books than the Nairs' flat. Thick volumes on every shelf, thinner magazines and pamphlets bursting out of every nook like weeds. Everywhere the patter of English. When Rukmini's mother switched to Malayalam, Ira knew it was bad news. She spent an afternoon or two each week at Rukmini's place. They were supposed to study together, but in reality, the girls read comic books or gossiped about their classmates.

Sometimes they had more pressing matters on their minds.

'Why was Sumit talking to you after the last period?'

'He had a question about the science homework.'

'Do you like him?' Ira dropped her voice to a whisper, afraid of being caught by Rukmini's formidable mother. 'I think he likes you. Let's play Flames to find out.'

'What's that?'

'I'll teach you. I need paper and a pencil.'

Ira took one of Rukmini's notebooks, opened the last page. 'You write down the name of the boy and the girl, S-U-M-I-T and R-U-K-M-I-N-I, cross out all the common letters between your names and count the remaining ones. There's U and M and I gone, which gives us S-T-R-K-N-I; that's six remaining letters. You cross out every sixth letter in FLAMES. First goes S, so you are not siblings.' Ira proceeded with surgical efficiency. 'Not friendship, not affection and not enemies either. And there goes M. Aha, L—that means you two will be lovers.'

'What rubbish!'

'It is decided. Lovers.' Ira made smooching noises.

'Shut up.'

'Love-Love-Lovers. Look, you're blushing! Did you imagine his lips making those sounds?'

'Stop it!' Rukmini buried her face in a pillow.

An adult voice punctured the giggling. 'I thought you two were studying.'

Mrs Nair snatched the notebook from Ira's hands and looked at the jamboree of letters on the last page. Next to the two names, LOVERS written in caps. Rukmini began to cry in anticipation.

'Rukmini, who is Sumit? I will not tolerate this nonsense in my house.' She slapped her daughter, vindicating the pre-emptive tears. A barrage of Malayalam poured forth.

Rukmini looked mournful. 'Sorry, Amma.'

'Ma'am, the game was my idea. Please don't scold Rukmini.'

'Ira, go home. I'll tell your parents if this happens again.'

'Sorry, Ma'am.'

Just when Ira was about to open the door to leave, Rukmini's mother called out to her. 'Ira, I want you to remember this:

first-rate people discuss ideas, second-rate people speak about events, and it's only the third-class who talk about other people.' She followed Ira to the door and let her out. 'Think about what kind of person you want to be.'

The question gripped her for days. What were these ideas? Did they include the recipes her mother devised, improvising for a shortage of this ingredient or that? The many ways in which Kusum maushi rearranged the photo frames, the porcelain figurines, the cushions in their drawing room? Were they the aphorisms printed on calendars or in practice books for cursive writing? *Aim for the stars, you'll end up on the moon. An idle mind is the devil's workshop.*

Or did the answer to the question lie, she wondered, in how Kartik spent his days? The coils of his mind were hidden from sight but his bookshelf was visible, a projection of his inner faculties on the outside world. The textbooks he read for pleasure, their spines as thick as fists. The novels which had begun to squeeze the Enid Blytons and the Russian storybooks into boxes under the bed: Orwell, Dickens, Oscar Wilde. The quotes and poems he had started copying neatly into a diary years ago—she had secretly flipped through its pages—whose concerns seemed to be narrowing with time. He was still seeking an answer to the question he had posed to her. Who am I? Other questions were emerging too: how to live, what is freedom, what is sin. The big questions of the world, a world beyond buying and selling, marriage and domesticity, beyond gods, gossip and groceries. Was that the address of the world of ideas?

Soon after, Kartik put up a poster of the Australian coat of arms, with a kangaroo and an emu, above his desk. Preparing for engineering entrance exams was taking up most of his time that year. His den was the balcony of his parents' bedroom.

Sliding glass windows served as its walls and the small space was fitted with a desk, a cupboard and a bookshelf.

'Both these animals, they can't go backwards, only ahead,' he said. 'Isn't that inspiring? No matter what, keep moving forward.'

Ira burst into laughter. 'This is the height of your scholarpana. You have outdone yourself, you nerd.' She picked up a fat red textbook lying on his table. The page she opened had a sketch of a monkey in a suspended basket trying to pull itself up. 'Here's a question featuring you.'

'Very funny.'

'Much funnier than you with your emus and kangaroos. Boys your age are building their biceps with such weights.' She did a bicep curl with his physics book, but had to use both arms. 'Not burying their noses in them.'

'Oh, really?' He snatched the book from her and took out a sky-blue twin from his bookshelf, taking one in each hand, curling his arms with no visible effort. 'You were saying?'

'Let me see those *musskulls*.' She pushed up his shirt sleeve and ran her fingers over his biceps. He flexed his arm, skin stretched tight over muscle. She clasped his upper arm with both hands, forming a circle with her thumbs and index fingers. 'Not bad at all.'

He grinned and, in turn, rolled up the sleeve of her t-shirt and grabbed her arm with his right hand, his fingers closing nearly completely around it. 'But you, on the other hand, have more work to do—you are a total delicate darling.'

At darling she blushed. Aware of his hand around her arm, his skin on hers. In her belly, a small animal leapt off its feet.

'Can you please leave now? I have to study.'

She made a face. 'No doubt you do.'

Oblivious to the rising colour in her cheeks, he waved her off and went back to his books.

❧

Ira FLAMES Kartik = Friends
Irawati FLAMES Kartik = Friends
Damn.

❧

She thought it happened suddenly, but it had not. When does day turn to night, bud to blossom? Never suddenly.

The hankering for his attention, the monopoly on his time, her unwavering loyalty. Love.

Chicken. Egg.

And so, when she overheard what Kusum maushi said to her mother some months later, it pleased her greatly. It was late in the afternoon, the heat in the flat was slowly thinning. The mothers were chatting in the kitchen. They must have assumed that Ira was taking a nap in the bedroom, but she was only lolling in bed, taking in the sweet smell of ginger and cardamom from the tea her mother was preparing. Hoping that Kartik's name would come up, she tried to listen to their chitchat—how little it took to inspire exhilaration in the early weeks of a crush—but her mind began to drift when it became clear he was not on their agenda.

Till she heard her mother assume a doleful tone.

'It's not right, telling someone the time of their death.'

'But Shobha, if you only had a few years left, would you not want to know?'

'Why live in fear like that, if there's nothing you can do— imagine the weight you will have to carry every moment.'

'She did not seem upset. Maybe he told her she would live to the age of ninety.'

'I hope I don't live to that age. Bedridden and dependent on others. God, please take me before that.'

'I must say she is brave, asking him to reveal when she will die.'

'Do you think she has told her family?'

'If she did not have much time left, she would have shamed that daughter of hers into finally marrying. Who doesn't want to see grandchildren before they go?'

'But Kusum, children these days don't believe in all this.'

Ira wasn't sure whom they were talking about. At first she was worried that somebody she knew might be unwell, perhaps even dying, but then realised that they were merely gossiping about a far-off prophecy. Even their idle chatter illuminated the shapes of their personalities. Her mother, seeking bliss in ignorance. His mother, seeing opportunity in adversity.

The ups and downs in the lives of the people they knew were the beats of their conversation, the music of their days. What would the mothers have left to talk about without the troubles of others? But that was not the whole truth, Ira corrected herself; they could always go back to their own lives, their losses and disappointments. These were their true favourite subjects. Each story had been repeated a dozen times with small variations, new angles. Like tales from the epics that one kept returning to for comfort and continuity. And then just like clockwork:

'What's not to believe? One by one what he said has come true. He said our destiny was to be right here and that's what happened. My brother had even started the paperwork for our German passports, but my brother-in-law dropped a bombshell on us at the last minute and we had to stay back,' said Kusum maushi.

'One child, he told us, only one. It took us ten years to accept it.' Her mother's voice trailed off. Ira guessed she had closed her eyes and was pinching the bridge of her nose.

'Forget it, Shobha. Who can change what is written? Ira is no less than any son.'

This too was an old story but it twisted Ira's insides, the knowledge that she hadn't been enough. Her parents had hoped for a son for many years. Second-hand stories of miracle children had kept this hope afloat, a son born after six years of marriage here, after ten years there. They had become willing to put their faith in anything, everything. She remembered her mother fasting five days a week for a son: Mondays for Shiva, Tuesdays for Ganesha, Thursdays for Sai Baba, Fridays for Lakshmi, Saturdays for Maruti. Her father walking to Siddhivinayak and back every Tuesday for years, four kilometres there and four kilometres back, and so on, perhaps adding up to a walk to the moon. Her anger simmered but she continued to listen as the two women aired their complaints and comforted each other with reminders that their defeats were not personal failings but acts of fate.

'Do not forget that he has given us good news too. Something to look forward to.' Ira detected hints of mischief in Kusum maushi's voice. She pictured her bobbing her head, a crooked smile stretching her lips.

'Shh, Ira might be awake.'

'Your daughter is incapable of sitting still without making a sound. Can you hear her? That means she is fast asleep.' Kusum maushi laughed. 'I can't wait to take her home.'

'In seven or eight years.'

'Oho, that's what I mean. They are only fifteen and seventeen—you think I want to get two teenagers married?'

Two high laughs mingled with other sounds from the

kitchen: the end of teatime, cups cleared from the table, a strainer full of boiled leaves emptied into a bin, a pot quickly scrubbed and rinsed.

'How wonderful it will be if it happens. Our daughter will live only one floor away.'

'Don't say if, Shobha. *When* the kids are willing.'

So it was destined! Winds whipped through her heart, stirring up new sensations, deeper joy than she had ever felt. What now, she wondered? He was barely aware of her presence. At least not in the same way that she was aware of him. Aware of his small mouth, of exactly how much his lips stretched when he smiled. The smile he was most likely to let slip accidentally, when he worked out an answer or unearthed a new question worthy of his time. Aware of the furrows that appeared between his eyebrows when he was lost in thought. Aware of each twinkle in his searching eyes.

Kartik, the crackpot. *Her* crackpot.

When Kartik got into the college of his choice Ira spent weeks agonising over his departure, over the crucial question of what to do next. He would study computer science at one of the best engineering colleges in the country, but he would have to move to remote Powai. Finally, a few hours before a taxi arrived to take him and his suitcases to Powai, she told him she had to speak to him alone. Why, he asked. She wanted to discuss something important, it would not take long, she replied. Fine, he said, and asked her to come to the terrace. They walked up together and he complained about how much he still had left to pack.

'Stop complaining,' she snapped at him. 'Powai is not even an hour away. You can come back if you forget something.'

'I can only return after a week. My classes start tomorrow.'

'Are you nervous about moving away?'

'Not at all, I am excited.'

'About what?'

'Living away from home for the first time.'

'Mister Scholar, what will you do with this freedom? It's wasted on you.' He frowned. She took a deep breath to recover some tenderness. 'Won't you miss your family, your friends? Me?'

Still smarting, he shrugged coolly. 'Why would I? Didn't you just say that Powai is only an hour away? And what did you want to talk about?'

'Kartik, I like you.'

Her heart was hammering so wildly she thought Kartik might hear it.

'So?'

'I mean, not only as a friend. I love you.' Only the last three words in English. How could she have said that in Konkani—it was the language of everyday matters, of ordinary things; how could it capture the riot in her heart?

'Okay.'

He stretched out the two syllables to the point of snapping. The furrows in his brow were deepening, his features setting into a troubled frown. She saw the distress on his face but it was too late, her limbs had already swung into motion. Before her head had finished computing that he did not return her feelings, she had stepped forward, her arms were around his neck, her lips on his cheek, and a feeling of horror had begun to sink in.

He pushed her arms away and wiped his cheek. His face was puckered, his mouth open in horror.

'Are you mad? Stop it, please. You are like a sister to me.'

At the word sister, uttered with such bile, she felt a lump in her throat and her eyes welled up. She could not let him see her cry, so she turned around and mumbled an apology. She broke into sobs even before she was out of earshot.

She cried herself to sleep for two nights. She filled a diary with declarations of love and heartbreak before tearing up the pages and throwing them away. At first, he had come home every weekend from Friday evening to Monday morning, but his visits slowly became shorter, erratic. Homework, projects, exams, internships. If they saw each other on the stairs, he smiled but did not look at her directly. Perhaps he was still embarrassed for her. His withdrawal from their friendship was smooth and skilled. A surgery with no visible scars.

She ran into him outside of Asha Nivas only once: when she went to his college for their student festival. He was walking with another teenage boy, absorbed in conversation, and when he saw her, he flinched and took a step back. Trees lined both sides of the main road which ran through his college campus. They appeared to slowly come together behind him, rows of giants vanishing into the horizon.

'This is my neighbour, Ira,' he said when he introduced her to his friend.

Neighbour, not friend. She wanted to ask him if that was his revenge.

Slowly, the declaration on the terrace became a feeble memory, an embarrassing footnote in her long friendship with Kartik, the second chapter of which only began over a decade later. All through her teenage years, there was a part of her that had thought it possible—inevitable, really—that Kartik and she would be friends again. But not even in her boundless optimism had she imagined that what she had seen as a teenage folly would one day be vindicated by a matching revelation from Kartik.

It had taken thirteen years for their friendship to mend,

for their time together to feel fluid again, so Ira was astonished when, within a month and some weeks of their first meeting on the terrace, Kartik proposed marriage.

8

A LIGHT SLEEPER AT BEST, Mumbai opened its eyes by 5 a.m. to the trundling arrival of milk trucks on the streets. Local trains started to ply around the same time, carrying fisherwomen, flower sellers, and sleepy revellers up and down the arteries of the metropolis. And along these arteries, Mumbai awoke in slow waves, the farthest suburbs stirring first, readying themselves for the long battle that was the day ahead. By ten, when Ira was leaving home, the city was fully roused. The mismatched rhythms of footsteps, cars and two-wheelers, a radio here and a television there, words spoken and shouted in half a dozen languages, motor horns and the cawing of crows, all blended into the gargling score of the city street.

Ira had to get to the office before noon for an edit meeting but had left early, with enough time for a second breakfast at King's Circle. The eponymous circular park, where several tentacle-like roads met, looked like the head of an octopus. It was rimmed by an outer circle of restaurants and shops.

At her favourite Udupi eatery, Ira found a table with a view of the park. Only three other tables were occupied. The morning walkers had eaten and left. The bachelors were already in office and the college students would come by lunch. Yet, the waiters, out of habit, moved nimbly. One wiped her table with a wet towel, while another took her order: a plate each of upma and rasam vada, and a cup of filter coffee. On the other side of the park was the only Irani restaurant at King's Circle. When she was a child, there had been at least three, but the others had shut down, become shops that sold suitcases.

Within minutes, there was a plate of steaming upma before her. She scooped out a ring in the hot porridge, poured sambar into this moat, and stirred. The steam rising from the plate, spice-scented, proved irresistible: she put a spoonful into her mouth, then another, the sear on her palate notwithstanding.

She waved her hand to get a waiter's attention. 'Can you bring my coffee too?'

'Now?'

The waiter frowned, but his expression could easily have been surprise. She could always have another cup of coffee at the end of her meal, as was the custom here.

Ira thought about the work day ahead. The city editor would be in a foul mood: the *Times* had broken two stories that they had missed, one on page one itself. Her friend Shefali Mitra had interviewed a corporator about the municipal corporation's plans to convert the Kala Ghoda area into a conservation zone on the lines of Trafalgar Square in London. It was rare for a civic beat reporter in Mumbai to write a hopeful story. Ira envied Shefali. Her fiery eyebrows and beautiful bass voice came to mind, along with her staggering collection of block-printed kurtas and colourful stoles. They had first met at a BMC press conference as junior reporters and had somehow become allies in the somewhat opaque quest for news. For some months they had hunted together, acting as each other's eyes and ears, making sure that between the two of them no stories were missed, and no leads went unshared. Edit meetings eventually proved to be the undoing of this partnership. There was immense pressure not to miss a story, but equally to break stories, beat the competition. It was hard to put your full faith in rivals, to share everything you knew and expect them to do the same.

From Shefali Ira knew that, had they missed a story, her counterparts at the *Times* would have got an earful from their editor before 8 a.m. At least for her team, the shit storm wouldn't start till noon and they could enjoy their breakfasts in peace.

Relatively speaking, of course.

Two days ago, her father had called her at work and asked her to come home early. She had returned to find her parents sitting in the drawing room, without the TV on, not even tea or snacks before them. What are they doing just sitting there, she had wondered, amused that the thought of her parents having a civil conversation felt suspicious. Nonetheless, it was unusual. Her mother usually started cooking before seven but there was no sizzling or spluttering from the kitchen. Ira put her bag down and turned the TV on, waiting for her mother's protestations—*at least wash your hands first, why do you have to watch TV first thing when you come home, you didn't fold your blanket this morning*—but none came.

From the corner of her eye, she saw her parents exchange glances, smiles germinating under their taut faces. She knew that look. Some hare-brained man somewhere was looking for a wife.

'Ira, we have some good news.'

It was her father who spoke first. He liked to be the one to open any conversation of import but avoided sticky follow-throughs. He looked at his relay partner, passing the baton with a slight lift of the chin.

Her mother: 'Promise you will listen and you won't get angry.' A toothy smile had sprouted on her mother's face. 'Promise?'

No, she would make no such promise. She wanted to tell her mother to wipe that grin off her face and leave her alone. Instead, Ira said as calmly as she could, 'What is it?'

'Kusum maushi and Ashok kaka were here this afternoon.' So, a friend of the Kinis was looking for a daughter-in-law. 'She comes over very often. She is your *best friend*, isn't she?'

'Yes, that she is, but they had another agenda today.'

'Kartik told me his aunt's visiting.' At the mention of Kartik, her parents traded smiles again. 'Whatever it was she said to you, I am telling you, she only wanted to get away from her sister-in-law.'

That would be her weapon, she would interrupt often, deflate the story and their excitement, pinprick by pinprick.

'What rubbish you keep talking, Ira.'

Ira was pleased, she had succeeded in flustering her mother. 'Guess why they came over. A hint—it's very good news.' She said nothing.

'They came with a proposal for you! She wanted to ask for your hand. For Kartik, our Kartik!'

Ira blinked, then scowled in confusion. 'Kartik?'

'You think we didn't notice how much time you have been spending together? Kusum said it will be a love-cum-arranged marriage.'

'I can't believe this.'

'Please, Ira, say yes, you will make us so happy. He's such a good boy. A true gem, he's a diamond, no, he's a Kohinoor who has turned down fifty girls. And they asked us. That is an honour.'

'Was Kartik here with them?'

'Of course not, it was four in the afternoon, he must have been at work, no? But Kusum said she asked him before she came to us. They are also broad-minded like us, why would they come here without checking with him first? We know we can't force our children the way our parents did. That time has passed.'

'Broad-minded? You think you are broad-minded?'

Her mother shook her head, she knew it was best to dodge the barb. 'So, what do you think? I thought you would be more pleased.'

'What do you want me to do? Shout yes and start dancing?'

'Why can't you say yes? You have known Kartik your entire life!'

Her father interjected. 'And by entire life, your mother means all of your twenty-eight years. Need I remind you that you will be twenty-nine soon?'

'You have both gone mad. I am not going to say yes just because I am turning twenty-nine.'

'Don't talk to your father like that,' her mother said.

Wow, thought Ira, this had put them on the same side.

'We won't let you say no right away, not this time. You have to promise you will think about this.'

But Ira had stopped listening, she got up mid-conversation. She wanted to talk to Kartik; this proposal made no sense to her and she was hoping he could explain. She called his home and asked him to meet her on the terrace. When he didn't ask why, she knew of his complicity.

Kartik was already there when she reached the terrace. He beckoned her to hurry up, then pointed towards the street below. A fight had broken out. Two men were swinging punches at each other and a small crowd had gathered around them. He began to explain what he had seen: one of the men had come in on a motorcycle with a woman riding pillion behind him. He had dropped her off in front of their building, but she had lingered, holding on the handlebar, leaning back coquettishly. The other man had appeared out of nowhere—

'Enough faffing around, Kartik. What is this marriage business? Whose idea was it?'

His voice dropped, or perhaps the temple bells got louder. 'I think it is a good idea, don't you?'

'I want to know how it came up.' *Did my parents go begging to yours? Please have our daughter, because nobody else will.*

'Fine, my mother brought it up, but she only came to your parents after I said yes.'

'Oh, ya? When have you said no to your mother?'

'I have been saying no for years. Every week, she wants me to meet the daughters and nieces of random people she runs into. I am sure it's the same for you.'

She shook her head. Her parents had nagged her a little but there had been no meetings.

'Lucky you. Last month, it was the sister-in-law of a woman she ran into in Crawford Market, a complete stranger she met while shopping for underwear, yes, underwear.' Ira imagined Kusum maushi and another woman holding up large panties, stretching the waistband in sync to test the elastic. 'I am out of excuses now, and women too, my mother will say, but the truth is—'

'Fifty, right?'

'Sorry?'

'I heard you rejected fifty girls.'

'No, that's not possible. There was no more than one meeting every month, on an average. Thirty-five or thirty-six, I think. And I got turned down a few times too. That my parents don't tell anyone, do they?'

Ira smiled. One couldn't use numbers loosely around him. Fifty was not a large number, not a figure of speech. It was a precise integer, one more than forty-nine, one less than fifty-one.

'The truth is that I am lonely, Ira,' he confessed. 'I am sure you understand that, the craving for a deeper companionship than what friends, even family, can offer.'

'So why did you reject those thirty-five women?' she asked, aware that it sounded like she was fishing for a compliment.

He flashed an exasperated look. 'I said lonely, not desperate.'

He wouldn't trade the loneliness for a partner whose life and story he did not wish to share. A spouse who commanded his respect, that was what he sought. One who challenged him and stirred him, whom in turn, he could spur and support.

'Nobody can do that without knowing who you are, where you come from. The two of us, we have known each other forever, we have the same roots. We have been friends, close friends. And the past few weeks have made it clear that we still enjoy that comfort with each other. Don't you agree?' She nodded sideways, meant to convey a measured yes. 'And it helps that you are beautiful,' he added, grinning, 'but that, of course, is not everything.'

Hence proved, she half-expected him to say. Q.E.D.

'My mother noticed how eagerly I looked forward to our meetings. And she knows no restraint—it's hard to believe sometimes that I am her son—she just asked me point-blank if I was interested. It only hit me in that moment. Yes, I am. I *am* interested.'

There was such a sudden spurt of spirit in his voice that she wondered if he had rehearsed the last part.

'I hope you were telling me the truth when you said you don't have a boyfriend. You don't, do you?'

Ira shook her head but felt words and memories collide, some sticking together and others drifting away. She hoped that the right response would form out of this entropy, as in a crystal ball.

'I need to think about this, Kartik. Give me a few days?'

He beamed, treating it as a small victory.

'I did not expect you to have an answer today.'

After looking over his shoulder at the door, he lit a cigarette. A few drags in, he blew a smoke ring, and into it a smaller one. She had not seen him do that before.

'Wow, where did you learn to do that?'

'Here and there.'

'Teach me, please.'

'There will be plenty of time for that, I hope.' He grinned boyishly.

'And if I say no?'

'Are you saying no?'

'No, but what if I do, what does that mean for us?'

'For *us*?' He raised an eyebrow. There was not much of an *us* between the two of them, only a weeks-old rekindled friendship, but there was something else she was worried about. 'I promise this won't affect our families.'

It was comforting that he had sensed what she was worried about, even when this was an amorphous worry at best. Maybe he could read her face, or her mind, at least parts of it. Their lives to that point had to have given them a shared shorthand. He spoke in a mix of English and Konkani, a few Hindi phrases thrown in too. How easy it was to converse with someone when you shared all languages.

'Take your time,' he said in parting.

She had told him she wanted to gather her thoughts before she saw him again. And here she was a day and a half later, having breakfast *in peace*. Peace was not having anybody breathing down your neck for an answer. Not feeling two pairs of desperate eyes locked on you every waking moment. Peace was a second cup of coffee.

The question had consumed her for a whole day and she

was no closer to an answer. How was one supposed to think about this? She conjured up the man who had paid the Desais a visit: gun to her head, what would she choose?

Surely this was not the way to decide.

Kartik was a good man, he made good money, he was handsome. Her parents liked him, their families were close. They liked spending time together. She didn't love him, not yet, but she was prepared to open herself to the possibility. And she had to admit that she was flattered, in spite of herself, at the things Kartik had said, at the way he had declared, *I am interested.*

What Kartik had said about loneliness, about the need for a deep companionship, she knew all too well: the stillness, the stasis one carried within, untouched by the kinetic city and its seductions. Even with Vinay, the good days—there had been more than a few of those—had felt like warm bliss. She missed that. This was hard to hope for with friends, and it became harder each year as all the competing claims multiplied: marriage, children, family, career. She wanted somebody to whom she could say, *we are in this together.* Could that be Kartik?

Even so, the thought of an arranged marriage rankled. She had never imagined that after a lifetime of making trouble, she would one day hand over the reins to somebody else. What she and Kartik had was muddled—this would be a match arranged as much by fate and by time as by anybody—but it was not love, it was certainly not passion. And without passion, how could she feel what she wanted to feel? How would she replace the one who had crept up on her a hundred times in the past two days, her mind drawn to thoughts of him like a moth to a flame?

She had recently purchased a hand-dyed notebook, an extravagant acquisition that she intended to use for a project on the history of Matunga, but she could spare the last page for this all-consuming question. Make a list, perhaps. When she opened her bag, she scowled: her new notebook was warped. The rains had surprised her the previous day, the zip of her bag must not have been fastened all the way through. The paper appeared ruined but, still hopeful, she made a squiggle in a corner on the last page. The ink did not smudge. The book would not go to waste—a relief!—though the warp would remain the first thing that caught the eye, even with the dampness gone.

A waiter rushed over to clear her table—a customer lingering with a notebook was not good for business. There was still a sip of coffee left. The other patrons were quiet that morning. Only the clank of spoon against plate was constant, only the droning whoosh of the ceiling fan. Otherwise, the room was empty enough for the sounds of the street to pour in.

Ira watched a young couple walk into the Irani cafe across the street. The Irani cafe, Kaiz had told her the day they met, was a counterpoint to the Udupi restaurant. The two establishments had some things in common—cheap food, casual settings, run by immigrants to the city—but the similarities ended there. The Udupi eatery was about quick service (here he had snapped his fingers) and it brought the rush of Bombay into mealtimes. It offered no respite, no refuge. The Irani cafe, on the other hand, was designed for leisure. It was a place for loitering, that rare, rare verb in Bombay. The Irani cafe was enclosed within brackets in the sentence of the city, he had declared, a part of it but also an island. It was a beautiful image, islands within an island, and she felt an old sadness come upon her. She pressed her fingers along the edges of the notebook again, tried to flatten it with her palm but knew it was futile. The warp remained, immutable, intractable.

She took a deep breath. Here she was, wallowing again, becoming one of those pathetic heartbroken women whom people mocked.

Fuck the Irani cafe, fuck loitering, fuck nostalgia, fuck him.

Ira waved to get the waiter's attention again, and asked for yet another coffee. The third cup of coffee was a special weapon in her arsenal, like the brahmastra from the epics, to be wielded occasionally and against the most insidious of enemies, one's own demons. She poured the filter coffee from the steel tumbler into a bowl for it to cool. After two long sips, she began to feel the surge of caffeine. The trusty Old Monk and Thums Up—which she would have picked had it been 11 p.m. instead of 11 a.m.—only left her head swimming, but after the third coffee, her lungs held more air, her veins more blood and, for a little while, anything was possible.

It felt possible, if not to put Kaiz behind, then to move forward with the weight. She had tried to replace him with others, but they had only doodled, left mere doggerel on the warped pages of her heart, unable to mask his presence, his absence. A possibility began to take root in her caffeine-sodden mind: perhaps she had got it all wrong, perhaps no new love could mend what an old love had torn apart, that passion was an unstable force and perhaps her life did not have to be in a constant state of flux. These pages had weathered love and loss. Now, she said to herself, it was in her hands to write here a new story.

9

IT TOOK IRA THREE WEEKS and two days to decide. All through this period, her parents were tense. Shankar and Shobha Kamat were of the belief that the family of an eligible bachelor should not have to wait too long for an answer to a proposal. To palliate the possible insult, her father agreed to finally listen to what the Kinis had to say about cutting a deal with their landlord, and accepted their invitation to visit one evening.

'The pugree we put down when we moved into the building was a third of the price of the flat at that time,' explained Ashok Kini. 'We have been paying rent for thirty years, too—we have practically already bought our homes.'

The women were dealing with the warm package that had just arrived from Saraswat Bhawan: hot medu vadas wrapped in an old newspaper, and packets of chutney and sambar. The food had to be unpacked, transferred to plates and bowls, brought out to the dining table and served to the husbands. Only then could the wives join the discussion.

'You tell me, do you want to live in a rented place again?' Ashok continued. 'Be at the mercy of another landlord at our age? I have earned the right to a home of my own and so have you. This is all we said to Naik and Rege. The Shanbhag father and son also agree with me. And—I'm telling you this in confidence—Ganesan and Krishnan are also going to move to our side. If everybody demands a flat, a flat is what we will get.'

His words were packed tight with logic, with the promise of untold riches.

'Oh, is that so—Ganesan and Krishnan both?' Shobha Kamat exclaimed. She was close to Pramila Desai, and Mrs Desai had told her that the two Tamil families were her husband's firm allies.

'It's plain and simple,' said Kusum Kini. 'Why would anybody settle for twenty or thirty lakhs when a flat is worth at least three times as much?'

'But it will work only if we present a united front. The residents of Sundar Sadan couldn't reach a consensus and the loudest voices prevailed. They settled for too little. Now they are scattered up north in the suburbs—Goregaon, Malad, Kandivali.'

'What if the landlord does not agree right away?' Shobha enquired.

'He probably won't. This might take a few years. Possibly two or three.'

'But what about the terrace, the Naiks' flat? What will we do if the roof collapses or a parapet falls?'

'We will take charge ourselves.'

'How so?' asked Shankar.

The Kini husband and wife looked at each other and smiled.

'If every family puts in a little money, we can cover the expenses together. The landlord will have no bargaining chip left.'

'How much money?'

'Not much. Thirty-five for the 1-BHK families. And we two-bedroomers will contribute fifty. It's only fair that we put in a little more.'

'Thirty-five *thousand*?'

'It's not an expense, it's an investment. You put in thirty-five thousand now, and it will turn twenty lakhs into sixty.'

'But—but, it's a lot of money,' Shankar stammered.

Ashok slapped his neighbour's back. 'Shankar, how is it a lot? You were a banker for forty years. You can do the math, can't you?'

Shobha smiled nervously. Her husband's ego was a metal detector, always scanning the sands of conversation for the sharp edge of a buried slight. And he was extra touchy on the subject of money, when he was forced to confront how much—or how little—he had saved. Let him not sulk or snap in front of them, she prayed, let him think of Ira. She was relieved when her husband smiled and said he would think about it. Perhaps the thought of seeing their daughter married had made him somewhat impervious.

'What's there to think, Shankar? Just say yes. It will be no work for you, I promise. We will take care of everything.'

'And what about Rajwade?'

'What about the professor?'

'His children have board exams. He does not want to disturb their studies.'

'Arre, his children are smart, they will manage. He respects you, he'll listen to you.'

As the Kamats got up to leave, Kusum Kini pulled her friend aside and whispered in her ear: 'Shobha, we are going to be family soon—what's a little money between relatives? Kartik will have no problem putting in the money for you. You just convince your husband.'

But in Shobha's eyes, it was her daughter who needed to be convinced.

10

THERE WERE FIFTY GUESTS IN the Kinis' flat for the engagement ceremony: family, friends and some colleagues of the couple. The women were dressed in silk sarees in various metallic hues. They wore strings of jasmine gajras in their hair, and gold at their necks, wrists and ears. The men were dressed like they would any other day, mostly in trousers and shirts, but a few were also in kurta-pyjamas. All the seating in the house that could be moved had been brought into the drawing room, and three other families in the building had chipped in with chairs. They were still slightly short, so plastic mats had been put on the floor. The men and the elderly sat on the sofas and chairs. The women pulled up their sarees slightly and adjusted the silk folds around the knees to sit down cross-legged. Children were scattered across the room, some sat with their arms around their mothers, others stood shyly in the corners with their fingers in their mouths. Some of the guests spilled over into the kitchen as well but both bedrooms remained bolted.

The ceremony started with a Ganesh pooja. The priest chanted Sanskrit shlokas in short breathy bursts. He sounded like an unwilling scooter being kickstarted. Ira sat next to her parents, with her right hand crossed across her chest to rest on her mother's upper arm, and her mother's right hand in turn touching her father's arm, like they were playing a game of chain tag. She looked at her henna-covered hands. Soon, there would be a ring, but for now her hands were light and bare, except for deep orange filigree. Across from them, about six feet away, Kartik sat with his parents in a line, also hand to arm, hand to arm. A cousin's toddler sat in his lap. Plates with coconuts, rice and bananas lay on the blue bedsheet between the two families, steel boats crossing a cotton sea.

She had seen these rituals before, now it felt surreal to participate in them. This wasn't a distant relative or friend whose betrothal she had been dragged to, it was she who was sitting with her hand on her mother's arm. It was she who was repeating strange lines after the priest and it was she who was mindlessly touching coconuts, flowers and fruits when she was asked to, as if playing soundless musical instruments.

It was as boring as she had always imagined.

Kartik was fidgeting even more than she was, shifting his weight, asking the kid to move from one leg to another. He finally lifted the child up and put him on the floor next to himself, and flapped his crossed legs slightly. She studied his face, his hair that was combed neatly into a side parting, the cut on his eyebrow from six childhood stitches, the thin lips on his small mouth, the points where his dimples fell. Her gaze lingered, trying to find the words to describe each feature on this face she would spend the rest of her life with. His face showed a trace of a frown, his eyes slightly squinted, alert, not willing to get even a single instruction wrong. When he leaned over to touch a coconut placed closer to the Kamats, there was no bulge at the waist of his kurta, no roll of fat. She would confirm after closer inspection in a few months. Maybe even sooner? The thought made her nervous, a new beginning, another nakedness to get familiar with.

Dada, or older brother, she had called him till she was ten.

'I am only two years older than you,' he had complained. 'Dada makes me sound old, I don't like it.'

'But you are an old man, you have always been one. What difference does it make what I call you?'

'Please, you have to stop!'

'Okay, Dada, I will stop.'

It had been difficult to go from Dada to Kartik just like that. She continued to call him Dada occasionally to irritate him but very soon Scholar became a more potent weapon, dripping with even more uncoolness. Was now a good time to revive the old tradition? How would the assembled guests react if she called out to Kartik, *Dada, it's time to exchange rings!* The thought made her chuckle. Her mother turned towards her and glared.

The priest was now speaking Konkani instead of Sanskrit, conversing directly with the gods it seemed, submitting a request seeking blessings for the health, wealth and well-being of Shankar Kamat, his wife Shobha and their daughter Irawati. She hadn't heard her full name in a long time and, for a brief moment, she thought she was at someone else's engagement ceremony, back on the sidelines.

Around the time she stopped calling Kartik Dada, she had also sloughed four letters off her late grandmother's name and gone from Irawati to the shorter, more modern Ira. Her father had not been pleased when she started writing the new appellation on her school books as well. He had seen it as an affront to the memory of his beloved mother, who had passed away when he was ten and paved the way for an indifferent stepmother. Shankar Kamat was a man of few words and, as is often the case with men of few words, his resentment was a moving, growing object which dissipated very slowly.

'I am sure your grandmother is pleased that you are calling yourself Ira. Why would she want the black sheep of the family to carry her name?'

Ira would fight back: 'Black sheep? What do you mean black sheep?'

Her mother tried to play the peacemaker between the two. She silently preached to Ira the age-old womanly remedy known to bury domestic fracas—silence. She would touch her right ear and tap the left, miming sympathetically, into one ear, out of the other.

Her mother had mimed the same advice to her a month ago, the day the proposal had arrived. When Ira returned from her meeting with Kartik without an answer, her father was left aghast. It started harmlessly enough, with the usual desperate needling, but when Ira refused to reveal even a morsel of her conversation with Kartik, her father's pleas turned to taunts, and her mother began to get worried. In no time they would be thundering at each other. *Let it go*, her mother gestured again and again, the helplessness in her face deepening till Ira submitted.

'We talked and I told him I need more time,' Ira finally declared. 'Kartik is happy to wait.'

That was enough to placate her father. After dinner, as Ira was making her bed in the living room—putting the pair of decorative cushions aside, laying a sheet on the divan, fluffing her pillow that was stuffed, by day, into a box stored under the TV—her mother appeared.

'Thank you for not saying no, Ira.'

'Don't assume I'll say yes.'

She lingered, patted down the corners of the bedsheet to remove creases. When Ira was ready to retire, her mother got up and turned off the light. But instead of leaving, she walked back and seated herself in the chair next to the divan.

'What?'

'You don't have to be afraid of marriage.'

'Okay, goodnight.'

Her mother remained seated. She stroked Ira's forehead. The tips of her mother's fingers were rough but she could not imagine a gentler touch.

'Your father was once a good husband.'

'Really? When was that?'

'He has had a tough life. Don't judge him too harshly.'

Ira did not think her parents had ever been happy with each other: the echoes of their latest argument seemed to reach all the way back in time. She struggled to find any happy memories of her own that featured both her parents. Either only one of them appeared, or neither did. It was possible that a part of her did not wish to see these moments, even if they had occurred. Perhaps she wanted to believe that only indifference, and not love, could turn slightly rancid in this manner. (The opposite of love, a friend had written in her high school slam book, was not hate but indifference.)

'When was he a good husband? Tell me one instance. Just one.'

Her mother thought about the question for a long moment. 'When he drew that pencil sketch of me.' She pointed, in the dark, at a frame on the wall. 'Do you know how long it took him?'

So exactly once. 'The best part of your marriage was a sketch?'

'No, dear, you were the best part of my marriage.'

Her mother leaned forward and kissed her on the cheek.

'And what was the worst?'

'The worst?' A brief hesitation.

Ira's eyes, better at sifting through darkness by now, took in a small figure sitting hunched with her arms clasped in her lap.

'Nothing.'

'No, you have to tell me—what is the hardest part of marriage?'

'That I can answer. The hardest part is washing the pot you boil milk in.'

Her mother shuddered comically and pretended to gag. It was typical of her mother to make light of the big things so easily and also, at other times, to make mountains out of molehills.

After the Ganesh pooja, the two families gifted each other milk cakes with the names of the bride and the groom written in icing. The cakes were cut into small pieces and passed around the room. Ira put a gold band on Kartik's finger and he gave her one with a small bright diamond. The guests clapped and cheered, and the photographer asked the couple to pose. As she smiled plasticly for the camera, she focused on the photographer's hand. Like a bird with a two-note call, the photographer's vocabulary had shrunk to two gestures: a pointed index figure when he was about to take a picture, a thumbs-up sign when he was satisfied. Over and over, his hand assumed these two shapes and she watched, enraptured. Suddenly she felt feverish, light-headed, as if a part of her were floating to the ceiling and taking in the scene from a distance.

She saw Kusum maushi walk towards her.

'God bless you, child, I can't tell you how happy I am.' Kartik's mother hugged Ira. 'And I have a secret I can finally tell you. When the two of you were children, your mother and I were told that we were sisters in a previous life and our children would make us sisters again. And look, it's finally happened!'

The prophecy!

'Told by whom?' asked Kartik. The mothers were busy giggling, taking each other's hands in their own. He turned to Ira and repeated, softly, with a look of arch amusement. 'Told by whom?'

There was such intimacy in his voice, in his expression, in the way he whispered to her in a room full of people that Ira felt a flood of warmth. *We are in this together.* She could not tell Kartik that she had known for years. And in a flash the photographs from her fifth birthday came to mind, of Kartik dressed as Krishna in a yellow silk dhoti with a peacock feather rising from his hair, his lips pressed against a wooden flute, and Ira playing his consort Radha. She considered the possibility that the mothers had already been guided by divination, that the little act of dress-up had been more than a spot of fun. An attempt to tailor a fitting history, a mythology, for an inevitable future. This future. A ring on her finger, henna on her hands, the sweet taste of cake in her mouth.

'We didn't want to give you any ideas when you were younger,' her mother said. 'And you modern children would have scoffed at us.'

Kartik's mother laughed and took her friend's hand. 'Modern or not, here we are. The two of us should have a picture taken together—sisters in this life and many others! Now where's that photographer?'

❧

Every day for three weeks and two days her mother had enquired if Ira had made up her mind. Every day she presented Ira with further reasons to say yes. One time it was the horoscopes the mothers had got secretly matched. She said the astrologer hadn't seen a better match in years. Another time it was because Kusum maushi had casually dropped into conversation how much Kartik earned: well above Vasudha's estimate. Yet another reason was the chance to settle an old family feud: one of the women that Kartik had turned down was the daughter of a relative that Ira's mother disliked. And bit by bit, Ira's protests grew feeble. Like naphthalene balls, vanishing slowly.

Perhaps the decision had already been made a long time ago.

The pressure on her to get married had been mild but persistent. Her parents had never tried to force her into the arranged marriage routine. They had refrained unwillingly, and only because they were a little afraid that she might embarrass them in front of a potential match, and by extension, the whole GSB community in Mumbai. It was a small community, closely knit by ties of blood, marriage and the possibility of future marriages. Even the needling only began after she turned twenty-six, so she had more years of peace than most.

When she was twenty-two, the family priest had asked her parents whether they wanted to float her horoscope in the matrimonial market, and they laughed the question off. He repeated the question every year and they dismissed it each time, but the timbre of their laugh betrayed a growing anxiety. When they finally brought it up with Ira, it was her turn to crack up. None of this horoscope business for her, she announced. If she found a suitable boy, she would tell them. After that, her parents started scavenging through conversations for names of male friends or hints of a romance. Stories of other people's engagements became sensitive topics, to be tiptoed around only after gauging the mood of the room. Then the relatives started asking, and the neighbours, and friends of the family. At first, they brought it up only with her parents, but emboldened by their evident helplessness, they fired the occasional salvo at her. They remarked how choosy she was, what a *bold* choice this was for a woman, how much freedom she had enjoyed but with such a feeble sense of responsibility towards her family. These comments were made within earshot of her parents, so that they could know that the speaker cared about the Kamat family. These exchanges were a curious mix of schadenfreude and concern. When her father's high cholesterol was diagnosed, eyes wandered to her as they discussed how stress could unbalance the body, even the mind. And wasn't the biggest stress of all an unmarried daughter?

But there had been no tears or drama, no pleading, no shouting.

It was a gentle assault that chiselled at your will, and chip by chip, your resistance fell away, sculpting a new you. When you acquiesced, you were left wondering why you had ever resisted. In some moments you were even convinced that it was your decision, that you were acting of your own free will—that mirage of a notion—because after all, any pressure on you had only been mild, albeit persistent.

But there was hope for happiness, too.

She had spent a lot of time with Kartik before she arrived at an answer. Catch-ups on the terrace, walks to Birdy's for chocolate mousse in the middle of the workday, even the occasional lunch date. It helped that they both worked in Nariman Point: they could meet in the day without having to tackle questions from eager parents who wanted a full report after each meeting. But the spectre of the proposal had hovered over them, even when they did not talk about it directly. It was she who had occasionally steered conversations to the essential questions of matrimony: where would he like to live after marriage (away from his parents), did he want children (yes, one or two), would he be supportive of his wife's long and irregular hours at work (ya! He was not an MCP!). His wife's career, not hers, that smokescreen felt essential. He would listen to her questions with a bemused expression, as if he had forgotten that each meeting was an appraisal, that they did not have the luxury of indefinite deliberation.

It was the little things that gave him away. The heartbeat-long hesitation, when they ran into his colleague on a walk, before he introduced her as a friend. Something in his voice revealed he wanted her to be more. The number of times he'd asked her what she thought of a passing vehicle, of its model and make, obliquely getting her input on the car he was no doubt planning to buy. And when she told him about Kaiz and Vinay, he said her past did not matter to him, but he lit a cigarette right after and began to blow smoke rings, telescoping one into another meditatively. This, she had come to know, he did when he was flustered. His new habits already felt familiar.

For instance, if they went to a new restaurant, he was almost certain to ask: 'So, how much do you think they make in a day with six tables?'

'Oh no, not again,' she would groan, in jest.

This was one of Kartik's favourite games now, he called them guesstimates: how much did businesses earn, how many pieces did they sell, how much profit did they make? His thirst for puzzles had taken a new form, one compatible with his new profession. She made fun of this habit but her teasing did not bother him. It was especially curious because he had never shown interest in the running of his own family restaurant.

As for the question of how much money the restaurant earned each day, he would break the puzzle into smaller pieces and tackle them one by one: the number of tables, the average bill, the length of each meal, the hours of business. Ira would sit back and wait for the scene to unfold, smiling as he went through the problem exactly as she had predicted. There was a quality of familiarity to these dates. At the end of the meal, he would offer to pay. She would protest, he would insist, but only once or twice, and in the end, they would split the bill.

These dates pleased her, even though they carried the burden of an open question. She was grateful for his quiet decency, his mutating curiosity, the warmth and comfort of his company, the occasional cutting joke. She could see them exchanging affectionate banalities which would fill the time, their years, and the small talk would slowly grow more loving, more particular to the two of them; there would be private nicknames and inside jokes, a deep companionship.

She watched her mother pose for photographs with Kusum maushi, an arm around her neck or hooked in her friend's arm. They were both beaming, excited like schoolgirls, their delight rolling off them in waves. Ira had not seen her mother this happy in years. When she caught Ira looking at her, Shobha came over and gave her daughter a tight hug.

'Thank you, Ira,' she said in her ear.

'For what?'

Her mother said nothing, only pulled away and smiled. Ira was prickled by irritation at her mother's behaviour, at the way she was acting like this was the biggest gift Ira could have given her. After what her mother had gone through, Ira expected better.

Shobha Kamat's parents had forced her to drop out after two years of college to get married, because a banker from Bombay was too good a match to pass up on. If Shobha's opinion had been sought, she would not have given up her studies, but she was a pragmatic woman who saw how marrying him could offer a better life for her and her future children, much better than what marrying a clerk or shopkeeper in her small town would. She repeated the story often but not with any strong emotion or regret, only hinting at a mild disappointment.

'That was a different time,' she would say if the story of a younger woman at a similar crossroads came up. 'There were braver women even then. My friend Shalini is now a professor of zoology at our college—and I was far ahead of her in all exams. She got married at twenty-five, which was very late at the time. I could have waited too but I just could not imagine it for myself.'

Their mothers' dreams meant nothing to children. Ira would be quick to interrupt: 'But you wouldn't have married Pappa and I wouldn't have been here.'

'Oh no, dear, I am very happy I did not wait.'

Her mother would hug her and kiss her on the high apples of each cheek. The reassurances comforted her, but Ira learnt early that a lack of imagination could be as crippling for the spirit as any poverty.

It baffled Ira that her mother had once wanted to become a scientist. She had seen no proclivity for science in her; it was her father who had watched over her studies. She had finally asked her mother about it a few years ago. 'To discover an unknown truth, to invent something new, so that people would remember me after I am gone,' her mother had said, dismissing her naive younger self with a laugh. She had gone on to build nothing, she had created nothing, she would leave nothing behind other than her only-born, and it seemed to Ira that all her mother wanted now, all she had wanted for years, was that her daughter take her place, play her part: become a wife, one day a mother. Maybe prophecies were redundant, Ira thought, because people like them lived the same lives over and over again.

At the end of the evening, after the guests had left, Ira's family stayed back to help the Kinis clear up. Some close relatives had stayed back too, so nobody noticed when Ira and Kartik slipped out. He had quietly asked if he could have a moment alone with her and they sneaked up to the terrace.

'I owe you a confession,' he said to her.

'What?' she asked, nervous and excited at the same time. She was alone with her fiancé for the first time.

'Remember my science project in school, the pinhole camera that was found broken?'

'What about it?' she said, smiling. She had an inkling of where this was going.

'It was me, I broke it. I was afraid I would lose badly, so I crushed it.'

'I know, I saw you sneaking out of your classroom that day. But why are you telling me now?'

'We are going to be married, we should be honest with each other, right? And we are friends, I should have never lied to you in the first place.'

It had rained all evening and a soft, cool breeze enveloped the terrace and their warm bodies, and thirteen years after the first failed attempt, she kissed Kartik.

11

IRA'S NEWSPAPER WAS GOING TO publish a series of articles about Mumbai to mark fifty years of India's independence. The City at Fifty, they were calling it. The editor wanted to push beyond the usual narratives: the city of dreams, heart of India, most cosmopolitan, capital of organised crime. Leave that to the *Times*, she said.

'I think we should do an article on Matunga,' Ira proposed in an edit meeting. They had already locked down most of the stories for the series, but last-minute cancellations had necessitated another brainstorm.

'What angle do you have in mind?' asked the editor.

'It was the first planned suburb of Mumbai, planned by the British. I want to compare their vision for what a neighbourhood in a city should look like with our new definition of development.'

Matunga had emerged from a dream of homes among parks and gardens, a vision of wide, shaded roads and open spaces, of a place not tainted by the spectre of factories, of work. The first suburb of the island city was the colonial government's response to the epidemic of plague that shrank Bombay's population by tens of thousands at the turn of the previous century. But, for the victims of the plague, families that slept gridlocked in rooms so small that when they dreamed at night their dreams overlapped, commuting was a luxury. And the wealthy, what could Matunga offer to lure them away from the sea? When the suburb was finally ready in the Twenties, only the middle classes came. First to arrive were the office workers, new arrivals in the city, eager to participate in its post-war economy: clerks, stenographers, typists, accountants. Then came professionals and small business owners. Doctors, lawyers, traders, restaurant owners. They found themselves collectively anointed the middle-class residents of the middle-class heart of Bombay. Over the years, the city had absorbed the suburb.

'If you had your way, Ira, every article in this series would link to redevelopment,' said her colleague Aman. Incidentally, the only man on the team.

'That is the story of this city at fifty.'

It was the story of Asha Nivas too. In the span of just a few months, the Kinis had convinced all the residents that it was perfectly reasonable to expect a flat in the new tower that would replace their building. Vastly outnumbered, Mr Desai had informed the landlord that he had dithered for too long and had lost the opportunity to settle with his tenants. The residents were now demanding a flat each. Mr Desai had also stepped down from his role as their representative. Ashok kaka was now in charge of negotiations with the landlord.

'We should write a piece on what this obsession with skyscrapers says about the city's men and their masculinity. Why this anxiety to see these phallic high-rises everywhere?' asked Aman. The two interns giggled.

The editor turned to Ira. 'Matunga used to be called Matungam. Even mini Madras. That might be an interesting hook too—its south Indian flavour.'

'And what about the middle-class angle?' added a junior reporter. 'Remember the Man from Matunga in the Eighties? He had become a stand-in for all of us middle-class people.'

This twenty-two year old, Ira noted, lived in Prabhadevi in a three-bedroom flat, drove to work in a brand-new Maruti Zen, a gift from her parents to celebrate her first job. Strictly speaking, in this poor country, Ira's own family wasn't middle-class either. But middle-class in this country was a state of mind, as one of Kaiz's unbearable friends had once declared. Not the filthy-rich of masala movies, not the dirt-poor of arthouse films, but everything in between. For some it was shorthand for middle-access, a separation from the corridors of power. For others it was middle-culture, a separation from the world of ideas.

'Ira, could you work on some of these for tomorrow's meeting? And has Amol sent you an outline for his architecture story yet?'

'He has promised to send it this week—I'll call and remind him.'

Amol Nadkarni was the director of a research institute her desk often turned to for help: the focus of its research was urban planning and conservation. He had offered to write an article on the history of architecture. He had also promised to help her with the statistics for an article on textile mills that she was writing. Nadkarni was an absent-minded man with a slippery grasp of deadlines. When she called him, she was not surprised to learn that he had not yet started working on the article; what worried her was that he didn't intend to.

'We have a brilliant intern who's working on something very similar—the historiography of architecture in Bombay. I have asked him to work with you.'

What on earth was historiography, she wanted to ask him, and why did he not have even an outline for an article that was going to be published in a week?

'Mr Nadkarni, you aren't palming off your intern on me, I hope?' Ira chuckled to soften the message.

'He's more an expert on this than any of us here. Great chap, he's been working with us for a long time, PhD student at Stanford.'

Ira sighed.

'In fact, why don't you come by the office and I'll introduce you to him. Friday at three?'

Their office was a rather unremarkable space with whitewashed walls and steel filing cabinets. It appeared deserted that afternoon, only a handful of people at their desks. The sarkari whirring of ceiling fans, fully audible now without the hum of conversation to dampen it, made the room feel even more shiftless. The receptionist told her that most of the staff were wrapping up a meeting in the conference room, that she should go ahead and meet them there. Ira waited outside for a few minutes. Nadkarni was still presenting. On the wall were two large charts, collections of squiggly lines in different colours. Just as he turned off the projector, he saw her standing by the door. He appeared surprised as he waved at her. She opened the door gently and entered. But the meeting was not over. A man with his back towards her raised his hand to ask a question.

When she heard his voice, even before he turned around, even with the short-cropped hair and the new beard that fell halfway between messy and trimmed, and even though almost four years had passed, she recognised him.

8 August 1997, six minutes past three in the afternoon.

'Ira, I thought we were meeting tomorrow? Oh no, I said Friday, didn't I? Sorry, sorry, give us two more minutes. And yes, meet Kaiz Dewani, the researcher I mentioned. Kaiz, this is Ira Kamat. The article you are working on, it's for her paper.'

'Hello, Ira,' he said, without looking her in the eye.

She managed to squeeze a response out of her throat. 'I'll wait outside till your meeting is done.'

Part Two
IRA

12

IN THE SUMMER OF 1992, Ira had been a beat reporter for less than a year. So when her editor asked for a favour, she could not say no. 'His mother is an old friend. The boy wants to see the inside of the municipal headquarters for a class project but says he can't get in. You'll take him along, won't you?'

The boy, who studied architecture at JJ College, called her to explain his project. Something about heritage structures from the colonial era. He sounds quite colonial himself, Ira thought wickedly, this rich kid from South Bombay.

South Bombay, Town, Old Bombay, the *real* Bombay, SoBo, sometimes even South Mumbai—but never SoMu.

Ira proposed a day with no standing committee or corporation meetings, when she would be able to show him around at leisure.

'Would I be able to go into the corporation hall then?' he asked.

'I am afraid not. It will be locked.'

'That won't work. Let's go on a day with a meeting.'

What a choot, thought Ira. Covering these meetings was her job, why did he think she would have the time to babysit a townie brat working on his homework? But he spoke with a confidence that admitted no other possibility, and she relented.

She picked a corporation meeting which she expected

would yield few surprises. Kaiz showed up five minutes later than he said he would but walked towards her at an unhurried pace. Sauntered, really. A grey kurta, two sizes loose, hung on his rangy frame. It was only the squared shoulders that lent his body some heft. His hair was wavy, unkempt, and covered his ears and part of his forehead. He had big hands with long, slim fingers and ragged cuticles. She felt he had a bohemian air. He looked like he played the guitar and smoked pot.

'It's a beauty, right?' It took her a moment to understand that he was talking about the municipal corporation building. Kaiz looked at the golden-brown Gothic structure with his mouth slightly open, his jaw slack. He took in its basalt rock arches as if he were famished and standing before a buffet spread.

'If anybody asks, you are an intern,' Ira said.

'Did you know the BMC building will turn hundred next year?' he said as they walked in.

'Really? I assumed it was older—two or three hundred at least.'

He tut-tutted at her. 'No, no. There was nothing here three hundred years ago. The Fort area wasn't even built then.'

A sharp intake of air suggested he wanted to go on, give her a quick history of Bombay perhaps, but decided against it. She was glad.

Ira led him to the corporation hall where the weekly meeting had already begun. About two hundred corporators occupied the wooden benches packed radially around the speaker's well. Most women corporators sat on the fringes. It was a sight that had stopped incensing Ira over time. It only disappointed her now. Peons dressed in formal white attire from head to ankle—white topi, white shirt, white pants—but shod in blue rubber slippers, handed out notes from the speeches being made. A fierce debate was underway, over contracts for the pre-monsoon repair work. There was shouting, clapping, banging on the tables. School teachers should say to unruly students that the classroom was not the parliament, not the state assembly, it was not the corporation meeting. The much-maligned fish markets, she thought, were comparatively civil.

She watched Kaiz to read his reaction but saw no horror at the antics of his elected representatives. He had tuned them out. She leaned closer to see what he was writing in his notebook. Sketches of columns and arches, careless yet confident. She tried to look at her hunting ground with fresh eyes, searching for what had captured his attention so completely. She had always taken the beauty of the corporation hall for granted, only a pleasing backdrop to the discussions and compromises that shaped the city. Had the carved wooden ceiling always been this regal, she wondered. The honey glow on the mint walls—surely the bulbs had been changed just that day. And those figures carved on the columns, how had she not paid attention before? She decided to ask him about them afterwards.

'Would you know the story behind the monkeys?'

'What?'

'The monkeys carved on one of the pillars inside—the ones playing among vines.'

'I am not sure,' he said, frowning. He seemed slightly displeased about not knowing the answer. 'But the Bombay High Court also has a sculpture of a monkey—a blindfolded monkey holding up the scales of justice. He has one eye open and the scales are not level. An Indian subcontractor had a dispute with the English architect. He lost the case in court so he extracted his revenge in stone, and declared that the law was not impartial. But in this case,' he pointed his thumb at the corporation hall behind them, 'I think someone predicted today's meeting.'

'Why do you know all this?'

'All this?'

'Trivia about these buildings.'

'I love history.'

'But this isn't proper history.'

'What do you mean *proper* history—what's in the textbooks? History is not just names, dates and events, you know? That's just the skeleton. Stories are the flesh and blood, the link between past and present. That's the reason we study history after all.'

She paused to absorb what he had said when she saw Pandu Mhatre, a senior peon, walking towards them. She waved at him and whispered to Kaiz that Pandu was her most reliable source. 'You can say he is the skeleton to the flesh and blood of my stories.'

'Namashkar, Madam.'

Before Ira could greet him back, Kaiz bowed before Pandu with folded hands. 'Boss, I hear you are the most important man in this building.' His Hindi was also slightly accented. *Townie*, judged Ira, but this time with a spot of affection.

Pandu chuckled. 'Who's this gentleman?' he asked Ira in Marathi.

'My boss's nephew.'

'What all you have to do, Madam.'

'No choice, Pandu kaka. Have to fill this wretched stomach, no?'

'Hey, I am not that bad,' Kaiz said in Marathi. She was taken aback that he spoke Marathi.

Kaiz began to tell Pandu about his project, in his townie mix of Hindi, English and Marathi, and showed him the sketches he had made in the past hour. He asked Pandu what his favourite room in the building was, how the building had changed in the years he had worked there and listened intently when Pandu spoke.

In another room, Kaiz was fascinated by the tiles, so he sat down on the floor to sketch them. People stared but it seemed to make no difference to him. The nonchalance has to be a performance, Ira thought, but she could not help imagining the kind of boyfriend he would make, attentive and sensitive, not one to forget birthdays or anniversaries. He would remember the shirt he wore on the first date, the conversation that led to the first kiss. And when the span of his attention became the length of a lover's body—her breath caught in her chest before she could complete the thought. She felt a wisp of anticipation rising in her heart as she took in the odd angles of his limbs, the floppy hair, the air around him suffused with his unmistakeable charm. This image of him sharpened before her eyes, coming into focus in a way that made her feel like somewhere, in another dimension, their bodies were already together.

'Give me one more minute,' he said.

'Take your time.'

She wished he would write more slowly, sketch with greater detail.

'Do you have time for a chai?' he said when he was done. 'I know a great place nearby. My treat.'

'I never say no to chai.' A lie. She was a coffee drinker.

He took her to an Irani bakery deep in the heart of Fort. He ordered at the counter and walked back with a plate of brun maska, a waiter following with two glasses of tea. They sat on a bench by a closed window, separated by a plate and two glasses. The wooden slats shredded the sunlight so that it fell on them in ribbons. Kaiz rubbed two crusty slices of brun together to spread the dollop of butter, and then dipped the buttered bread into his tea. A crumb or two glistened on his lips before he licked them away. When he saw her looking, he smiled with his mouth full, without a hint of self-consciousness.

Walking to the bakery, he had told her half-a-dozen stories about the buildings they passed. *This landmark was a gift to the city by a trader who nearly brought it to financial ruin. This used to be a brothel. Here was the neo-Gothic style of architecture, there was Indo-Saracenic.*

'What about that one? What school of architecture is that?' She pointed at a modern office building, only half-seriously.

'Generic.' His lips turned down a little. 'That's modern architecture for you, no imagination, no soul.'

'No *soul*? You are too much.' She laughed at him; he took no offence.

Ira wondered whether these buildings he admired had once been called generic, if they had inspired similar disdain in those who abhorred the new. And how had they acquired souls, become interesting? Would Asha Nivas develop a soul one day, or were souls reserved only for old buildings in some parts of the city?

She saw that his was a Bombay of the past, of lore and legend. When he told her over tea that he had spent the first ten years of his life in Delhi, she was astonished. It would make sense to her much later, that you needed some distance from a city to be able to worship it the way he did. It had also been his way of belonging: learning its mythology was one of many paths to calling a city home.

All these signs already made her certain that he would love Irani cafes. He said the Irani cafe was the more open counterpoint to Bombay's other budget restaurants, the south Indian lunch homes and the Udupi eateries, which he thought had an unspoken brahminical air.

She was puzzled by that word he used, brahminical. What did it mean—serious? respectable? strict? Her twenty-three years in a brahmin family made it difficult to entertain an alternate definition. Yet, his tone alluded to something cruel, oppressive.

'That's ridiculous. What do you townies have against Udupi restaurants? You think they are unglamorous because they are vegetarian?'

'Precisely.'

'Let's settle for different but equal. How about that?'

He shrugged.

'There's another way in which they are different but equal too,' she added.

'What's that?'

'The Irani chai and the Udupi filter coffee. Only a fool would order coffee at an Irani or tea at an Udupi.'

He raised his empty glass in agreement and she lifted hers to meet it. She felt their fingers touch. He ordered more chai, another plate of brun maska.

'I have a theory.'

'You have a theory,' she said, a nip of teasing in her voice.

'The Irani cafe was one of Bombay's first cosmopolitan spaces. Everybody was welcome: prostitutes and poets, mazdoors and communists, all classes and castes could mingle in this democratic eatery. Who else would have taken them in? This mix of people, all in one place, this was Bombay. And this *beautiful chaos*,' he said the last two words with a beatific smile, then drained his face of all expression, 'got *too* chaotic to handle and that is the secret behind the famous signs at Irani cafes: no loitering, no arguing, no fighting.'

She laughed, not at the punchline of his silly theory delivered with mock seriousness, but to share in his happiness, the giddy joy in his eyes.

She told him about her first byline, the highlight of her first year on the job, thanks to Pandu the peon.

'Madam, I have some news for you,' Pandu had reported two months ago. 'Corporator Shivraj Raut might be in trouble.'

'What happened?'

'He lost his temper and slapped one of the junior overseers this afternoon. His party is trying to hush it up because they don't want union trouble.'

'When did this happen? Will they be able to suppress it?'

'Last evening, when the corporator was in his ward. They are trying their best but the union is going to get involved. No one will break the story tomorrow, that's for sure. It's yours to print.'

'Tell me more. Who is the staffer?'

Pandu gave her a name. 'He is the Junior Overseer of the Rats Department.'

She stifled a giggle. 'What did you say? I heard rats.'

'Yes, rats. Undir, mooshik, Ganpati's vehicle, you heard right. Junior Overseer, Rats. What is so funny, Madam? This is the municipal corporation of Bombay, of course they have to deal with rats. The most fearsome sena in this city is the undir sena, and the only forces keeping this army of rats under control are the Rats Department of the BMC and the NRK.'

'NRK?'

'Night Rat Killers. You don't know about them?'

The Night Rat Killers were contractors who beat rats to death under the cover of the night. These killers were paid 25 paise for each rat they killed, but only if they hit their weekly quotas, and only for rodents that had been beaten to death, not poisoned (from her notes: WHO'S DOING THE POSTMORTEM??!). They reported to the Junior Overseer (Rats) and got only Sundays, Republic Day and Independence Day off. Every NRK she spoke to aspired to join the official BMC Rats Department, she told Kaiz, in a permanent job, where not only did they have no monthly targets to meet but also enjoyed the freedom to poison and trap rats in addition to bludgeoning them.

His face went through a gamut of expressions as she narrated this story, and he punctuated her telling with little sighs and chuckles. She was left wondering whether what she had narrated in three minutes was an epic tale with deeper allegories. Or perhaps he was just someone bursting with feeling.

The afternoon was a crafty animal she tried to hold on to but that slipped away. She had to leave to file her stories for the day.

'Thanks for the tour. I hope I get to see you again.'

Not used to so many cups of chai one after the other, Ira's heart leapt out of her throat like a frog. 'You are welcome,' she said.

Ira spent the night replaying the afternoon, dawdling on the goodbye; her heart skipped each time he said he hoped to see her again. But when she tried to conjure up his face, she couldn't summon a focused image, just a grey kurta, a big smile, eyes like espresso, a mop of wavy hair. Her eyes, diligent cartographers, wished they had spent more time running over his face, recording to memory its contours. When sleep came, she dreamed of him, of his body entwined with hers like freshly washed laundry. She woke up breathless in the middle of the night. The details of his face remained hazy but the idea of him had taken root.

Even years later, she would wonder if her life would have taken the same course had it not been for this dream, whether it was the dream that had cemented a passing fancy into something concrete.

A few months later, Ira was asked to cover a protest at Azad Maidan. The organisers expected three hundred citizens to join hands to form a human chain against communalism. Her newspaper was doing a month-long series on the Babri Masjid issue: the court case to decide upon the fate of the disputed mosque in Ayodhya, Advani's rath yatra around the country to gather support among Hindus for a temple in place of the mosque, and its aftermath. Her two hundred words on the event would go into a piece about citizen movements for communal harmony. It was the kind of journalism that won awards and made enemies. Ira was thrilled to play a small part in it.

Earnest in her escalating responsibility, she showed up before the announced meeting time, only to find a sparse crowd of out-of-towners and other first-timers. Over the next half hour, people began to trickle in. An artist or two, a couple of art film directors, some theatre actors. Handloom sarees, long earrings, large bindis. Here were the trade unions: SSS, INTUC, AITUC, other collections of letters that were vaguely familiar. Some people held up large posters, not having thought through the human chain angle of the protest which would soon occupy their hands. A young boy walked around with a large pot on his head, pouring out glasses of cold water for a rupee. A group of housewives who had come to the event together took each other's hands, except the two women at the ends who shyly held hands with strangers. Men and women were soon swapping places to try and minimise the number of male–female pairings without veering far from their original companions, as if guided by an invisible mathematician.

And then she spotted Kaiz. He was among a dozen-odd young men and women, all students from his college. He didn't see her, so she took quote after quote from the section of the chain around him, till finally, fifteen minutes later, he did. He waved at her, breaking the chain for a moment.

She tore herself away to go cover other parts of the demonstration but was back before the protest ended, waiting for him.

'How have you been?'

'Good. And you?'

'Very good. How did your project turn out? The one you came to the BMC building for.'

'Very well. I did get an insider's view after all.'

She could see his friends getting impatient behind him. Finally, one of them called out to him.

'I have to go, but I am glad we met again.'

From the flush in his cheeks through the vacuities they had traded, she already knew he was glad to see her. Maybe even more. She could not wait for another coincidence. Bombay was a big city, there were no third chances.

One, two, three, go.

'Kaiz, do you want to go out for dinner sometime?'

'I would love that.'

In the days leading up to the date, she made Kaiz her raft in the sea of small talk that was her workday. A symbol to meditate upon, a distraction she could shape into any fantasy. Had he had a different name, or had she truly been interested in architecture or history or the other topics he held forth on, perhaps this idea of him would have crystallised into something other than sex, but as things stood, desire clasped her like a vine in the days leading up to the dinner.

Kaiz picked a Lebanese restaurant in an alley off Colaba Causeway. The restaurant welcomed guests with a window full of skewers on which roast chickens glistened, naked and wanton. She had walked through this very alley years ago, with her mother and Kartik. At the end of the lane, her mother had spotted a group of hippies passing a chillum around a circle and had immediately covered the children's eyes with her palms before making a quick exit. In the Eighties, when Arab businessmen had started appearing, the warnings continued, this time about abductions and slavery, and the alley had remained out of bounds for the gullible and well-behaved young, the children of prejudice.

Inside, Kaiz and Ira sat across from each other at a little round table at the back, Kaiz out-speaking Ira four words to one, his elbows on the table, his face less than two feet from hers. He was still a fount of stories whereas her own words seemed to have flown away. At first, all she gave to the conversation were questions. Fibre to let him keep spinning yarn. When their beers arrived, he leaned back into his chair to make room on the table, palms interlocked behind his head, cool, cool, but she saw he tapped his feet furiously from time to time. This sign of impatience kept her on edge. She was afraid he might be bored, that her questions were not good enough.

She had spent days thinking of the things they would speak about, of how she would make him laugh and how her fingers would graze his hand, but now found herself under a spell. Does the share of words spoken on an early date reflect the balance of infatuation, Ira wondered, and thus the balance of power, set in stone for the length of the relationship? And what about the volume of words thought but not spoken, was the algebra reversed, for her mind had become a bicycle racing downhill. How was he so confident, how did he never fumble or falter? How come he knew so much, what did he have to forget to make room in his head for the past?

He told her later that when he got nervous he babbled. Even his prattle, it turned out, was self-possessed.

Between sips of beer, Kaiz began to tell her how he was nearly killed a few days ago when he was walking home with a book in hand, fully absorbed in the pages, and did not see a bus that had come dangerously close. It had stopped only five feet from him.

'That happened to me too—just last week! But unlike you, I am an expert at crossing roads with one arm out.' She found herself returning to her body, felt her voice coming to life again.

'What were you reading?' he asked.

'What?'

'Last week—in the middle of traffic. What book were you reading?'

A potboiler, which she knew was not the correct answer.

'*Midnight's Children*,' she said without a second thought. 'Salman Rushdie is such a terrific writer.' Shit. 'I'm only talking about, umm, about this particular book, of course.'

A long pause.

She bit her tongue: why did that have to be the first book that came to mind? It was unlikely, but what if he was the type of Muslim who was baying for the author's blood?

Then he began to grin. 'It's alright, it's one of my favourites. And Salman Rushdie is a Malabar Hill boy like me.'

'Thank god. And what book did you nearly kill yourself over?'

He named a book she had not heard of. It followed the events leading up to the First World War, he reported. 'I was *this* close to becoming the latest casualty of a war that ended seventy years ago. Who is to say when wars really end, right?'

'And you were reading this for fun?' she asked, teasing. Ira could not imagine reading history for pleasure, military history even less. She was neither a bore nor a show-off. Even in school, history had been one of her least favourite subjects. Names and dates learnt and repeated mindlessly like a chant.

'As opposed to?'

'For a project or a college course.'

'As an architect? What course would that be?'

'I never read non-fiction. It's so *boring.*' It was the beer, for a moment she had become herself.

'Wait, you find all non-fiction boring? *All* of it? That's a sweeping statement. And if you don't read any non-fiction, how do you learn about the world?'

'I use my eyes and ears. I read the newspaper.'

'You think that's the same?' He rolled his eyes, and added after a pause, 'I had you down as a more curious person.'

'I also read BMC press releases and tenders, but they are closer to fiction than not.'

He smiled. 'I still can't believe that a journalist says she doesn't read *any* non-fiction.'

'I deal with reality all day, all week. There's just so much of that one can take.'

She didn't know why the conversation had rattled her, it had been no more than banter about books. She was embarrassed by her white lie about *Midnight's Children*, her evident need to please. How do you learn about the world then, he had asked. The truth was she had never gleaned any lasting ideas from the books she had consumed, most were thrillers and romances she bought at the roadside stalls at King's Circle.

'I will pick a good thriller over a boring, serious book any day,' she declared with theatrical confidence. 'And I am a beat reporter, not an editor: I don't need to use big words or quote French philosophers.'

He laughed. 'Call a spade a spade. So, why did you become a journalist?'

She bristled at the suggestion the question contained. 'What do you mean?'

'Why a reporter? Why the civic beat?'

Alright, just a question then. So, she told him: she was nineteen, studying psychology in college, when she had come across a food stall outside a children's park which spewed its exhaust right into the play area. It did not make sense to her, that somebody could get a permit for a stove in that spot, it felt hazardous. She had written a letter to a newspaper, a rival to her current employer, and a few weeks later, the food stall switched to selling cold drinks and snacks only. The stove was gone, it had been illegal after all. She had made a difference— or had been part of a remarkable coincidence—and one thing had led to another.

'And why did you become an architect?'

He raised his fork in the air. 'Whoever is born a poet becomes an architect.'

'What does poetry have to do with architecture?'

'Victor Hugo?' He blinked slowly, a little embarrassed. 'It's from *The Hunchback of Notre Dame*.' He shook his head as if to say, *never mind*. 'I have always loved buildings, that's why.'

He put a large piece of meat into his mouth and began to chew slowly. To not have to speak, perhaps? Every second of silence felt like a sentence. She was keen to change the topic.

'These kebabs are really excellent. Good choice, Kaiz.'

'My boys know how to cook.'

'Your boys? You know the owners?'

'No, ya. I do know the owner but I meant my boys, my Muslim bros.' He smiled.

When Kaiz brought her to the restaurant, he seemed to know it intimately already. With a guiding hand on the small of her back, he had walked to the smallest table and smoothly pulled out a chair for her before seating himself. He had not looked at the menu when he ordered—she had asked him to recommend what to get—and when the food arrived, he ate it without comment or compliment, leaving her to do the gushing. Every couple of minutes, he picked up a fry or two from her plate, no permission sought. It was as if he had lived everything already, many times over, like this evening was his own house and he knew where everything was and how it was arranged. Nothing impressed him or surprised him, his fidgety feet announced.

This confidence distanced her, made her feel out of place. It sat between them carrying a blade in its pockets, a weapon it hinted it was not afraid to wield if challenged. But his smile made him vulnerable again, human and lovable, it made his small eyes sparkle and crinkle and go into hiding like a pair of children playing pranks on her.

'And do you also cook well, like your boys?' she began to ask, but before she could finish, he raised his arm to wave at someone. He put up two fingers, *two minutes*. He walked to another table and she was left mid-sentence, mid-smile, eyebrows partly arched, mouth half-open, as if somebody had shouted 'Statue!'

Ira carried a pocketbook and a pen for such times, to occupy herself as well as to appear occupied. After a few minutes, which felt like an eternity, she sensed that he was back, standing behind her, trying to see what she was writing. When she did not look up, he leaned in and blew into her ear. His scent, of citrus and spice, stole over her. It slithered in and wafted through her body, summoning to attention every molecule, every atom, till it found its mark, the centre of her existence. In that moment, there was only desperate longing. If he touched her then, it would flood her being with all the colour there was and the world would turn black-and-white and fade into nothingness.

'Sorry, I saw someone I knew. You were saying?' He slid back into the conversation as smoothly as he had left.

They talked till all the other customers left, till one of the waiters sheepishly turned the fan off and brought them the bill. She offered to pay for dinner because he was still a student. To her dismay, he did not protest. When they were about to get up to leave, an insect crawled up her hand. He brushed it away. Slowly. The unexpected touch of his hand left her skin covered in goosebumps, rising and begging to be touched, poetry in Braille. Perhaps he noticed.

They walked to the nearest bus stop. There were no other waiting passengers and they had the entire bench to themselves. They sat down comfortably apart, but inched closer over the course of conversation. They pretended not to see this invisible dance their bodies were performing till her bus arrived, ten minutes later, fifteen inches closer. When she got up, a strand of her hair caught in a button on his sleeve. Ira felt a tug on her scalp and was filled with a familiar irritation and an unfamiliar urgency. She turned towards him and he stood up and kissed her, putting his lips on her answering mouth.

They were lovers within weeks of their first date; how she let it proceed at that pace she did not know. When she thought about the weeks after the kiss at the bus stop, what she remembered most clearly were scattered sensations. Running her fingers through the shock of his hair, the smoothness, the softness, cotton where she expected coir. How her toes tingled each time their mouths met. The vast distance between his door and his bed. Their impatience and the dusty cold of his tiled floor on her bare back, on her buttocks. It was her body that remembered more clearly than her mind. She thought it was a borrowed pleasure, weightless and absolute. It made even his cockiness delicious, it rendered invisible his untrimmed nails, black crescent moon on each finger, the clothes repeated two days in a row. It made lighter the weight of his name. Too much, too soon, what about, what if, what if, those doubts did come up from time to time, but his hold over her body flattened her reservations. Everything was fine the way it was. Pleasure of the body over spinning of the mind.

At least it was in the beginning.

She had believed that the heart was like a house and when you let someone in, they were only a guest. You could entertain them in the living room while keeping the bedrooms shut. You could limit their footprint to a minimum. But she had not suspected that Kaiz was a shameless, over-familiar guest who took a tour of the house on his own, opening doors and walking in unescorted, uninvited.

Sometimes when Kaiz looked at her, she questioned the story she told herself. When in the middle of a conversation or after making love, he looked at her as if she was all there was, as though his five senses were a bowl in which there was room for her alone and nothing else. She didn't remember when desire started competing with affection, with more. Perhaps it was the day she first saw his silly side, when he told her how much he loved dabba gosht as a child because he thought the mutton dish was, in fact, dabba *ghost*, a spirit in a box, and that anybody who ate it was possessed by the spirit of the goat for the duration the curry remained in the body. And then he had bleated like a goat, a spot-on impression that had startled her. He had rolled over, overcome with laughter at his own silliness, and she began to laugh too, both seized by paroxysms of laughter till they recovered and did not remember what they had found so funny in the first place.

Or the first time he called her jaan—when at dinner one evening, he picked up the bones from her plate and started gnawing at them. Her face betrayed her horror.

'Kaiz, that's disgusting.'

'Don't make me say it.'

'Say what?'

'Aren't we exchanging enough fluids already? You are terrible at eating mutton, see how much you have left behind. Why let good meat go to waste? An animal died for us, jaan, show some respect.'

Or perhaps it was when he told her his parents separated when he was eight and he only saw his father, who was a senior advocate at the Supreme Court, a couple of times a year. His college professor mother had brought up her two children single-handedly, he told her proudly. But to Ira it was incredibly sad. She didn't know anyone who was divorced. The word divorce evoked in her a funereal melancholy. Die-vorce, her parents pronounced it.

And as if he read her: 'It's fine, Ira. Don't feel sorry for me, alright?'

She kissed his forehead, she could not help it. 'Was it hard for you?'

'I don't know, I was only eight. But I do remember the shouting and screaming in the years before. They fought so bitterly that I think I was relieved when it ended.'

'Really?'

'Let me tell you how bad the fighting was. In an English exam in school, we were asked the masculine form of bitch and I wrote bastard.'

'No!'

'Yes.'

She started seeing him more often, off and on became every day. A little secret, a small rebellion. Nothing more. When they were apart, memories of him would arrive unannounced to keep her company, snatches of a kiss or a bad joke, and remind her that a portal to him might still be inscribed on her skin—he liked connecting the moles on her back to create constellations: Theseus, the ark, Vulpus Minor, the little fox, and her favourite, Amora Amora, the geometric heart. A temporary tattoo marking a temporary intimacy.

One evening, he was reading a book of poetry next to her, in his bed that was too narrow for two. They were curled up like two commas placed together, a typo in the story of the universe. She felt their heartbeats pulsing under their skins, slightly out of sync but scrambled up, how hard it was to tell which was whose. His face pressed against her hair, fine lines etched into his cheek. A book of poetry in one hand, a finger tracing circles on her thigh. He read aloud, the poem was in Spanish: he was practising for a language test. Those alien sounds carried by his velvet voice rose and fell and washed over her gently. His words threaded through her half-dreams as she drifted in and out of sleep. She glanced at the clock. It was almost nine. She winced, she had to leave, how had time flown so quickly? When she started to get up, he put his arm across her shoulders to pull her down and shook his head. She relented, lay down again, and to be sure she wouldn't leave, he placed the book, and an arm, across her chest. Kaiz came to the end of the poem he was reading, turned the page and read aloud, *aqui te amo*. Here I love you, he translated for her. The narrowness of the bed, the angle of his torso, the pace of his reading and all the interruptions, the rotation of the earth, the hands of the clock, they had all conspired and culminated in this. Here I love you, and her heartbeat right below.

Still, there were moments of questioning. They had such

little in common. For her doggedness and ambition, there was in him a corresponding unflappability, but his intellectual need for precision contrasted with her comfort with ambiguity. He looked comfortable and content in his skin and in his life; in her there was a volatility, a thirst to climb. It was telling, she thought, that she liked coffee while he preferred tea.

I am proud to be a kept man, Kaiz started saying in a few months, even though brun maska, a plate of idli-vada or dosa, and the occasional fish thali were all that Ira could afford. She took him to the Press Club, to Samovar Cafe at the Jehangir Art Gallery, favourite haunts of journalists. Kaiz introduced her to bombil fry; it was a sticky, smelly fish that was transformed when fried, a fish her mother never cooked at home because she said it was a poor man's food. Ira was glad, her four thousand-rupee salary welcomed it with open arms. Most of her salary she handed over to her mother anyway, who gave it to her father to deposit in Ira's bank account.

Kaiz insisted on meeting the owners and cooks of the places he liked, he asked them for recipes and made up stories of failed attempts at replication. He noticed small changes in the menu, asked about their families back in their villages. The occasional freebie, like two bottles of Thums Up or a caramel custard or two, was a small price for such attention, a reminder that you were visible. But even though he seemed to know how to stretch a ten- or twenty-rupee note, he did not pluck money out of his wallet with the same deliberation that her parents did. She was used to watching them count each note slowly and carefully as if bidding it a painful adieu. That kind of frugality made sense to her, not his thriftiness.

It was clear to Ira from the beginning that Kaiz's confidence was developed over not just the twenty-three years of his life but longer. The soft-footed English accent, his choice of books and his turn of phrase, the generous patronage of those who served him, these signs did not just sit on his skin, they came from his flesh and bone. They had to have been accumulated over decades of a rolling inheritance (correct), she had surmised, a generation or two of foreign educations (incorrect) and a childhood where English came before the mother tongue (correct).

At his Malabar Hill flat, she came across an album of pictures from his childhood. One that stayed with her was of a dinner party at his Delhi home, which Kaiz and two other young boys appeared to have crashed. Her parents had never thrown a dinner party, her flat had never seen men in suits and women in sarees and pearls. The room in the photo was decorated with Madhubani paintings. A carpet sprawled across half the floor. More remarkable were the huge bookshelves, row after row of tomes patiently awaiting their turn behind children still playing with toy trains. He had grown up in a home steeped in culture, in a cocktail of art and history and politics which had radiated from the bookshelves and leaked into everyday conversation and bedtime stories, it bounced off guests at dinner parties, perhaps it was even exhaled by the potted plants at night. It was a world she was familiar with, also somewhat enveloped in—some editors at work carried the marks of its citizenship—but in his company, she came to know it more intimately. The world of ideas, of analysis.

Her parents, like many of their generation, were good at a different kind of analysis. All Shobha and Shankar Kamat needed was a name to glean intricate insight from.

Did you say Sanjay Deshmukh? Is he very fair? He must be a CKP, Chandraseniye Kayastha Prabhu. He has light eyes, no? No? Hmm, most CKPs have them, not all. They have very bossy women, beautiful but bossy. And even though they go by Prabhu, they are not brahmins.

Your friend's name is Anasua? No, no, it's Anasuya, like the sage's wife. Or she must be Bengali, they change spellings sometimes. V becomes B. A becomes O. Such funny people when it comes to names, but very cultured overall. Very well educated too, just a little lazy.

That's not the point, an exasperated Ira would think, but they could not help it, it was a tic of personality. What would they gather from his name? What would Kaiz Dewani mean to them? Shia or Sunni or Bohri? From the north or the south? What were the faults of his blood, what graces was he heir to?

Perhaps it would suffice for them to know he was Muslim, enough to paint a portrait.

In December that year, after a mob of Hindu hardliners tore down the Babri Masjid in Ayodhya, riots broke out in different parts of India, including Bombay, killing and displacing thousands. Police turned on citizens, mobs on the innocent, neighbour turned on neighbour. In many parts of the city, what mattered was not how long you had lived together or how many meals you had shared, it came down to how you prayed, and even if you never did, it came down to how you were *supposed to* pray, to what was decided for you generations ago. There were two waves of violence and, by the end of January, the riots were over. But once you were taught to reduce a person to just one piece of their identity, it took a long time to learn to fill in the other details, to make them whole again and see them as fully human. Once you sow this mystery seed, who knows what you will harvest centuries, years, or even months later?

On a Wednesday in early February, the weather was lovely. At midday, the sun was mellow and streaks of wispy clouds covered the sky, like a milk spill mopped badly. It felt wrong to stay indoors, so Ira and Kaiz, ducking out of office and college respectively, decided to meet at Chowpatty for lunch. The beach was bursting with young couples, greedy for breeze, for the salty sea, for time together. Ira and Kaiz walked close to the water, hand-in-hand. Under their feet the sand sank; they left a trim of footprints along the billowing hem of the sea. They talked about nothing in particular, speaking only so they could be enveloped in the sound of each other's voices. This was happiness, thought Ira, these minutes and hours spent with him, gazing at his face, at the slant of his smile, his vanishing eyes. Then it was time to go.

The taxi they hailed had plush velvet seats and tiger-striped padding on the doors. A many-coloured array of religious idols and bobble toys stood on the dashboard. Always nodding, ever approving, this peanut gallery.

'I think we need sunglasses,' she whispered to Kaiz.

'What a taxi, boss!' he said aloud.

Ira glared at him.

The taxi driver, a chatty middle-aged man, told them he had given his taxi a makeover the previous week. You like it? he asked, barely able to contain his pride. Kaiz nodded vigorously, he praised the driver's taste, said the taxi really stood out. The irony in his voice was lost on the driver.

He used to work at one of textile mills that had shut down in the Eighties, the driver told them. For a decade he had struggled, working at one odd job after another. Some of his fellow mill workers succumbed to the lure of easy money, they joined gangs, turned to crime. But not him. 'We have to show our faces to Him one day,' he explained, pointing at one of the idols on the dashboard, 'so I stayed away from all this 420 business. And look, it took longer but here I am.'

Kaiz was in no mood to listen to the driver's entrepreneurial escapades. He moved his hand over her leg, under her skirt, and prised her knees apart slightly. She took his backpack in her lap and slid forward. As his fingers moved, her breathing began to get knotted. But when a cool breeze blew through the open windows of the taxi she caught a whiff of herself. She quickly pushed his errant hand away. Kaiz looked annoyed but whispered, fine. He put his arm around her and she rested her head in the nook of his shoulder, her fingers locked with his to keep them from further mischief. On the radio, a romantic film song, a new hit.

The taxi driver turned the radio volume up. 'Perfect song for the lovebirds.'

They laughed, nuzzled again. Ira hummed along, a little out of tune and, for a change, Kaiz did not make fun of her singing. Ira wished the ride could go on longer, she prayed for a red light or two. When the taxi stopped at a traffic signal, a girl tried to sell Kaiz red roses. The world seemed to know that the taxi was carrying a couple in love.

'Don't buy them, Sir. They are all picked from graveyards,' said the taxi driver, looking out for them again.

Just then the azaan started, first from one mosque, then another, and another, each muezzin slightly out of sync with the others.

'These Mohammedans are a nuisance, aren't they?'

Kaiz laughed. 'Yes, such awful singers.'

The taxi driver turned around and nodded. Once again, he had heard the ironic remark as an endorsement.

There was a mole on his cheek that Ira had not seen before.

'Not just that, Sir. Who do they think they are, with these

blaring noises five times a day? Is the city the property of their fathers? Too bad we could not teach them a lesson, even after two tries.'

Kaiz took his arm off her shoulder. 'What do you mean?'

Ira noticed among the paraphernalia on the dashboard saffron stickers of a roaring tiger.

'December and January. Twice we tried, but they are a resilient bunch, aren't they? Like cockroaches. Even an atom bomb can't kill cockroaches, I have heard.'

Ira turned to Kaiz, she saw him draw a deep breath, his nostrils flared. She knew what that sharp inhalation was—the rumble before the rage. Ira clutched at his arm, pressing her fingers into his skin. He exhaled.

'Kaka, please pull over,' she said.

'Here? Didn't you want to go to VT?'

'Not anymore, just drop us here.'

The ride ended but his anger did not cool off.

'Who the fuck does the taxi driver think he is? What makes him think the city belongs to him—does he even know how old Bombay is, does he know its history? Bombay has seen *centuries* of plurality and only a few *years* of bigotry. It is the likes of him that the city does not need.'

'Jaan, I know, but it was not safe.'

'You should not have stopped me, Ira,' he said. 'I wish you hadn't.'

She tried to make him see reason, assured him that, had she been alone, she would have protested too, picked a fight. But she knew that at best she would have used levity to impart a gentle lesson: in Marathi, from the safety of the backseat, the safety of her name. Only if she had been alone. But there, then, the stakes had been higher.

'That's just like you, Ira, picking the expedient over the imperative.'

'Sorry, what over what?' She scratched her head in exaggerated confusion, hoping to distract him from fury.

When he saw the look on her face, he sighed. 'Never mind.'

What Ira did not tell Kaiz was that she was terrified when he had lingered by the front door of the taxi, his hands on the window, his anger still simmering. So she had grabbed his arm and pulled him away. 'Kaiz, let's go.' Upon hearing his name, the taxi driver had sneered and looked at them up and down before driving away, but Ira had felt his gaze chiefly upon her, questioning and accusing.

A month later, Kaiz asked Ira to celebrate his birthday with him. His mother would be in college till the evening. They spent the morning together and, after an early lunch, they decided to watch a movie, a matinee show in Fort.

The first explosion was at 1.30 p.m. It was a very loud bang, like crates had fallen out of the sky and crashed to the earth. Thunder in March? No, this was too loud. The entire theatre broke out in panicked murmurs.

Kaiz turned to Ira. 'What's going on?'

'It sounds bad. Should we leave?'

They rushed out. On all sides people were running out of buildings. Someone pointed towards the Bombay Stock Exchange building. She saw a plume of smoke rising from the tower. When she heard the word bomb, she knew that she had to get to work as soon as possible.

There were thirteen bomb blasts over the next hour and a half. Five days after Holi, the streets were painted scarlet, drenched in glass and shrapnel, bones and limbs. Major roads were blocked, so Ira and Kaiz had to snake through the

Fort area, through the thick crowds, relying on each other's knowledge of alleys and passages. By the time she reached her office an hour later, even without a radio or a TV, she knew what had happened, she knew at least three versions of what had happened.

At Nariman Point, as she had heard already, she found the bottom of the Air India building gutted, the lobby hidden by a still-thick curtain of smoke. For a few moments, she was only a Bombay girl in mourning, crushed at the sight of her muse and home violated and wounded.

Kaiz put his arm around her, it's okay Ira, it's over. His voice trembled.

In the many versions of truth she heard that afternoon, only one thread had been constant. *Those haraamis, those landyas, this was their revenge for Babri.*

No, Kaiz, it's not over.

13

FOR MOST PRACTICAL PURPOSES, the bomb blasts turned out to be the last chapter of a dark period of communal unrest in the city. Among the blast sites was a Muslim neighbourhood, Bombay was told, so this was not a communal attack. Smugglers wanted to cripple the newly open economy, Bombay was told, they wanted to attack this lush, booming, blooming city, the spirit of the nation, *Urbs Prima in Indis*, strike fear into its very heart, the Bombay Stock Exchange, so that money would move underground again and lubricate the shadow economy of gold, havala and drugs. But at the same time, there were murmurs of arrests, hundreds dragged out from their homes, from their shops and mosques; there were whispers of torture and humiliation, of unspeakable things forced into unmentionable body parts. These hushed voices grew louder till everybody heard aloud what they already knew. It was a revenge attack after all, and the perpetrators were safely hiding in Pakistan and Dubai. But Bombay was tired, Bombay was battered already, and the cycle of an eye for an eye did not continue. For most practical purposes, the communal violence that started after the Babri Masjid fell came to an end after the blasts. But there were other casualties.

This toll became clear at dinner tables around the city, at bus stops and in the corners of trains, over rocks abutting the sea and over cups of tea, wherever people gathered and confided in each other. It emerged in safe spaces where latent misgivings could bubble up at last. These suspicions were a seam being stitched into life in the city, not always visible but shaping its form and fit. When you got into a rickshaw, you inspected the insides for markers of faith: a red-and-gold cloth or a green-and-gold sticker. You also learned to read between the lines of their absence (wait, perhaps you always did). You began to hear that when one was looking to rent a house, one's surname determined one's pin code (wait, perhaps it always did). Around the city, and in Asha Nivas, the bearded face of Shivaji and the visage of a roaring tiger began to appear on the round behinds of scooters, as did stickers on car windows saying Jai Shri Ram. Politics, hardly a staple of conversations before, became the main course at dinners with an increasing frequency.

Even in Ira's own house. Ashok kaka and Kusum maushi in her living room, over for tea on a Sunday evening.

'Why haven't they imposed President's rule yet? How has this government not been dismissed? They were quick to dismiss four BJP state governments after Babri Masjid. Our lives mean nothing to the Congress.'

'Why would they dismiss the government? The BJP was responsible for the demolition. This government did not engineer the blasts.'

'But they can't catch the culprits. That's as bad as being responsible.'

'You think they can't get Dawood back from Dubai if they tried? They are too weak.'

'Don't forget, there is a vote-bank angle.'

'All religions are the same, they are all different paths to the same destination, the One above,' said Ira's mother, refilling a plate of biscuits. 'We have been sending money to the Ajmer Sharif dargah for over twenty years.'

In your hope for a son, thought Ira. Only one prejudice can cut another.

'See Shobha vaini, either everyone is secular, or no one is. Why is it a load only on our heads? Do they ever come to our temples, celebrate our festivals? Never. They say it is haraam for them. Do you know how many temples were demolished in Pakistan and Bangladesh in retaliation for one Babri? Hundreds. It is all the meat they eat, I tell you, it makes them very aggressive. Look at the Pakistan cricket team, world champions, and look at ours, bloody bailas.'

Her mother, having seen the slow rearranging of Ira's face, looked at her and shook her head. *Let it be.* Her mother, defuser, enabler, changer of topics.

'Why don't you two stay for dinner? I'm frying pomfret, there is prawn curry too.'

'Some other day, Shobha. We have to leave soon.'

'I'll send some up with Ira at dinnertime in that case.'

Ashok kaka continued. 'We Hindus are too soft, we need

to become more like them. Tell me, is it too much to ask for, to be respected in our own homeland?'

'Too soft? What are you talking about? Who demolished the Babri Masjid? Who started the riots?'

'But, Ira, who started it all?'

'Yes, who started it all? You tell me, Ashok kaka.'

'Who partitioned the country? Who built the mosque over the Ram temple? Who invaded us nine hundred years ago, brought our age of glory to an end?'

Ashok kaka, what a bag of contradictions he was. Of late, he spared no opportunity to talk of the glory days of India, of Hindus. This nostalgia remained unlived at two levels: never had he lived what he longed for, nor did he appear to want to. He wore tailored shirts and trousers, peppered conversation with English phrases, even recounted fondly how he had taught himself the language. Indulged his wife like no other man in Asha Nivas did. Enjoyed—no, savoured—a good tandoori chicken or seekh kabab. Ira remembered his hands dancing around the sharp spike in his restaurant, unafraid, all in play, the kind of man her father was not, would never be. The spirited uncle, the self-assured sophisticate. Ashok Kini, tall and sturdy, with a keen wit and hooded eyes. And a hooded mistrust which he was now comfortable uncloaking.

So for most practical purposes, the communal violence that started after the Babri Masjid fell came to an end after the blasts, but the spell of peace that followed felt like hate was only shedding its milk teeth.

But in spite of all the ups and downs in the city, it was his social circle that remained, in Ira's eyes, the impediment in her relationship with Kaiz. His friends were an eclectic bunch. Among them were aspiring filmmakers and theatre actors, lawyers, economists and NGO workers. Some were biding time at internships or on research projects before they left for doctoral studies and a life in academia. The gang usually met at Kaiz's house on weekends. There was Old Monk and beer on offer, biryani and kathi rolls to eat. If his mother were away, marijuana too. Up to four people on the three-seater sofa, some leaning against the sofa or a wall and, in their laps, more friends resting their heads. Handloom cushions were strewn around, cigarette burns hidden among their bandhani dots. Most times this group met, heated debates broke out. A few hours into the evening, once the pot had dulled their sharp edges, the debates were forgotten and a strange, shared obsession with bad puns surfaced.

These debates had a revolving door of participants but a few faces remained constant. Among them was Neel Sen, a pugnacious lawyer with thick glasses and a ringing, sibilant laugh. Kaiz and he revelled in needling each other, hurling fond insults with smirks on their faces. In the beginning, Ira was alarmed by the intensity of the arguments, but after spending time with this bunch, she sensed that behind what felt like great tension lay a cool, compulsive need to debate. But perhaps Neel did take these arguments to heart, for his hair had begun to grey early: at twenty-six, he appeared to carry a head full of cobwebs. When Neel was in one of his moods, nothing was spared; the smallest thing could become a symbol for more than itself, worthy of assault, worthy of defence.

The Babri Masjid had once not been taboo, not till it was felled and the terrible violence broke out. She often thought about an evening a few weeks before the demolition, when Neel had decided to play the contrarian. The call for a Ram temple in Ayodhya had reached fever pitch; volunteers from around the country had been asked to assemble at the mosque on the sixth of December and erect a makeshift temple while the Supreme Court dragged its feet on delivering a verdict. It was the opportunity to right a historical wrong, the saffron leaders had announced, and reinstall a temple at the birthplace of Ram.

'If you look hard enough and go back long enough, you can find justification for every act of violence. History can become a wholesale shop for excuses—that's why you need a statute of limitations,' Kaiz had said to Neel.

'And who decides what that should be? The victims never get a say, do they?'

'What victims? We are talking about something that happened five hundred years ago.'

'I will never condone violence but could you pause to consider that attacking symbols might be different from attacking people? You have to recognise the element of catharsis, admit the possibility that it might help a wounded people heal.'

'Hmm, right, because these wounds that you speak of are real, they have persisted unhealed for five hundred years. Where else would they come from—hatred cannot be manufactured, right? And it's not like anybody profits from this idea of revenge, it does not unite a fractured Hindu vote bank.'

'Look, I believe that you have to move past the past to go forward, you can't just keep prodding old wounds. You and I get that, but you have to understand why it's not easy for many to do that.'

'There you go again with your old wounds. Are you comfortable with what that means for the idea of India? That this sense of justice—in quotes—can be secured not in courts but through rabble-rousing and violence?' The slightest of pauses, the lightest of frowns. 'Are you comfortable with what that means for me?'

Ira had asked him later whether Neel's line of argument had hurt him but he had played down her concern. 'That's how we talk. You can't take this personally.'

'Chill, dude,' said Neel with his hands up. 'I am only playing devil's advocate.'

'And you are doing a great job for your employer, you scuppie.'

'What?'

'Saffron-clad yuppie.'

'Fuck off.' Neel burst out laughing. 'Actually, I like the sound of it. Scuppie. But it won't scupper my chances with the liberal ladies, will it? What do you think, Ananya?'

'You know what—people have long memories, far too long. Everyone has these old grievances, Hindus against Muslims, Shias against Sunnis, but don't these people have more happening in their own lives? My roommate doesn't pay for her half of the groceries and I suspect she steals pads from my cupboard. My father threatens to disown me unless I let him find me a husband. And apparently, my ex is now bisexual. Who has time for old complaints when there are so many new ones to fume over?'

'Another one for the books,' Kaiz declared with a laugh.

Ananya Rajaram was one of Kaiz's closest friends, who had arrived in Bombay from Bangalore via New Haven. Ananya worked at an international aid agency and had a penchant for handloom sarees and serpentine bindis. She was stretching out on the sofa that evening, leaning ostentatiously on the armrest with a spliff between her fingers and the pallu of her black saree draped around her neck, laying bare her midriff. The lamp beside the sofa cast a lambent halo around her. None of the men—or even a less attractive woman—would get away with saying something that flippant, but on Ananya, irony became an irresistible perfume, a pheromone. It was only one of her many affectations.

Of all his friends, Ira liked Ananya the least. The first time the two women met, soon after she started dating Kaiz, Ira mentioned that she preferred the paneer version of a mutton dish at a popular restaurant. Ananya gasped.

'Oh no! I was loving you till you said that,' she said.

That comment, with its implication of camaraderie, had pleased Ira. She cringed when she thought about the day they met, how desperately she had sought Ananya's approval and how thrilled she had been with the scraps thrown at her. A few weeks later, Ananya left Ira bewildered.

'Kaiz, I did not expect you to fall for such a *conventionally* gorgeous girl,' she said. 'It takes away your street cred, you know. You can't be a jholawaala with a light-eyed hottie on your arm.'

Ananya was the queen of backhanded compliments, Ira learnt, backhanded with a tight fist and knuckle armour.

'Meow,' another friend chimed in, and made a clawing motion in the air.

'Didn't you call me a bitch yesterday? Make up your mind, am I canine or feline?'

Everybody laughed, Ira louder than most so nobody thought she was offended. Later, she remarked to Kaiz that Ananya was like an eccentric character from a movie or novel.

'She's a character, yes,' Kaiz said, 'but a character in a movie? No way. She would be *the* movie.'

Ananya was mercurial. One evening she was friendly, and frosty the next. Sometimes, she liked to pretend that Ira did not exist, or she would merely smile plasticly when Ira greeted her and immediately turn her attention to someone else, leaving Ira nonplussed. Her favourite move was to pull Kaiz away when he was talking to Ira, whisper in his ear and either appear grave or burst out laughing, leaving Ira in the dark either way. If Ira asked what they were talking about, she would wave the question away. Too silly to repeat, she might say.

His other friends were better, they made an effort to make her feel welcome and asked her about local politics, the inner workings of the city. Ira sensed from their pinched smiles that they were disappointed with her answers, for all she offered were facts, refraining from commentary or exposition. 'Generally speaking', 'Taking a step back', 'The bigger picture', those phrases did not come to her naturally. She could speak more comfortably about acts and budgets, clauses in tenders, the common loopholes in municipal contracts. So, somebody else had to play that role, bring in political and economic theories, link the small troubles of one BMC department to bigger struggles, provide *context and perspective*, make the discussion *interesting*. There were times when somebody would take something she said and use it as a springboard to launch into a tangential argument, which another person would then rebut fiercely, and thus interrupted, she would be left watching from the sidelines. If she sat down to reflect on these conversations, her head began to hurt and it became difficult to think clearly. It felt as if her brain had a film on it that obscured clear thought, like the crinkled skin over a cup of cooling tea.

It had to be clear to them as well, she feared, that she was a fish out of water in their gatherings. Did they wonder what their friend saw in her?

By the end of the summer, they had been together for over a year and a new side of his personality began to emerge. His mood could darken without warning, he would swing between listlessness and peevishness in no time. His ire was directed at the government, at monsoon rains and potholes, at traffic jams and traffic cops, sometimes at all policemen, at the droning jobs and low pays offered to fresh architects, at his mother who had taken early retirement from her teaching role and was at home all day. His mother had been in San Francisco for the first six months of their relationship, and was planning to return to help her daughter with her one-year-old as soon as the required window of waiting between two visits passed. This meant that Ira and he had little privacy, and there was no sleeping together, just kissing at matinee shows.

Kaiz had graduated from college some months ago and appeared to be in no hurry to find a job. Perhaps he had been bored in college as well, she thought, but classes and projects had kept him distracted. His explorations of the city, the dabbling in history and philosophy, his debates with his friends, these had been enough to consume the rest of his intellectual energies. It bothered her that he felt no need to earn a living, that his parents did not expect him to start working right away. His cavalier attitude would not have flown with any family in Asha Nivas. Perhaps this is what happened when you have never had to strive for anything; when there was nowhere or nothing you had to escape, you were propelled only by higher yearnings.

'Beauty is nothing but the promise of happiness,' she once heard him say, 'but in this city, only misery is guaranteed. Nobody can promise happiness here, just different shades of misery.'

Enough with the moping, she wanted to say to him. What were these shades of misery he was talking about, were they like the ad jingle about all the different shades of paint from which to choose *mera vaala blue*. A blue to call my own.

Then suddenly, he brightened. His father asked him to

spend a week in Delhi and Kaiz said yes immediately. He was excited about the change of scenery.

'He is going to introduce me to some of the architects I grew up admiring.'

There was a burning question on her mind. 'Do you think these are job interviews, does he want you to move to Delhi?'

'No way, I don't want to live there. It is a fuck-all city.'

'Good. I love you.'

'I love you.'

Kaiz never said I love you too, he said it sounded like an afterthought, mere reciprocity. Ira had found this irritating at first but had slowly made peace with it, that some people were unwilling to be followers, even in declarations of love.

He spent his time in Delhi meeting his heroes, among them an architect who had won the Padma Shri the previous year. When he returned, there was a glimmer of his old self again. He knew the root of his dissatisfaction, he told friends, his expectations of his vocation had been shaped by a different era. Architecture had once played a key role in forging a national identity. There was a time when the architect's role was not limited to built spaces only, it extended to urban design and civic planning as well. But today they were reduced to designing elevations for high-rises. And worse, the synergy between tradition and modernity had given way to a rigid binary: Shanghai or bust.

'Architecture,' he declared, 'needs a revolution.'

'What's with all the pontificating, dude? Have you come back from Delhi with a farzi PhD?' Ananya interrupted flatly. 'Or are you secretly getting one by correspondence?'

She said what many were thinking, and Ira wished she had been the one to point it out, not Ananya. But around him Ira found herself indulgent, unarmed.

Kaiz laughed but glanced at Ira, almost nervously. She thought he wanted reassurance that he was not being a bore, so she smiled and blew him a kiss. Immediately he launched into an anecdote, about a poster he once saw for an engineering and architecture college that required no mark sheets, no aptitude test or entrance exam; it offered admission on first-come-first-served basis only.

A weekend in early September, when the rains had turned erratic in slow preparation for their exit, he turned downcast again. His mother had left for San Francisco, but Ira had been unable to see him before the weekend. She planned to spend the weekend at his house; arrangements and excuses had been made. To her dismay, not only was he gloomy all evening, he had also invited his friends over.

Another soiree, Ananya complaining once again.

'I thought he was doing this only to humiliate me, but he's on serious boyfriend number two, so it can't be just that.' Ananya's ex-boyfriend had started dating a famous writer a month ago. Everybody who knew her had heard a detailed dissection of this relationship. 'Three years we were together and now he says he is gay—not bisexual—gay. I hope he got AIDS from one of the tourists he picked up at The Walls. He told me that's what gay men call the sea wall outside Gateway of India. What am I saying—I don't want him to *actually* get AIDS but a false scare would be mighty nice.'

Ira had no patience for Ananya's performances that evening. She flitted from guest to guest, making sure glasses were full, that everybody had tasted all the food Kaiz had ordered, but Ananya's voice followed her wherever she went.

'Some people are just ordinary and they can't bear that, you know?'

What a joke, Ira thought, she was playing hostess while the

host had made himself comfortable with one guest. Ananya was also making herself comfortable, she first crossed her legs on the sofa and then stretched one leg out and put it across his knees. In her lap was a small plate with a burra kebab which she was only nibbling at. Ira looked, again, at her leg on his knee. She poured herself a large peg of rum and took a swig.

'He was a relentless self-improver, Kaiz, even when we were together. He took an anthropology class—ONE class—and for three months, he could not have a conversation without dropping highfalutin words—modernity this and modernity that, post-colonial blah blah.'

Ira made her way to the sofa where they were sitting. To make room for her, Ananya had to put her feet down. She scowled and made a small noise of displeasure, then continued her story, without bothering to fill Ira in on the conversation thus far.

'Someone should tell Mihir that intellect is not sexually transmitted. You can't fuck your way to culture, you know?'

Ira put her hand on Kaiz's arm but he barely stirred. He was busy chuckling at Ananya. Another long sip of rum brought summer to her body.

'His family is so bourgie, man. He's probably the first in his family to pick up a book that is not a ledger. And try as hard as you may,' Ananya said, 'the first coat of paint shows.'

Kaiz snickered. 'You are pure evil, Ms Rajaram.'

Ira suddenly felt ill. Her stomach tightened into a clump and she found herself trembling a little. The warmth of the rum was now a burning in her chest. Had he found what Ananya said outrageous but nothing more? In that moment, she hated him more than she hated Ananya and she knew that even after the memory of this evening was gone, a crust of this hatred would remain, calcified in her memory as doubt.

What was her first coat of paint? And had she shown it to him?

Ira had only spoken Konkani till she started school. On the field, she used a khichdi of Marathi and Hindi and, in the office, a mix of Hindi and English. She still spoke Konkani at home and filled the many gaps in her knowledge of her mother tongue with other languages. But around Kaiz, she felt compelled to speak a single language: English. Sometimes, when she fumbled for the right word, as if looking for a one-rupee coin in the loose change at the bottom of her purse, Kaiz finished her sentences, producing the fitting phrase in an instant. She hadn't used a knife and fork till she met him. He had laughed at her: *don't hack at your food, use a sawing motion, like this.* Only one of her grandparents had been to college. Her father was stuck in a dead-end job, a clerk for over thirty years. Her mother rinsed and saved plastic milk packets so she could sell them to the raddiwala at Rs 5 a kilo. Their flat was decorated with McDonalds Happy Meal toys that Kusum maushi had palmed off on them, gifts from her relatives visiting from abroad. And their home had not been painted in fifteen years. The paint was peeling off, and in some places, even the first coat was gone, baring the plaster.

'You are evil, Ananya, but you know what's worse? You don't know how to eat a kebab,' Kaiz added, holding up her half-eaten kebab before he finished it off. 'Look at all this meat still on the bone.'

When he came to bed, she turned towards the wall, feigning sleep. She waited for his arm to rest on her side, his breath to fall on her skin but he turned the light off and left the room.

She clenched her fists till she fell asleep. When she awoke, he was already up. He made coffee and they ate toast and jam, reading two parts of a split newspaper in silence. He spoke first.

'I am going to visit Ayesha for some time.'

'Good for you,' she replied coldly.

'I'll finally get to meet Zara.' His niece. 'Uh, I leave Wednesday.'

'This Wednesday? In three days?'

She thought trips abroad had to be months in the planning. Of course he had no need for that, she should have known he already had a long-term visa.

Or had he known about the trip for months, but kept it from her?

'When will you be back?'

'In a few months, maybe two or three.'

'Two or three months?' She thought she had misheard him.

'It will be good for me to spend some time away.' Then he added, softly and wryly, 'It's not the best time for my *boys* here.'

She felt her anger from the previous evening return: what fear did a Malabar Hill boy have, how could he compare himself to Muslims on the streets, in the slums? Had he forgotten the coat of varnish that set him and his friends apart? He asked her to stay longer but she left after breakfast. The words *first coat of paint* continued to ring in her head, as did his laughter that had followed, masking any melancholy the news of his being away for two months would have brought on.

Still smarting, she saw him only once before he left for San Francisco, when she took him to Crawford market to shop for a suitcase. They said goodbye that evening, but on the day of his flight, he called her and begged to see her again, so she went to see him off at the airport. She was glad she did as soon as she saw him with his bags. He held her hand while he waited in queue to check in—for an hour and ten minutes, in the middle of arguments and negotiations over extra baggage, amidst disembowelled suitcases, crying infants, parents giving advice to departing students, talk of connecting flights and airport shuttles. She was thankful for the noise, the chaos, his hand around hers.

I'll miss you, she said when it was time for him to go. I love you, he replied, and finally, she felt it: saying I love you too did sound like an afterthought. So she hugged him instead and held on for as long as she could, trying to commit the moment to memory: the warm embrace, his t-shirt damp from her tears and her fingers from wiping his, the scent of his skin, his collarbone on her cheek and his heartbeat in her ear and, above all, his tangible struggle against the impulse to crack a joke and make light of the moment.

They wrote to each other every week and spoke on the phone occasionally, managing a proper conversation for every three or four aborted attempts when her parents were within earshot. There was never enough time or paper for everything they wanted to tell each other: Zara's antics, the weirdoes of San Francisco, the vagaries of weather and of politics in both places, new friends, intimate words, promises and reminders.

Ira settled into this new routine but a long-distance relationship came with challenges. She found herself going over her own day continuously, distilling it into anecdotes and insight to be served at a later date, then packing them tight for international calling card rates. Often, she forgot to tell him something she had carefully held on to for weeks, only to remember it after she had hung up; it would be stale by the time they spoke again. It was also hard not to read into pauses or hesitation, into an innocuous remark about a new acquaintance. The possibility of his infidelity occurred to her often. Some days, she dismissed it at once, and even if it did happen she reasoned she would forgive him eventually, she loved him too much to let go. At other times, even the thought wounded deeply, she knew she could never bear to see him again if he were unfaithful.

What bothered her the most was that she could not paint a picture of the new world he talked about, the backdrop to his days and nights. This world he described—the blue waters of the San Francisco bay, its hills and winding roads, the rows of colourful houses each different from its neighbour, a place soaked in fog and the haze of marijuana, where one could walk from one end to another in mere hours—what was it, city, town, or dream?

Kaiz spent a weekend in Los Angeles, a week in New York, then one in Florida. He returned from these trips breathless with stories, of how the art deco buildings in Miami were different from their cousins in Bombay, of a free meal he was fed by a Pakistani restaurant owner and a mutton dish there that was exactly like their favourite dabba gosht, and how even the sea of humanity at Times Square on a weekend was not a patch on Dadar station. She wondered if he felt he owed it to her to anchor his accounts in Bombay, in the life they had shared till he moved away. It reminded her that his world had been set in motion while her life was right where it was a year ago, bookended by BMC wards A and F North.

Two months became three, then four, Kaiz still had no answer for when he would return. From his letters, she learnt that he had cut his hair short, Zara had learnt to speak in sentences. In one of his letters, Kaiz sent Ira a picture of the two of them, the little girl in her maamu's lap, her plump face lovingly turned towards his. Even the faint resemblance between uncle and niece delighted Ira. How wonderful it was to see a shadow of the face you loved, to see its essence reflected in a different person, its presence in the universe multiplied. She imagined herself in the picture and it became a blueprint for the future. The price for this family would be a lengthy battle with her own but happy endings were not unheard of. A third cousin was marrying a Christian man. A distant relative had eloped with a Parsi woman and the family had come around eventually. Perhaps the harder divide to bridge would be the chasm between her family and his, broken as it was: how would they overcome the differences in their coats of paint?

Ira had been unable to speak to Kaiz for a month when her parents decided to go to Kolhapur for a wedding. It was only for three days, but it was the first time in her twenty-five years that she would have the house and the phone to herself, day and night. She called him from a phone booth to tell him, and spent the next week thinking up the naughtiest things to say when he called.

It was the day after Valentine's Day—still the fourteenth for him—and she thought about pointing out the date to him. She smiled when she imagined his reaction: eye rolling, mock gagging. The phone rang.

'Hello?' She kept her sexy opening lines at the tip of her tongue, in case it was someone else.

'Ira? It's me.'

'I know, I am wet just from hearing your voice.'

'Ira, I need to tell you something—'

'Tell me where you want to touch me first.'

'Just listen to me.'

'Uff, what is it?'

'I applied to grad school and I just heard back. I've been accepted to the school of urban design at Berkeley.' Silence, then his voice returned. 'I start this fall. In September.'

'Grad school? What is that—a masters' degree?'

'No, a PhD.'

'A PhD? Isn't that five years? What—how—why didn't you tell me before? Kaiz, how could you make this decision without asking me—without even letting me know?'

'I didn't think I had a chance, I wrote my application essays in a hurry.'

'That's bullshit. You know it's utter bullshit.'

Suddenly, it all made sense: the trip to Delhi, his speeches about architecture and the role of architects, so finely worded as if they were part of an admission essay.

'Ira, I am sorry. I am very sorry, but—' His voice trailed off. He sounded abject.

But what? He had never sounded this miserable in the time she had known him, not even at the airport the day he left. Such was her surprise that the anger disappeared, like water hitting a hot pan and sizzling into steam. In its place she felt a wisp of fear. 'No, listen, I am sorry. I promise I'll be more supportive. And congratulations, I am proud of you.'

But what?

'Ira, I can't do this anymore. It's not fair to either of us.'

'What do you mean?' She spoke slowly, the blood leaving her face.

'You know what I mean.'

14

AND JUST LIKE THAT, IT is over. Fifteen months together, five months apart. One phone call.

She does not get out of bed for fourteen hours: she has no sense of time, but the clock says so. She just lies there, boneless and hopeless. Her mouth is dry; she rolls her tongue around her teeth and feels moss. How gross, she thinks, distracted for a moment. A smile slips through the picket lines and perches itself on her face, till it is blown off by remembrance. She waits for him to call again, she craves it, wills it, but the phone does not ring. She calls instead, knowing fully well that an international call will draw questions at the end of the month. He does not answer. She calls again, and again.

Finally she leaves the house and walks. The city changes around her, from tidy rows of apartment buildings to the chaos of commerce to flat, smushed sprawl. And the cycle repeats till the sea bursts into view, over two hours later. At first, it is only a strip, blue tape holding sky and sand together, then it becomes its own thing. Rippled, certain, endless. She fears the yellow-and-black phone booths on the way. The letters STD ISD PCO beckon, they promise false hope. Tears come, like local trains, every couple of minutes. When she cries, people look, then look away; it's the code of this city, to look away from someone in private distress, a code as solid as 022. She carries her bloodshot eyes along the seafront. The breath of the sea is salty. It has turned white buildings grey, the colour of old men's teeth. Salt makes grey, salt makes red. Salt heals, slowly.

She keeps walking, into the early evening. The city turns orange and incandescent. Hawkers pack up, shops down their shutters, the buzz moves to where the food is, where drink is. Human flies drawn to the sweetness of escape. She hears shreds of different conversations one after the other—a car radio scanning for a station. Here and there, between honks, she can hear crickets. When she is tired, she walks more, to a bus stop. The ache of muscle distracts from other pain, so she walks the next day too. Day after day, week after week, after work and before. February is lost. March will vanish too.

How is one supposed to nurse a broken heart in Delhi,

she wonders, in Patna, in Kashmir, in Jaffna, where one cannot walk like this?

She writes to him, putting her pride and promises into sentences on blue paper, letter after letter, till she has none left. He does not reply. One night, she dreams that he has sent her an empty telegram with a single word: OVER. She will take anything, even that. What is he doing with her letters, she wonders, does he put them away, shred them or set them on fire?

People offer aphorisms. You will get over him. It's all for the best. It will be okay. You will be okay.

How long can you nurse a broken heart? Nurse is not the right word. Indulge, obey are more suited. First, the friends give up. They have jobs, families, their own heartaches. Then someone says what she needs to hear. *Are you the first person to have your heart broken?* Slowly the loss becomes an injured muscle which gives trouble from time to time, but she learns to adjust her movements, her life, around it till it heals; she has no choice. It will be okay, you will be okay. They call this the spirit of Bombay.

15

8 August 1997, six minutes past three in the afternoon.
Hello, Ira.
I'll wait outside till your meeting is done.

Fifteen minutes and a formal introduction later, she found herself alone with him. For fifteen minutes, she had taken long breaths, clenched and unclenched her fists. When Kaiz emerged, she had to continue to remind herself to breathe, to not let her face betray the rattle of emotions inside.

'Weren't you at Berkeley?' she asked when Nadkarni left.

'I transferred to Stanford two years ago when my advisor did.'

'You look different.'

He wore his hair short, a length at which it looked almost straight. His face had not changed much except some faint lines around his mouth and eyes. Her eyes wandered to his abdomen as she spoke. Its concavity had given way to a fuller flatness.

His hands sprung to his belly. 'Oh, this? I succumbed to freshman fifteen—even as a grad student. But you—you look the same.'

'You put on fifteen kilos?'

'Fifteen pounds, about six or seven kilos. It's a popular phrase there. I have come to learn that Americans have a lot of phrases. It's almost a national pastime, coming up with these. Did you know what hangry is? It's when you are hungry and irritable. Hungry-angry. Hangry. So the average college student gains fifteen pounds in the first year. I might have put on more, to be honest.' He proceeded to explain his diet in university, the heavy drinking and cheap pizza, the lack of exercise, an Indian aversion to sport that took some time to correct, the Californian love of the outdoors, bumbling on as if he were afraid of stopping.

What was he even trying to say? These things he was speaking about made no sense to her. She heard disconnected words, an assortment of sounds. The thread of meaning, of comprehension, that was supposed to string them together, was gone, snapped by the force of seeing him again.

At some point, he stopped. 'How are you, Ira?'

'Good. And you?'

'Doing alright. I must confess I have thought about—'

'You owe me an outline today. Should we go over what you have?'

He was quiet for a moment. 'Let's go to my desk.'

Ira walked with him to a musty far-off corner where all the interns sat. Kaiz tried to pull a chair for her but she stopped him and picked it up herself. She put the plastic chair across the desk from him, as far as was possible. A column of light rose from the wooden desk to the small window next to it; this pillar of dust separated them. He pulled out a typed sheet from a folder and began to explain the work he had done.

Don't look at his eyes, she said to herself. If he looks back, it will shatter you. Don't look at the lines on his face, ledger of the times he laughed without you. Don't look at the cloth on him, you know the skin it conceals. Don't look at his skin either. Don't look where he is, don't look where he isn't.

There was no place left to rest her eyes. Rain drummed on the window, the world outside was a blur.

But work was work. His outline, to her surprise, was a solid first draft. The writing was lucid and precise. A part of her had hoped that his writing would peddle cheap nostalgia, but there was a gentle balance in what he showed her, of love for the city and a scholar's rigour. She pointed out parts where his arguments were too academic and others where he needed to spend more time. He listened attentively and took notes. She thought about how much he had complained about his first job, the ten-day break he had taken a month into it and how he had quit soon after; even through the soft glow of love she had harboured no illusions about his work ethic. Perhaps she had been wrong.

As he spoke, her fingers kept returning to the spot on her left hand where there was now no metal, only skin. She had slipped her engagement ring off while she was waiting outside the meeting room. She did not allow herself to dwell on this, just like she did not allow herself to ask him about the other story she needed his help with, not till they ran out of time, not till he told her he had another meeting to attend.

'But what about my article on mills? Should I go back to Mr Nadkarni?

'We can work on that tomorrow,' he said. 'If you can come back. You start work after eleven, right?' She nodded. 'Can you come here early—around ten?'

'I'll try.'

All evening, she was fine. She kept herself busy, filed her stories, gossiped about editors old and new with a senior crime reporter who carried a resignation letter in his pocket at all times. At home, she helped her mother prepare dinner and discussed the stock market with her father. The Sensex had reached its pre-scam highs again, nearly fifteen thousand. Because of foreign investors, her father explained. After dinner, she took out old photo albums and went through them with her parents, and asked lots of questions. Where was this taken, who is this child in the background, what happened to this aunt. Finally, at the end of the evening, when she turned off the lights and turned into bed, her body began to shudder as if seized and she had to take deep breaths, again, to calm herself. She counted each breath like a chant to distract her mind, to shorten the night, dark and empty, that stretched before her like a yawn.

She made time to see Kaiz again the next day, after dispatching an intern to cover a minor press conference at the BMC. The bulwark she needed for her story on mill lands would come from his institute, from him. She had no choice.

Or so she told herself.

Textile mills had been the lifeblood of the city for over

a hundred years, but blow by blow, they had been rendered unviable. The five hundred acres of land in the centre of the city where the mills once stood were in the eye of a storm, caught in a custody battle between the mill owners and the state. Kaiz had done his homework: on his desk was a stack of reports on mill redevelopment, a paper tower surrounded by a bed of loose sheets and sketches, textbooks, brown rings from years of chai glasses. He took her through sections he thought she might find interesting, and they discussed various angles and points of view: the mills were central to the idea of the city; the toil of thousands had to give the public some equity in the lands; some equity, but how much; how much of the city can one rightly claim, in exchange for sweat, for blood, for life itself?

She wondered if his colleagues took note of his easy chemistry with a journalist he had just met, the ease with which they threw ideas at each other, the long smooth volley.

In talking about the city again, the poison she had kept at the tip of her tongue she found receding. She would not allow herself to be at ease in his presence, but the anxiety which had gripped her the previous day was loosening its hold, admitting the possibility of social graces, of polite conversation.

She asked him about his research. His focus for his doctoral studies was the Bombay Improvement Trust, a body formed by the colonial government to develop the city after the plague epidemic of 1896. He was looking at how the Trust, through architectural codes and policies, had shaped the city's visual identity. Nadkarni had been right, his research did fit right into the article Ira was having him write. Kaiz went into the details of the chapters he had already written, taking care not to use much jargon.

'I am not boring you, I hope?' he asked twice. Not something he would have done four years ago.

Ira shook her head. She was masking her delight; she had been reading about the Trust herself, how it had gone about creating the first planned suburb: Matunga, her home. She did not know what form her research would take, but it slaked her curiosity and for the moment that was enough. She didn't tell him about her project in case he thought she had just parasitically taken his interests.

She didn't tell him about the fate of her own building either: a small piece of the Trust's work that was going to be undone within a few years. The Kinis had finally prevailed. After uniting the residents in their demand for new flats, they had got two mid-level local politicians to ring up the landlord to persuade him to be reasonable. How the tables had turned in three months: the muzzle of the gun now pointed the other way. The landlord was willing to give each resident a new flat if he found an amenable builder.

Ira looked at her watch, an hour had passed. *Why did this feel so familiar, why could he still change the chemistry of time with his incantatory words?* Perhaps he read her mind, because as he was about to wind up, he began to fumble.

'Ira,' he started, and when he wavered and blinked, she already knew what he was going to say. 'I want to apologise for the way I ended things.'

'There's no need.'

'There is. It was a tough time for me. I was depressed and confused. And I was a coward. I am sorry.'

Not one letter, one call? But a single wrong word could become her undoing, so she willed herself to be a robot.

'Thanks for apologising.'

'I don't want to make excuses. I should have written back. The truth is I never opened your letters, I just could not. I am sorry I was a jerk.'

'I would have picked a stronger word.'

'Fair enough.' He looked down, struggling to continue once she'd shown a hint of resistance.

'I was joking, Kaiz. It's been a long time, I am fine.'

He smiled thinly. 'Didn't miss me too much, I hope?'

She smiled too, every muscle in her face weary with the effort. 'No, not much.'

No, she had not missed him much, not thought of him every day for months, for years. She had not stood outside his house hoping for an impossible glimpse, and never had she wondered whether he had finally started saying I love you *too*, or to whom. She did not see him imprinted over every street they had walked on, her heart was completely rid of him, and now, when he was standing before her again, she was okay.

The lines of a poem came to mind: like a saw it cuts when it goes, and it cuts again when it returns. She did not remember what the *it* was. Had to be love, she told herself, it had to be love.

16

IRA AWOKE BREATHING HEAVILY, and looked around to make sure that she had indeed been dreaming. There was nobody next to her, she was on the narrow sofa in her living room where she slept every night. Her heart was beating faster, her skin was still warm. She wished she had not woken up, that the dream had gone on. Even thinking about it shortened her breath and made her skin tingle. A tumble of images kept falling before her eyes: her breasts in his palms, her tongue in his mouth, his warm breath on her back, on her throat. He had trailed down her like a flush of heat, he understood the language of her breaths, read her smallest movements like a map to lead her further into the folds of pleasure. Her breath rose and fell, a furious march towards oblivion. They had repeated each other's names gently; he had called her Ira but what name had she called out? It was Kartik that she saw in her dream, she told herself. She replayed her dream and touched herself, Kartik's face now firmly on the imaginary lover's. A few minutes of blissful nothingness followed, like sliding into a warm body of water.

She got up to pour herself a glass of water and the doubts began to crawl up her spine again, as they had every day since she saw Kaiz again. She and Kartik had not slept together yet. They had kissed, there had been some necking and petting too, but no more. They both pretended that it was a matter of privacy, but that had not stopped her before, had it? Once when she let her hands wander, Kartik had nearly jumped. He told her about a painful break-up he'd had in Bangalore, hinting that it was the reason he had moved, but how was she supposed to ask if it had been an intimate relationship? Ira considered the possibility that he was still a virgin. So, she decided to take it slow, let him take the lead, set the pace. But he had done nothing and she discovered, to her surprise, to her alarm, that she did not mind. She liked spending time with him. She enjoyed being let in slowly into his mind, into his life, so different from hers and yet familiar. His body was less interesting.

She'd always had great love for Kartik but falling in love was a different matter. It was made harder by the commitment they had already made to each other, which loomed over them every moment that they were together. Once they were husband and wife, they would overcome this awkwardness with each other's bodies but the passion that she had witnessed in the dream was harder to hope for.

That word she dreaded. Passion. Was it even important, to love each other that way, to be consumed by it?

Passion was the opposite of power. Passion was the forsaking of power. In passion, she had offered herself as a canvas for somebody else's pen, mutely receiving his designs on her skin. In passion, she had allowed herself to dream of a new name, adding his name to her own, chopping off a part of herself as an offering. In passion, she had cut herself up, lost herself, lost days, lost months.

She hated the word.

Passion was temporary, she repeated to herself, like ink over the skin, like the memory of a dream; what she and Kartik had—a shared history, common roots, a common ground to build upon—was the foundation of marriage, of family, of life itself.

His article on the history of architecture in Mumbai was the first in the series to be published. What set apart colonial architecture from what came after it, Kaiz posited, was not individual marvels but the visual harmony of neighbourhoods. When people thought of the Fort Area, they might think of iconic buildings first, but it was the way the different buildings fit together, the unified street fronts that made single structures look like they were part of a bigger whole, that created a sense of awe. It was the same story in some parts of Matunga and Dadar, on Marine Drive. Individual buildings were often of different styles but, through proper planning and regulation, the built environment had been lent coherence. In contrast, the office buildings of Nariman Point were disjointed high-rises, and only someone compelled by scale alone, he argued, would find himself in awe of the modern office district.

Ira read it twice, the second time only to look for his signature, rummaging through the names, dates and facts for familiar turns of phrase. There was a passage in particular that caught her attention, one about how important it was even for a building to be a good neighbour, a good citizen, a responsible member of the community, a part of a whole; but eventually, buildings were built by people, for people. When the social fabric of the city itself had undergone such upheaval in the past decade, he argued, how could one hold bricks and mortar to higher standards than flesh and blood?

How deftly he wielded ideas and how beautifully he spun words. Spun them into cotton candy, sweet on the senses, but the illusion of fullness persisted for mere moments, only to vanish leaving no more than some grains of sugar.

Good building, good neighbour, good citizen. Bad boyfriend.

She made plans to have breakfast with Kartik at King's Circle. She brought the newspaper with her, and left it rolled up between them. The brisk waiter at the Udupi restaurant resented the small obstacle on their table that slowed him down for a split second when he put down their dishes. It forced him to aim with more care when he poured refills of sambar and chutney. The newspaper had been placed there for a reason but Kartik paid no attention to it.

'Did you read the paper today?' she asked him finally. 'The first part of my City at Fifty series is out.'

She wondered why she was playing with fire like this.

'Not yet, show me.'

She opened the city section and pointed at the article. He read it, nodding from time to time.

'This is very good, you write well. You write really well.'

The masterly speed-reader had not seen the byline.

'Thank you, but I didn't write it.'

She nudged his eyes towards the newspaper again. This time, Kartik looked at the byline and, as she had hoped, his eyes widened. The walls were tiled to the height of a grown man: they were prepared for children's fits and lovers' spats, for a bowl of sambar to be flung or a cup of coffee to be knocked over.

'Did you not have a boyfriend by the same name?'

'It's him.'

'Ah.'

A sweet singe, just what she wanted.

'Such a small world, no?' he said.

'What do you mean?'

'Of all the papers in all the towns in all the world, he walks into yours.' He spoke with an air of indifference but the pitch of his voice told a different story. 'Did he get a PhD at Berkeley to become a journalist? Not that there is anything wrong with that—it's just surprising.'

Ira laughed. 'He doesn't work with me, Kartik, he is an intern at an organisation my desk collaborates with. And I just found out he's at Stanford, not Berkeley.'

'Stanford,' Kartik repeated and nodded twice, slowly. 'So how long is his internship?'

'Hmm, jealous, are we?' She shook her head in exaggerated disbelief. 'He returns to the US next month. Happy?'

'Does he know you are getting married?'

'Oho, you don't trust me?'

'I do, I do. I am sorry.' Then, after a pause, he added, 'Are you alright, Ira?'

'Of course. It's nothing, ya.' She took his hand, pressed her thumb on the engagement band he was wearing. The memory of the previous night's dream returned and made her blush.

'He sounds like a total socialist. Now I am worried about what you think of my five-star office.'

Ira laughed. She derived some satisfaction from Kartik's responses, from the muted passion in his questions. The first hints of jealousy, after all, were the green shoots of love. She was also glad he had not repeated his previous question, whether Kaiz knew she was engaged.

There were many reasons why she had kept her engagement from Kaiz. The day they met, she had taken her engagement ring off without thinking about it, but each time they met after that, it had felt like the right decision. No occurrence escaped his scrutiny. His unsparing gaze could reduce any event to a political act. What would he make of an arranged marriage to a man of the same caste? How could she expect him to see the many shades to every choice, the tug of love, of belonging? Kartik, however, could stake a greater claim to the truth.

She told herself that there was no need for guilt, Kartik now knew that Kaiz was back and that she had met him. These were two separate parts of her life: the relationship she was trying to build with her fiancé and the short professional link with Kaiz. Their work together was almost done and she could soon retreat into her old world like a crab. A world without Kaiz. An absence that she had made peace with, that had ceased to unsettle her, unlike this new presence.

Kaiz called her that afternoon. It was not immediately clear why.

'The article turned out quite well, didn't it?' he said. 'My mother has never been prouder of me. The phone's been off the hook since morning. Have your parents got used to it? Seeing your name in print?'

'This is what I do for a living. You can't expect my parents to celebrate every byline.'

'Wow. Thanks for bursting my bubble.'

She didn't tell him that her first-page stories still thrilled her parents, even after six years and scores of bylines. Her mother had a set of rituals for those days: she would fold the newspaper till it fit into the wooden shrine in their kitchen, rearranging lamps and idols to make room, and at the end of the day, the article would be clipped and stored in a folder stored along with her mother's jewellery.

'Was there anything wrong with the data you shared on mills?'

'No, why?'

She didn't know how else to put it. 'Why have you called then?'

'Right. I am having some friends over this weekend. I wanted to invite you.'

'What's the occasion?'

'None. My mother is going to Pune to visit my grandparents. So I thought of throwing a party.'

'I am not sure I can make it.' She made an excuse about a deadline.

'On a Saturday over a long weekend? Come for an hour. Or for fifteen minutes, but do come. You remember my address, right?'

Pulling over in front of his building, walking to the lift, the names of his neighbours on their wooden letter boxes, the sudden start with which the lift cage moved, the short tune it played when opened, seventeen steps and—there!—his door.

Ira had not forgotten any of it. Kaiz answered the doorbell. He stepped forward as if to hug her but held himself back. She recognised faces from past evenings spent in the house, but so many years had passed that she did not wish to reacquaint herself with his close friends. Kaiz stood with her for some time, then left to attend to other guests. She was talking to a journalist acquaintance when a familiar voice called out from behind.

'Look who's here!' Ira turned to see Ananya walking towards her. Ananya Rajaram, whom she had not seen since that horrid evening. Ananya was even more beautiful now: either her skin exuded a new radiance or she had become more skilled at applying makeup. She put her arms around Ira warmly. 'Kaiz told me he was working with you, but he didn't say you were coming. I am so happy that you did. Come join us.'

She took Ira by the hand to a corner where many of his old friends stood chatting. Ira saw a few expressions of surprise. Clearly, nobody expected her to be there.

'Ladies and gents, those of you who need your memories refreshed, meet my friend Ira Kamat. Scourge of the corrupt, Superwoman of the civic beat.' She turned to Ira. 'Is that still correct? Still a beat reporter? Same paper?'

And there it came. Whack. Still a beat reporter. Not an editor, not a political commentator. Ira told herself she was being paranoid.

Introductions done, Ananya launched into a story: she began to tell the people around her about her first meeting with a young businessman from Delhi. She called him a 'man-friend', which Ira took to mean someone between a friend and a boyfriend, also clearly neither.

'So,' Ananya narrated, 'I ask him, "What's with the people of your city? Why are Delhiwalas so aggressive—don't you care about the reputation you have around the country?" He was really attractive so imagine my surprise when he smiles and says, "It's a city of refugees, one that is still hurting from the wounds of Partition. We take time to trust people, to let them in. As for this friendly city of yours, Bombay is a place of pleasant aloofness, full of small talk and token kindness, but selfish and closed when it really matters. But Delhi, it lives on abrasive warmth." And I thought, wow, this man is the total package. That's it, I decided, here are the keys to my heart.'

Ananya was still a consummate performer, her narration did not have a beat out of place. As if it had been told several times already, perfected over repeated tellings. It seemed to Ira that she still went about life with the sole purpose of collecting stories, fashioning people and emotions into anecdotes, into punchlines for the entertainment of an admiring audience. Although a part of her wanted to walk away, Ira also felt compelled to participate in this performance, throw in a clever line or an innuendo.

So she said, 'Only the keys to your heart, Ananya?'

'I keep nothing else locked up.'

A round of laughter.

Somebody asked, 'What happened then?'

She sighed. 'We had a few months of *great* abrasive warmth and then the inevitable unpleasant aloofness.'

Ira could tell that Ananya was drunk, from the sway of her body, from her light slurring. She told Ira twice that she *adored* her bag, an ordinary cotton jhola she had picked up on Hill Road. As soon as the two of them were alone, she said, 'I am glad you could put everything behind you, Ira. I didn't think you would forgive him.' She squeezed Ira's hand. 'And I never thought you should either. I love Kaiz but he was an asshole to you.'

'Water under the bridge,' Ira replied, irritated that Ananya seemed to know so much about the circumstances of their parting.

'Long-distance is awful and you would have broken up sooner or later but he should have been nicer, you know? And look, I have put away the better part of a bottle of wine, I should drink some water.' She held up her empty glass. 'Or finish off that bottle. The bar beckons.'

But instead of the bar, Ananya walked over to Kaiz, interrupting his conversation with a very pretty woman, someone he was spending a lot of time with that evening. Ananya pulled him close and began to whisper in his ear. She pinched his waist, as if she were teasing him. His eyes darted in Ira's direction. She looked away. Same old story, she thought, and felt a stab of resentment.

She had slowly come to be wary of the world he inhabited, so why was she at his party? What was she hoping for—to show him that she had forgotten the crush of her broken heart? For months after he left, that heartbreak had refused to be relegated to the past, to distant memory, it had seemed much closer. A wound with no scab. The pain had very slowly turned to grief, and the grief had become fury.

Sometime in the long period when she was consumed by anger, there had been a spate of slum demolitions in the city. One had been particularly egregious: a colony of over a thousand had been made homeless overnight. Bulldozers had razed hundreds of houses and even a makeshift clinic in their zeal to flatten. In the confusion, a fire had started and obliterated whatever had remained. In the wake of the broad public support for these demolitions, especially from the middle classes who harped on about the illegality of the shanties, Ira had proposed to her editor a series covering other illegal constructions around the city. She had cast the first stone: her target was Golden China, a Chinese restaurant in Malabar Hill. The restaurant was closer to the sea than it was allowed to be and in spite of being embroiled in a long-standing but low-profile legal tangle with the municipal corporation, it had recently added a floor as well as a patio, both illegally. Does the patronage of stars, socialites and politicians change the law for some, she asked in her first-page story. Other papers picked up the case too and the spotlight compelled the restaurant to close for a year and reopen in a different location. She had relished the closing of the restaurant, then questioned her glee because she liked to think of herself as an objective reporter.

One evening at Kaiz's house, he and his friends had reminisced about evenings at this restaurant: the crispiness of the wontons, the eccentricities of the chef-owner and the prices that they found *bizarrely low* for a place as good. Mr Lang had brought authentic Chinese food to Bombay, one of his friends had gushed, the *whole* city had discovered the cuisine because of him. Ira had not made anything of the exchange then, only a mental note to eat there someday when she could afford it. Afterwards, she had scoured her memory for anything that could turn sour, the memories she found fit she had prodded and aired till they fermented. There had been so many things she associated with him that she lost track of them, but from time to time an unpleasant association resurfaced and rankled, like this Chinese restaurant. She had been furious that she had let him continue to hold the puppet strings and there was nothing she could do but strike back at empty symbols.

The Monday after the party, Ira went to his office to thank Mr Nadkarni for the help the institute had provided. He had read every article in the series. Another excellent example of civic journalism from your paper, he told Ira.

'I appreciate it, Ira, but there was really no need to come down.'

She wished he hadn't pointed that out.

'It was no trouble, your office was on my way. And I want to thank Kaiz too.'

She found him at his desk, three different research reports open before him. She tapped him on the shoulder and he looked up, annihilating boredom written all over him.

'Mondays,' he said, mustering a feeble smile. 'How come you are here?'

'To thank you and Mr Nadkarni for your help.'

'So how about one last round of fieldwork?'

'What fieldwork? The series is done.'

'Look outside, it has finally stopped raining. Let's go for a walk, please?'

'And your work?' She pointed at the sprawl on his desk.

'This? I was just pretending to be busy, yaar. Who reads three reports at once?'

After many rainy weeks, the sky was clear, the streets were satin. Buildings looked burnished and newly-cleansed leaves shimmered like foil. The air was still moist. A coolness, an optimism sprung from the earth, and his face was awash with the glow of happiness.

'Chai?' he asked.

It was something to celebrate: they had reached the end of the project without incident. They sat down at the first chai shop they spotted, one that was located next to a new McDonald's. Happy faces streamed in and out of the bright red building. Many children carried packets with the toy of the month. Even on a Monday afternoon, the place was packed.

'Did you have a good time at the party?'

'I did. Thanks for inviting me.'

'Ananya said you two spoke for a long time. She was glad to see you.'

'Me too.' The mention of Ananya brought with it a flood of mixed feelings.

'What did you two talk about?'

'Oh, did you want to know? I am sorry I didn't take notes.'

He burst out laughing. 'You sound just like her. After what, ten minutes together?'

Ira felt a knot of irritation forming in her chest. Did Kaiz think Ananya was the only funny woman in all of Mumbai?

Their chai arrived. After a few sips, Kaiz looked towards McDonalds and said, 'It's the beginning of the end.'

'What is?'

'Fast-food chains. I thought we could hold out. What else is this son-of-the-soil government good for?'

'The formula has always been son-of-the-soil plus America. Remember Michael Jackson and the toilet?'

'I just can't bear to watch Bombay become like every other city in the world.'

She was sure he was joking but she detected no trace of irony in his voice. 'Are you serious? It's just a restaurant. Our own street food isn't any healthier.'

'I hope you are right, but it's never just one restaurant, is it? Don't you wonder why these people are grinning like that? What are they losing their minds over? The colourful made-in-China crap that will be in our landfills within months?'

Or end up in glass cabinets in Matunga and be preserved for years. A dash of colour in a dull home, cheap and cheerful.

A family of four exited the restaurant. The son, a large-toothed boy of about eight, was wearing a paper birthday hat with the chain's logo and was visibly beaming from his birthday celebrations. Both he and his sister wore bright, ill-fitting clothes with a mishmash of logos and captions that declared their provenance: Fashion Street, Hill Road or some such roadside market.

'And look at that family. For your birthday, I gift you clogged arteries and diabetes, wrapped in mediocre flavours,' he said. He had hints of conspiracy in his voice and looked to her to take his act forward, but Ira did not wish to join him in belittling the hapless eaters. In their clothes and manners, she recognised something familiar.

'Leave them alone. They are just trying to have a good time.'

'Yes, yes, but you have to admit this is sad, if not downright pathetic.'

The knot in her chest was returning, only now there was a touch of anger in it. 'Pathetic? Not everybody can afford an evening out at the Taj.'

'Taj? I had more modest alternatives in mind.' He pointed at a little Afghani eatery across the street. 'Like that. They'll eat much better and spend less, but it doesn't have the flash, the name.'

'I guess nobody knows Mumbai as well as you do. Happy?'

He bent forward, took a small bow. 'I remember eating quite well on a budget, don't you? When did we ever spend more than a hundred rupees?'

'What I remember are your stunts—*this is the best biryani I have eaten, there's no kebab like this even outside Jama Masjid, this kheer reminds me of heaven.* All for a free drink or a plate of dessert. That wasn't pathetic?'

He narrowed his eyes at the turn the conversation seemed to be taking. 'Don't hate on my skills. Charming people is not easy, it requires imagination.'

'Oh, really? And what was the secret of your brilliant imagination?'

184 | AMRITA MAHALE

'My empty wallet. I was a student and nothing spurs the imagination like poverty.' He smiled, and his eyes nearly disappeared again.

Only partly true—Ira would have pointed out in different circumstances—because both poverty and wealth did. But imagination, much like AIDS as the popular story went, was not the lot of the middle classes. Imagination was the force that freed the mind, unchained it from reality. If you were poor, you had much to escape from, so you needed imagination. If you were rich, your reality needed little tending to, you could afford to dream away. But the ones in the middle, where was the room for it in their lives? It was action, not imagination, that was their best shot at a big step forward. For the middle classes, the mind and the body had to run along together, like railway tracks, to let them move forward.

Instead, all she said as she leaned back in her chair and looked him in the eye was: 'What bullshit.'

He raised his eyebrows, 'Excuse me?'

'What you said. It's utter bullshit. What do you know about poverty?'

'I was being facetious, Ira.'

'How can you joke about being poor? You'll never be poor. Or even close. Have you forgotten your first coat of paint which won't change no matter how many cheap kebabs you eat? Though I must add that the question begs to be asked: will the *first coat* stand up to the corrosive powers of a Maharaja Mac?'

'What are you talking about—this is not at all about burgers, is it?'

'I have no patience left for your snobbery, no, your snobberies. You live in Malabar Hill, you study in California, you travel around the world. You rail against capitalism when you have every kind of capital there is. But that isn't enough, you also want to feel superior to that poor family over where they eat, over their lack of taste. Don't pass this off as nostalgia for a simpler time and please don't joke about being poor. It is an insult to half of Mumbai.'

He brought his hands up and touched the outstretched fingers of one hand to the other palm, forming the letter T. 'Okay, time out. What's bothering you?'

She wanted to take a deep breath, count to ten, blame PMS, blame her editor or a truant colleague, lie about a family member being in hospital, say sorry, but she could not.

'You are. This city that you claimed you loved so much, that you left at the first opportunity, how much do you know about it? When was the last time you took the train, or went north of Worli? Yesterday, I was in the basti next to the train tracks in Mahim. All the shanties in the basti are flooded. Do you know why? Because the BMC *forgot* to dredge their drains again. In the luckiest homes, the rainwater is ankle-deep. But it isn't water, it is sewage. Brown, green and black waste in every house, and the people who live there, they eat, sleep and cook through it, in the middle of this filth. The poor in Mumbai are living like sewer rats, they are leading a subhuman life. This city that you say you love, it is crumbling, Kaiz, faster and faster every year. Mumbai is not *going* to the dogs, it's already there and it's not because those people just ate at McDonald's.'

She made sure she said Mumbai not Bombay.

17

FOUR MONTHS AFTER THE MEETING on the terrace, the residents of Asha Nivas assembled again, this time in the Kinis' flat. The circumstances under which the second meeting was called were less dire: Ashok Kini had invited his neighbours home to share good news. Good news for most.

A twenty-seven-inch television set was the pride of the Kinis' drawing room. It was flanked by two sets of shelves, one full of books and the other of CDs. About a dozen small Ganesh statues, in a mix of sizes and materials, crowded a wooden side table. The decorative cushions on the five-seater sofa set had Kashmiri needlework embroidery, every other cushion perched on its corner like a diamond. On the window sill, money plants grew in empty bottles of imported whiskey. There were back issues of *The Economist*, *India Today* and *Femina* to read. On one hand, the Kinis were trying to hasten the fall of the building on the grounds that it was crumbling, but on the other, a glimpse of their home weakened their case. Their flat was tip-top. They never failed to repair seepage in the walls or paint over peeling patches.

Ashok Kini established that he was a generous leader by being a generous host. The guests were served snacks delivered from his restaurant along with cup after cup of masala tea. The moment he stood up, he had everybody's attention.

'I spoke to the landlord this morning and have some good news to share. He has a serious offer from a builder. Now this new builder is an ambitious fellow,' he said. 'He wants to build luxury flats here. Marble floors, French windows, fully modern A-grade houses.'

In a flash Ira knew what was coming next. There was no market for one-bedroom luxury flats.

'This one too wants to build an eight-storey building,' he continued. 'And put a penthouse at the top.'

Penthouse! The word was repeated around the room in chorus.

'But you see, people who want to buy luxury homes don't

want to live in one-BHK flats. He wants to build only two- and three-bedroom flats.'

This declaration invited collective gasps.

'Wait, let me finish. I was aghast too—and I told the landlord as much. All of us, whether we live in a one-bedroom or two-bedroom flat, deserve a new home in the same location. He had an interesting proposal: he is going to offer all of us the additional space at 10 per cent less than market rate.'

'But Ashok, market rates in Matunga are through the roof. How have we gone from asking the landlord to pay us to now talking about paying him?' asked Mr Desai, looking somewhat triumphant, convinced that he was soon to be vindicated.

'First listen to me, Bipin. For those of us who don't want to pay the difference, he has agreed to buy back our tenancy rights at half the market rate for a new flat.'

'I thought we weren't going to settle for anything less than a new flat.'

'This is only the first offer, baba. I will get more out of him. But there is another problem.' He paused. 'He will only offer this to those of us who have lived here for over twenty years.'

So this was why the meeting was called on a day when both Professor Rajwade and his wife were out of town, thought Ira.

'What are you saying? How can that be?' exclaimed her father.

'Rajwade did not have to pay a pugree like we did. He moved in nine years ago after the pugree system was done with. He doesn't have the same claim as us.'

'But he paid a security deposit. Same beast, different name.'

'Not at all. He did not buy tenancy rights like we did. He only signed a lease with the landlord.'

'Rajwade is one of us. Tell the landlord and the builder to get lost.'

Ira was proud of her father for jumping to his former ally's defence, even though she suspected that Ashok kaka was correct: new leases did not give tenants the same rights as the older ones did. Still, calling the meeting when the professor was out of town was an underhand move.

'Kamat, be reasonable. There is a lot at stake. Maybe we can persuade him to offer Rajwade a good deal too.'

'It's simply out of the question.'

'Think about the nine families here,' said Kusum Kini, sweeping her hand across the room. 'Between all our family members, we have lived here for over a thousand years. Over a thousand.'

'Kusum maushi, what does that have to do with anything?' Ira interrupted. 'Does someone with three children have more claim over the building than you or my parents because their years add up to more? Should we really be discussing this while Professor Rajwade isn't here?'

All eyes in the room darted between her and her future mother-in-law. This little tussle was no less dramatic than a finger gun.

'All I am saying, Ira, is that this is the best offer we've had in five years of negotiations. Let's not shut any doors till we have thought about it properly. With cool heads.'

She sounded collected but Ira saw a slim flash of fury in her eyes.

Ira had begun to admire Kusum maushi at a young age. She admired her fierceness and unflappability, her taste in fashion, her frank narrations of domestic battles with her own mother-in-law. Born Nirmala Pai and rechristened by her mother-in-law, Kusum Ashok Kini had arrived in her husband's Matunga flat with four suitcases, one full of only shoes, clutches and make-up. Ashok kaka's mother had had misgivings all along about whether a girl from a rich home would fit into their family; the suitcases had fanned her doubts further. Battle lines were drawn at once. Only one woman would prevail, could prevail. Kusum maushi loved to tell the story of how at first she had tried to divide up household tasks so that each woman had her domain of influence. She was the better cook, so it seemed obvious that she be in charge of the kitchen. To balance that, she was happy to let her mother-in-law handle the family shrine and the rituals of daily worship, which most people would consider the ceremonial seat of power anyway. The plan had not worked. 'The house is mine, the shrine is mine, the kitchen is mine,' the older woman had thundered. 'I will decide what I do and what you do.' She made sure to delegate only those tasks to her daughter-in-law that the younger woman had little interest in or aptitude for.

Ira's flat had then become her refuge every afternoon, an escape from her mother-in-law and also a canvas for her domestic aspirations. She had taken Ira's mother under her wing, guiding her through the maze of wifely duties she had been thrust into at the age of twenty. She taught her how to use a pressure cooker, where to find the freshest vegetables in Matunga, and even which days of the week to fast on for the blessings of various gods and goddesses. She had once told Ira's mother that she understood why her mother-in-law resisted conceding any territory to her: imagine investing decades to build your position at the heart of the household, only to have it snatched by an upstart. 'But this will mean nothing to you, Shobha,' she had added. 'Only the mother of a son knows this feeling.'

It was unfair, Ira thought, that men had always had the run of the city but women like Kusum maushi only had the four walls of the household within which to exert and express themselves, where one woman could only be powerful at the expense of another. Men lived under the same roof as their fathers and brothers, so any jostling for power was done with their own blood. Women had little choice in this matter, air-dropped into new arenas a couple of decades into their lives. Giving a woman a new name or a new home did not erase the years before, the person before. It did not suddenly turn strangers into family, it did not give her an appetite for their oddities and patience for their faults.

Here was a case in point. Ira was appalled that the Kinis thought that betraying one of their neighbours was alright. This would not change in two months, when Kartik and she were married. She had protested now and would object again if needed.

The meeting went on. Ashok kaka explained what would come next. The builder would come back with a more concrete offer and the residents would get till the end of the year to sign away their leases. They would not have to leave their homes for another year at least.

'All I ask is that you do not discuss this with Rajwade yet. Let me inform him, let me persuade the landlord,' said Mr Kini in parting.

'Greedy buggers,' her father said when they got home. 'Every one of them.'

For the rest of the evening, she shared her father's crossness. Not a single person had said a word in support of Professor Rajwade. They had bubbled instead with ideas on how to take the discussion forward. They must demand that the landlord cover their rent while the new building came up, they deserved a bigger discount than the 10 per cent on offer. Each time her father tried to steer the discussion back to the matter of the Rajwades, the others told him to focus on the more important issues. Mr Naik even reminded her father that the professor had been the last to join hands with them, as if that were sufficient grounds for their loyalty to be rationed.

The memory of her outburst at Kaiz was still fresh. Would any of the people at the meeting give a fuck about those who lived like sewer rats? It had taken them just a moment to toss a neighbour aside. It was not just her neighbours. All week she had been reading letters to the editor at her paper: there were varied responses to their City at Fifty series. A few were enthusiastic, some were openly snarly and a handful simmered with a peculiar disquiet. The ones who reacted to the article on slum rehabilitation were the most predictable.

Giving someone a free flat in exchange for a shanty built on encroached land is a slap in the face of the hardworking people who toil for a lifetime paying off home loans. And for what—just so they can rent the flat out and move to another slum?

and

Be prepared to expand your newspaper's crime section in the coming years. If the government keeps handing out flats, we cannot expect the tide of unemployed migrants to stop.

and

Your reporters have a lot of sympathy for the homeless. Why don't they adopt them and take them home? It will take some burden off the streets and off the shoulders of honest taxpayers.

These were her people too, no different from her neighbours. Once, she guessed, they had only known their narrow worlds. Their gods, their families, relatives and neighbours, what they said, what they thought. They had known want, they still remembered the small struggles to get from one month to another. Now, when their worlds had opened up somewhat, they had stumbled upon an old toy, the anger they had been too busy to play with before. They had decided their deliverance was too late and too little. They felt cheated. Everybody was stealing from them, they had come to believe, even the ones who truly had nothing.

But the people she felt kinship with were alien to her as well. For weeks, years, she had thought of Kaiz and his friends with a mix of contempt and longing. The ones born to the world of ideas, who had inhabited it for so long that it had settled in their imagination, their speech. She agreed with them more often than not but if she borrowed their shiny phrases, they would sit poorly on her. No amount of self-invention was enough, even the effort would mark her as a climber, a striver. She would only be a poor imitation. What was her place in all this, she wondered, was she fated to be stuck in limbo, not contained by her roots anymore, unable to grasp the world beyond either?

18

IRA SLOWLY GATHERED THE courage to apologise to Kaiz. It was clear to her that that there were subterranean forces at work behind her outburst, forces which she did not fully understand, but these were her demons to slay. She had no right to foist them upon Kaiz.

On the phone, he was cool and distant. He made vague, distracted noises of agreement till finally he said, 'You can do better, Ira. A phone apology?'

She agreed to meet him at Marine Drive the same evening. Couples of various ages sat along the sea, close together, evenly spaced, like laundry on a clothesline. Head over shoulder, hand in hand, eye to eye, some under umbrellas. Ira and Kaiz sat an arm's length apart. Someone cracked the sun open and orange yolk spilled out into the sky.

'I am sorry,' she said as soon as they sat down.

'Care to explain what brought that on?'

'It's not important.'

'That's not an answer.'

'It was a bad day at work,' she lied.

'And you thought it was alright to take it out on me?'

'What you said was very condescending, so I snapped. But I shouldn't have.'

'That's some apology. I'll still accept it,' he said, 'but only if you come to Alibag with me this weekend.'

'Alibag? Why?'

'One of my school friends—remember Puneet Mirchandani?—has a bungalow by the beach and he is throwing a party. I can't tolerate that bunch for that long, not by myself, you know how they are. But I need a break from the city. Might as well go, no? We'll leave Saturday evening and be back by Sunday afternoon. Please say yes.'

Everybody straddled two worlds, Kaiz was no different. He had always had two sets of friends: the more intellectual bunch, and the schoolmates and neighbours he had grown up with. The latter was a breed Ira was more familiar with, the South Bombay kids with their familiar but grating accents, their casual references to gymkhanas and foreign vacations, their practised indifference. These friends of his usually dabbled in their family businesses: industrial parts, diamonds, real estate, law. Occasionally, his worlds collided when a schoolmate or neighbour dropped in, another Malabar Hill or Marine Drive kid, when his core gang was around. Brats, the latter group called the former behind their backs. Jholawaalas, the former tittered in their turn.

'I never liked your school friends.'

'Now you tell me.'

'Don't act like you didn't know. I can't come. Take Ananya, take somebody else.'

'I don't want to spend time with Ananya or anybody else, I want to spend time with you.'

'Kaiz, please.'

'I fly back to San Francisco in ten days. When will you see me again?'

She said nothing.

'Bas, you are coming with me.'

Once again, he spoke with a confidence that admitted no other possibility. She relented.

They drove to Alibag in his mother's Maruti 1000, which would be the most modest vehicle at the party. Ira had proposed taking the ferry but Kaiz said he was prone to seasickness, which she had not known. It delighted her that new facts could emerge about somebody one had known for a long time. She thought of Kartik, how little she knew about him. All the more to learn in a lifetime together, she told herself, and felt her heart wrench. She had told her parents and Kartik that she was going to a team outing over the weekend to celebrate the success of the Independence Day series. If only newspapers were that generous. The city slowly fell away. Their car barrelled past a landscape of hills and villages made lush by the monsoon.

His friend's bungalow was one of the largest houses Ira had seen. It was right by the beach, and a section of the coast behind the house had been cordoned off. A cobbled path twisted through a vast lawn towards the entrance of the house. The main door was inlaid with brass chevrons and the facade was decorated with plaster angels flying over a mesh of creepers. Inside, one of the walls of the living room was painted a deep orange. There was artwork of various sizes and styles. The largest one was an oil painting of a knot of village women carrying earthen pots.

'Sindhi baroque,' Kaiz whispered to her.

'What?'

He pulled her aside into an alcove. 'This gaudy mishmash, the hideous stucco work, the orange accent wall and that eyesore of a door. Have you seen anything uglier?'

His hand was still on her wrist. She freed her hand to put a finger on her lips. 'Somebody might hear you.'

Over the next few hours, servants moved most of the furniture and the decor out of the room. Whatever valuable remained was covered with plastic sheets. A DJ console was set up in one corner, a makeshift bar in another. She counted the bottles and plastic cups: the party would not be a small affair. What kind of music will the DJ play, she asked the host. Trance, house, techno, some jungle, he replied. She wondered if these were names of bands. Large electric lamps were set up in three corners. Upon being switched on for testing, they filled the room with multi-coloured lights, shredded rainbows. The room got warmer at once. Around 10 p.m., after dinner had been served to the friends who arrived early, large groups of people started to appear. Ira changed into a crinkled black skirt and a strappy mirrorwork top, brushed her hair and left it open, put on eyeliner and lipstick. She wished she had carried something less ethnic. When she came down from their room, Kaiz was talking to his friends. She went out to the beach for a walk just as the DJ began to test his apparatus.

She walked up to the sea slowly but when she returned the cacophony hadn't ended. What she assumed was a round or two of sound testing turned out to be the actual music. A scramble of strange sounds, somewhat muted by the sound of the sea. At least the night was beautiful, she told herself as she sat down on the steps of the porch.

A tap on her shoulder.

'There you are.'

Kaiz. Two of his school friends had followed him to the porch but they stood at a distance. Kaiz and she had been given a room with two separate beds. She wondered what he had said to his friends about her.

'What is this music?' She clapped her hands over her ears.

'Oh well,' he grinned. 'But here, I have something for you.'

Kaiz put his hand out, he had a white pill in his palm.

'What is this?'

'Say hello to Miss Molly.'

'What's that, a hard drug?'

'A *hard* drug? Jesus, yes, it's Ecstasy.'

Years of anti-drug ads on Doordarshan flashed before her eyes: syringes and smoke, orgasmic eyes, bad decisions, followed by spirals into death and shame. She lowered her voice so only he could hear her.

'What is wrong with you? When did you start using drugs?'

The stark disapproval on her face made him laugh. 'Don't look at me like I am a junkie.'

'But you use hard drugs.'

'I don't *use* hard drugs, no, but I might have tried some. I did go to Berkeley.'

She imagined the worst. 'Heroin?'

'Are you crazy? Of course not. When did you become so self-righteous anyway? You've smoked up at my house, haven't you?'

'Yes, but only four times and I didn't inhale.'

'You kept count?'

'Marijuana is not addictive, Kaiz. Hard drugs are terrible, you know that.'

'Please stop saying hard drugs. And Ecstasy is not addictive either, but none for you, I presume?'

'No way.'

'Alright, fine, but do ask yourself where this resistance is coming from.'

'Hard drugs are—they are beyond my limit, okay? Don't force me,' she blurted out crankily. *Beyond my limit*, what a ridiculous and tacky choice of words. She regretted it at once. Had she shown it again, her first coat of paint?

'I won't force you, of course not, but I will warn you that you won't like the music much if you are sober.'

She bit her lip. 'Okay, fine, I'll try it. Just this once.'

'You don't have to, Ira. No one's forcing you.'

'I want to.'

'Are you sure? I'll hear no end of it otherwise.'

'I am sure.'

'One hundred per cent?'

'Yes.'

'Great. Trust me, you will love it.'

'So it's called Ecstasy?'

'Also E. You should write about it, then you can think of this as research. Here's a headline: "Ecstasy is the New Agony of the Narcotics Bureau".'

'What will it do to me?'

'It won't hit you immediately, give it half an hour. You'll feel a surge of energy and joy—hence, the name—but no hallucinations.'

'Side effects?'

'A bit of a crash tomorrow, but don't think about it now. Your jaw might clench too.'

'Nothing permanent?'

'No, baba. Don't be such a phattoo. This is a small dose. Here.'

Her heart thrashed like a mad animal immured in her chest. But she didn't feel different, pounding heart notwithstanding.

'Okay?'

A thumbs up sign.

They went inside the house. Visible between the dozens of swaying feet was the marble floor, now a muddy brown from shoe marks and spilled drinks. The makeshift bar table, manned by a liveried bartender, was covered with liquor bottles. Next to the DJ, a man dressed in formals was dancing with abandon. A woman in her early twenties, possibly even in her late teens, was dancing next to him and licking his cheek. Ira looked around keenly. The commentary in her head distracted her from her nervousness. The music, if one could call it that, made no sense: like taking a note and setting mad dogs behind it. Frantic one moment, meditative the next, it slowed down before it reached fever pitch, as if to catch its breath, and then it dashed again. She could not move her body to this erratic beat, the arrhythmia, so she picked a graceful woman at the far end of the room to copy. Kaiz danced next to her but her attention was elsewhere: on the stranger's swaying hips and looping arms. She continued to mimic the woman's dance moves till about twenty minutes later when—like in a romantic comedy in which the leads pretend to be in love only to actually fall for each other—she realised her limbs were moving of their own accord.

The music, with all its rises and falls, clicked into place. It spoke to her body directly. It told her to be joyful, to expand and become everything, to become everyone. Kaiz was no longer next to her but it did not matter. She danced for hours after that, or was it days, or perhaps just a few minutes; time was a ball of jelly, now flattening to a disk and now bouncing back. When she finally spotted him, Kaiz was standing alone by an open window looking at the beach. She walked up and put her arms around him. She saw his eyes widen before she closed her eyes. There was a slight chill in the air, even the stars shivered in the sky, but together they were warm.

Ira, he said, I need fresh air. He wanted to walk to the beach. They took their shoes off and held them in their hands and walked towards the sea. Sand crusted their toes, fish ready for frying. The beach was theirs, only theirs. It brought to mind another walk on the beach before everything went wrong. She also remembered a red frisbee from a class picnic to Alibag long ago, and the first swim in the sea, going under a wave, enveloped by darkness and greenness, the taste of brine, thinking this is it, this is the end, then suddenly surfacing to light, gasping, lungfuls of air. The thrill of being alive. She felt now the sum of all those joys, this moment contained every moment like it. The drug stapled all of it together, all happiness.

The sky had so many stars that it was like looking at a lamp through a sieve. The night sky in Mumbai was often blurred, like uncorrected vision, but here the night was sharp and clear. She looked up and felt ready to explode from beholding such brilliance. This thing of heart-breaking beauty was not hers or his or even theirs, it belonged to everybody, to anybody who looked up at that moment. If the most beautiful thing in the world was being given away for free to anyone at all, who were they to decide who got the trifles?

'Are you okay, jaan?'

It was messing with his mind too, with his sense of time: he must think it was years ago, that he could call her jaan again.

'Doesn't looking at the sky make you think that we are all equal in the eyes of the universe? Why can't people put their small differences aside and focus on this: we are all the same, all one.'

But once she had put the sentiment into words, it sounded trite. Telling some stories robbed them of their essence, stripped them of power. Like leaving a perfume bottle open to smell it. She wanted to take her words back, melt the cliché into pure feeling again.

'Is that so?' he said coolly. 'We are all the same, is it? You and me, at this moment in time, we are equal? Brilliant.'

He made no effort to disguise his condescension. Without warning, her eyes welled up.

'I didn't mean to say it like that. I am sorry,' he said.

'You think I am silly.' She blinked to fight the tears.

'Not at all.'

'It's the drug.'

'I know. I know.'

He put an arm around her, she put her head on his shoulder. The dull throb of electronic music from a hundred feet away. Why was she here, she asked herself. For closure? Or for him?

'Ira, I need to tell you something.'

'What is it?'

'About the way I left, why I ended our relationship.'

'It's alright. We are good, Kaiz.'

'But I haven't told you the full story.' Another side effect of Ecstasy, he hadn't told her, was honesty.

'What do you mean?'

'When I went to see my sister, I knew I wasn't coming back.'

'You knew?'

'I had made up my mind about applying to grad school. I did not want to return to this wretched city.'

'This *wretched* city was your home. I thought you loved it.'

Loved *it*, not me. How easy it was to talk about cities. First-rate people talked about ideas, only the third-rate talked about people.

'You know I lived in Delhi till I was eight. When I moved to Bombay, I decided this would be home. Why do you think I know so much about its history, its streets and buildings? I spent years making up for the decade I lost out on, thinking I was putting down roots, earning my right to call this city home. But when the time came, it wasn't enough.'

'How was it not enough?'

'I had the wrong name, so how could it be my home? They wanted to expel people like me.'

'Those hateful people and their hateful ideology, that is not our city, they don't get to decide who is a legitimate citizen and who is not.'

'I was a citizen, yes, but was I at home?'

'Of course you were.'

'Ira, come on, how would you know?'

'Your neighbours—the Damanis—they gave you and your mother harbour for a week after the riots, didn't they? They believed this was your home. Other families in the building took out your name plate from the lobby so the goons, when they came, wouldn't know that a Muslim family lived here. And the mohalla sabhas that brought back peace—the people walking from door to door pacifying the scared and the angry, they did it for everybody who calls this home, people like you. They were from this city, weren't they? That's also a face of the city, Kaiz, its true one.'

'I am grateful to all of them, I am, but would you want to live like this? Having to be hidden? Having to hide who you are? Your name and your faith?'

She did not have an answer.

'It's hard to describe how angry I was in those months. I asked myself what my love for this city amounted to. Zilch. It was not this love that protected me, my address and my privilege did. How could a place that offers such a conditional protection return my love? What I held dear turned out to be pointless—the poetry, the stories and symbols. It took me years to start asking myself why I read those books or why I went on all those walking tours, what had I been anxious to prove? I had an intellectual notion of home. It was a flimsy relationship—all in my head. How could that stand up to any violence?'

A door to despair opened inside her, even without what he said next.

'But none of this excuses what I did to you. I was an asshole. If it's any consolation, I broke my own heart too. I loved you, Ira, I still do.'

'But why didn't you tell me before?'

She had carried her bitterness for years, fashioned it into a weapon, a shield, this animus. Even without it, there was no relief, only the taste of hopelessness. Guilt that she had not known. Wrapped in her own heartbreak, she had never guessed. Wrapped in her own privilege, she had not even tried.

'What would I have said? That I got scared and ran away? That I gave up? Even this—what I just told you—I know I'll regret tomorrow.' He looked at her and grinned, half foolishly, half sadly.

She wrapped her arms around her knees and put her face down. She did not want to look at him or have him look at her. This knowledge was overwhelming. He rubbed her back to comfort her and her skin came alive. Emanating from him was a familiar heat, a warm abyss she could disappear into. Time slowed to a trickle before it began to flow backwards. His hands lingered on her back; she felt his fingers move from one clothed mole to another, guided by memory. She could not tell what celestial pattern he traced on her skin: the ship, the fox, or the heart.

This made no sense, she thought, why was she making him comfort her? She turned to look at him and he gave her a sad smile. A sudden urge to touch him, to hold him tight and shield him. She stroked his forehead, his cheek. Was that the drug too?

'Is there anything I can do now?' she said.

'Will you give me another chance?'

She looked at him and blinked, certain that she had misheard the question.

'You are leaving next week.'

'We'll work it out.'

'How?'

'I am going to spend at least six months here next year, maybe even more. So, will you? Give me another chance?'

Yes, she wanted to say, she would give him another chance. And she wanted more than that. She wanted to kiss his face, his salt-rimmed eyes, his sandpaper chin. She wanted to kiss his throat and its bobbing anticipation. His stomach and its new topography. Pay no attention to his great ache, skip to the vale of his thighs. Trail her tongue lightly upwards from the inside of his knees till the torment made his face scrunch up. She wanted to watch him thicken in her hands and taste again his twitches and throbs. To be on her knees, to be kissed along the length of her spine. And to feel the small fear that came with this position, the anticipation of an unpleasant surprise. As he entered her, he would put this anxiety to rest. And the years in between would disappear.

She saw the same hunger in his eyes. He, too, wanted to bridge the gulf of the years.

All she had to do was say yes and lean into him.

Say yes.

He had asked her a question.

'I can't answer your question, Kaiz,' she said and turned away. The moment passed. 'Not now, not like this.'

She did not know she was capable of such strength. Had she leached away the iron from her blood, the calcium from her bones in uttering those words? All that was left was to collapse into a pile of dust.

'Fair enough. I can wait. I will wait.'

The sky was a petri dish someone kept dropping pink dye into, drop by drop by drop till it erupted with colour. After some time, he lay down in the sand and she put her head on his chest. Her head rose and sank with each breath he took, his ribs pressed softly into the curve of her neck. The clarity brought on by the drug, by his confession, slowly gave way to fog, to fatigue. The sun rose further, and a small ball of unease started to unspool inside her, seeping through her mind and body. Her muscles felt tight, her jaw was a brick. Is this what he had warned her about? She turned her head to ask him, but he had fallen asleep, his eyes gently shut, his mind already out of her reach. A helium balloon floating in dreamland. The sunrise was slipping away from her too, so she closed one eye and tried to push the coin-sized sun back into the sea. Her finger slipped smoothly down the canvas of the sky. She was reminded, again, that she could not turn back time or stop dawn from breaking into day.

She sat up to stretch her arms and back. Kaiz stirred from the shift in weight. She ran her fingers through his hair, his inexplicably smooth, soft, twisted hair. Her fingers still expected coir and were surprised when they found cotton wool instead, even after five years, as if they were back at the beginning. The amnesia of her fingers aside, she knew, she remembered. She knew that five years had passed and that this too would, that he had once left her and broken her heart, and he would leave again in a week, that this was a borrowed happiness, an overdraft against eventual pain, inevitable pain. Their worlds were too different. The brief overlap was enough, more joy than what most got in a lifetime.

She lay down next to him. She pulled his hands, always cold, between her thighs, just above her knees, where they would be warm, and clasped them. Still asleep, he buried his face in her hair, his nose against the back of her head. He would wake with a skein impressed upon his cheek. This, more than anything before, was bridging the gulf of the years. Against the early morning warmth of his body, she fell asleep.

On the drive to Mumbai, there was no talk of his confession, of his question. There was not much talk at all. She was disappointed, then surprised at her disappointment: did she want to mean something to him or not? The next day, she went to see him again. He beamed when he saw her. He asked her how she was feeling, whether she had experienced any after-effects, any mood swings. She mumbled her answers, she was fine, that she hoped he was feeling okay too. He offered her tea but she only shook her head and asked him to sit down.

'Kaiz, I have kept something from you.'

'Tell me.'

She put her engagement ring on the table.

'What's this?'

She picked it up and put it on her ring finger. She saw his face redraw itself as he worked out her secret.

'Oh.' He kept nodding his head, she noticed. 'Who is he? When did this happen?' He spoke softly and kept nodding.

'His name is Kartik.'

'Kartik what? Kartik who?'

'Kartik Kini. He's a childhood friend. We were engaged in July. I am getting married next month.' *But the cards have not been sent out yet,* she wanted to add; no, even the thought was ridiculous.

'Arranged?' He had sunk into the sofa, shoulders slouched.

'Yes and no, but mostly yes.'

'Hmm, mostly. So, do you love him?' His face darkened. 'Of course you don't love him. Why would you not mention him to me if you did?' She looked away, she could hear the rising anger in his words.

'Kaiz, it's not like that. I am sorry I didn't tell you—I just couldn't bring myself to do it.'

'And you let me make a fool of myself on the beach?' He put his head in his hands. 'So this is how you return my honesty. Why did you do this, Ira?'

'I screwed up. Like you did when you left.' As soon as the words left her mouth, she knew she had erred.

'Ah, this was your revenge? You were getting back at me. What a plan.'

'I did not mean for any of this to happen, but it happened because I still love you.'

She paused, startled at her own words.

He scoffed. 'That's precious coming from you. Is that how you explained it to this Kartik—that you still love your ex-boyfriend and so you led him on? Spent a night with him? You are a terrible person.'

'Excuse me. What did I even do to you? It's my fiancé I should be apologising to. You are leaving this weekend, just think of this as a missed opportunity for a hook-up and forget about it.'

'You think that's what this was to me? Fuck you, Ira.'

'I think it's best if I go.'

'It is, because I don't want to be in the same room as you. I don't want to see you again, do you understand? Just get out, please leave.'

She left his house feeling wretched. Outside, a downpour. It had started raining in the ten minutes that she had been with him and she was forced to wait in the foyer of his building for the rain to abate. She wondered if he would follow her down.

She did it because she still loved him.

The grey sea across the road made her dizzy. It foamed and seethed with violence under the spell of the rain. She leaned against the stucco wall of the foyer, its protrusions pricking her like ants. Comforted by the sharp pain, she pressed her skin against it harder till her mind was empty. The alternative was to succumb to the tumult building up inside, growing more feral. To surrender and be ripped to shreds. When the rain dwindled to a spray, she made her way to the bus stop. Slowly, stepping around puddles. Thunder rumbled, the sky cracked its knuckles before the next set of blows. Near the bus stop, a pair of puppies, brown and black, emerged from under a car and tumbled towards her feet. She sat on her haunches and petted them, running her hands over their wet, matted fur. The brown one rolled over and looked expectantly at Ira. She looked at its soft belly, speckled and heaving. How easy it was to win someone's trust, how much easier to kick them in the gut.

She did it because she still loved him.

To love was to protect, even from yourself, and yet, she had crushed him. She had said nothing when the truth was called for and spoken the truth when saying nothing would have sufficed.

She did it because she still loved him.

There was no bus in sight for twenty minutes, so she took

a taxi to Nariman Point. She rolled the window down all the way as the cab gathered speed along the sea. The salt in the air stung her eyes, carved a moist trail down her cheek. Teardrops, diamonds melting in the sea breeze, a great pressure undone. Even at work, her mind was in disarray. Images from her time with Kaiz, with Kartik, kept swimming in her head while a half-written article blinked on the computer screen. She found it impossible to put sentences together, as if her words had turned to magnets that repelled each other. She did not have to feign illness. Her editor noted she looked pale and asked her to go home. On the train ride back, she sat with her eyes closed, opening them long enough to see a well-dressed young woman ask loudly, three times, which side of the train the Dadar platform fell on. Lest anybody believe that she took the local train often. Lest anybody think that she lived or went anywhere but town.

Part Three

KARTIK

19

'Aeroplane'—'Feather'—'Submarine'—'Rabbit'—'Amoeba'—
'Crown'—'Inkblot'—'Cheater! Cheater!'

Of all their childhood games, Kartik was certain that this particular one captured his personality best. Ira and he would climb the water tank on the terrace to watch clouds. They let the flimsy lacy ones scud by and when a more ample specimen appeared, they began: in turns, they came up with different things the cloud resembled till it drifted out of sight. Ira rarely won. She stood no chance because Kartik had a protean stash of words for when his imagination failed him. Cracked egg, amoeba, inkblot, words that worked almost each time. He used them towards the end of every game till Ira caught on, at which point he came up with a new set, and the cycle repeated.

Amoeba. Inkblot.

He pulled the heavy velvet curtains aside and looked out of the window. The sky, grey and matted, offered no clear shapes. *Idli batter? Wet dog? The fog in his brain?*

This fog was inexcusable: five kinds of coffee and eight kinds of tea were a phone call away, as were four-storey club sandwiches, three varieties of fried tubers, half a dozen grilled meats attesting to the plunder of land and sea and, slathered with a whole sixty-five spices, glorious chicken wings. The bountiful snacks section of the five-star room-service menu lay open before him. He sat at a large mahogany dining table with three colleagues; a taupe silk sofa accommodated the rest of his case team. Above him was a crystal chandelier, the glint of a thousand frozen teardrops. All this opulence, and the absence of sunlight, made the living room of his office suite look like a villain's den, the lair of a smuggler from a Seventies movie.

'Does anybody mind if I draw the curtains open?'

'Noooo! My anti-glare screen is broken, I won't be able to work!' cried Anuj, the youngest analyst on his team.

All the better, Kartik thought, I will save at least an hour if I don't have to fix your junk spreadsheets. Anuj appeared to have studied something like psychology or political science before business school: he could barely calculate a compounded annual growth rate.

'Anuj, it's not even that bright outside. And come on, some perspective?' Kartik drew the curtain and ran his hand along the long curve of the Arabian sea. 'The Queen's Necklace, versus—,' he pointed at Anuj, who was slouched over his laptop, '—whatever you are screwing up today. Guys, a vote? Who wants the view?'

The young analyst's face shrank, grape to raisin in seconds, as hands around the room went up. 'If everybody wants the curtains open, I can go sit on the sofa.' Anuj sulked as he lumbered to the couch, but found a silver lining almost immediately. 'Well, I am going to put my feet up. Not so bad, huh?'

Kartik drew back the curtains. How sweet this small victory tasted. But within minutes, he was feeling bad about his needless—but admittedly funny—jibe at poor Anuj. He wished he could bring himself to be nicer to him: what the lad lacked in quantitative skills he made up in eagerness and hard work. If only Anuj could see how easy it was to strike at his Labrador-like good cheer, if only he could understand how important it was to not be the weakest link in the room.

It had been a long week at work and it was just Wednesday afternoon. Kartik was the project manager on a team of consultants advising an American car company on how to enter India. He had been working on the case for a little under two months. Two more months to go.

Over eight weeks. About fifty-eight days. Nearly fourteen hundred hours.

Kartik stared at his laptop screen and counted the number of times the words *middle class* appeared in the presentation his team was working on.

India's middle class was growing, expanding in size and influence, and in spending and aspiration too. Blah blah. After nearly five decades of austerity, the economic reforms of 1991 had made this new middle class open their eyes, and their wallets, to the wonders of comfort and luxury. Blah blah. They had waited long enough, now they wanted to show they had arrived.

Twenty-two times.

And it wasn't over yet. He had to regurgitate more drivel from an older report his firm had put together for foreign companies trying to enter India. *India: Namaste*, the report was called. On the cover, a collage of stock images. The Taj Mahal, smiling faces of dark children with very white teeth, a young woman working at a computer, a modern office district which could have been Nariman Point. Inside, statistics about India's demographics, results of consumer surveys, passages on the regulatory landscape, case studies on foreign companies that had seen success. Kartik thumbed through the report repeatedly, the pages dissolving into a blur. The paper breeze was delightful.

He read through his slides again and yawned. This was truly third-rate stuff, but that's what his boss insisted the clients wanted. And it was his boss who wrote his performance reviews, not the chutiya voice in his head that asked him why he was wasting his time at such a soul-crushing job.

The stinging irony was that he did not own a car. Even two of the analysts had Maruti 800s. Their own, not family vehicles. Going by the consumption pyramid on one of his slides, he would not even qualify as upper middle class. *What car do you drive, Kartik?* A question he dreaded, one that he knew would come up sooner or later at lunch or over drinks. He had taken the train to work for a month, then switched to taking taxis. The first-class season pass he still kept, no taxi could match the frisson of a crowded local train compartment. Only for occasional use, of course. It was time to buy a car. Preferably of foreign make, certainly not a hatchback, but nothing too conspicuous or flashy either. He was not north Indian. His money might be new but it did not have to scream for attention like new money was wont to. He only wanted it to introduce itself with a firm handshake.

Just three months ago, his eyes had widened when he heard that his new employer did not have a proper office but had leased a suite in a five-star hotel. Their team in India was still small—two partners, three project managers and nine analysts, many of whom worked from their clients' offices—so the year-old American consulting firm saw no need to invest in an actual office yet. Besides, the name of the hotel made a strong impression on their clients and, against all intuition, it made it easier for these clients to digest the fattened bills they were sent at the end of each month. To celebrate his first day on the job, the whole team had gone to the Chinese restaurant at the Taj Mahal Palace for lunch. The senior partner ordered a bottle of champagne, and Kartik furtively looked for it in the menu. The bottle cost a fourth of a month's salary. He listened carefully for every item that was ordered and kept a running sum in his head. Even without taxes, the bill had run up to a five-digit number.

Kartik was seated next to the senior partner, Raghu Kapoor. Sir—no, Mr Kapoor—no, Raghu ('*We only use first names here, young man*') was in his forties and had returned to India after two decades in Chicago and London. He was a tall man with a spine so erect that he could be in a tableau on the evolution of the *Homo sapien*. His thick black hair had a single ribbon of silver, reminding Kartik of Indira Gandhi. He hung on to every word that his silver-tongued boss uttered.

Raghu spoke to the two new analysts—among them Anuj— only weeks-old at the firm, about what they should expect from the job. It was the first job for both of them. He described the illustrious history of the firm, dropping big names from their roll of clients across the world. A good consultant was not just a doctor for struggling businesses, he explained, but also a coach and mentor. And a career in management consulting was a springboard to any job in the industry. It made the world of business your oyster.

A waiter arrived with the champagne and poured Raghu a sip. He swirled it in his mouth and smacked his lips before nodding. It was the signal for the waiter to serve the champagne to the table.

Raghu continued, 'Now I come to the best part of the job—the possibility of a new you. The true *you*. Use your time here to learn about something that fascinates you. It could be anything you find interesting, like whisky, or Cuban cigars, or fine coffee. Or even Persian carpets.' The analysts looked puzzled but nodded with determination. 'What is important is to have a passion *and* to be able to talk about it at length. It marks you as a—as a certain kind of person, someone who invests time and energy into what they care about. This job will allow you to become that person.' He rolled his fingers over the rim of his glass. 'I want to urge you to find your passion and hone it. Come to me if you need help on that. For your case questions, please go to my boring colleague.' With another half-smile he pointed, with his chin, at the junior partner, who raised his glass. He knew his place in the skit.

Raghu continued to unburden himself of one dictum after another. Instant coffee was rubbish, Ethiopian roasts were more flavourful than Central American varieties. Essential lenses for your first SLR camera? Prime over Zoom, and thanks to Mumbai's famed mugginess, it was wise to invest in a dehumidifier as well. The right brand of shirt? (Here, Kartik's hand went to the cuff of his Arrow shirt; no luxury label but respectably posh.) Always bespoke. It was a trick question. The BMW vs Mercedes conundrum, and what your preference said about your personality.

Kartik listened, fascinated. What a day it had been, he thought, and this was only the beginning. At first, he had tried to look unimpressed, tried to stop his eyes from wandering over every wall, dome and ceiling, from ogling every piece of furniture in his new habitat. He strived to remain unfazed but now he could not help himself any longer. He gulped mouthfuls of luxury, champagne-flavoured, and told himself that he was finally at the base camp of Mount Success. And he was going to scale the fuck out of it.

It had taken less than a month of twelve-hour-plus workdays for the euphoria to wear off: his enthusiasm was no different from a sweatshop garment that can only take a certain number of washes. When he returned home after midnight for the sixth day in a row, he decided that he did not like his new job very much after all.

The seed of doubt was planted the first time he presented

his work before Raghu. They were about two weeks into the project when his boss asked to see what progress had been made. Kartik had stood before both partners and his whole team, and presented their first draft of fifteen slides. He was certain that it was an impressive amount, and calibre, of work.

'It's only our first draft,' he said at the end, in a burst of fake modesty.

'I understand,' said Raghu. At once Kartik recognised that the afternoon was going to go spectacularly off script. 'It's only been two weeks and it's an all-new team.'

Raghu cracked his knuckles. First one hand, then another.

'Can I ask you why you chose this colour scheme?'

'Colour scheme?'

'Do you have a strong reason for picking shades of green for your graphs? I don't like that colour. So, unless you have a strong reason, could you redo them? How about blue? Or even purple? It's a *bold* choice—it captures how ambitious our vision for the client is. What do you think?'

'Right, purple. Anuj, are you taking notes?'

Three nods where one would have sufficed.

'Also, I don't love pie charts,' Raghu continued. 'To be honest, I hate them.'

Kartik waited for Raghu to laugh, or at least grin, or convey in some other way that he was joking, but Raghu's face remained steady, serious.

'But these are market share charts,' Kartik explained. 'How else do we show relative sizes or parts of a whole?'

'Be creative, Kartik.' A half-smile. 'How about doughnuts?'

'Doughnuts?'

What on earth?

'Yeah, just put a hole at the centre of the pie. Make a regular pie chart and put a smaller white circle over it. Voila, a doughnut. It's not a pie chart anymore.'

'Okay, we will do that.'

'Great.'

'So is that all? We are good?' he asked Raghu.

'No, of course not. We have to redo the whole thing. But good start, team. Good start.'

Over the next fifteen minutes, Kartik saw the tidy slide deck he had printed get massacred with a red pen: Raghu severed slides into two, slashed whole paragraphs, flayed his dear graphs and disembowelled the poor pie charts. And he was handed the bloody remains to rebirth like Frankenstein's monster.

'Let's discuss the next draft tomorrow morning?'

It was already eight in the evening.

'Sure, no problem.'

This was the first of many such evenings, the first time he had to stay in office past midnight. So Kartik had decided to chase the silver lining in the cloud looming over his life: airline miles, all the books he wanted to buy, a swish five-star gymnasium.

A little before three, the four analysts on his team left to conduct consumer interviews. Solitude brought relief, as if a part of him, cramped in company, could spread out and be comfortable. He stood up and stretched his neck and back. He walked to the window and looked at the grey sea curving into a question mark, the city curled around it. And with fresh eyes, decided to look at the presentation again. He thought it looked fine. And it told a clear story: there was a burgeoning demand for cheap cars in India because of the growing middle class, while competition in the sector was still limited. But Kartik had also thought that the presentation looked fine a week and six drafts ago. The changes his team had made in the past week had all been cosmetic. Some shuffling of the slides, a change of font here and a realignment of charts there, small pieces of new analysis. They had done exactly what the boss had asked for.

His boss disagreed.

'This isn't working, Kartik,' Raghu had said. Thankfully, when it was just the two of them. 'Your presentations need to be more visual. There's too much text. Put more graphs, more pictures.'

How about a visual of a man bending over while a sedan covered in stars and stripes hovered around his ass? Was there a clipart image for that, Kartik had thought acidly.

He tinkered with the presentation till four, when it was time to walk down to the coffee shop. An anniversary, albeit a small one: a month since Ira said yes. Kartik had asked to steal Ira away from the newsroom for half an hour.

'The coffee shop in your hotel?' Ira had repeated on the phone, incredulous.

One coffee, Rs 100.

'Yes,' he replied with a laugh.

'Wow.'

Dark cloud, silver lining: swish gymnasium, airline miles, all the books he wanted to buy, hundred-rupee coffees.

Stripped of cultural context and natural lighting, the five-star coffee shop could have been situated in any part of the world, at any time of the day. Yellow and purple lights embedded in the ivory walls lit up row after row of abstract art. Rattan chairs were packed cosily around marble table-tops, each table with a small bunch of fresh flowers. Kartik ordered two Ethiopian coffees. They arrived in bone china teacups with a plate of complimentary cookies. He wanted Ira to say the coffee was excellent but she sipped it without comment. She was telling him about a special Independence Day series she was working on for her paper. The way her eyes lit up when she talked about her stories both delighted him and made him feel small and sad. To love your work, to tell yourself it mattered, how did that feel?

'How do you like the coffee?' he asked finally, unable to hold himself back.

'The coffee is very good. It better be, no?' She smiled and added, 'This is my first time in a five-star hotel. Thank you.'

'This is my first time outside of work too.'

'I still can't believe you work here. What a life!'

'Yes, what a life.' He popped a cookie into his mouth and chewed on it slowly. His jaw felt heavy, suddenly aware of the lie it had to repeat every day. 'Can I tell you something? Promise you won't laugh. Remember those superhero comics we used to love?'

'What about them?'

'Every panel, every figure was made up of small dots.'

'Red, blue and yellow dots, the primary colours.'

'Right. And the three placed next to each other created the illusion of different colours. I remember I used to bring the page very close to my face till the pictures dissolved and all I could see were the dots. Heroes, villains, the scenery, all reduced to the same coloured pixels. And when I moved away, the patterns would slowly re-emerge and the drawing made sense again.' He paused for a moment, took a sip of coffee, felt a prickling in his eyes. 'But now when I take a step back and look at my life, it's like seeing only dots. There are no patterns, no meaning, no bigger picture.'

'Why do you say that?'

He lived in two stories. One, public, in which the judgement on his life had been delivered: here he was, reaping the fruit of decades of hard work and discipline, a catapult loaded as much by his own application of his gifts as by the spring of the new economy. The other narrative was fractured, where effort and excellence, intention and reward, even sense and meaning, were no longer linked. Surely it had to amount to more?

'I have a job that pays well and hires the smartest people. I should feel lucky, no? Not complain about the long hours or the fact that the work seems meaningless. I mean, who loves what they do every single day, every hour? Do you?'

'No, not all the time.'

Ira leaned forward and combed her fingers through his hair, the tips grazing his scalp. He found his shoulders melting under her touch, melted by the memories of head massages from his mother. He took her other hand in his.

'If you hate it so much, why don't you quit? You will have no trouble finding a job you like. You are the smartest person I know.'

He recoiled without meaning to, annoyed at the unsolicited advice. It was not her fault, he told himself, what other advice could she give him? Someone more ambitious, someone who knew more about the kind of work he did and the future that was expected of him would have asked him to be patient and work harder, get a promotion or two and save up to buy a flat in Worli by the sea, keep at it for a few years before looking for another job. A three-month stint on the resume looked terrible. It raised questions about your work ethic. Someone like his father would have told him to stop complaining, to man up.

'Shit.' He looked at his watch. 'I forgot that I have a meeting upstairs in ten minutes. Let's finish our coffees soon?'

A lie.

'Kartik, it's alright to admit that you don't like your job.'

'No, it's nothing, just a bad day at work. Please remind me I am too old to throw tantrums.'

'You are never too old to want better.'

Want, want, want: the story of his life.

He smiled at her. 'True.'

They finished their coffees, after which he paid the bill.

Kartik took the lift back to the highest floor. The carpet was lush, dazzling. Yellow paisleys in a maroon sea. He dragged his feet along the endless corridor, identical doors on both sides with only brass numbers to give his body a locus. He stopped in front of one of the doors and swiped a key-card. A green flash and a click. The office suite was empty except for the administrative assistant. The partners were out of town, the other project team was working from their client's office and his own team was out doing market research. A familiar stirring arose when he found himself alone. He had the computers to himself, perhaps a visit to some chat rooms? No, he said to himself, you are better than that.

20

KARTIK TOOK IN THE COOL, damp August air. He tried not to think about the muddy tiles under his feet, slippery and dusted with mould. The low gurgling of the water tank was pleasant to his ears. The tank was ten feet high and connected to a jumble of pipes and tubes, a nervous system turned inside out. He considered climbing up, like he and Ira used to as children, to be briefly removed from the bricks and mortar of his life, but it was impossible—the tank was covered in rusty acne, not safe to go near anymore. The children in the building didn't seem to have noticed. Who had time to climb up a water tank when you had eight television channels to choose from every evening?

What a privilege, he thought, to have this jagged corner of the city all to yourself. So far, Ira was right: nobody came to the terrace anymore.

The terrace had become a venue for their assignations, a place to catch up on each other's days, to hold hands and exchange a kiss or two, to perform a courtship. But Ira wasn't with him today. He was by himself, spending a few minutes doing nothing. It was the first time in two weeks that he had left work before eleven. He had come straight up to the terrace, his heart beating a little faster as he tiptoed past his flat to climb two more floors.

Even as a child, his favourite hours of the day had been the ones spent doing nothing in particular. He was happiest at the end of the day, at home. After dinner, he would retreat to his room—he had claimed the balcony of his parents' bedroom for himself long before the occupation was recognised by higher powers—and spend an hour or two alone with his books. He read till his mother put him to bed at ten. The books themselves were immaterial, he needed no more than pencil and paper to occupy himself. He might fill the margins of the previous day's newspaper with nesting geometric figures, as many layers as the sharpness of the pencil allowed. Or he studied the patterns in the old tiles on the floor, tracing familiar irregularities from memory and finding new imperfections. On some days, he just sat by a window and listened to the sounds of the street rise and ebb.

After a tiring day, he still liked nothing better than simple mechanical tasks, finding comfort in the persistent low humming of his mind. To not be discovered, to not be interrupted, that was all he asked for. In moments of clarity, when he let it sink in how ill-advised the career path he had tumbled down was for someone with these tendencies, he became depressed.

Since the move back home, he savoured any time he could steal for himself. His engagement had turned his home into a circus. Relatives, jewellers, cooks, decorators wafted in and out all the time. One aunt had seen the perfect tent design for the reception, another had just attended a wedding with a Chinese food counter. They brimmed with questions: how were the cards coming along, how many starters had they decided upon, had the gold sets been ordered, where would the out-of-town guests be put up? When there were no visitors, his mother complained to him that she was doing more work than any mother of the groom had ever done, but she could not help it: she wanted her only son's wedding to be a grand affair and the Kamats, good people as they were, were simply not capable of pulling it off. Thandi istri, she called them. A cold iron, easy on wrinkles. Or his father would launch into one of his rants on unholy alliances and Vatican conspiracies, a new passion of his, fanned by the rabid discussion forums he had discovered via their month-old internet connection. There was not a moment of peace. This was the rent he paid, his room and board.

Not that things were any different before the engagement. When he had arrived from Bangalore three months ago, his parents were preoccupied with the redevelopment of Asha Nivas: they could not stop chattering about the landlord, about the opinions of their neighbours and what it would take to persuade each of them. For five years, the landlord had been offering his tenants a few lakhs to vacate their homes. It was his parents who had first demanded that the settlement cover the deposit for a flat in Matunga. By the time all the residents were convinced that it was a fair ask, the Kinis had moved their sights to a bigger prize: new flats.

All credit to his mother. It was she who had heard about a family in Dadar that had been promised a new flat for vacating the flat they had lived in for forty years. She had asked around and learnt of other examples, more precedents. It had taken her no time to convince her husband; when it came to grand designs, they were kindred spirits. His mother had worked like a bee, buzzed from one home to another to pollinate the minds of their neighbours with the promise of a new flat. Even slum dwellers are getting new flats now, and look at us, begging for a few lakhs, she said to Mrs Shanbhag. Just the thought of another rented home, another landlord, increases my blood pressure, she told Mrs Rege, the hypochondriac. Selling a one-bedroom flat in Matunga, she suggested to the space-starved Mrs Naik, will buy a three-bedroom flat in the suburbs.

It was a touch ironic, he thought, that his mother should spend her days trying to secure a flat in the building that she had plotted escape from for half of Kartik's childhood.

The intruder who had scared Mrs Desai with his finger gun had proved to be a blessing for his parents' mission. Even the most conservative residents found their faith in fairness upended by this gross violence and found themselves more amenable to the Kinis' proposal. Demanding a new flat from the landlord did not feel like screwing over a decent man anymore. His parents had moved steadily and swiftly and, within months, everybody was on their side.

How on earth did they have all that energy, he wondered.

It was hard living with his parents again after thirteen years away. He had already started making enquiries about where his colleagues lived, how they had found their apartments. Raghu Kapoor lived in Cuffe Parade, the junior partner had an apartment in Worli, as did the two other project managers. None of them lived with their parents. The analysts were scattered across Bandra and Mahim, living with one, two, even three flatmates. Where is Matunga, Anuj had asked him the day they met, is it one of the suburbs between Andheri and Borivali? Anuj had only lived in Mumbai for a few weeks then. He had probably taken a quick look at the local train map and mixed up Matunga and Malad. It annoyed Kartik nonetheless. It's south of Mahim, you idiot, he wanted to say, it's not a suburb.

You needed two things to succeed in this city, Kartik had heard, dress and address. Who can peep into your pocket and see how much money you had? This was all the world had to go by. Dress and address.

He had hinted to his mother that he might move to a flat of his own. She had dismissed the idea at once. 'Move when you are married if you really want to. I am not letting you out of my sight till then. You work so hard, who will look after you?'

So he worked even harder, trying to delay coming home to the madhouse for as long as he could. At work, when he was overwhelmed, he went to the bathroom and sat on the five-star pot for twenty minutes, letting his team think he was taking a long shit. At home, the terrace of Asha Nivas had become his refuge.

The Kini family had lived in Asha Nivas since 1948. In the early Forties, Kartik's grandfather, Shrikant Kini, had left behind his wife and young children in the coastal town of Kumta to earn a living in Bombay. He had worked as a delivery boy, a waiter, a cook and a caterer before he opened Saraswat Bhawan. Only then had he summoned his family to the city. The family had been penniless in Kumta, mother and children living off scraps, off relatives and their dwindling generosity. Kartik's grandmother, he had been told, would eat only one and a half meals a day in those years, claiming it was good for the constitution. Her father was a village priest, her husband was an avowed Gandhian, she must have known a thing or two about self-abnegation. Shrikant Kini visited his wife and children a couple of times a year, bringing with him a little money and many stories of the big city, of his work in the Congress Party and the freedom struggle. He had been to jail twice—arrested briefly for taking part in demonstrations both times—even though he had been no more than a cog in the wheels of the fight for Independence. That had been enough for him: wearing a white hand-spun kurta, attending meetings and marches, shouting a few slogans and being near the Mahatma every few months. It could not have been a coincidence, Kartik's father liked to claim, that the family was summoned to Bombay only in 1948, some months after Gandhi was killed, when the senior-most Kini's heart was finally open to his mundane duties again.

Only when the nation is free. That had been Shrikant Kini's answer to most questions about his plans and intentions: why could he not focus more on his jobs, why did he not ask someone from the community for steady employment, when would he be able to take his family with him? Only when the nation is free. If his children demanded new clothes on the occasion of his visits, he preached the Gandhian virtue of simplicity. To his wife's muted protests on his odd jobs, which she implied were unfitting for a brahmin, he replied there was no indignity in any labour.

Ashok Kini had grown up believing that his father was lazy, that politics was a ruse to mask his inabilities, that Gandhi was the magic word that squared his beliefs with his limited means, his aspirations with his obligations. He had concluded, at a young age, that one's worth as a husband, as a man, was best measured in gold. He had gleaned this from the women around him: this one was a great husband, his wife had more tolas of gold than there were years in their marriage; that one was no good, his woman died with not an ounce more than the gold threads in her mangalsutra. His father hadn't come out well on this test: Ashok's mother had seen little material comfort.

It had not been Ashok Kini's plan to marry rich. It was a distant relative who had put the two families in touch. At first, his future wife herself had not been keen on the match, especially on account of his pin code.

'Matunga? That's barely Bombay. Don't you remember my conditions?'

She had laid down two conditions before her mother: she would marry an eldest son, and only a man who lived in Bombay. Her oldest sister had married the youngest of four brothers and had to live under the thumbs of four women. Another sister had been married into a family in Halliyal, a village with no electricity, and worse, no cinema halls.

'No, no, it is proper Bombay, it used to be the last tram stop. The suburbs start only at Mahim,' her mother reasoned with her. 'Besides, he has three sisters who are already married and his brother is much younger. You'll establish yourself in the household before another woman comes in.'

When Ashok saw Kusum bring out a tray of tea into her Colaba drawing room, he was besotted at once. With her bouffant bun, manicured nails and convent-accented English, she was precisely the wife he wanted, a partner and driving force in the life he sought to build for himself. Her family was above their station, his mother protested, she wouldn't fit in with the Kinis. It made little sense that her family had agreed to this match in the first place, they had to be hiding something. One of his sisters said her long face and big teeth made her look like a horse. An old horse, the other sister added, almost twenty-five years old, no decent woman remained unmarried that long. He could not care less what they thought. But when his father said he did not think she had the virtues of simplicity and modesty, Ashok decided he had met the future Mrs Kini.

Over the years, there were many other things the two Kini men disagreed on: the importance of English, the limits of simple living, whether Gandhi ought to be called Mahatma or not and, closer to home, whether Saraswat Bhawan should sell packaged snacks and sweets like Irani cafes did, whether a few north Indian dishes could be added to the menu as an experiment, whether *any* kind of change, really, could be made to how the restaurant was run. On some days, the tension between them had filled the house, it crept up the walls and hung from the ceiling like stalactites.

Things came to a head in the summer of 1977. That was the year that Nandan mama, Kartik's uncle, visited Bombay. It was his second trip to India since he moved to Germany several years ago. The first had been for Kartik's parents' wedding. This time too, he had brought a suitcase full of gifts: porcelain figurines that required new glass shelves to be put up, bottles of chocolate milk his mother numbered before they were put in the fridge so none would be *accidentally* given away by his grandmother to her relatives, a new set of teacups she refused to keep in the kitchen.

Kartik had never been unhappier. His cousins, a pair of twins a year younger than Ira, spoke Konkani but no English. They spoke to each other only in German, and the rasp of their words left Kartik certain they were mocking him. The brutes thumbed all his books and put them back in their shelves out of order. They rifled through his toys and played tug-of-war with his once-precious stuffed bear. They shuffled his deck of cards in a clumsy, handsy manner that left every card greased with sweat. They jumped on the bed, and from the bed, leaving dusty footprints everywhere. His heart was smushed with anxiety for two weeks. He thanked god that he had no siblings.

They stayed for two weeks. As soon as they left, before

Kartik could even sit back and savour their departure, the cessation of violations, his mother drafted him into a game of her own. His uncle had gifted him a children's guide to West Germany, a glossy book bursting with maps and illustrations. She asked him to read it from cover to cover and, when his father returned from the restaurant, she quizzed Kartik on the contents of the book.

'What is the capital of West Germany?'

'Bonn.'

'Very good. Where does Nandan mama live?'

'Frankfurt.'

'And when you go to Frankfurt what will you eat?'

'Spätzle, schnitzel, sausages and black forest cake.'

'Doesn't that sound delicious?'

'It does!'

Water in his mouth, a glint in his eye, an idea for a new game.

His grandmother interrupted: 'Why will you eat all that, boy? Won't your mami cook *proper* food for you? Or does she not know how to?'

'In some places, food has to be tasty to be called *proper*. In other places, one has to make do with boiled pumpkins.'

'In some places, Kusum, proper behaviour is worth much more than tasty food.' Dragging her closed fist over her mouth, his grandmother mimed tearing meat off the bone, a gesture that suggested wantonness. 'Places where a married woman wears only maroon bindis—and does not match her bindi with her saree like a cheap film heroine. But those places, I suspect, you are not familiar with.'

'That's enough, Kusum, Ayee,' his father said sharply. 'You women have the whole day to bicker. The men are home now. Please put an end to it.'

A game that was being played out for his father had prodded his grandmother. Her taunt directed at his mother was conveyed to him. A squabble between women had to be settled by a man. And Kartik would have to sate his craving for delicious exotic foods with dal, rice and boiled pumpkins. To Kartik, family life appeared to be a series of cross-connections.

He slept on a roll-up mattress on the floor next to his parents' bed. That night, sleep evaded him. He waited for his limbs to slacken, for his leg to twitch and kick on its own, which signalled a leak of consciousness, the nearness of slumber. His parents' conversation, carried out in whispers after he had been put to bed, kept playing in his ears.

'You have to stop it, Kusum. Don't bring up Germany in front of my parents again.'

'If you decide to go, they will find out anyway. It is best that they are prepared.'

'You think these things are simple. It is not easy to start over in a new place.'

'Nandan has promised to help in every way.'

'What would that make me—a ghar jamai? Will you respect me if I live off your brother?'

'We wouldn't be living off him, he will only help us get started. I am confident you will be on your feet in no time.'

'You don't understand, Kusum. We will be nobodies there.'

'Nobodies? And what are we here? Arvind is getting married soon, where will he and his wife stay? In the kitchen?'

'He is an engineer, he can afford to take up a flat.'

'Then why should we be stuck in Matunga? Let your brother also perform his duties as a son, let him look after your parents.'

'You talk like you are suffering through hell here. Am I not providing enough?'

'I can see that you are suffering too. You are forty years old and your father treats you like a boy. You should be a leader, an entrepreneur, not a mere manager.'

'Kusum, please.'

'This is not a country that wants people to move up, not people like us. Think about what this move could mean for Kartik.'

For Kartik, this move would mean hell. Even the thought of his twin cousins becoming a fixture in his life was terror. He slept poorly for weeks. He prayed more fervently, morning and evening, he lingered before the gods even after the minimum prayers were said. Anything, he bargained, he would give anything in order not to move.

(And he remembered this promise for years. When those images of men began to invade his dreams, his waking moments, he wondered if he had cut a terrible deal.)

Soon after, a miracle happened: his father's brother told the family that his fiancée's uncle had offered to sponsor his Green Card to the US. The uncle ran a chain of motels and was looking to diversify into real estate. He needed a civil engineer on his team and his favourite niece's husband was the ideal candidate. As the oldest son, Ashok Kini had no choice but to stay behind. But it didn't mean that he could not tell his father about the offer from his brother-in-law, about how much he was tempted to move to Germany with his family.

And so, at the end of the summer of 1976, Ashok Kini took over the reins of Saraswat Bhawan.

Kartik hoped his parents would not still be awake when he returned home from the terrace. He had no interest in recapping his day for them or asking them any corresponding questions about theirs. He loved his parents but he was an adult man—

was it so bad that he found their company tiresome? Kartik found the company of most people tiresome, and the number grew with time. It was as if the ground beneath his feet was shrinking. Every year there was less he had in common with the people he had once been close to: uncles, aunts, cousins, neighbours. When he looked at them, he saw middling people with middling concerns. They shoved their children before him and asked him to share the secret of getting into an IIT or an IIM. Put your hands over my child's head, they would tell him, only half-jokingly, maybe that'll get this wastrel to study more. As if this was the crux of his identity: he had once been good at entrance examinations.

Kartik had no older sibling to tease him that he was adopted, or torment him by saying that he had been picked up from a dumpster. So he had done it himself. For years he had agonised over whether there had been a switcheroo in the hospital, for there was no way he was the spawn of these gregarious, big-talking, fast-moving parents. As a child he had experienced this disconnect with his family as a deep fear, but with time it had morphed into an existential disappointment. But as different as he and his parents were, their planes of existence did intersect. At one place alone: success, his success. Perhaps that was the reason he believed that it was all that mattered. And look where that had got him.

Kartik glanced at his watch. It was 11.15 p.m. He felt sorry for the poor business analyst who was no doubt still working on their client's market opportunity model and would continue for a few more hours. He had hinted that he wanted the next draft by the following morning. Only if possible, he had emphasised, but the foolish woman was too eager to please. This trait he had seen in many young women at work. They were hard-working and sincere, driven by a fear, he suspected, of earning a bad name for womankind. He surmised that the small number of women at business schools—and their biggest feeders, the top engineering colleges in the country—had something to do with these women seeing themselves as representatives for their gender. He had seen it first-hand in college. There had been five women in his class of two hundred. If a male student struggled in a course, either he was called a duffer or the subject itself was declared too hard. If one of the women did, the class would gleefully conclude that what they had heard about females was true: they were no good at the fundamentals of mathematics and science, their presence in the midst of geniuses was an aberration. He had shared this theory with Ira one evening, expecting her to be impressed by his perceptiveness, his feminist sympathies.

But she had told him he was being patronising, something about how he could not extrapolate the experience of a few female classmates to all women in the professional world. How was that different, she argued, from his friends who had generalised one woman's wrong answer to a weakness of the whole gender. Why could his analyst not simply be ambitious, why did her work ethic have to be a response to sexism? Why did men get to take the credit, however indirectly, for her hard work?

There was no pleasing women, thought Kartik, feeling robbed of his well-deserved kudos. He was on her side, wasn't that enough?

But there was some truth in what she had said. He did tend to look at women as a slightly inscrutable monolithic unit. If asked to describe women, he knew he would put forward a list of adjectives—strong, smart, emotional, impulsive, dramatic, cunning, kind, loving—a rich mix of good and bad, distilled from the exceptional women he had grown up around. But if somebody were to ask him to describe men, he was certain that he would reply with a question: which man?

21

THE BIG CLIENT PRESENTATION, the one that Kartik had to make to the senior vice-president of the car company his team was working for, was a reasonable success. There was no standing ovation, but Kartik's worst prophesies hadn't come true either. Raghu took the team out for a dinner at a new European restaurant that evening. The restaurant called itself a bistro and had white stucco walls and warm, honey lighting. The wooden tables and chairs looked unfinished, the menu was handwritten and the prices inexplicably steep. Raghu ordered for everybody except the vegetarians, who were asked to order for themselves. After they had finished eating, the chef came out to ask if they had liked the last course. It was his third trip to their table: thanks to the two expensive bottles of wine that Raghu ordered, no doubt. The chef, a bronzed, sinewy Italian in his thirties, indulged in small talk in a lilting accent for a few minutes before he recommended desserts to the table.

Only one recommendation was offered directly, with locked eyes: 'You must have the panna cotta, it is *heavenly.*'

His shoulders stiffened and his heart began to pound; he knew he should not have let his gaze run away unchecked before.

'I'll have the chocolate cake, thanks.'

After dinner, Kartik and the analysts stayed behind to smoke outside the restaurant. Even the non-smokers hung around, he noted, such suck-ups.

He really ought to not smoke so much but smoking had become a workday ritual. When time moved so slowly that it seemed to stand still, it was important to mark its passage: the cigarette break celebrated the passage of time. It was his shield, his armour. It created the illusion of camaraderie, made it possible to be social without eye contact, without deep conversation. Look, we have something in common, it announced. In large groups, he sometimes felt naked without a cigarette between his fingers. It had become his spirit's sustenance.

'Is that Kartik Kini—what a surprise!'

He turned to see who had called his name. Bile rose in his throat. Before him was a face he had tried to forget for years. Pinkesh Panchal, old rival, arch-scoundrel, asshole.

Pinkesh walked up to him and slapped his back before he shook his hand. His grip was still like a vice. His face, too, appeared unchanged by time; his features, when he wasn't speaking, were composed like an equation, spare and precise. But even one word out of him and his stratospheric arrogance would mar everything.

'How have you been, buddy? I haven't seen you in ten years.'

Eleven, thought Kartik. He summed up the decade in a few lines, shaving down to the bone—an MBA after college, three jobs, Bangalore, now Mumbai, the consulting firm, the team dinner. Pinkesh nodded with a sincerity that made Kartik suspicious but also compelled him to return the question.

'I am also here on work,' said Pinkesh. Before Kartik could probe further, Pinkesh turned to his colleagues. 'We used to be quiz rivals in college. Wait, not rivals, I always kicked his ass. Didn't I, Two-Piece?' Kartik cringed. 'Don't worry, I'll spare your ass this time. Unless one of your friends has trivia questions on hand.'

What was Two-Piece, someone asked. One of his many college nicknames. Kini had become Bikini had become Two-Piece. The febrile imaginations of young engineers had churned out worse; better Two-Piece than Pondy, Despo. Better, also, than the names that had not stuck: Mandakini, Muggoo, Daddy.

'Can I get a light?' Pinkesh put a cigarette to his lips and leaned forward.

'You are smoking a cigarette.'

'Ya, so?'

'Didn't you only smoke beedis?'

'You expect me to smoke those cheapda beedis at thirty-two? I am not *that* chindi, yaar.'

Pinkesh had once been an unlikely star quizzer at inter-college festivals around Bombay. Unlikely because he was a state board-educated boy from Kandivali in the bastion of brats from ICSE schools. Even before Kartik entered college, Pinkesh was an icon on the college festival circuit. One of his signature moves had been blowing smoke rings, making ash and vapour bend to his will. Beedis, with their thick smoke, had been his preferred medium. It was Pinkesh who had taught Kartik how to blow smoke rings, although when Ira asked, he didn't say this. He didn't want to talk about Pinkesh, let alone talk to him, but now that the man had appeared out of nowhere, Kartik had little choice. What does the bully want, he wondered, and was glad when Pinkesh said he had to rush. But before he left, he slipped a card into Kartik's hand. Too afraid to look right away, Kartik waited till he was alone, his heart hammering in the minutes in between. The paper was very thin, Kartik nearly cut his finger on the edge before he read it.

It was only a business card.

Pinkesh Panchal
Private Investigator
Discretion guaranteed

Kartik had first met Pinkesh in the early months of college, in the final round of an inter-college quiz competition. It was not his loose-limbed strut, or the square-jawed smirk, or his steely, pointed gaze that struck Kartik, rather the fact that Pinkesh had single-handedly clobbered him and his team. Kartik was captivated by his opponent's catholic mastery of trivia topics: he could answer questions about Woodstock and Oscar-nominated pornos as smoothly as those about former Governor-Generals of India. The second time they faced off, Kartik answered an easy question that Pinkesh could not, about an Indian bowler with a polio-withered arm. Pinkesh looked at him and gave him a sly nod. He had a wide, severe face with a high forehead, deep-set eyes and a thin, sharp nose. His lower lip protruded in an imperious pout while the upper lip was scant, like a curly bracket. The cursory nod from Pinkesh wasn't accompanied by a smile, nor had his severe expression softened, and Kartik's team went on to lose the quiz by a wide margin. Still, it felt like the biggest reward, worth more than any numbers on the scoreboard. Kartik decided he would do anything to see a look of frank respect on that smug face.

To best Pinkesh then became his singular ambition. Kartik had learnt at a young age to forfeit a race if it looked like he wasn't going to win. This time, though, he had found a formidable opponent and even the thought of vanquishing him left Kartik breathless. He began to study Pinkesh's performance, the questions he answered with ease, where he faltered and where he failed. Kartik wanted to assess his strengths and look for openings, opportunities to strike him, to seize his records, his reputation.

The quizzers in the city all knew each other: it was the same ten or twelve faces that ended up on stage after the elimination rounds. They called each other by the nicknames college friends used—in an approximation of actual friendship—but usually did not meet between quizzes. Kartik found himself admitted to their ranks in no time.

'Mr Polio,' Pinkesh remarked when Kartik introduced himself. He felt an acceleration in his heart. He had looked up the events calendar and learnt of the other competitions that Pinkesh was participating in. He hovered casually around the venues till he saw a hand wave at him. Kartik noticed how Pinkesh tore away from his teammates to speak to him. The next month, at another inter-college quiz, Kartik asked him if he wanted to try out the famous spring dosa at a nearby roadside stall. Five of them went. Pinkesh said he was not too hungry, so Kartik offered to share a dosa with him and asked for a spoon to cut it into two.

'Why, dude?' Pinkesh responded. 'Will you make me pay two rupees more if I have a little more than half?'

They ate from the same unbroken roll, slowly working their way towards the middle. Under these twin assaults, the spring dosa spilled its guts into the plate. Kartik watched the other boy's fingers closely, plotting to reach for the same piece of capsicum or onion at the right instant. Pinkesh turned out to have quick hands; only once did he manage to make their fingers meet.

Before they finished eating, a beggar accosted the group. He was a badly deformed man, as if a broken doll had been put together by a child. Extending a bent claw before each of them one by one, he repeated the same benedictions. May you do well in your exams. May you always prosper. Whatever you give, god will give you back a thousandfold.

If Pinkesh were a girl sharing a plate with him, the man might have said god bless the couple.

Kartik thought of him constantly. He lay awake in his hostel room, with its musty smell that lingered for months after the rains stopped, thinking about the impossible questions he had seen Pinkesh answer. He counted the days till the next meeting while operating the lathe machine in his workshop class, while poring over his physics, mathematics and economics textbooks, while the rest of his hostel indulged in a water fight with the neighbouring hostel, hurling buckets at each other. Around Pinkesh, he was desperate to make a good impression: his sincere and probing questions, the esoteric topics he researched to drop into conversation, the hungry pause that followed when he thought he had said something clever. Pinkesh sensed this admiration too and must have enjoyed it, for he spared Kartik the mocking that the others he vanquished were subjected to, and when he could not hold his barbs, he softened his cruelty with a dab of affectionate irony.

By the time the inter-college festival at Kartik's university rolled in, the two had become good friends. On the first day, neither was participating in any events, so they strolled around the campus taking long sips of the winter sun. Kartik showed him the library, the canteen, workshops and laboratories, his hostel, his room. Pinkesh showed no special interest in Kartik's world.

What is this smell, he asked loudly in the hostel corridor. Sweat and socks, Kartik replied, it is a boys' hostel. Pinkesh put his nose up and sniffed loudly. And semen, he added with a wink. Kartik blushed.

In the more crowded hostel lobby, Pinkesh began to bat with folded hands, practising different strokes in a game of imaginary cricket. It amused Kartik that his footwork was all wrong. Kartik asked him to stay the night, he had to return for the quiz the next day anyway, and if he stayed, they could have breakfast at the crack of dawn. Dosas at a ramshackle canteen across the road from his college campus, run by a Tamil family.

'It is an essential experience in these parts of the city,' he explained.

'City? No way,' said Pinkesh. 'This is more like a jungle. People who live in the actual city come to the lake next to your campus for a mini-vacation.'

'Forget breakfast and stay for the lake then', Kartik pleaded. 'I'll show you the lake at midnight, and a spot that none of your vacationers would know about.'

His guest relented and called his parents from a phone booth to let them know he was staying with a friend.

They attended the last event of the day together, a classical music concert: a jugalbandi between two maestros, one on the tabla and the other on the sitar. The ground was packed like a local train, bodies squashed together in a daze of vices: cigarettes, bootlegged rum and whisky, marijuana. The evening was electric. The sounds of the two instruments rose and fell together for the most part, in step. Then suddenly, one seemed to take the lead and rise to a crescendo, only to part the air for the other to come roaring in—and the cycle repeated. Neither was the lead nor the accompanist, it was a meeting of equals, each one stirring and spurring the other.

After the concert, they walked to the lake through a thicket behind Kartik's hostel. He led the way, as he had promised, with a torch in hand. Their feet ruffled up dry leaves like someone crunching toast. Pinkesh followed a step behind. When he nearly tripped on a dried bough, he grabbed Kartik's hand for support and held on till they reached the wooden pier that jutted out into the lake. Whispers of love songs played on a distant radio. Or was he imagining the music, Kartik wondered. The boys sat down at the edge of the pier, their feet dangling over an old boat. The night was feverishly beautiful. The bloated moon, a few days shy of fullness, illuminated a long strip of the lake.

Pinkesh lit a beedi. 'It's so peaceful. You guys are lucky to live here.'

There, again, the smoke rings. Kartik was reminded of a circus master's hoop, one that even mighty lions jumped through.

'Teach me how to do that.'

'You have a cigarette?'

'No, I'll try it your way.'

'Really? You don't look like a beedi smoker. Do you even smoke?'

'I don't look like a lot of things, but you'll be surprised.'

'Is it so? There isn't much that surprises me, let's see what you can do.'

He took a second beedi out of his pocket, but instead of lighting it for Kartik, he took the one he was smoking and put it between Kartik's lips, grazing them with his fingers.

'Okay, watch.' He lit the other one for himself and moved closer so Kartik could see him in the dark. 'Purse your lips— like this—and push with your tongue.'

Kartik watched his lips move but he saw no smoke, no rings, only his mouth. Opening, closing, opening. His throat was on fire but he did not complain.

'Dude, pay attention.' Pinkesh looked into Kartik's eyes and blew smoke into his face, making him cough.

He tried again and failed.

'You are not even trying, man. Okay, try this method: someone told me it's a little like resisting giving a blow job. Imagine that.'

Kartik nearly burst out laughing but his laughter caught in his throat. Pinkesh had placed a hand on his. The weight of skin, the pinch of gravel, dark waters under the silver of the moon. The shiver of his heart.

'I am having trouble imagining it,' he said.

'I thought you were a good student. Not giving up, are we?'

Pinkesh kneaded Kartik's hand, pressing down his fingers in the gaps between the knuckles. Like a river fills its bed, leaving no empty spaces. When Kartik did not flinch, Pinkesh reached for his thigh and began to stroke it, first with his fingers, then the whole palm of his hand. Kartik's leg stiffened and he accidentally nudged the wooden boat at their feet. In an instant the lake was covered in ripples. It was a ritual he would remember, this act of testing the waters. An accidental touch, lingering fingers, a grope, a squeeze.

'I am not giving up—it's like resisting a blow job, you said?'

'Resisting *giving* one. What do you think?' Pinkesh took his hand and placed it in his lap.

In a thump of anticipation, Kartik leaned forward to kiss him. He was going for a peck but Pinkesh prised his lips open, ran his tongue along Kartik's teeth.

'Alright,' said Pinkesh as he reached for his trousers. 'but you have to promise to *resist*.'

'I will try my best.'

While waiting for Pinkesh to unzip, he was reminded of a spelling bee competition at the previous year's student festival, where the host had asked the only female finalist to spell fellatio and the auditorium had erupted in sniggers. He couldn't remember if she had managed to spell it. Then it was time. It's happening, it's happening, he thought giddily, it is happening. It was a few more hours before he learnt how to blow a smoke ring.

There was a new project manager in the office suite, James Arnett—Jim—on loan from the New York office. The Harvard Business School graduate had worked with the firm for a total of six years and had amassed a bit of a reputation as a star. He was six foot three with peach-and-gold skin and dark brown hair. A booming, gravelly voice made it even harder to not pay attention to him. He was two years younger than Kartik. To Kartik's chagrin, Jim's most recent client in New York was the same automobile company that he was working with. His boss had asked the American visitor to look over their India entry case as a quick favour.

'You need to know that Ted is a numbers guy,' Jim declared. 'Your models have to be shipshape. The slides, your deck, those are less important.'

Ted? Who the fuck was Ted? Kartik was at a loss for a moment. Ah, Edward Wilson, his client, the senior vice-president of international expansion. Americans and their mapped nicknames made little sense to him: Jim for James, Ted for Edward, Peggy for Margaret and the most ridiculous, Dick for Richard.

Jim continued, 'I took a look. Your deck is fine, the analysis looks alright too, but I would have structured the presentation differently.' He explained that Ted preferred direct communication. So he would have started with the size of the opportunity and left some of the market context for the appendix. Kartik himself had tried to push the presentation in that very direction several times but had failed to convince Raghu. This time, he noted, Raghu listened intently.

'In fact, why don't I take a stab at coming up with a narrative for your next check-in? It's in two weeks, you said?'

'I appreciate the offer, Jim, but surely you have a lot on your plate.' On Raghu's face, a half-smile. *I see why everybody says you are a star.*

Kartik interrupted before Jim could answer. 'I have already prepared a storyboard for the next presentation. Why don't we discuss—'

'I am sure you do,' Jim said curtly before turning to Raghu again. 'It'll only take me an evening. It's alright if you end up using none of it.' He looked at his watch. 'If you don't mind staying a little longer, I have some ideas we can thrash out right now.'

Kartik had an inexplicable urge to hiss. His chest was clotted with rage. He did not want to test the bounds of his restraint, so he offered to call room service for coffee. The phone was in another room. As he picked up the receiver, it struck him that he was not a fucking secretary, it was not his fucking job to order coffee. He put the phone down and decided to walk to a different room where he could tell an *actual* secretary to make the call instead. He had earned that right, that privilege. It was the privilege you earned from doing as you were told for thirty years. This privilege, he had thought, was the finish line of a race. You started with different handicaps but you ran as fast as you could and once the line was crossed, you were done. You had made it, you belonged to the club. But no, it turned out that privilege was a ladder, no matter what you achieved, there would be others above you making you feel small.

Like these white men with their foreign MBAs.

Did Raghu not know that the colleges that Kartik had been to were far harder to get into than any of the Ivy League universities? The acceptance rate at American universities was over 10 per cent: they practically admitted *anybody* who applied. He, on the other hand, had taken some of the most competitive entrance exams in the world and had excelled. He was the crème de la crème of India. Raghu knew nothing, he was a foreigner in his own country. A brown-skinned Jim Arnett. Raghu was a fool not to treat Kartik like the treasure that he was.

His assistant waved at him before he could ask her to call

room service. There's a call for you, she said, and handed him the phone.

'Hello?'

'Kartik.' It was Pinkesh.

'How did you get my number?'

'You know what I do for a living, right? I have been trying to call you for days. Are you never in the office?'

Kartik asked the assistant if he could have a minute alone. When she left, he cupped the receiver and whispered, 'This is not a good time. Why have you called?'

'I want to meet my old friend, is that a crime?'

'*Friend?* What are you smoking?'

'What else were we then?' He chuckled before switching to a more measured tone. 'I am sorry about the dreadful things I said to you in college. Happy? We were kids, yaar, just let it go. I need to meet you, it's important.'

'I don't want to see you.'

'I already apologised, didn't I? Believe me, you will be glad I called.'

'I don't give a fuck.'

'Please, Two-Piece. I said sorry. Don't be so heartless.'

Kartik wished he had learnt to say no as a child, it was too late to pick up new habits. He agreed to meet Pinkesh at his office the next afternoon. And since he had the phone in hand anyway, he decided to call room service and place the order for coffee himself.

Pinkesh's office was on the third floor of an old building in Ballard Estate. When Kartik arrived, he was buying cigarettes at the paanwala around the corner. They walked into the building together. The wooden staircase inside was dark and damp, and smelled of mould and cat piss. There were columns of red splatter on the walls as far as he could see. The sight

of so much red made him uneasy even though he knew they
were only paan stains.

'Let's take the lift, please?'

In the small lift, he stood as far from Pinkesh as he could,
pressing his back against a slightly sticky wall. Suddenly, a hand
darted across his face. 'Boo!'

'What the fuck?'

'I won't bite, you know? Why are you acting strange—
standing that far?'

Kartik didn't say anything till they got out of the elevator.
Pinkesh shared an office with a travel agency. There were also
two stockbrokers, a marketing agency and an environmental
NGO whose offices were on the same floor, all busy at work.
They filled the corridor with a stream of mismatched jargon.
Pinkesh locked the door behind them. Technically, his office
was just a wooden booth in a corner of the travel agency. The
only furniture in it were a large desk, a few chairs and a steel
file cabinet. A noisy wall fan surveyed the room from wall
to wall, making the loose papers on his desk flutter violently
every ten seconds. Pinkesh was using as a paperweight a desk
calendar issued by the neighbouring NGO: it had children's
drawings of trees and wildlife.

'This is my humble office. What will you have—tea, coffee,
or me? Oho, don't look so distressed, I was joking. There's no
canteen in the building, so no tea or coffee.' He winked at Kartik.

'What did you want to talk about?'

'Cutting to the chase, I see.'

'I have to get back to work.'

'Fine. I know you are a big man now, that is why I wanted
to meet.'

'I am not a big man,' Kartik rejoined, fear roiling in his chest.

'You work for an MNC with its office in a five-star and

claim you are not? Anyway, I don't want anything from you. But others might—then you will find my services useful.'

'What do you mean?'

'This city is not very safe for people like us, you have no idea how many blackmail and extortion rings there are these days.' He played with a second paperweight, a glass orb with specks of red and yellow. It looked heavy, capable of smashing a skull. 'Or maybe you already do.'

'What do you mean by "people like us"?'

Pinkesh raised an eyebrow and smirked. 'People in this *line*, as they say. Men who love men. Men who fuck men.'

Startled, Kartik stood up. 'What are you talking about?'

'Don't worry, the fan guarantees privacy,' he said, reading the alarm on Kartik's face. 'And I said, people like us, didn't I? Not people like you.'

'Really? I thought you were a *normal hot-blooded man*. And those days are behind me. I am getting married in four months.' He paused before he added, 'To a woman.'

'Who else would you marry? A tree?' Pinkesh burst out laughing, visibly pleased with his own joke. 'Welcome to the club. You thought you were the only one?'

'You too—?' he began to ask before he shut up.

'No, but many of my clients are married.'

'What do you do for these clients of yours?'

'I offer the usual detective services, spy on a cheating spouse, make sure your new tenant has the bank balance to pay rent, et cetera, et cetera. Bread and butter stuff. But I reckon what you will find more interesting is my work with our community. We are easy prey, you know. You pick up a guy at the railway station and the next thing you know, there's a knife at your throat. Or you find photos of your encounter in the mail. If you are lucky, you pay up once. We have had to deal with some amount of blackmail for decades, but now there are entire rackets. You will be squeezed for months. And not in a good way.' Kartik cringed. 'Whom will you go to? The police? Of course not. Matters of the street need to be settled in the street.'

'And how do you settle these matters of the street?'

As Pinkesh was about to speak, the phone rang. 'Good morning, Firoz bhai, how are you?' *One minute,* Pinkesh gestured to Kartik. 'You got my message yesterday? Yes? Good, good. Please send it home, I'll arrange the payment tomorrow, okay? Thank you so much! Khuda hafiz.'

'What was I saying? Yes, about blackmail—I have people in my networks who can make the problem go away and I make this introduction for a small fee. The actual intervention happens without my involvement. I am only the middle man,' he said with his hands in the air. His hands were clean of any violence, he meant to convey. Kartik saw the cross-stitched lines on his pale palms, rivers and tributaries, the long love lines he had briefly examined so lovingly.

'Just now, on the phone—was that one of those people?'

'Who—Firoz bhai? Just because he has a Muslim name and I called him bhai? That was my father's chemist, you fucker.'

The morning after their tryst by the lake, Kartik awoke when Pinkesh was still fast asleep. He held his face close to his friend's to watch him as he slept, mouth half-open, his nose and eyelids twitching, gently protesting his morning dreams. His breathing was pinched into a soft snore, a faint sour smell on his breath. When Kartik leaned forward to kiss him, Pinkesh woke up. He looked around the room in confusion before he remembered where he was. He looked at his watch, which he had worn to bed.

'Shit, our quiz starts in forty minutes.'

He scrambled to find his clothes, a mirror, then some toothpaste and soap, babbling about something or the other the whole time: where was the bathroom, would there be a queue, was it clean, was he even allowed to be there, were guests permitted to spend the night? Half asking, half thinking aloud. Kartik found his panic amusing. Nobody in his wing woke up more than fifteen minutes before the first lecture. With half an hour, one could even take a shower, but bathing in the morning was unheard of in the school year.

They both made it past the elimination rounds. At the finals, questions and answers flew about furiously. *How many limbs does a squid have? What was the name of the spaceship in the 1979 film* Alien? *What kind of a musical instrument is a piccolo?* The better the mood Kartik was in, the easier the quiz questions usually felt; that day, he was floating. Points stacked up, in his square and Pinkesh's. At the end of the last round, their scores were tied. It was a first, a crack of hope. The tie-breaker, the quizmaster announced, would be settled with a buzzer. Kartik groaned. Pinkesh was the champion of buzzer rounds, his fingers moved faster than sound. It was a lost cause, he knew, but he did not mind. Today of all days he would not mind losing to Pinkesh. And today of all days, a victory over him would be sweetest. He kept a finger on the buzzer. Oh, it's an easy one, said the quizmaster when he looked at his card.

The question arrived like a gunshot: 'This child of the Roman god Mercury was born with both male and female sex organs.'

Both buzzers rang before the words were fully spoken. Two bells piercing the brief silence between question and answer. When Kartik saw the red light at his table, he thought he was dreaming so he looked towards the table where Pinkesh sat, his team's bulb unlit. *No, it couldn't be.* The quizmaster looked at him and blinked rapidly, equally surprised that somebody had faster fingers than Pinkesh.

'It's Hermaphroditus,' said Kartik, his heart thumping as wildly as it had the previous night.

The quizmaster said nothing, looking around the room for effect. 'And it is Hermaphroditus, indeed—we have a winner!'

The teams shook hands and congratulated each other but Pinkesh had already left. Kartik looked for him and saw that he and his two teammates were sitting on the steps outside the auditorium. He made his way towards them.

Pinkesh waved at him. 'What a *sixer* of a performance today, Two-Piece! Chhakka, total chhakka.'

Titters ensued.

Kartik's teammate made a face and said, 'Very funny. Congratulations on coming *second*.'

'Thank you, but the question still remains: how did our friend know the answer so fast? I guess it takes one to know one.'

Kartik felt a tightness in his chest. This was how these boys spoke, this was how he had spoken to this very group in the past, the ribbing, the mocking, but those words had been harmless, performed for laughs. What Pinkesh said sounded barbed, as if he meant to draw blood.

He knew better than to bite, but he could not help it. 'If it takes one to know one, what did you ring the buzzer for?'

'Chaayla, look how upset Two-Piece is.'

'Looks to me like you are upset. You are a sore loser, you know?'

Kartik stormed off, his footsteps echoing through the corridor, a few decibels louder than the round of laughter in the background.

Kartik confronted Pinkesh when they were alone.

'Why did you do that? You were horrible to me.'

'Grow a thicker skin, dude. I was just teasing.'

Kartik looked around. A group of students sat a short distance away, out of earshot, but he dropped his voice anyway. 'I would have been happy for you had you won.'

'What is wrong with you? You are a homo or what?'

'Should I refresh your memory as to what transpired yesterday?'

'Don't get any ideas, Two-Piece. A mouth on my cock is a mouth on my cock. What does it matter if it's a woman's or a man's?'

Kartik winced. The Hindi word Pinkesh used, lund, was coarse to his ears. 'And later at night? In my room?'

'It was dark, I couldn't see a thing. How do I care whose body I was rubbing against? It's all the same when you are horny. I hope you remember I never touched your cock, but you seemed quite eager to touch mine.'

'So that's what you are going with?'

'It was just some masti, yaar. I am a normal hot-blooded man, not a homo, okay?'

Kartik grabbed his wrist. 'Why are you saying all this?'

Pinkesh pulled his hand away with a sharp jerk. He raised his voice when he said, 'Listen, Kartik, your fuck-all college has no girls, so your wiring has got mixed up. Please spare me.'

The students looked in their direction. Pinkesh took a large step back—the hand that he had pulled away he kept suspended above his head—as if his whole being found Kartik repulsive.

Kartik dropped out of the quiz team till Pinkesh graduated, so he would not have to see him again. He told his team he was not happy with his first semester results, he had stood second in his class. That had earned him a new nickname: Muggoo, the mugger-upper.

For nearly eleven years their paths had not crossed. But he had met the likes of him many times over the years and learnt to avoid them too, these macho men, hot-blooded bullies who claimed a mouth was a mouth, a hole was a hole, reducing you to your parts. In the best case, that is. They might also belittle you, blackmail you, even extort sex for others in the worst. The latter he knew only from cautionary tales, and now Pinkesh had given weight to this fear. Of course, he would have no further opportunity to learn first-hand, he reminded himself.

Never again, he had already said to himself before. With less than total success.

The first time he made that promise was after Pinkesh. Never again. The humiliation, the rage simmered in him for months, purging desire. But desire is resilient. It returned, like a virus, demanded attention. He found release in the gent's toilet at Andheri station. Sufficiently far from home and college, he calculated. On a Friday evening in late March, he boarded bus number 422 from Powai towards Andheri. Through Chandivali and Marol and Chakala, he trembled in the belly of the bus, pressed by flesh on all sides, sour metal on his palms. A rising ache in his groin from the lick of anticipation. Just before Gokhale bridge he got off: he knew a shortcut to the eastern end of the railway station. Sparks rose from a welder's shop at the mouth of Teli Gali. Its neighbours were mechanics, carpenters, metal-workers. Kartik heard a stampede of hammer-hooves under the drone of electric drills. He crisscrossed through a warren of huts and small homes. Children peered at him from behind grimy curtains, flashing glimpses of life in the kholis: steel, plastic, cloth and skin. The shortcut deposited him across the street from the ticket counter. Another short walk—he only had to follow his nose—took him to the men's toilet he had been told about.

He entered to see two men masturbating each other and an audience of three around them. When they saw him, they stopped. He didn't flinch, so one of the performers looked him in the eye and raised his chin. *Aap bhi? You too?* When Kartik nodded, they resumed the performance. He returned the next two weekends. The third time, he let someone touch him. It was a sultry night, the air thick with expectation and the smell of waste. He took deep breaths, he wanted the obliterating stink to remind him of what he was doing, of where he was. When it was over, he was sticky with shame. He stepped out of the restroom and went into a corner store to buy soap and two bottles of water. He washed his face, his neck, and then his hands and his arms as far up as his shirt sleeves would roll up. He emptied the second bottle on his head and boarded a Harbour Line train to go home to his family. Passengers stared at the well-dressed young man whose head and clothes were drenched. He had gone too far, he told himself, never again. But beyond every vow of never again lay the promise of a warm, hard, pulsing body. He broke the resolution the week after. And then again, and again. He needed soap and water each time but in smaller measures every passing week. Slowly, the shame evaporated. Only a thin patina of guilt remained.

But this time, he meant it. Never again.

22

AS EVENING FELL, SKY AND earth were thrown into frenzy. Sheets of birds billowed overhead; more squawking masses rose like steam from treetops to join them. Traffic spilled from the main roads to the narrow lanes where eternally frustrated drivers had to now contend with hawkers and shoppers. There were puddles of murky rainwater everywhere and unwary pedestrians were splashed. People cursed a lot. The climbing moon dawdled above the roofs of buildings.

And on the roof of Asha Nivas, concealed by the rust-covered water tank, Ira and Kartik. His fingers were laced with hers, his other hand in her hair, hers on his hip. Her mind was elsewhere: she was looking at the moon, at the sprinkling of stars, everywhere but him.

Hey, he said.

One moment she was wearing a faraway, forlorn look and the next, she snapped to attention. Ira appeared to alternate between anxious distraction and maniacal attentiveness that evening. He asked her if she was thinking about work and at once her lips were on his neck.

Does it look like I am thinking about work, she said.

She leaned into him and her words grew muffled: she was speaking into his skin. He felt the thrum of her laugh in his collarbone. They had been engaged for over a month but these trysts had not stopped feeling weird.

They met here several times a week. They held hands, mashed mouths, indulged in feverish necking. Feverish, though, felt like the wrong adjective, the wrong ailment; the words common and cold were better suited. He was trying to make it work. Each time they were together, Kartik tried to imagine that he was a teenage boy again, relearning the dictionary of desire. What did lips feel like? Cool, soft. How did tongues taste? No longer reptilian or graceless like in *actual* teenage kisses. Asses were asses, topographical marvels, but breasts were trickier territory. What was the big deal about them anyway? He had discovered, however, a more tortuous route to arousal:

thinking about what they did to other men, women's breasts. Perhaps that was the problem, too much analysis. He longed to feel the heat of desire but his penis remained reluctant even as her hand strayed dangerously close to his crotch.

She deserved better. Ira was his friend, she truly deserved better. He resolved to love her and respect her and support her more than any husband in the history of marriage to make up for his shortfall of passion. His shortfall of passion for *her*. Otherwise he had always been an explorer, had freely given in to the wanderlust of his eyes and his hands and his mouth, propelled by a curiosity for pleasure, for sin.

'Your ring. Where's your ring?' he said suddenly, pulling his mouth away from hers. He held up her left hand, their fingers were still knitted together. He was glad for the small diversion, a ruse that allowed him to look through her supplicant caresses.

'Oh, here. Wrong hand.' Ira appeared flustered at the interruption. He wondered if she might have been enjoying what was happening moments before. Was that the reason for her agitated appearance? 'I must have moved it accidentally.'

'As long as it's on one of your hands.'

Again, her expressions changed rapidly as if she were browsing through a catalogue to find a look she liked. She stopped at mischief.

'As long as it's on one of my hands. I see,' she repeated. 'But where would you like my hands to be?' She dragged her hands up his thighs.

'Whoa, stop. Not here, not here.' He glanced at the door and back at her. 'Sorry,' he added with a sheepish, nervous smile. Thirty years of general skittishness made this a convincing act.

'Oho, my scholar,' she said as she mussed his hair. He thought she looked equally relieved.

He had loved Ira like a little sister all through childhood. She was a constant appendage to his person in most of his memories, a thread stitched into the cloth of his early years. Like the love between siblings, it was an unconditional affection tinged with exasperation.

He had first climbed the water tank on the terrace at her insistence. It was hard to spot the sign under the rust now, but one side had a skull-and-crossbones sign painted on it, which to Kartik had said clearly: stay away. Only to Kartik, not Ira. How old had she been then—five, six?

'It's not like you'll be able to see anything new from up there,' he had said, trying to reason with her. 'And it's almost dinnertime, let's go home.'

'I want to try it just once.'

'Do you see the skull, stupid? It's the sign for "Danger". It means you can't climb up.'

'It only means that you are scared. I am not.'

He bristled at the insult and grabbed her by the shoulders to push her towards the tank. 'Fine, go.'

Ira put her hands on the ladder hanging off one side. Kartik was sure she would change her mind. The ladder teetered even at a child's touch; climbing it was madness. Ira put one foot up. Then another.

'Stop! If you are going to do it anyway, I should hold the ladder. I don't want you to fall.'

The ladder rocked with every step. Kartik tightened his grip and pressed it down, and asked Ira to go slower. She scampered up. Under her frock, she wore yellow panties with small pink flowers. He looked away. The smell of metal filled his nose, it would remain on his hands till he washed them before dinner. When she reached the last step, her small figure disappeared from view as she ran across the top of the tank, her footsteps jangling across the terrace. He asked her to be quiet. Ira reappeared, cast in a purple light. Above her the setting sun was pressed between clouds like a dried flower.

'Kartik dada, come up.'

'I don't want to. And you come down. Now!'

'It feels like an earthquake, see?' She jumped up and down a few times.

'The sun has almost set. Our mothers will come looking for us. Hurry up.'

He told himself, again, that the climb was not worth it. Why take the risk of getting caught, of flouting the warning painted on the side—and for what reward, it was only a water tank. Why did the silly girl think it was thrilling? He put a hand on the side of the tank and felt its metallic pulse, the cool throb of the water inside. What would it be like to take the ten or twelve steps to the top, he wondered. With his longer legs he might be able to skip a few rungs. But before he could peel his desire fully, Ira was on her way down.

'Dada, you should have come up. Go now, I'll wait.'

'Are you deaf? I don't want to go up the stupid tank.'

'If you are scared that the ladder will fall, I'll hold it for you.'

'You? You'll hold it up?' He scoffed. 'Go home or you'll get two slaps from your mother.'

'Okay, bye,' she said, hurt, and skipped down the stairs without waiting for him.

He was dismayed at the absence of gratitude. Not one thank you she had offered him. Had she fallen or injured herself, or if somebody had walked in on them, it would have been his fault. He was the older child, the responsible one, her safety net and insurance. He resented her recklessness that made her blind to this, that made her blind to all care, let her do as she pleased. Then quietly, with an eye on the door, he climbed the ladder to see what the top of the tank was like, only half aware at the time that he wouldn't have done this were it not for Ira.

The first time he came to realise how much she meant to

him was after he shoved her in front of their friends and she stopped talking to him. In the beginning, he experienced her absence as a sidekick-shaped hole in his life. His other friends were louts: there was nobody but Ira he could play games like teacher–teacher with, where he gave her math questions to solve or let her read aloud from his story books so he could correct her pronunciation. No one else with whom he could read side-by-side, whom he could interrupt to discuss something interesting he had just learnt, like the size of the universe, or how bombs worked, or why wounds healed. He missed her but not too much. He was a lizard with its tail cut off, disoriented but unhurt.

What he longed for was order and continuity. It was a year of tumult. As hard as he tried, he found that he could not keep his mind from wandering to the open-air gym that stood opposite the children's park his friends often went to. All this small square of land contained was a rack of iron weights and about a dozen wooden clubs, all arranged in order of increasing size like a poorly composed group photograph. Every evening, a posse of young bodybuilders put on a limber display at the barebones gymnasium. They swung clubs around their heads, curled dumbbells the size of their heads, twisted their shiny torsos this way and that. Bands of muscle were already hardening on their bodies—lightly oiled with sweat, compact and bronzed, charged with static electricity. A tingling across the street, where the children of Asha Nivas conducted their evening games.

When his classmates drooled over a cabaret dancer with her ass-skimming feathered skirt, he found his heart marching to a different beat: the tall, dark hero with his two left feet. And how his insides burned if the new boy in his class, a raffish older student who had been held back in class six for two years, smiled at a girl. Kartik was frightened and perplexed, unable to pin down the import of what he felt. Troubled by these fits of confusing jealousy, he apologised to Ira and he was less alone once again.

They remained close friends even though one part of his life remained hidden from her. Some matters couldn't be discussed even with the closest of friends. Only books, gossip and guesswork could help. When Ira confessed her love to him, he wondered if he had led her on, somehow suggested to her that her infatuation was reciprocated. Perhaps other teenage boys comported themselves differently. He wished he had pulled away from her sooner.

When he returned to Mumbai, his mother pushed him towards her. At first, it had felt like an annoying but harmless mission. The day after the incident with the Desais, he had walked in on his parents discussing the matter of rallying the neighbours. He was about to sneak out for a cigarette but when his mother patted the chair next to her, he joined them. They were trying to make sense of Shankar Kamat's behaviour. Their families were close, they knew that the Kamats could do with a financial leg-up. Why then did he refuse to join their side? Perhaps he was turning senile, they speculated.

'Ira called me this afternoon to tell me she spoke to the landlord. She told him what he did was illegal, that we will not tolerate such antics.'

'What did he say?' asked Kartik in English. He was still getting used to speaking Konkani again, his tongue could slip into English without warning.

'Of course he denied,' his mother replied, also in English.

'But look, Ira promised she'll speak to the landlord, she called him the very next day,' said his father with a touch of admiration in his voice. 'That's rare in this generation.'

'Very efficient girl. I wonder where she gets that from,' his mother added cattily. 'Kamat and Shobha? No chance.'

'Sometimes the apple falls far from the tree.'

Kartik wondered if they were throwing daggers at him. Suddenly his mother turned to him.

'Kartik, you must ask Ira why Kamat won't move.'

'Me? But I haven't spoken to Ira in years.'

'Didn't she come up to you after yesterday's meeting? You two were so close once.'

'That was in school. I can't just go and ask her about her father.'

'Ask her about other things first.'

'Like what?'

He found his parents staring at him. They both looked aghast.

'Have you forgotten how to talk to people? Do I need to make a list of topics for you?'

His father scratched his chin. 'Let's see. She won an award last year for a corruption story. Do you remember what it was about, Kusum?'

'It was something big, no? Who can keep track of all the scams these days. But yes, you can talk to her about the award.'

'Her office is in Nariman Point too. Ask her which train she takes to work.'

'Our son won't take the train. He'll only travel by taxi,' his mother said. 'Or are you going to buy a car, my darling?' She pinched his cheek and gurgled at him.

'Yes, yes, but as a topic of conversation, trains are gold. You can't bring up trains or buses with a Mumbaikar and run out of words.'

'I have never seen Ira run out of words on any subject. And look at our boy here—he hasn't gone after his father or his mother.'

Kartik wanted to tell his parents that his remark was rhetorical. He did not need a list of topics to construct small talk around. He was, in fact, very good at it; he just did not enjoy it very much.

To his surprise, when he ran into Ira some days later, he learnt that it was still easy to talk to her. The film of childhood had lain unexposed for years, there was a long roll of memories to develop. Memories of a fonder time, a simpler time. Asking a question or two about her father was no trouble at all. It also helped that Ira was curious without being intrusive or pushy. She was comfortable with his silences and did not always rush to fill them with banalities. This made their conversations feel like a cosy space that he could step into little by little.

These warm pockets of comfort, what more could he ask for from marriage?

The idea came from his mother but it was his decision to marry her. He did not want a lifetime of skulking and stolen pleasures. The merry-go-round would one day get tiresome, in some ways it already had. He was good at seeing the ripples running forward from each action: pleasure, he knew, was deferred pain. His most serious lover, a French expat, had lived in India for a year and two months and they had spent ten of those months together. When it was time, he left without fanfare and Kartik was left behind to pick up the bill. Run away with me, he had foolishly hoped Damien would say. Ten months of bliss but how many of deferred pain? He was still counting. *Run away with me.* And then a thought occurred: perhaps Damien had been hoping that Kartik would ask him to stay back. The last time he cooked coq au vin for Kartik, their final coupling, through the long lingering goodbye kiss, one thought. *Ask me to stay.* In this possibility Kartik found equal parts comfort and torment.

Ira switched her engagement ring to the correct hand. Happy, she asked him. In present company, always, he replied. Soon it was time to leave. The sky was turning to slate, the temple bells had died down. They walked towards the staircase, holding hands, when they ran into Vasant Naik on the landing outside the terrace. Their plump childhood friend was now properly paunchy, as if he had borne his two children himself. Domestic bliss settles in the belly, Kartik had heard a relative tell his father. He was glad this bliss would elude him.

'Getting to know each other?' Vasant said to the couple with a slow, suggestive bob of the head. He winked at Kartik when Ira wasn't looking.

'I'll see you tomorrow,' she said before they parted at her doorstep.

'Tomorrow? Did we make plans?'

'It's Sunday, baba.'

'So?'

'Tea at your place?'

The Kinis insisted that Ira come over every Sunday evening. His parents, too, got to see him only on weekends. They wanted the youngsters to spend time together but did not want their son to spend too much time away from home either.

'Right. *Chai pe bulaaya hai,*' he attempted to croon, making Ira laugh. He continued to hum the song under his breath as he walked down another flight of stairs. He could hear Ira sing the first two lines to herself, aloud, while she waited for someone to answer the doorbell. She was a far worse singer than he was.

Opposites attract, most people had said of their friendship and left it at that. And what had she thought of him, he wanted to ask her. From the time he stood over her, rocking her cradle, she had grown up in his shadow. She must have been told that Kartik had spoken his first word at eight months, his first sentence at one year, he could count to ten and recite the alphabet by two, and read and write before he turned five. Even two years were enough for memory to start turning to myth, and Ira might have spent her childhood being compared not to Kartik but to an embroidered prodigy. Perhaps she had been able to see this entity as separate from her flesh-and-blood friend. The specific virtues of his that the adults extolled probably held little appeal for her—good marks, good behaviour, good prospects—and yet he was surprised that she harboured no resentment against him. He would not have brooked any comparisons with a friend.

He envied Ira. There was a clarity, a certainty of purpose behind everything she said and did; it could only come from knowing your place in the world. Take away his degrees, his mark sheets and medals, take away the jobs he'd held along with the decades of accolades, take away his sexuality too for good measure, and he was left with no conception of who he was.

At the same time, it was entirely possible that Ira believed that he was a sorted man. She might even see herself as the confused one, the one in tatters. When you looked at yourself, you saw a tangle of fiction and feeling. You only began to make sense under the lingering gaze of another.

23

KARTIK'S SUNDAY SIESTA WAS INTERRUPTED by a doorbell. Gautam Doshi, his neighbour from upstairs, had arrived with a stack of pamphlets in hand. Neighbours remembered Gattu, now twenty, as the chubby, friendly baby that everybody had pampered. Most of that description still applied. In spite of the squarely middle-class fortunes of his family, nothing less than Lee jeans lined his muffin top, and the best of Tantra's witticisms were stretched to distortion across his chest. Even in getting no exercise, he made sure that only Nike and Adidas workout gear, purchased at the factory outlets in Parel at half-price, lay unused. And it was a Timex timepiece whose exhortations he ignored each morning, missing at least one or two lectures at college. His parents were finally running out of patience. Tired of being called a duffer and a wastrel after years of being indulged, Gattu had joined a social service organisation to hone his leadership skills. And here he was, in the Kini home, raising funds for a blood donation camp.

When he revealed the name of the organisation, Hindu Youth for National Advancement, Kartik was worried but decided not to judge too soon. Gattu explained that his organisation was very new, so they had to fund their camp through donations. But more important than the fifty or hundred rupees they might collect from a donor was the chance to sit across from a community member and talk about their mission.

'Most blood donation camps in college are organised by funded Christian groups like YMCA, so we thought, why should we Hindus be left behind, we are not useless, you know? We don't need anybody else to help us.'

'Who called you useless, Gattu? How dare they!'

He made an exasperated face. 'Kartik bhaiyya, you are so *jokey*. But you don't know what they say about us behind our backs. *What, men, these Hindus, men, in their most holy book, brothers kill their own brothers. Such a rubbish religion it is, no wonder that they don't help each other.*'

Kartik burst out laughing. 'Come on, Gattu, nobody says that.'

The mocking shut him up. Kartik felt bad for the kid and passed him a plate of biscuits. 'Tell us more about your organisation.'

'Hindu Youth for National Advancement wants to empower young, urban Hindus to restore the glory of our great motherland through selfless service—'

'Wait a minute. I just realised that the name of your association abbreviates to HYNA. Not an animal you want to associate yourself with, is it? Famous for its cowardice.'

'No, certainly not,' he mumbled.

Kini Senior came to the boy's rescue. 'That's enough, Kartik. Nobody calls YMCA Imca, do they? Why will they call these people hyena?'

'Thank you, Uncle, good point,' he said. 'Uncle, you know who the biggest enemies of Hindus are?'

Ashok Kini smiled, he had an answer. He had many answers.

'Hindus only. We, ourselves,' Gattu slapped his chest, 'are our biggest enemies.'

'Oh, trick question,' said Kartik.

'No, Bhaiyya, it is true. We care more about caste and status than about each other.'

'Hmm, that I agree with.'

Armed with this scrap of approval from someone who had only challenged him so far, Gattu grew strident, as if he were at a college debate. 'I have many examples. Did we stand up for our Kashmiri Pandit brothers? Did we help our poor tribal brothers before they were tempted away by Christian missionaries? We are too divided to be a true force and that is why we are seen as weak.'

'Very true, Gattu,' Ashok Kini said. 'But *who* sees us as weak? *Who* has exploited this weakness? Have you heard of the 5M Axis?'

Kartik groaned inwardly.

'No, Uncle.'

'The 5M Axis is the Axis of Evil in India: Marxist, Mohammedan, Missionary, Macaulay and,' he hesitated, stole a glance at Kartik before he said, 'the Media. All these forces remain ever-ready to ridicule us, to weaken us and break us apart.'

Kartik thanked his stars that Ira had not dropped in early. His father continued to tell Gattu about his theories, and even offered to write down the names of some websites he could visit for a more thorough discussion.

'Uncle, where will I surf the internet? Cyber cafes charge a hundred rupees an hour. We don't have a computer at home, my father thinks it's a waste of money. Not all fathers are cool like you. You are so *young at heart*!'

This was his father's favourite genus of compliments. He smiled as he handed Gattu Rs 250. The student beamed broadly, his calculation had paid off.

'Make us proud, Gattu. Self-reliance is the first step to self-respect. Give your blood, your all to the country! Restore the glory of our motherland!'

Restore the glory of the motherland. Just that morning an op-ed along those lines had caught his eye. Perhaps his father had read it too. The writer of the article had been a lawyer in another life and appeared to be angling for a prominent role in the government if a right-wing coalition came back to power. Hindi had one word, kal, for yesterday and tomorrow. Not only was the path to the future through the past, the columnist wrote, the past was the future. She claimed that, for fifty years, the party in power had not allowed Indians the right to be proud of their past (huh what, he had thought), but systematically destroying and denying the past did not mean a clean slate. Take the name Mumbai for instance. Liberals wrote opinion pieces every month on what the city lost in going from Bombay to Mumbai (this was true, he had to concede). For these people, Mumbai was the land where forces of chauvinism and nativism were winning over the cosmopolitanism and uneven modernity that Bombay stood for. They acted as if the name Mumbai was pulled out of nowhere, as if the city had never been occupied or colonised and had been called Bombay since the beginning of time. This hubris, this ignorance, is what the right wing was seeking to counter, the columnist argued, and replace with national pride and self-awareness. Kartik did not particularly care for politics but had read the piece twice so he could discuss it with Ira later. See, he was making an effort.

After Gattu left, Kartik's mother began to set the table for tea. She asked Kartik to climb on a stool and take out the nice tea set that was stowed above the cupboard. The box was covered with a film of dust: the set had not been used in years. His mother asked him to wipe each cup and saucer as a precaution.

'What is wrong with you, Kusum? Ira will be here any moment. Don't make him do all this in front of his wife-to-be. This is not a man's work.'

'Oh hello, those days are gone. Husbands can't get away with not knowing how to boil an egg anymore.'

Ashok Kini clicked his tongue and guffawed. 'Stand up to your mother, Kartik. Before you know it, you'll also be called a joru ka gulaam like your father.'

Any man who did not keep his wife under his thumb was called a joru ka gulaam, thought Kartik, a slave to his wife. It was true that his mother was assertive and opinionated, and his father was admittedly devoted to her, but he was no blind devotee, no slave. It was his mother who had forsaken her own name, who did not even say the name of the husband whose name she had taken. It was she who would never retire from her indentured job as a housewife. So who was the real gulaam? This line of thinking would please Ira, he thought, giving himself a pat on the back. Immediately a sharp voice in his head pointed out that he was incapable of having a single thought without also considering whom it might please.

When Ira arrived, Kartik was afraid that his father would bring up Gattu's visit. Mercifully he began to tell her about his latest conversation with their landlord; this was not a topic from which Ira would allow digressions. A builder had sent the landlord an interesting proposal for the future of Asha Nivas. If the driveway could be removed and the setback between the base of the building and the compound wall trimmed, an eight-storey building could be erected in its place.

'Even Sundar Sadan—Belle View—has only six floors,' Ira pointed out to her future in-laws. 'We'll cut off the light for both the buildings next to us.'

'Sunlight comes from all sides. At worst, we will block only one side, no?' his mother said, nudging Ira towards the tray with tea and snacks. She had poured the tea next to the stove itself and had wiped away any stray beads that might have landed on the lip of a teacup or the rim of a saucer. The aluminium pot with its blackened bottom and the bright green plastic strainer would have been unsightly at the dining table.

'But it's a big change, Kusum maushi.'

'What nonsense, Ira,' said his father, less patiently. 'It's only eight floors. Look at New York, Hong Kong, Singapore. They have forty- and fifty-storey buildings. You think they live without sunlight? Like bats? Anyway, what would you pick, Ira—sunlight for your neighbours or a flat for your family?'

'It's not only about our immediate neighbours. What will happen to Matunga if it becomes a collection of tall buildings cramped next to each other?'

Kartik had cultivated a habit of nodding vaguely when Ira and his parents disagreed. He was truly a neutral party. He had no opinion about this redevelopment business. All he wanted was a large, well-located, elegant home. It did not matter to him how many floors lay above or below it.

'Where else will people live? The next building to come up will be even taller. This is progress—six becomes eight becomes ten becomes twenty.'

'Six might become even sixty, but if the streets, buses, trains, parks all remain the same, how is that progress?'

'That will change too. All in due time. One has to start somewhere. Once you become a Kini, you'll have to learn to be more optimistic. What do you say, Kartik?' he said as he slapped his son's back. 'Haven't you started training the future Mrs Kini yet?'

Kartik flashed his father a small uncomfortable smile. He looked at Ira and shook his head slightly and sighed. She knitted her brows into a question. Ira had told him that she was not going to change her name after marriage. She hadn't asked for his opinion, or his permission, she had informed him of her decision; he, in turn, had not informed his parents.

'It's up to you, of course,' Kartik had said to her, 'but indulge me for a moment. What's the difference between choosing your father's name and my name? It's a man's name either way.'

'True, it's a man's name either way. It's a choice between my father's name and *your* father's name. Right? In that case I'll stick to mine.'

He had put his hands up and admitted defeat. He knew Ira would not hesitate to repeat this piece of reasoning before his parents.

On a couple of occasions, the conversation about her name being one of them, Kartik had wondered if he had taken on more than he had bargained for by agreeing to marry Ira. He loved her, she was fantastic and, importantly, he liked what this choice of wife said about him. But there were issues that hinted at bigger problems in the future.

There was the Muslim ex-boyfriend. He had seen the hardness in her eyes when she recounted this affair, the stillness in her limbs, as if she were transfixed by this memory. Why reveal such a transgressive relationship, what had she hoped to say about herself and her past? Why bring up such a relationship at all, why not comfort your future partner that your heart would belong to them like it had never belonged to anybody else before? Perhaps it was one of those truths that chopped you and tossed you, changed the recipe of your life. To deny it was to deny a part of yourself. To conceal it was like trying to hide your shadow in the day. Rubbish, he thought, dismissing his own theory, there was no such thing as a truth too big to hide. Or a lie too big to tell. After all, he had made up a great love story of his own for her. He was not one to be left behind in these matters.

Then there was the beef-eating.

A week ago, they had eaten lunch at a small restaurant in Colaba that served continental cuisine. Continental translated to food from all the continents bar the Indian subcontinent, whose flavours still managed to haunt each dish. The hand-painted menu on the wall was different from the printed one in their hands. A third menu, with the weekly specials, was pinned to a board on the wall by the kitchen. The specials had a Soviet ring to them: chicken à la Kiev, beef stroganoff, pork chop Valdostano. By the entrance was a small fridge with their famous desserts. Many kinds of cheesecake, Kahlua mousse, lemon tart, blueberry pie.

'I'll have the chicken lasagna.' Kartik pointed at the paper menu.

One lazaag-naa, the waiter repeated.

'And a pepper steak for me.' A weekly special.

One pepper steek.

'Ira, I think that might be beef.'

'It better be.'

'Oh, you eat beef?' He was taken aback, but quickly recomposed his face.

'And you don't, hmm?'

Kartik shook his head. 'When did you—how did you start?'

'I accidentally had beef vindaloo at a friend's house in college. I loved it but couldn't bear the thought of spending my parents' money on beef, so I waited till I had a job.' She rolled her eyes at her own silliness. 'It is a very tasty meat, you know? I hope you don't mind.'

'Of course not. I am not even sure why I don't eat it, there's no reason not to.' He pushed his straw into his tall glass of fresh lime soda, it popped right back up. He pushed it in again, it popped up again. He had once refused to kiss a man who had eaten beef, flinched from him when he mentioned what he'd had for dinner. But that was a long time ago.

'Remember the Saraswati and fish story?' she said.

The fable was repeated generation after generation, it was a bedtime tale, origin story, legend: in the beginning, the Goud Saraswat brahmins had been strict vegetarians, settled on the banks of the river Saraswati. One year, the river flooded, fields were destroyed and people began to starve. And magically, the goddess of learning, Saraswati, appeared before an elder from the community and said: *Your people are special, the world needs your wisdom, you can't die of starvation. Look around, fish is abundant. I give you permission to eat fish.*

'What all we cook up to justify our follies! Couldn't they say they just wanted to eat fish?' Ira said.

'If only Saraswati had seen a herd of cows first. I might have been sharing your pepper steak today.'

'In that case, I am glad for how it turned out.' She made a swatting motion over her plate. 'Stay away from my food.'

And then she confessed that the story had made her uncomfortable for years, it carried a serrated edge of implication that her conscience snagged on without fail. To think that she had once relished telling this tale, she said, with irony but without self-awareness. *How silly my people are, ha ha.* But their unassailable belief in their own exceptionalism spilled over beyond the silly legend. Was this real-world spillage funny too, and to whom?

He had grown up hearing his grandmother say that their caste was the highest of the high, prime even among brahmins. This is where his father must derive his supreme self-possession from. Like a borewell, he managed to tap into deep reserves of privilege; it had to be the source of his ambition, his resilience. An immutable sense of superiority. A sense of superiority that demanded acquiescence.

He had hoped that marriage with Ira would be a bed of complicity, but the more time he spent with her, the less likely it seemed. He had learnt to process his father's opinions with a dash of irony. He wondered whether Ira would ever be comfortable doing that. Hearing selectively, seeing what you wished to see, waving away the rest. He would have to make sure that Ira did not mingle with his parents, especially his father, any more than she had done before the engagement. It was only his cross to bear. He had made his bed and he would have to lie in it.

And while on the topic of beds, hmm. Hmm. Pinkesh had asked him the day he went to his office, do you think you will be able to sleep with a woman? Of course, he had replied, his voice filled with indignation. But will you be able to satisfy her, are you that good an actor? Shut up, Pinkesh. And even if you can't, you can both have your own side dishes, right? A scowl. Dude, have you even slept with a woman? It's none of your business—but as a matter of fact, yes, I have. (It was a different matter that it had been, to put it kindly, less than fantastic.) Seriously, tell me, what do you know about women? Do you know how they taste? Don't squirm. Do you know how they smell? Women, they smell of the sea. (Lines from a poem. But why had he indulged Pinkesh? Why had he given an answer at all? It happened all the time. He spoke so little, hoarded words like pearls, so sometimes these words spilled out like seed.) A cackle. You are a Bombay boy, Kini, what is the smell of the sea? Be specific. Is it the salty hopefulness of Gateway? The rotting mangroves of Carter Road? Or the fish stink of Sassoon Docks?

24

THE OTHER PROJECT TEAMS WERE out again, it was just his team in the suite. Kartik asked his analysts to work from the living room so he could focus on sketching a new strawman to present at the evening's meeting with Raghu and Jim. A strawman was a short visual outline of a slide deck. Rows of boxes with titles, doodles of charts, the central idea of each slide. Each box would then painstakingly be translated into a full slide by his faithful lackeys, the analysts he had banished to the common room while he sat at the desk in one of the two lavish bedrooms. Privacy was doing nothing for his focus today.

Ira had surprised him early that morning. She had called to ask if he wanted to meet at one of the Udupi restaurants at King's Circle. His mother had already made an omelette for him and he could not gather the courage to refuse it. So he had met her for a second breakfast. At the restaurant, Ira had sprung another surprise on him. Her ex-boyfriend—the *Great Love*—was back in town and was working with her. The bastard even went to Stanford. (It's no Ivy League, he thought.) There was a calculated casualness to this reveal—leaving the newspaper with his op-ed in front of him—that made him more suspicious. This was the kind of shady move he would pull. In front of Ira, he had tried to appear unruffled but as the hours passed, he got more mad at her. She had been working with Kaiz for at least a week. She'd had plenty of opportunities to tell him. They had spent a whole hour on the terrace on Saturday talking nonsense, for god's sake. Had she been thinking about the other man when they were making out? Even the thought was infuriating. All day two theories had sparred in his head. One, that Ira wanted to make him jealous, that this was some kind of a feminine ploy for his heart, and another, more worrying possibility, that the return of this old flame had reminded her of what Kartik had not been able to give her thus far. Might that be the reason, he wondered, she had appeared flustered over the weekend?

When he looked at his sketch sheet ten minutes later, all he had drawn were nine boxes, all empty. His fingers felt restless as his eyes darted to his sleeping computer and back. This meeting was everything, he could not afford to be distracted. A few minutes of browsing might put him at ease, he said to himself. If Ira could spend hours with her ex for work, he reasoned, he should be allowed a brief flirtation for his own peace of mind. It took about a minute of deliberation before he popped in a privacy screen onto his laptop. He was alone in the bedroom of the office suite but locking the door would raise suspicions. He unlocked the computer and typed the address of the chat service. From the list of chatrooms that popped up, he clicked on Mumbai. This was not cheating, he repeated to himself. A few minutes turned into twenty. He had raj_chembur in one window and raj_bandra007 in the other. He decided to ignore matunga_raj_8inch and sexywadalaboy.prem, too afraid of the thought of wanking off with a childhood acquaintance. It made little sense, he knew people all over the city. This was only a relic of his old habits in the physical world. He had never cruised near Matunga or Wadala stations, he had stayed away from King's Circle on Sunday evenings when it turned into a meat market. The city was rife with desirable men, these small embargoes had made no difference. But there would be no more occasion for the wicked thrill of a chance encounter. This was all he was going to allow himself. To replace the currency of glances, thrown and returned, with clicks in a browser.

These filmi pseudonyms were a pestilence though. A glut of usernames with Raj, Rahul and Prem in them; an outsider might believe that this was what most gay men in the city were called. It was the flood of romantic Bollywood films in recent years that was to be blamed—*Dilwale Dulhaniya Le Jaayenge* was the biggest offender—and the limited imaginations of their makers. Raj, Rahul, Prem. No one in these chat rooms called themselves Shah Rukh or Salman, they were more interested in the characters the stars played on screen, in the fantasy of the handsome star-crossed lover.

Chembur Raj had a way with words but Bandra Raj had a webcam. Kartik's work computer did too, but it would be too risky to use it. He let it slip that he had a webcam but was at work. Bandra Raj was impressed, he asked him the make of his webcam, and also where he worked, whether he worked in IT or at an MNC. When Kartik said MNC, he enquired if he had an MBA degree. Kartik sighed, was this turning into an arranged marriage meeting? What would he be asked next—his caste, his salary? Picking up men at railway stations and in parks had been much more efficient but none of those men would be able to afford getting into these chat rooms. He swelled with desire at the memory of some of those men: dry heels cutting into his shins, dark, thin bodies, the ripe smell of cheap polyester.

His fantasies were cut short when Bandra Raj typed that he was turning his webcam on. It was the week before Independence Day and the header of the website carried animations of fluttering tricolour flags. Kartik turned to look at the door again, to make sure it was shut. The video was closely cropped and grainy, he could not pick up any details about the room, only a seated figure who looked much older than Kartik had imagined. Bandra Raj had wrapped a saffron dupatta around his face and had a body that was soft and dimpled like dough. Kartik's eyes moved downwards, only to be disappointed further: his cock was less tumescent than his belly, it stood only at half-mast.

Four. Four out of sixteen: the number of his slides that Raghu picked for the next big client meeting. The rest would all be Jim's. So Jim Arnett was three times as good as he was, three times as worthy. Jim and Kartik had gone head to head, each had presented a mock slide deck, and Raghu had delivered his verdict. Kartik had no doubt that his version was better. His analysis was tighter, the commentary more relevant to the market. Jim had only been in India for three weeks—what did he know about the automobile market here, or the middle-class consumer? But Kartik had been unable to demonstrate that simple fact to his boss. He had simply keeled over. Capitulated without a fight. I'll ask the team to start making the slides at once, he simpered at the end. It was the path of least resistance. He wished he had a knack for confrontation but going with the flow was so much easier.

Kartik felt the nerves in his forehead tighten. He had a splitting headache, like he was wearing a crown of thorns. The memory of his online tryst, only hours old, had already receded to a point. He pressed his fingers into his temples and rolled his thumbs over his eyelids. His head kept throbbing from all the voices inside. Only four, only four.

He had also failed to confront Ira properly about Kaiz, afraid of even a shadow of rejection. He was convinced that she was drawn to Kaiz again because of him, because he had failed to make her feel desired, failed to make himself feel desire of the right kind. Just like he had failed to impress Raghu or Jim, failed to shine at this new job. He had once been good at *not* failing but those days felt far behind: college, school, the childhood playground. He replayed his life backwards and forward, replayed it a thousand times till the tape in his head began to squeak.

Damn, he had peaked early.

That thought, he knew, was the canary in the coal mine. It signalled the coming of darker thoughts, of a weighing of one's triumphs and defeats on tampered scales. It announced a spiral into despondence. Every shortcoming would become a referendum on his life and his choices, and a deluge of his deficiencies would hit him all at once. He lit a cigarette and tried to still his mind, focus it on blowing rings, but the smoke sputtered out in puffs. All the while, a voice raged at him, called him names, told him over and over that he was a failure in every way. Even through the fog he could see which way the tracks bent, what the carriage of his mind was hurtling towards. That final whisper: what was the point of going on? It had happened for years, but this intensity was new, sharpened by his loathing of the job. He was still taking deep breaths, waiting for the long dark moment to pass, when out of nowhere an idea presented itself.

Kartik pondered over the matter before he called Pinkesh, knowing fully well that the detective would pick giving him grief over lapping up an easy case.

'Are you sure you don't just want a way out?'

'Why would I get engaged if that were the case?'

'Perhaps this is for the best. You can screw men and she can screw her old boyfriend—isn't that what you management folks call a win-win?'

He wished he knew other private investigators but this smug prick was all he had, and oddly, the only one he would trust.

Pinkesh assumed a more serious tone. 'And didn't you say she is a close family friend?'

'That she is.'

'You don't need to do this, Kartik. Talk to her, tell her how you feel.'

'Why will she tell me the truth?'

'The truth is overrated.'

'Will you take the case or not? I can find somebody else too.'

'Okay, fine, meet me tomorrow at nine at Satkar.'

The next morning, Kartik waited for over half an hour outside Churchgate station but Pinkesh did not show up. He left for work unwillingly. The rest of his morning was spent with two scouts that his client had hired as a makeshift local team to start clearing the way for approvals and licences, to grease the right palms. Worried that his friend might be in trouble without any means of reaching him, Kartik found his attention shredded to confetti. He could focus on the meeting, on the slides being presented for no more than a minute at a stretch before his mind returned to Pinkesh. To his dismay, even these scraps of attention proved sufficient, such was the level of the strategy discussion unfolding around him. Somehow the hours passed.

When he got back to the office, his assistant informed him that a friend had left him a message. Pinkesh's home phone number on a Post-it note. He called immediately. Pinkesh told him he was stuck in a family emergency, his father had slipped in the bathroom and broken a leg. He was not going to come in to work till after the Independence Day weekend. Would Kartik be able to come and see him at home in Kandivali, he asked. Kartik agreed reluctantly. He did not particularly like travelling north of Bandra and certainly not north of Andheri, but he did not want to wait any longer. Pinkesh asked him to bring a photo of Ira.

Pinkesh lived with his parents in a small flat near the Kandivali railway station. His mother was a small, wiry woman, dressed in a floral pink nightie at four in the afternoon. She wore a petticoat underneath but the outlines of her spindly legs were still visible when she moved around the bright room. She brought out a tray with three cups of tea and a plate of biscuits arranged in a pretty star pattern. The tea was only a shade darker than the chipped white teacup. Kartik took a sip. It was also sweeter than the accompanying jam biscuits. Pinkesh was quiet while his mother made polite conversation.

She asked Kartik if he was married. He hesitated before he told her about his engagement. From the corner of his eye, he saw Pinkesh smile with a wicked gleam in his eye.

'Beta, do you have your own house?'

'Yes, Aunty, I mean technically no, we live in a rented flat in Matunga. But my family has lived there for almost fifty years and the building is going into redevelopment soon.'

'2-BHK?'

'Yes.'

'So you will get a three-bedroom flat after redevelopment?' Kartik gave a tiny shrug as if to say, *who knows?*

'And after marriage? Where will you stay? On your own?'

'We will rent a flat.'

'You should buy, my boy.'

'But who can afford a flat in Mumbai at our age, Aunty?'

'Don't say that! Pinku said you have a good job. Touch wood. And your wife must be in service too, no? Is she also an MBA?'

'She's a journalist.' And an only child who would inherit her parents' flat. As if he had not thought about this, as if his parents had not made that calculation before they asked him to put in the money on her father's behalf.

'Still, you must buy as soon as you can. We had a choice to buy this flat or a two-bedroom one in Borivali and we chose this. That flat was not close to the station, you see. This one is only a ten-minute walk. Minimum fare by rickshaw.'

Kartik nodded politely and sipped at the cloying milky tea.

'No girl wants to marry someone who lives with his parents in a 1-BHK. Poor Pinku, how will he find a wife without a flat of his own?'

And with a love for dick. It was the perfect moment to drop his cup of tea, or spit out a whole mouthful dramatically, killing two birds with one stone. Instead, Kartik gave Pinkesh a long, doubtful look. To his credit, the man did not flinch.

His mother continued, 'In our community, even a rented house will not do. Package, bonus, CTC, these words you see in the paper every day, we don't understand all that, and as for this detective line of work, don't even ask. But your own home, that's a solid thing everybody understands. It tells people that you are settled.'

Why was this woman talking so much? He was here to talk to her son, not to listen to her babble on about flats. And look at her face, thought Kartik shirtily, how ironic that its vast real estate was largely unoccupied: close-set features on a tall, wide canvas. It struck him how much Pinkesh looked like her.

'Enough, Ma, please don't bore him with this flat business. We need to talk about work, we are going down for a walk.'

The apartment complex that held Pinkesh's building and its two siblings was small: between the parking area and the compound wall there was only enough space for a child to ride a tricycle. They walked to the park across the road, which was full of children wearing tricolour pins on their shirts.

'Plotting your freedom on Independence Day, huh? I want to say this again, just drop the idea.'

'I won't, it's a matter of principle. I can't marry a dishonest woman.'

'And what are you—pure and washed in milk?'

'I didn't come all the way to Kandivali to listen to your lectures.'

'*All the way*? You make Kandivali sound like Nala Sopara. It's not a bad idea to come north once in a while, boss, it will help you stay down-to-earth. That is important, you know, when one earns in lakhs.'

'What do you mean?'

'I know how much these new foreign companies pay. So tell

me, what's wrong with your wife having a side dish? I thought all this was fine in high society.'

Kartik scoffed. 'Unbelievable. Do you want to work for me or not? I thought you were saving up for *your own flat* so you can get married to a nice Gujarati girl.'

'Alright, tell me everything you know about this guy.'

The rush of this open question gave Kartik a new zeal for work. He worked through the weekend and wrapped up the slides for the next big meeting three days ahead of schedule, surprising even the analysts who had quietly taken the long weekend off. When the team got together to discuss the deck, he left no openings for Jim to interrupt. He was a ball of manic energy. For the first time, even Raghu was impressed.

As soon as the meeting ended, his assistant told him that there was a message from Pinkesh. Kartik called him back immediately and they agreed to meet in the evening. Pinkesh didn't say anything till they had ordered two glasses of ganga-jamuna, orange juice mixed with sweet lime.

'What did you find out?'

'I am not a hundred per cent sure yet, but my gut says there's nothing. She's met him just once in the past three days and that was in a public place—at a chai tapri in Fort of all places. People having affairs don't do that.'

Independence Day was gone, her city series was done. What reason did she have to meet him at all? But a roadside chai shop? Huh. He thought of the fancy Ethiopian roasts they'd had at the coffee shop.

Pinkesh had followed Ira for three days and she had done nothing but work. He had tailed Kaiz too. He, at least, appeared to lead a slightly more interesting life. Pinkesh had even managed to ferret out his address and paid a visit to his building in Malabar Hill.

'Malabar Hill,' Kartik repeated slowly. *Only two things mattered, dress and address.* 'How do you know it was his house?'

Pinkesh made an expression of exasperation that said, let me finish. 'There was a name plate with his surname. So I befriended the watchman of the building, who confirmed that his mother lived there and that Kaiz had been back from the US for a few months. The watchman did not recognise Ira.'

'And?'

'There's really nothing else.'

'How do I know they didn't meet outside of the hours you followed her? Late at night? Early in the morning?'

Pinkesh rolled his eyes.

'I want you to go on for a little longer,' Kartik said. 'There's something going on, I know there is.'

The M-word was anathema to the Kini family. His grandfather, the Gandhian, had advocated the peaceful coexistence of the two communities, but only at a polite distance, while his grandmother had harboured a mistrust of all castes and religions but her own. Only one *secular* utterance had ever escaped her lips: the way she pronounced alarm. Alaaraam. An accidental Allah–Ram.

To his father, the word was malignant. Of all his imagined enemies, the Axis of Evil and beyond—and what touchstone of vigour, of strength could one have in the absence of any enemy, even an imaginary one—the Muslim was the worst. It was not hatred as much as suspicion, a historical aversion, a memory of injustice and defeat kept alive through the centuries. Even the hint of a liaison with a Muslim man would make Ira irredeemable in his father's eyes. Kartik knew that, oh he knew that.

To his surprise, it was his mother, not his father, that Ira managed to grandly piss off.

'She talked back to me in front of fifteen people. The gall!' she roared. 'If she disagreed with me she could have told me in private.'

'This house is a magnet for strong women,' his father chuckled. 'Beware, son!'

Kartik grinned foolishly. This was the beginning, he knew, of a new headache. The next day, when Ira came over for tea, his mother sulked openly. She brought out old melamine teacups and steel plates, did not put cardamom in the tea. The plates were placed on the table with a little more force than needed, the difference of a few decibels intended to speak volumes. Ira was immune to the tantrum. She acted as if nothing was out of the ordinary but addressed no questions to his mother, giving her no opportunity to snub Ira further. But as she was leaving, Ira gave his mother a tight hug and she had no choice but to unloose her old self.

Kartik was mighty annoyed with Ira and her father in the weeks that followed. It was their fault that he had got pulled into his parents' latest machinations. He remained stuck there even after their anger at Ira abated. Now his mother felt compelled to report every small development to him: the landlord's latest offer, Shankar kaka's objections to the Rajwades not being offered the same deal, the grumblings of the other neighbours about having to pay to move into the new flats they believed they were owed.

'Not everybody deserves to live in a prime part of Mumbai. It is no fundamental right. If you can't even spend twenty lakhs then go live in the suburbs—clearly that's your *aukaat*.'

It amused him that she used the street word for station, for social rank. His mother was full of surprises. She had shocked him a couple of days ago by confessing that she had tried smoking a cigarette in college. Did women even smoke in those days, he had cried out. Some did, she said, there are always some women who do as they please.

Would she forgive Ira, he wondered, for being unfaithful?

Pinkesh called him every couple of days to report that Ira had not met Kaiz, not even once. He had shadowed Kaiz too, to find him on coffee and lunch dates with other women. Kartik found his old listlessness returning with each call.

Case closed, dude, Pinkesh said finally, after three weeks, but Kartik heard in his voice a note of tentativeness. Or was he imagining it?

Kartik had not expected to feel thwarted by this finding. He felt like a child whose toy had broken. He just hated to be wrong, he said to himself.

'You sound disappointed, yaar.'

'Not at all. I am just surprised. In a good way, of course.'

'If you say so.'

'Does this happen a lot? Has a jealous fiancé been wrong?'

'More people are wrong than betrayed. But god bless doubt, it pays my bills.' Pinkesh nodded slowly, either lost in thought or buying time. 'Look, it's none of my business, but you don't have to marry her if you don't want to.'

'You are right.'

'I am?' Pinkesh looked astonished at the absence of protest. Kartik grinned. 'That it's none of your business.'

This was his year of rekindling strained friendships, thought Kartik, first Ira and now Pinkesh, though his old equation with Pinkesh might be more accurately described as poisoned.

'You could have easily gone to America. I am sure half your classmates did. Why didn't you?'

'I am not sure. A vague sense of duty towards the country, I suppose.'

And a sense of filial duty. And an ineffable self-awareness, a secret he could not confess to: he'd rather be a big fish in a small pond.

'You work for an American company that helps rich businessmen get richer.'

'Indian businessmen.'

'Ah, yes, I can see the patriotism in that decision—if I squint my eyes enough. But the fact remains that if you lived somewhere else, you could be yourself. Marriage, fiancée, the ex-boyfriend, all these problems would go away.'

'Be myself? You think being gay is the full measure of who I am?'

'I am not saying that. Just that you have a choice that most of us don't.'

'The choice to put myself in exile.'

'Whatever you may call it, it is an option.'

It was his turn to pause, think.

'So,' said Kartik, 'I have wanted to ask you for weeks—what changed after college, after all the horrendous things you said to me?'

'About that I'm truly sorry.'

'What changed?'

Pinkesh raised an eyebrow and was about to speak when he stopped himself. The smirk disappeared. A new gravity, almost melancholic, set into the symmetry of his face.

'I was twenty-five, still in denial. It was a Saturday night and I was partying at Mojo. I met a student from Ahmedabad there. It was the first time I had spoken Gujarati at Mojo, the first time I flirted in my mother tongue. It was oddly moving, wonderful. The boy was staying in a guest house in Dadar. His hotel was ten minutes from the station, but we began to fool around as soon as we got out of the train—you know how it is—and the toilet was right there.' He did not continue.

'What happened?'

'Cop.'

Neither of them had seen him, where had he come from, how did he spot them in the dark, the policeman with his lathi? Neither of them saw him till the rain of blows and abuses started. A blow on the shoulder. *Perverts.* Two blows on the back. *Eunuchs.* He had felt searing pain everywhere the lathi had touched him, a skein of flames moving up and down his body. A primal instinct had kicked in and Pinkesh had pushed the constable away and fled, without a thought for the boy he had found exquisite just moments before. It was only after he got into a taxi that he remembered that the boy had found himself thirty rupees short for his second drink, which Pinkesh had then bought him. The kid had no money for a bribe. He might have to go to jail or get beaten up further. Or perhaps, he would offer a barter for his safety: get on his knees. For days Pinkesh had dreamed of that young face battered. Purple contusions, an eye swollen shut, crimson lines streaking the face like a highway map. After some months, the face was forgotten but the wounds remained.

'It was hard to forgive myself, I was a coward. No more running away from the truth, I decided after that.'

'Is that also why you got into this work?'

'No, no.' He waved away the question. 'That happened two–three years later. It's decent money and I get to use these old juices.' He tapped on his temple. 'I have a good memory, an eye for detail, and an ear for gossip. So here we are.'

This work must be slightly easier for a gay man, thought Kartik. How did gay men find each other, how did they find the portals to their secret world embedded within the visible one? He had once thought it was like learning a language as a child, that it came naturally. How could anybody explain how that happened? But now he knew there was more to it. It required a deeper awareness of one's surroundings, of subtleties the broader world deemed imperceptible. To catch a gaze held for a second too long one had to pay attention. And once the attention was sharpened, it could glean so much more from the detritus of the everyday.

He called Ira as soon as he got home and asked to meet after dinner. He owed her some amends for his lack of faith. They walked to King's Circle for ice-cream. When he asked her if they could have dinner together on Saturday, she told him that she was going out of town, her paper was sending everybody on the city beat on a team retreat that weekend. How nice, he remarked, was that common? In the brief but unmistakable hesitation before she said that it was rare but that's what made it an honour, he knew she was lying.

He searched through his wallet to find the chit with Pinkesh's home number. 'Hello, it's me. You might have to reopen your assignment.'

Friday raced by, a whirl of meetings, conference calls, PowerPoint. For the first time, he was glad he had to work on Saturday too. When he returned home, he called Ira's house and asked for her. Her mother told him she was away on a team retreat. Hadn't she told him about it, she enquired. She had, it must have slipped his mind, he replied. So she had gone after all, thought Kartik, but with whom he did not know. He called Pinkesh's office a few times, nobody answered. Was he on her trail or somewhere else—if she had left with her team, Pinkesh would have called him and dismissed his fears. He paced around the house like a zoo animal, nearly jumping each time the phone rang.

Around nine, Pinkesh called.

'Only the two of them?'

Kartik heard a sharp intake of breath at the other end. 'Yes.'

'And whose bungalow was it?'

'Someone with private security outside. I tried but there was no way a man on a motorbike would have got in, it might have been a big party. But this was not a team retreat for journalists. Definitely not.'

'Bitch.'

He left his home after dinner, his head still a whirlpool, and headed to Mojo, a bar in Colaba where Saturday nights were gay nights. The air-conditioned section of Krishna, a restaurant and bar two blocks from Mojo, was another place where gay men had assembled for years. He had never had a chance to become a regular at either congregation, having moved out of the city right after college. In Bangalore, he had had his haunts, his rituals and a small group of friends that cut across generations, or at least across decades. A family, almost. During his internship in Delhi, he had learnt of a coffee house where you carried a red rose in the evenings to mark yourself. One red rose, a worthy investment, for he had quickly found company and comfort, then become a regular for three months. Here, in his own city, he had no such home.

It was only ten, the dance floor still had room, but the music was already loud, a mix of Bollywood and Billboard hits. The DJ was remixing all the tracks using a single formula, adding the same untz-untz beats to each number so the playlist sounded like one continuous song. That didn't stop the younger patrons from changing up their steps entirely every couple of minutes. Kartik felt sorry for a middle-aged man who was dancing by himself, he had managed to clear out a section of the dance floor around him. Young men who looked like models, or gym instructors at the very least, carried trays of drinks around the room; they shimmered under the disco lights. Kartik took a table across the room from the DJ console. He did not want to rule out the possibility of starting a conversation. The queens were sitting at a table close to the DJ but he could still hear their shrieks of laughter over the music. Every second man appeared to be wearing Drakkar Noir, like Kartik himself.

What did Kaiz look like, he wondered. He had asked Pinkesh to describe him, but the detective had come up short. Not very tall, curly hair, looks average. Not exactly a hero, he had summed up, I would say you are more attractive, definitely more handsome, but the heart has its own logic, doesn't it? The cuckold was more attractive. So what?

He had come to Mojo once, three years ago. The day after he was rejected by a prospective match: Janaki Pai, a physiotherapist who lived with her parents, her brother and his wife in Thane. Kartik and his parents had to squeeze into a small Rexine sofa in the drawing room, their knees brushing against the snack-covered teapoy. Kartik and Janaki were exiled to the small balcony to speak in private, where they chatted for fifteen minutes. When Janaki said no, Kartik was furious. He could not fathom why she would reject him, unless he had somehow given himself away. Why else would someone like her turn down a match like him? He pondered whether he had accidentally let his wrist go limp or spoken too animatedly, neither of which he was otherwise wont to doing. Had he been too kind, should he have challenged her more when she told him she was vegetarian and would not cook meat even after marriage? Perhaps no straight man would have acquiesced so easily?

That had been his first time at Mojo. A few stiff drinks would help him get over the sting of rejection, he had thought. He had come home from Mojo relatively sober but with his ego repaired.

Kartik had two drinks and was in queue for a third when someone tapped him on the shoulder to introduce himself. Diego was a short man, barely five foot four, a bass guitarist in a Nirvana cover band. He was in Mumbai for only three days and had heard about Mojo from his friends back home. Their queer nights were legendary across the country. Diego said he was twenty-one but looked sixteen. With nearly no hair on his face or his arms, he was not Kartik's type, but the Long Island iced teas were cheap, Diego had a beautiful smile and it had been a long time. The dance floor was packed and they struggled to hear each other, even pressed together, even with Diego on his toes. All Kartik heard was that Diego was staying in a hotel near Flora Fountain, a fifteen-minute walk away. Would he like to leave and head there? Leave together. Head to Diego's hotel room. With Diego. Where things would happen. Pleasure be given and taken. Kartik considered the offer. Diego took his arm and they left Mojo together. A cloudy night, unusually cool for September. It was past midnight. Hookers in bright lipstick were out in the streets, looking into passing cars, willing them to slow down, to stop. Before long, there was a clap of thunder. Let's hurry up, said Diego. They picked up their pace. A flash of lightning. They walked faster, but not fast enough. It started drizzling and within no time, it was pouring heavily. The sky had ambushed them with silver gunfire. We should wait it out, said Kartik. They found shelter outside a closed menswear shop in an alley near Kala Ghoda. It could have been the buzz from the drinks at Mojo, or the sweet smell of rain, or even the muscle on the unclothed mannequins behind them, but Diego decided he couldn't wait till they got back to the hotel room and when he got on his knees, Kartik found his own guard dissolving like a cardboard fortress under rainfall. This, this, this is who he was. Not a cuckold.

25

IMAGES OF HIS TIME WITH Diego swam in his head all day. In the middle of breakfast, in the toilet, also while his mother massaged oil into his scalp. Each time the memories resurfaced, he felt that familiar churning of lust. The images grabbed him by the throat, left him briefly choked with desire, then mocked and challenged him: so you still think you can be somebody else? The truth could set him free, a calmer voice in his head suggested from time to time.

But *whose* truth?

It was too much to keep it all to himself. Around his parents, he stared into space for long intervals and then sighed for no apparent reason but failed to elicit any questions from them. He wondered whether this behaviour, the sulking and the distance, was so within the realm of ordinary for him that they hadn't even noticed. He had fewer expectations of his father but where was the motherly intuition everyone went on about? There were many moments where he resented his mother for not seeing through his act at once, for not guessing what he was unable to tell her, for not taking charge and forcing him to put an end to the charade. So the charade went on.

Coming out to them was not an option but from time to time he had wondered how they might react to it. Would they even understand, at a minimum, what he was confessing to? A year ago, his curiosity had got the better of him. He had come to Bombay for Diwali to spend a week with his parents. In his suitcase was a magazine with an article he wanted them to stumble upon.

He had hoped one of them would browse through his magazine and find the story on the handful of European countries that had begun to recognise same-sex unions: marriage by another name. An inset carried an interview with the most famous gay man in India at the time, famous because he had once been assaulted by a star son. Kartik left the magazine lying around. To no avail; he had forgotten that he was the only reader in the family. Finally, on the last day of his trip, he left the page open on the armrest of the sofa. It worked.

'Two men marrying? What is this new trend?' said his mother, squinting at the picture of a newly-wedded couple surrounded by rainbow balloons.

'It says Sweden is the third country to allow two men or two women to have a legal marriage.'

'But why?' Genuine bafflement on her face.

'That's how some people are born. They only love those of the same sex.'

'Good we did not move outside India,' she said. 'This is madness.'

'What does your country have to do with it? There are gay people everywhere. Look,' he said pointing at the interview with the star activist.

'Rubbish,' she snapped. She closed the magazine and put the day's newspaper over it. For the remainder of his stay she avoided meeting his eyes. But perhaps some part of the hint stuck, for if he described a male friend even a speck too fondly on their weekly phone calls, he could tell that she stiffened at the other end, the phone line carried the loaded packets of silence thousands of kilometres to him.

When his mother told him that the wedding cards would arrive from the printers the following day, the first question that came to his mind was whether the card would read Bombay or Mumbai. It had been almost a year since the city was renamed, but it was still Bombay that rolled off his tongue. He didn't think he would get used to the name change anytime soon, even though he'd always heard his family say Mumbai while speaking Konkani. The families would start sending out the invites soon, his mother reported, right after Ira's parents got the card blessed at a Ganesh temple. The families believed that a blessing from the elephant god was an auspicious start to the final leg of wedding preparations and would smooth out any obstacles like a road-roller.

Kartik weds Irawati in Bombay.

Kartik weds Irawati in Mumbai.

Come to think of it, it really made no difference.

He left for Delhi the next evening for a meeting with a senior bureaucrat. They landed as the sun was going down. It felt like falling gently into a pink bowl of dust. 'Let me take the lead tomorrow,' Raghu said on the way to their hotel. Kartik nodded. He had no energy left to feel slighted.

The photos that Pinkesh showed him were far from incriminating, they only showed Ira and the other man in a car and then outside a bungalow in Alibag, his hand on the small of her back, an easy intimacy between them. The detective had also called two of her desk colleagues and confirmed that there was no team outing. So she had lied. It was a whiff of scandal. Only a whiff but it suggested scandal nonetheless.

Kartik ordered room service and watched television till he dozed off half-seated, slumping against the cushions. He woke up with a crick in his neck. The TV was still on, tuned to a religious sermon by a rapturous woman in a white saree. His notes for that morning's meeting were scattered across the room and his laptop, which he had left on as he cycled through a dozen channels, was now discharged. He cursed aloud and turned on the kettle for a cup of coffee. Caffeine brought clarity: the knots in his neck, the messy room, his laptop that he would certainly not be able to charge in time for his meeting, none of it mattered because he was fucked. His fiancée was cheating on him, he had cheated on her, and their wedding cards were going to be sent out in a few hours.

He picked up a sheet of paper from the floor. WHAT IS THE OPPORTUNITY HERE? said the heading. His heart jounced. It was a sign. What had Pinkesh said? *You can both have your side dishes.*

He picked up another sheet looking for a new omen. PROPOSED ORG STRUCTURE. Hmm, maybe. Another one. REGULATORY CHALLENGES. Yet another. APPENDIX. This is ridiculous, he thought. He gathered the notes and put them into his briefcase.

The meeting with the bureaucrat went well. There was half a day to kill before he caught a flight to Ahmedabad. He requested a late checkout so he could work from his room.

Just after lunch, his cell phone rang. It was his mother.

'Call me back. Bye,' she said rapidly.

'What happened? Are both of you okay?'

'We are fine. But this is sixteen rupees a minute. Bye.' Again, her words tumbled out in one long breath.

'For a whole minute, Ayee. It'll cost the same if you disconnect in five seconds.'

'Alright. Your father-in-law has gone mad.'

'Who?'

'Your Shankar kaka, Ira's father. He sent a letter to the builder—directly, without consulting us! The builder that your father and the landlord have been talking to.'

'But why?'

'The man has lost it. He told the builder his daughter is a top journalist with connections in the BMC, that she can order an enquiry into his business with a snap of her fingers and shut it down. Unless he and the landlord were fair to all residents.'

'That can't be true.'

'Of course it's not. She's a reporter, not Bal Thackeray.'

'I mean I don't believe Shankar kaka would do that.'

'The builder said he does not want to deal with such mad fellows: today they are sending letters, tomorrow who knows what they will do. He has taken back his offer to buy the building. The landlord is livid, that's over a month of work down the drain. What a nuisance. And for what? For that bore of a man, the professor.'

'Did Ira know about this?'

'She had no idea—she was very embarrassed when I called her. Wait—oh no!' his mother cried out. 'It's been over a minute. Look what you made me do!'

'It's okay, it's only sixteen rupees. Might as well finish what you were saying, no?'

'Hmm. So Ira—she was shocked at her father's behaviour. At the end of the day she's a sensible girl. Please tell her to knock some sense into him.'

'How can I tell her what to do?'

And if he could, he had more pressing instructions before he got around to the matter of her father. Stop fucking your ex, for example.

'Or you talk to him. You are the future son-in-law, that comes with some standing.'

'Don't worry, Ayee, there will be many more offers from many other builders.'

'I know that but it's infuriating—a madman can just shoot off a letter and cause so much drama. What a world we live in.' She sighed. 'So, how is Delhi?'

'*That* can wait,' he said. 'Sixteen rupees a minute.'

He had two missed calls from Ira too. He did not call her back.

～

He continued to avoid Ira even after he returned. Finally, one evening she landed at his home as he was about to finish eating. There was no hiding or running away. She chatted with his mother for a few minutes before asking if he wanted to go for a walk.

'So that's the real reason you are here,' his mother teased Ira. Some of the tension that had arisen from her father's letter appeared to have eased. Or his mother had many chambers in her heart and Ira's quarters in his mother's life were separate from those occupied by her father. Kartik, on the other hand, could not meet Ira's eyes.

Ira proposed they walk to a nearby park. On the way they passed a Jain monastery, one that had fascinated him for years. In school he had heard that the nuns who lived there were supposed to have shunned all aspects of modernity, including toilets. They were said to skulk around Matunga at night looking for spots to relieve their bowels. Some of his classmates claimed they had spotted turds of human provenance in their building compounds. After these accounts were seen to be well-received, another classmate said he caught a nun in the act, a small figure in a white saree squatting in the dark. A few days later, another boy insisted he had seen not one but three of them on their haunches next to each other, the women clad all in white, like a row of ghosts.

Kartik looked up and a nun appeared in one of the windows. She wore a white saree with a cloth mask covering her mouth:

she had sworn to do no harm to any living creature, however small, even unconsciously. *No, she would not betray a friend under any circumstances.*

Ira was a strong woman, he said to himself. Much stronger than he was.

It was then that he noticed how pale Ira looked, anxious and unsettled. It caked her face like stage make-up. She had not spoken since they left Asha Nivas.

'Are you alright?'

'Yes, yes,' she said. 'How was your trip to Delhi?'

He found her sudden interest in his life insincere, a cheap ruse, but decided to wait till they reached the park before asking her again what was wrong. The park was empty and they seated themselves at a bench next to a jasmine tree. The sweet oily scent of the evening blossom enveloped them.

'I know there's a lot going on this week but there's something I need to tell you. I went to Alibag with Kaiz.'

'Oh yeah?'

He looked at her evenly till he absorbed what she had said. *Wait, what was happening? Why was she telling him this?* He had been so stunned by her admission that he had forgotten to feign surprise. Ira looked up for a moment and looked down again, her face twisted in anguish.

'Kartik, I am not joking. My ex-boyfriend, Kaiz, he asked me to go to his friend's party with him last weekend. He's leaving for the US tonight and I couldn't say no. I am sorry I lied to you.'

'Shit shit shit,' he said with his head in his hands, unable to resist the call of drama. Even the tips of his fingers tingled with adrenaline. Now that she was confessing, he didn't want her to get away with a half-apology. He wanted to make her squirm, to confess in full. And how was a man supposed to react to his fiancée's infidelity: was he to grab her wrist, or seize her shoulders, shout insults, walk away in a huff? He began to prepare himself for the performance he would have to deliver. 'How long did this go on? Had your affair started when you published his piece?'

'What? No. No, nothing happened. There was no affair-vaffair.'

'You didn't sleep with him?'

'Of course not. I didn't even kiss him.'

Shit, shit, shit. For real this time.

'Why did you go to Alibag with him? In what world is that normal?'

'I knew I would not see him again so—,' she said and took a deep breath. 'It was a stupid decision. I am sorry. But believe me, nothing happened.'

Had she said that she knew she would *never* see him again instead of just not, he might have suspected this was all a lie.

'How do I know you are telling me the truth?'

'What do you want me to do? Say mother-promise? Walk through fire?' She smiled feebly.

He wished that the earth would swallow *him* whole. He believed her. It was possible that there was more to the story than she was letting on, but what had he done to deserve the whole truth? Even this measure of honesty she offered he had not earned.

'No, I trust you, I really do, but it is a little upsetting.'

'I know, I am sorry, but I couldn't not tell you.'

It was too late to undo what he had done. Only one question consumed him now. 'Why did you tell me, Ira?'

'You are my fiancé and my friend. Remember what you said to me—we should be honest with each other, right?'

26

To: Kini family of Matunga

Irawati Kamat is not of good moral charactar. She has Muslim boyfriend that she has relations with. She told she was going to company picnic but she went to Alibag with boyfriend last week. PFA photos and university page of boy for proof of affair, name & religion.

She will bring bad name to your family and son if marriage happen. This marriage will mix your esteemed family name in mud.

Warm Regards,
Your Well Wisher

EPILOGUE

THERE IS A STORY BREWING IN Five Gardens. The BMC's war on couples. Benches are being replaced with single seats, there is a policewoman on patrol in the evenings. Signboards have come up in all five parks warning couples that any harkat will not be tolerated. I interrupt a middle-aged couple on their evening walk to ask how they feel about the crackdown on romance. From their fair complexions and wide mouths I guess they are Parsi, which the lilt in their answers confirms.

'What is there that we have not seen? We have been married for twenty years, we know what couples do.' He grins at his wife, who blushes. 'I say do something about the obscene ads on TV instead. Is romance only allowed when it is used to sell things?'

His wife has different ideas on what should be dealt with first: the litter in the park, the homeless men who do heroin outside after dark, the teenagers who drive their cars much above the speed limit and puncture the evening calm with their loud music.

The older gentleman I talk to next wants to advise the BMC to bring a priest to the park, ask young couples who are caught cavorting if they are married, and threaten to get the unmarried ones hitched immediately. It takes me a moment to digest that he is serious. What if couples use this trick to get married against their parents' wishes, I ask. He does not think they are the type who want to get married.

So what if they aren't?

Is it okay for them to indulge in such mischief behind their parents' backs, he rebuts, the youth must deal with the consequences of their flirtations.

They must, they must. They often do.

I decide to get a bite at King's Circle before I head back. Soon, there will be a flyover at Vincent Road, rending into two the circular market and the park at its centre, the beauty of the eighty-year-old boulevard returned to dust. Standing taller than the proposed flyover is Santorini Towers. A private island, they had called it. It appears occupied, some of the windows have clothes hanging in them. I wonder if this is where those teenagers live, the ones with fast cars and loud music.

In other lanes, teenagers occupy themselves another way. A group of children play cricket in the driveway of a building I walk past. The bowler's run-up begins on the footpath across the street. He looks right, he looks left, runs across the road. When he reaches the gate of his building, he jumps and releases the ball. I hear the whack of wood against a rubber ball over the horn of a speeding taxi that swerves around a fielder. The empty plots are gone and parked cars have pinched the streets. Yet, cricket games continue. The papers are full of stories about admissions and exams, how everything is harder for students these days. But kids are kids; they find a way to come together.

I had resolved not to but I walk to Asha Nivas anyway. There is scaffolding around the edifice, on which three scrawny workers are perched. The terrace and the third floor have been broken and chunks of masonry are scattered around the base of the building. They are working their way down. Walls will be smashed. The railings from the balconies will be torn off for French windows. The floors will be stripped of the speckled terrazzo tiles to make way for marble. They will not stop till the building is uprooted, till the soil it stood in is turned over and its memory erased.

Fifty feet away, an older building still stands, but barely. Its walls are a mottled brown and grey. Hunks of concrete have fallen off the weather shades over the windows, protrusions which Kaiz once told me were called eyebrows. I can see a whirring ceiling fan inside one window and two scooters are parked by the entrance. The building has not been abandoned yet. It's not come to that here, but in Bhiwandi and Kalbadevi, old buildings have fallen while their residents slept soundly inside, some never to wake up.

These are the only choices we have, this lane seems to say, we can choose between different kinds of violence.

Asha Nivas went into redevelopment a year after we left. We settled for too little, folded too soon: what we received bought us a one-bedroom flat in another old building in Borivali, forty minutes further north on a good day. Those who held out, everybody but my family, will get flats in the new high-rise that will come up in its place. But let alone thirteen months, it's hard to imagine that we could have lived there even a week longer than we did. The landlord knew that. He too had heard about what happened; why would he have given us a single rupee more?

I remember that day in vivid, warm detail. I remember it with all my senses: the phone call, the howling from my flat when I rushed home from work, the four times I rang the doorbell in alarm, the sting of my father's palm on the flesh of one cheek and the blankness on the other that felt like an itch, his second blow blocked by my mother. When he finally held up the letter, I knew what it said even before the typed words came into focus. It's not true, I said. But Kartik's parents had already called the wedding off.

Some days later, the landlord called Pappa. I guessed immediately that he had heard about the letter too. They spoke for a few minutes and I heard my father grunt a few times. All he kept saying was, 'It is all false, it is a conspiracy.' After he put the receiver down, I heard him breathing through his teeth.

'Bloody bastard,' he said in English.

It was the first time I had heard him swear. 'What happened?'

'He sent it, that letter. I know it was him, he wanted me out of the building,' he cried, his nostrils flared. Mid-sentence, he ran out of breath, he clutched his chest as he coughed violently, as if anger had entered his lungs and left no room for air. But he continued, 'It was him, he ruined your life.'

'How did he know—what did he say?' my mother asked.

'He said Ajit Shanbhag told him. If Ajit knows, everybody in the building must know too.' His words continued to come in wheezes, like the cries of a wounded animal. I brought him a glass of water and patted him on the back to calm him. I felt the knots of his spine through his thin shirt, over and over like rosary beads. By the time his breathing returned to normal, my mother was also on the sofa next to him, one hand around his to comfort him, the other in mine for reassurance. I squeezed it tight. I was once handed to them by a nurse, wet, helpless, flailing. Now my parents have been given to me, frail and afraid, crumpled.

After that, the calls began to come every day. *It is horrible what they are saying about our dear Irawati. We know it's not true but what will she do now, how will she marry?*

My parents had carried their village with them to the city and in a village there are no secrets.

It took me a year but last September I wrote to Kaiz out of the blue after finding his email address on his department website. I typed out a long confessional and then deleted it line by line, fearing his email might be inactive, then fearing that it might be active. What I finally sent was anodyne. It was an awkward letter, too cheerful perhaps, and I was surprised when he wrote back within hours.

Over email, I learnt, he is sunny, evasive, a little foreign.

After a few emails, he asked if he could call. Perhaps out of pity: he asked only after I told him about the circumstances of my broken engagement. There again, on the phone, was a glimpse of the Kaiz I used to know. His voice, his words, his pauses were still familiar. He was livid about the letter and called Kartik feckless. This was the bigotry he wanted to get away from, he said. His mother had sold their Malabar Hill flat. His sister, an American citizen, was sponsoring her Green Card.

'I suppose that means I have no roots in Bombay anymore,' he said with only a hint of regret.

On a Sunday afternoon some months ago, he called me unannounced. It was late in the night in California, I could tell from his voice that he had been drinking. I felt my heart pounding. My parents were watching TV outside. He had never called when they were awake. We still played this new game by the old rules. I asked him if he was okay. A moment of crackling silence. Static on the line.

'I screwed up, then you screwed up. In a much smaller way but let's say we are even. Can we move forward?'

'Haven't we already?' I asked. What else were these tentative emails and phone calls, the fact that we were speaking again?

I heard him clear his throat. 'Would you consider moving here? Or you could come as a tourist till we figure things out.'

I nearly dropped the receiver. Even though I knew, I asked him, 'Figure what out? What are you talking about?'

'About us. Why can't you come here—come live with me.'

'Are you mad? Go to sleep, Kaiz.'

'You could apply to grad school.'

'I don't want to go to grad school.'

'Then come for me.'

I laughed, but feebly. Each laugh felt like a punch in the gut. 'You have lost your mind. How much have you had to drink?'

'I want us to be together again. Whatever it takes. We could get married.'

'Kaiz, you are drunk, good night.'

When I told my friend Vasudha of our calls, she was thrilled, hopeless romantic that she is. And I have never seen her as flustered as she was after I told her about the half-proposal, which she had predicted, and my response, which she had not.

From time to time, she enquires if I have changed my mind. When I say no, she shuts her eyes and squeals, 'Where is your heart, Ira?'

Indeed, where is it? Sometimes, when I go to bed, I hear the pulse of my heart in my ears. I feel it in the pillow under my head. Its fat, percussive thrum fills my head and fills the room. I can't sleep because everything feels heavy and I am afraid of waking up to another day where nothing has changed.

But on some days, my heart also begins to throb when I am working on a big story, when disparate facts begin to fit together and a bigger picture starts to emerge. These are the days when the work I do feels not like paragraph after paragraph typed into a computer. I know then that what I do is more than the sewers and scams I write about. My work feels like a part of a long arc that bends towards an answer to that fundamental question: how should our society be?

A question whose answer we both sought in the form and landscape of the city where we met.

This city was our common ground, I want to tell Kaiz. Not simply its soil, nor its salt or tides, not lines on any map, nor buildings and streets. Something else entirely. An image, a dream, an idea that beguiled both of us: a magical place with chaos in its code, where our stories collided briefly. That romance with the city he carries with him wherever he goes. What it means to me, though, goes beyond what we had in common, it can't be packed up and transported tidily. Mumbai for me is two people who moved from small coastal towns to this metropolis by the sea and made it their home. My home. And that is how the city is different for the two of us: for him both Mumbai and home were abstractions. Abstractions are at once more fragile and more hardy than reality.

He still hopes I will change my mind. A few months ago, he was convinced, now he only hopes. And with time, that too shall fade.

Last month, I was in the queue to take the lift at work when someone tapped me on the shoulder. It was Kartik, whom I had not seen in over a year. I moved to the end of the line so we could talk. His company finally had an office, he said, they were moving to the tenth floor in my building. He asked if I wanted to get coffee. I reluctantly said yes and only because I was certain that he was talking about a vague coffee date in the future. Let's go now, he said. I could not take back my answer.

There was a thrum of tension under our words as we sat and sipped our coffees. Neither of us brought up the broken engagement but each pause felt fat, pregnant with accusations, with explanations that were left unsaid.

I succumbed first. 'Did you get married?'

He chuckled, he sounded relieved when he said, 'No, I think I bought myself some time. You?'

'I did too.'

'Hmm, but what about Kaiz?'

'I told you there was nothing going on.'

He was quiet for some time, then seemed eager to change the topic. After we paid for our coffees, we promised to keep in touch. It was not a promise I intended to keep but I heard from him again the week after, asking to meet again. Then again, a few days later.

Each time we meet, it feels like a weight is slowly being lifted. Like archaeologists, we are delicately brushing off dust in order to excavate what remains of our friendship.

Last week, we finally spoke about the letter. He maintains that he would have forgiven me and put my confession behind us but he could not expect his parents to accommodate my transgression. He added that he admired how bravely I had handled the whole episode. This man, he always says the right thing. Even if he had been mad at me and wanted to call off the wedding, would he have done it? How would he have gone about it, I ask myself, would he have confronted me or spoken to his family first? I flirted with the idea that he was behind the letter—how did it appear the day after I told him—but no, he would never do that to me. Besides, the postmark was from the day before I confessed to him. I suspected his parents too, especially Ashok kaka, who might have worked out that it was best to have my father's claim out of the way. Once or twice, I even thought it might have been Kaiz who sent it but it's hard to imagine him capable of such cruelty. Even harder to picture him use such atrocious grammar.

After visiting Asha Nivas, I walk to the station and catch a train to Churchgate to meet Kartik. Last week my aunt told my mother that Kartik might be getting engaged again. He has been meeting prospective brides, she reported, or has met at least one. This girl is a dentist from a small town near Mangalore and a relative of her husband's brother-in-law. According to the girl's family, the meeting went very well. My mother couldn't meet my eyes after she told me. Her struggle to contain her emotions made me laugh. That upset her further.

When Kartik phoned me this morning and asked if I could meet him at the Gateway of India at five-thirty, I wondered if he wanted to tell me about the girl, break the news in person.

I take a taxi to Regal Cinema where I see him waiting in his too-formal clothes. I ask him what he has in mind.

'Let's sit by the Walls.'

'Where?'

'The Gateway sea face, the wall across the Taj?'

We walk through the park abutting the seaside monument. Families are spread out on the grass on both sides of the cobbled path we walk on. Little striped parachutes carrying plastic soldiers rain upon us, launched and collected by teenage toy sellers. Younger children are easily tempted by the latest Made-in-China rage. The toys won't work as well in the children's hands and will be immediately discarded in the park itself. A hawker stands under the Shivaji statue at the centre, a grey plume rising from his basket of peanuts. Kartik buys roasted peanuts for both of us in rolled-up newspaper cones. We find an empty spot on the stone wall by the sea and sit down, warm cones in hand. The sight of the basalt arches of the Gateway of India before us is the city announcing itself. I decide not to ask him why he wanted to meet, not till he brings it up first.

'Ira, there is something I want to tell you.'

So there it was. 'Ya?'

He sounds unsure. 'Actually, never mind, I'll tell you after the sun sets.'

'Uh, the sun will set behind us. East.' I point my index finger forward and then a thumb behind us. 'West.'

'It will still set, right?'

'But why—what is it?'

'It's not important, I can also tell you another day. But look how beautiful it is.' He points at the sky, where the light is already honeyed.

I am about to protest when a large wave sprays salt into my face and recedes. It is high tide and the sea is rough. My eyes sting and for a moment, I forget about what Kartik is saying. Two children sitting next to us squeal; it had caught them by surprise too. The receding wave reveals the debris the sea had kept hidden. Scattered on the rocks under our feet are plastic bottles, snack wrappers, a soiled diaper. Refuse that the water had obscured, like love does. The walls, Kartik called this spot. The name sounds familiar, but I am not sure where I have heard it. In a magazine, perhaps? I feel the unpleasant tug of a sour memory. Ananya comes to mind, but why? The walls. The walls. In the distance, large oil tankers stand still. Closer, fishing boats bob up and down, anchored but still moving. It's ten past six, sunset is at least ten minutes away.

The Walls. Oh.

Kartik has changed his mind. 'Ira,' he begins, 'I am sorry.'

ACKNOWLEDGEMENTS

My publisher, Karthika V.K., and my editor, Ajitha G.S., for giving my book a home, for whipping it into shape, for their warmth and encouragement. And all those at Westland who gave the book their time and energy.

Everybody who helped me recreate the Bombay/Mumbai of *Milk Teeth*; I would not have been able to tell this story without the generosity of: Sanjiv and Damayanti Shanbhag, Kunal Purohit, Nauzer Bharucha, Pramod and Radha Mahale, Rashmi Kaushik and Pushpa Mahale, Nemchand and Bansari Shah, Karima and Nasir Plasticwala, Ram Kamat, Smita Deshmukh, Sharad Ganoo, Sudha Ganapathi, Sachin Kalbag, Bhavya Dore, Suhail Abbasi, Sridhar Rangayan, Harish Iyer, Pallav Patankar, Jaimini Pathak, Radhika Singh, Akhil Katyal, and many others.

Friends who read the manuscript, gave invaluable suggestions: Aditi Rao, Anant Sudarshan, Manu Pillai, Pritam Sukumar, Supriya Nair, Tamara Sanderson, Vivek Shanbhag, and many others. Special thanks to Aparna Hegde, who read draft upon draft with unfailing faith in the book and in me, and to Rahul Soni, who believed in the book when I was close to giving up.

The Sangam House team, for the privilege of spending a month at Nrityagram, and my Sangam House cohort, for all the wonderful (whisky-soaked) conversations about literature and life.

Borderlands Cafe, Valencia Street, and Cafe Turtle, Nizamuddin East. For coffee, and shelter from wifi.

My parents, Asha and Sateesh Mahale, and my brother, Aniruddha Mahale, for a lifetime of love and support. And inspiration.

Akshay Saxena, for love, laughter, carbs, endless patience.

ALSO FROM

cntxt

From the author of The House with a Thousand Stories

HIS FATHER'S DISEASE

stories

ARUNI KASHYAP

Through tales that root up love, violence, motherhood and sex, Kashyap appears to ask: what are the stories about a place that are told, which ones are worth telling, what do we really want to say?

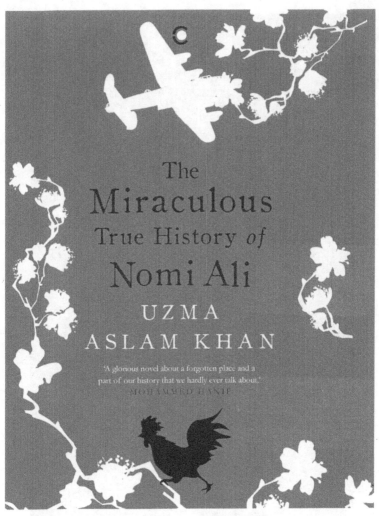

The
Miraculous
True History *of*
Nomi Ali
UZMA
ASLAM KHAN

'A glorious novel about a forgotten place and a
part of our history that we hardly ever talk about.'
MOHAMMED HANIF

Ambitiously imagined and hauntingly alive, the book writes into
being the interwoven stories of people caught in the vortex of history,
powerless yet with powers of their own: of bravery and wonder,
empathy and endurance.

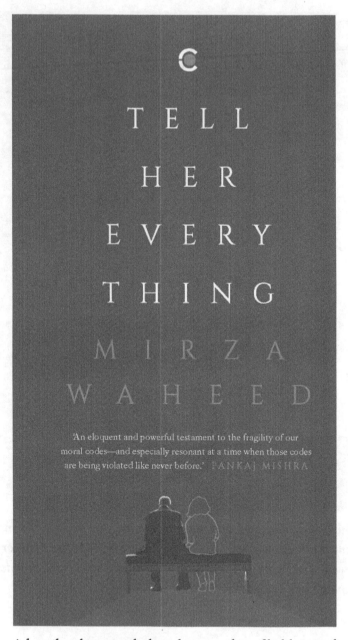

C

TELL

HER

EVERY

THING

MIRZA

WAHEED

'An eloquent and powerful testament to the fragility of our
moral codes—and especially resonant at a time when those codes
are being violated like never before.' PANKAJ MISHRA

*A heartbreaking novel about human ethics, filial love and
the corrosive nature of complicity.*

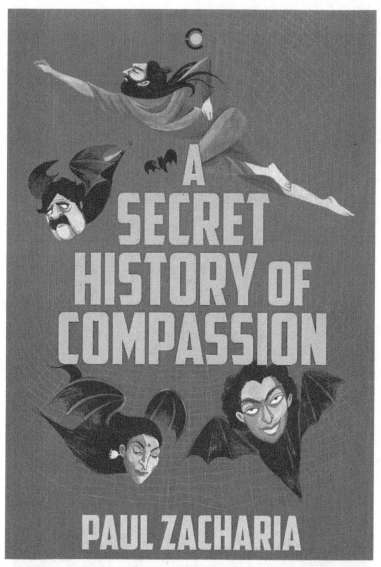

A SECRET HISTORY OF COMPASSION

PAUL ZACHARIA

By one of India's foremost writers, widely known for his wicked turn of phrase and unfailing irreverence for the Establishment, this is a novel in brilliant, irresistible freefall.

POONACHI
OR THE STORY OF A BLACK GOAT

PERUMAL MURUGAN

TRANSLATED BY N. KALYAN RAMAN

A delicate yet complex story of the animal world, about life and death and all that breathes in between.